**Tansy Burna felt the familiar mixed rush of battle
fear and battle joy spread along her limbs.**

She yelled *"Come on!"* to her squad as she squeezed her heels
into her mount. The cat lurched and Tansy thundered across
the plain, faster than most humans ever travelled, surrounded
by other cavalry all urging their beasts ever faster. Immediately beside her were the five other riders in her squad, holding wooden staffs, bows with blunt arrows and catch nets.
Varying degrees of smile played on their lips.

Behind them came the hundred moose cavalry, some carrying bows and blunt arrows, some with catch poles, and others
holding nets between two. Following them were six Empty
Children riding bighorn sheep; the surprisingly speedy animals were very nearly keeping pace with the galloping cats
and moose. The Empty Children were there in the unlikely
event that a dagger-tooth cat lost its shit and attacked its rider
or any other Badlander.

Tansy wiped away wind-whipped tears. Birds flew and
beasts scattered as they charged up the rise. The scout Nya
Muka had reported seventeen walkers, including two children. The seventeen were going to get an almighty shock
when over a hundred mounted warriors sprung out of the
Ocean of Grass.

The brow of the hill was nearer and nearer. They'd be on
their quarry any moment. Tansy squeezed her legs all the
harder. She wanted to see the surprise on their faces.

"Shoot their archers only!" called Rappa Hoga, dodging the
first of the enemy's arrows.

Tansy Burna shuddered. Battle was on!

THE LAND YOU NEVER LEAVE

West of West: Book Two

ANGUS WATSON

orbit

www.orbitbooks.net

Copyright © 2018 by Angus Watson
Excerpt from *Seven Blades in Black* copyright © 2018 by Sam Sykes
Excerpt from *Age of Assassins* copyright © 2017 by RJ Barker

Cover design by Ceara Elliot LBBG
Cover images by Larry Rostant
Map by Tim Paul
Cover copyright © 2018 by Hachette Book Group, Inc.

Orbit
Hachette Book Group
1290 Avenue of the Americas
New York, NY 10104
orbitbooks.net

Simultaneously published in Great Britain and in the U.S. by Orbit in 2018
First Edition: September 2018

Orbit is an imprint of Hachette Book Group.
The Orbit name and logo are trademarks of Little, Brown Book Group Limited.

The publisher is not responsible for websites (or their content)
that are not owned by the publisher.

The Hachette Speakers Bureau provides a wide range of authors for speaking events.
To find out more, go to www.hachettespeakersbureau.com or call (866) 376-6591.

Library of Congress Control Number: 2018936933

ISBNs: 978-0-316-31739-9 (paperback), 978-0-316-31740-5 (ebook)

Printed in the United States of America

LSC-C

10 9 8 7 6 5 4 3 2 1

For Jasmine and Napa

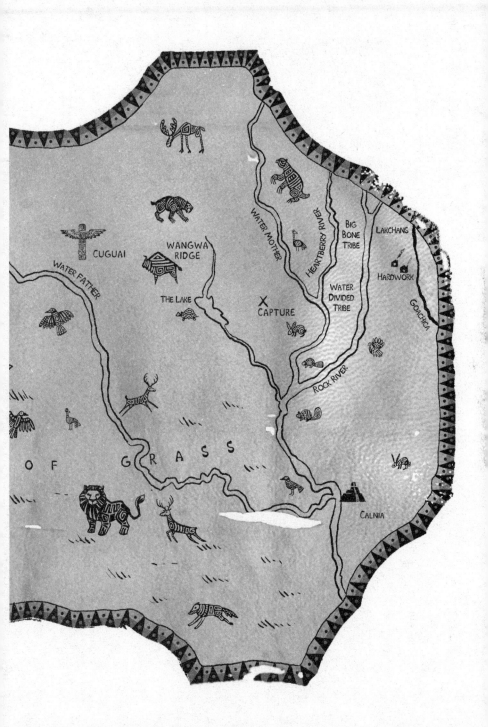

Part One

Heading home and into the unknown

Chapter 1

The Reluctant Nurse

Luby Zephyr was pretty sure that her nursemaid Caliska Coyote was going to kill her.

They hiked through fragrant woods busy with wildlife and across grassland abuzz with insects and shining with pink, blue and yellow flowers. The lovelier it was, the sourer Caliska's mood became. She spoke only to insult Luby, left camp-building and cooking to her and seemed to have forgotten about the unguents that the warlock Yoki Choppa had given her to aid Luby's recovery. When Caliska did deign to look at her patient, she gripped her throwing-axe handles and twisted her face like a parent whose child has walked fox shit into the hut for the third time that day.

Luby sympathised. Owsla captain Sofi Tornado had promised Caliska she'd be forgiven for her part in the attempted coup if she escorted the injured Luby back to Calnia unharmed. If Luby was harmed, Caliska was to be executed and have her soul destroyed by being eaten.

Sofi might officially forgive, but she wouldn't ever forget Caliska's plotting, so her place in the Owsla would never be comfortable again. Caliska would probably have a much better life if she abandoned Luby and set off south to hawk her alchemically enhanced fighting skills to some jungle emperor. Allowing Luby to live would leave a trail, so Luby had to die. It was what any stone cold killer would have done, and Caliska was about the stoniest and the coldest.

Now, six days after the Owsla mutineers had whacked her on the head with a stone axe during their short-lived attempt to assassinate Sofi Tornado, Luby had almost recovered. However, she was feigning sluggishness so Caliska would think she was an easier target. She was almost disappointed when her ruse worked. She'd fallen behind, as always, because Caliska did not have the patience to dally for the infirm. Rounding a corner on the woodland track, she found Caliska waiting for her, throwing axes in hand.

"I saw a bear." Caliska was scanning the dark woods. "I think it went round there and—" she gasped. "Behind you!"

Luby span as if she really believed there was a bear behind her, and dropped. A throwing axe whizzed overhead. Luby dived off the path, came to her feet, checked as the second axe flashed past her face, then rolled, bounced and swerved away through the undergrowth, as silently as her zephyr namesake.

Caliska's skill was the ability to throw with extraordinary power and accuracy. Luby Zephyr's skill was stealth. Given a suitable environment, stealth beat throwing power every time. And the middle of the woods was about as suitable as it got. Caliska had missed her chance.

Luby wasn't going to give her another one.

Caliska walked back to retrieve her axes, peering into the undergrowth. "Sofi doesn't love you, you know!" she shouted. "She was using you. She'll be with someone else by now. Probably Paloma Pronghorn. She's much more beautiful and—"

There's no need to shout, I'm much closer than you think, thought Luby as she dropped from a tree. Caliska turned. Luby slashed her first half-moon obsidian blade across her thick neck and the second blade across her exposed midriff, then dived back in the bushes and stole away silently as the dying Caliska stumbled after her.

Caliska had failed to follow Sofi's orders, the punishment for which was meant to be execution and soul death. So Luby should have lit a fire with an Innowak crystal, cooked Caliska and eaten some of her flesh to kill her soul. However, Caliska had brought her this far.

So Luby built a normal fire, burnt Caliska's body and, instead of eating part of it, shed a few tears.

Luby walked south, bow on her back, half-moon obsidian blades at her hips. Slung over one shoulder was a small leather bag containing a waterskin and the alchemical supplements and healing salves that Yoki Choppa the warlock had left with Caliska.

She walked a long way that day and further the next. She expected the rest of the Owsla warriors to catch up at any moment, returning south after dispatching the Mushroom Men, but there was no sign of them. She wondered what could have happened. Had they met a superior force or been tricked into their doom?

Worrying, however, detracted from her enjoyment of the walk, so she banned negative thoughts and decided that the Owsla's mission must have taken them further than expected. Their quarry had probably fled west away from the lake. Sofi, Paloma Pronghorn, Sitsi Kestrel and the others had surely followed them, killed them, then taken a more westerly path back to Calnia where they'd be waiting for her.

The following morning she awoke and breakfasted. She stretched, felt her pre-injury power fizzing in every muscle, and knew that she'd be able to run back to Calnia that day if she wanted to.

But she didn't want to.

In her years growing up in Calnia, then becoming Owsla, Luby Zephyr never had any time on her own. So she walked, slowly, taking detours to enjoy the view from small hills, to discover waterfalls and to investigate anything else that caught her interest. She told herself she was lingering to allow the rest of her squad to catch up, but knew it wasn't true.

She was as happy as she could remember being, wandering through the world alone.

She paced along, her head in the air and her feet on the ground. She inhaled the scents of the wood and moseyed along to the music of its creatures. When she started walking every day, worries flew in and batted at her mind, but soon it seemed that her troubling thoughts fluttered away, mingled with nature and returned, combined with the rhythms of the land and its animals. After a couple of miles she was just another creature making her way across the earth; a minuscule but valuable part of a huge, teeming system.

She hunted, foraged, ate, washed and slept, elated and cushioned by a peace so deep that she felt she could sink into it and stretch right out.

She arrived back in Calnia's immediate territory fourteen days after she'd left and seven days after killing Caliska Coyote. She hadn't realised how loud the background chatter of animals in the woods and grasslands had been until she emerged from the trees into Calnia's farmland and the world fell eerily silent.

Luby Zephyr was fully recovered from her head wound and sad to be home.

Up ahead the Pyramid of the Sun shone high and gold. Farmers looked up from their work and hallooed cheerfully. She hallooed back, unsure if she'd met any of them before. After the Swan Empress Ayanna, the women of the Owsla were the best-known people in Calnia. Strangers would walk up and start conversations as if they were old friends. Some of the Owsla were seriously irked by this unsolicited chat. Morningstar, Caliska Coyote and Sadzi Wolf had all punched people for talking to them unbidden. It didn't annoy Luby—she could have used her stealth skill to walk around unnoticed if it did—but it was disconcerting, because she had a bad memory and was never sure if her interlocutor was a childhood friend or a presumptuous unknown.

As if responding to her thoughts, an elderly farmer-looking fellow walking in the other direction stopped and opened his arms: "Luby Zephyr! Well I never. What are you doing out here in north Calnia? How *are* you? Do you need anything?"

"Hi, I'm fine. How are you?" *Why were his arms open like that? Did he expect a hug?* She settled for opening her own arms in a sort of *wa-hey!* greeting.

"Mustn't grumble," he said, closing his arms, apparently satisfied.

Did she recognise him?

"I suppose not," she said. "Unless you've got something to grumble about?" She peered at him and tried to look as if she wasn't. He did look a little familiar.

"You'll hear no complaint from me."

"Good. Any news in Calnia?" she asked.

"How long have you been away?"

"Two weeks."

"Well well, yes, I should say there's some news. A lot of news!"

"Such as . . . ?"

"Empress Ayanna had a baby yesterday. A boy!"

"A boy? That's great." *Was it great? What were you meant to say?* She wished she'd never left the woods.

"Yes, it nice to have some cheery news, given the war."

"*The war?*"

"Oh, of course, two weeks away, you wouldn't know."

"Wouldn't know what?"

"We're going to war. With the Badlanders."

"The *Badlanders*? Those sadists? Why?"

"Dunno. But they're nearly ready to go. Biggest army ever, that's what they're saying. I've had to give a quarter of my stores. I was promised payment of gold and porcupine quills but I haven't seen them yet and I'm not holding my breath."

"Do you know where the rest of the Owsla are?"

"They're not with you? Last I heard, which was yesterday,

they were still missing. There are rumours. Some say they've joined the Badlanders."

"And Yoki Choppa?"

"The warlock's with the Owsla, so they say."

"I've got to go."

"Of course you have! It's been wonderful talking to you, Luby Zephyr."

She ran towards the city wall and, after about twenty heartbeats, remembered who the farmer was.

Luby's parents, a teacher and a wall engineer from Calnia, had been pretty clear about what they thought of Emperor Zaltan choosing their daughter for the Owsla. Like the rest of the Owsla, she'd been chosen for her looks at least as much as for her athletic ability. "We are ashamed of Calnia, and of you," her mother had said as she'd left their hut with a small bundle containing all her possessions.

She hadn't seen her mother or father, nor heard from them throughout the gruelling training. It had been an agonising few years, physically and mentally, and some parental input might have been a comfort.

Then the Owsla had won a few battles, defeated some powerful enemies and bolstered Calnia's standing in the world. Opinion had turned. By the time the captive-killing displays began in the Plaza of the Sun, infamy had become fame. The people who hadn't been able to say the word *Owsla* without spitting now thought that the ten-strong squad of alchemically enhanced women warriors were the greatest thing since mashed corn. Some would cheer as they walked by. Some would try and touch them—which resulted in more than a few broken fingers.

After years of silence, Luby's parents reappeared and threw a party to declare their love and unflagging support. All their friends and extended family had turned up. Luby had gone along with a smile plastered on her face and had the most excruciating afternoon of her life. That was where she'd met the farmer before. His name was Eeyan and he was her mother's cousin.

Cursing herself for not recognising Eeyan, Luby Zephyr ran to the Mountain of the Sun and bounded up the log steps. Behind her the Plaza of Innowak, the place where she and the other Owsla killed enemies to entertain the citizens of Calnia, was covered in collapsed skin tents, piles of spears, heaps of stone axes and other campaign provisions. The Low milled around, marshalled by the higher orders, enlarging ordnance piles and generally moving stuff about.

Luby had always relied on Sofi Tornado, captain of the Owsla, to tell her what was going on. The next person she'd have gone to was Yoki Choppa, then maybe Chamberlain Hatho. With the first two missing and Chamberlain Hatho killed in the Goachica attack that had been the cause of their mission to the north, the only option was to talk directly to Empress Ayanna, even if she had just given birth.

She walked across the top of the pyramid, nodding confidently to the guards. A couple took steps towards her then seemed to think better of it. She was Owsla. One did not mess.

As she passed the sweat lodge, a voice from the bathing pool called out: "Luby Zephyr!"

The voice belonged to a young woman—a girl—who was immersed in the cloudy, mineral-rich water of the steaming bathing pool, with only her head visible above the silky surface. Her hair was plastered to her small head as if she'd just risen from beneath the water. She had a pert nose and her eyes twinkled.

Who could the girl be? Only the empress was allowed in this pool. And why was there so much steam? It smelled herby, almost intoxicating.

"Who are you?" Luby asked when it became clear that the girl was just going to carry on smiling at her as if she knew all her secrets and found them amusing.

"You'd like to see the empress," replied the girl. "She's asleep with her baby. You've come a long way and you're tired. Why don't you slip off those dirty, worn clothes and wait in here? You can tell me all about your adventures while I soothe your weary feet."

The girl was confident and persuasive and Luby really was tired now that she thought about it. And the steam smelled lovely. "Who *are* you?" she asked again.

"I'm Chippaminka. I'm the new head warlock."

"What happened to Yoki Choppa?"

"He's fine. He's just not here. You were separated from the Owsla nearly two weeks ago and cannot know what happened to the rest of them."

"Yes, but how do you...?"

"I'm a warlock. Take off your clothes and step in. I promise you'll see the empress as soon as possible, ahead of all the other people who've been waiting a good deal longer than you."

Luby Zephyr did as she was told. She removed her clothing and lowered herself onto the submerged wooden bench opposite Chippaminka. She sighed. The hot water was wonderful.

"Give me your foot."

She lifted her leg. The girl clasped the Owsla woman's foot and directed it gently but firmly onto her slick lap. She squeezed her thumbs into its road-beaten sole and kneaded. Luby could not help but sigh again. The girl's touch was even more soothing than the water.

"Do you know," Luby asked, "where the rest of the Owsla are and why we're about to march on the Badlands?"

"I do," said the girl, with a smile that made the breath catch in Luby's throat. "But why don't you relax for now?"

Chapter 2

An Uneasy Alliance

"I saw a tornado once, over Olaf's Fresh Sea," panted the Mushroom Woman, lolloping up to Sofi Tornado at the head of the procession. A gang of glossy blue and white swallows skimmed past southwards over the shifting green sea. High above, flotillas of brilliant clouds traversed the overarching blue.

The woman was Bodil Gooseface, Sofi knew, even though she didn't care about their ridiculous names. Her resolve to slaughter all the Mushroom Men the moment this fool's mission was over stiffened every time one of them spoke to her.

"And we saw another tornado just a few days ago."

The captain of the Owsla didn't show the dimmest flicker of interest. Gooseface blathered on regardless: "It lifted Chnob the White up and up and up and he didn't come down. Is that why you're called Sofi *Tornado*? Do you throw people into the air? Is that *your* special power?"

The fiercest warrior in the most fearsome fighting squad in the world deigned to turn her head. Bodil's eyes were wide and her mouth hung open like a head-whacked fish. She actually expected a reply.

Sofi sighed. This was the sixth day walking west with the Mushroom Men. She was buggered by a bear if she was going to call them the *Wootah tribe* as their leader Wulf the Fat kept insisting (*Wulf the Fat*, for the love of Innowak. What was wrong with them?).

"Yes, I'm called Tornado because I spin round and throw people into the air. I also destroy huts, flatten crops and when I'm done I disappear into the clouds."

"*Do* you?" The woman wasn't much brighter than a goose. Was that how she'd got her name? Sofi didn't care.

"Yes. Most often I attack when I'm walking point and listening out for trouble and I'm interrupted by—"

"My mum *used* to call me Bodil the Loquacious. I think it means that I'm a good swimmer because I am." Sofi was not used to being interrupted. She may not have consumed her power animal for a few days, but even without alchemical powers she'd be able to kill this woman and slaughter the rest of them before they'd realised she was attacking. Her fingers tightened around the shaft of the weapon that she'd taken from one of the Mushroom Men; an astonishing piece of metal called a sword.

"I used to swim in Olaf's Fresh Sea every day. I'd go quite a long way out but not too far because—"

The warlock Yoki Choppa had stopped feeding the Owsla their power animals and destroyed his supplies on purpose to weaken them. He'd justified his actions, but there was no escaping the truth, that if he hadn't sabotaged their powers, they'd have caught and killed the Mushroom Men on the east of the Water Mother, back in Calnian territory. They wouldn't have needed to cross the Water Mother and Talisa White-tail wouldn't have drowned.

No matter how justifiable his reasons, Yoki Choppa had acted without consulting Sofi and his actions had led directly to Talisa's death.

Despite her anger at Talisa's death, Sofi believed that letting the Mushroom Men live and escorting them west was the right thing to do; not because she *just knew* or any crap like that, but because Yoki Choppa said it was. He was the most intelligent, reasonable person she knew, free from ego and ulterior motives, as near to infallible as made no odds. If he said that guarding these freaks was the right thing to do, then, annoyingly, it was.

One of the Mushroom Men was a boy with a damaged mind called Ottar the Moaner. Yoki Choppa had seen that this boy would destroy a force far, far to the west at a place called The Meadows. They knew little about this force, other than that it was bent on destroying the world. If they didn't escort Ottar there, every man, woman, child and animal on earth would be killed. Sofi didn't give the tiniest of craps about most men, women, children or animals, but saving them all did seem like the right thing to do.

First of all, however, if she was going to get this gang of idiots through the horrors that no doubt lay ahead, she'd have to replace the power animals that Yoki Choppa had destroyed.

The warlock had tracked down some caribou meat in the Water Divided tribe's market, so they had their stamina back, but they were still missing the diamondback rattlesnake and tarantula hawk wasp which gave them speed, strength and other qualities.

As well as the three power animals that all the Owsla were conditioned to eat, each of the women had her own special animal from which her distinct skill was derived. Sofi Tornado's was the burrowing owl.

Apparently burrowing owls were easy enough to catch, but you had to be in their territory and that territory was a few hundred miles to the west. Already her hearing had suffered greatly. At the pace they were going it might be as long as a moon before they found her power animal. Without it, she felt disarmed and nervy. These were two entirely new sensations that she was not enjoying.

On the brighter side, they'd already found Chogolisa Earthquake's strength-giving dung beetle, Morningstar's punch-powering mantis shrimp and Paloma Pronghorn's speed-fuelling pronghorn, so those three women's special powers were almost back to normal.

Without the diamondback rattlesnake and tarantula hawk wasp, however, they were all weaker and slower than before. Moreover, as well as Sofi Tornado's own power animal, they were still missing Sitsi Kestrel's chuckwalla, which gave her extraordinary eyesight and ability with the bow. The chuckwalla came from the Desert That You Don't Walk Out Of, on the far side of the Shining Mountains. They were headed there, but, at best, given the snail pace of the Mushroom Men, it would take them weeks or even a few moons.

If they got there.

The Owsla were still a stunningly effective fighting squad but as well as being weakened, they were reduced from ten to five. If the Badlanders found them then—

Someone was running up behind. Bodil's constant blather—it seemed the woman used the musician's technique of circular breathing to speak continuously—had almost masked the sound.

Sofi's hand went for her weapon, but it was only Gunnhild Kristlover, oldest and possibly most useless of the useless Mushroom Men.

"Bodil, shush for a moment," said Gunnhild, "I'd like to talk to Sofi."

Bodil stopped talking mid-word, unoffended.

"And do try to remember, Bodil, *Listeners learn, talkers stay stupid.*"

Bodil nodded and fell behind, no doubt to find someone else to talk at.

Gunnhild strode along, keeping level as Sofi's pace accelerated.

"I saw you sewing last night," said Gunnhild.

Sofi didn't reply. She had been sewing, a frustrating business. She was not a good sewer, but she was not interested in sewing and did not require a lecture on how to improve.

"You were making small bags. I guess they're for your women to store their power animals, in case Yoki Choppa loses his supplies again."

Sofi shook her head. How did Gunnhild know about their power animals? She should have banned her women from talking to the Wootah. Paloma, Chogolisa and Sitsi were all far too friendly. Morningstar got it right. Don't talk to them and don't answer if they talk to you.

Gunnhild wasn't going to go away, however, so eventually Sofi said: "I made two bags."

"And you tossed those on the fire this morning because they weren't good enough?"

Sofi nodded.

"How many do you need? Five? One for each of the Owsla?"

"Yes."

"I'll make them for you. Rabbit leather will be better than the fawn you were using. You'll want them light and waterproof?"

"That would be . . . useful."

"I'll leave you to yourself now, Sofi," said Gunnhild, "but please remember, *enemies are people whose tales you don't know.*"

"No, Gunnhild. Enemies are the people that my empress orders me to kill."

"*Rulers order. Sheep follow. Lions question.*"

Sofi remained silent. She didn't want to encourage the woman.

"If I see Bodil pestering you again I'll come and get her." Gunnhild fell back.

The captain of the Owsla strode on, scowling.

Grass, grass and more boring grass.

Finnbogi the Boggy trudged along, glowering at Foe Slicer, *his* sword, bouncing on Sofi Tornado's astonishing thigh. Finnbogi had been attracted to strong women for as many of his nineteen years as he could remember. When he was tiny, he'd wanted to please and impress them. For the last couple of years, Wootah women like Thyri Treelegs and Sassa Lip-chewer had left him confused, as horny as a goat and doomed, it seemed, never to do anything about his passion other than stare at them and dream.

So, teaming up with five magic-powered female super-warriors who'd been selected for their good looks from an entire empire should have been the pinnacle of Finnbogi's fantasies. But it hadn't worked out like that. Six days with them and not one of the Owsla had even acknowledged his existence, let alone talked to him, and he was far too awe- and lust-struck to approach one of them.

Their leader had taken Foe Slicer that first night, without even *looking* at him, let alone asking for it. The sword wasn't really his; it had been looted from the grave of Olaf the Worldfinder, and it wasn't as if he knew how to wield it, and a magic-powered super-warrior would definitely get more use out of it. But, still, she could have *asked*... But she'd just taken it and tossed her crappy little stone axe at his feet and made him look like an idiot in front of Thyri Treelegs and the others.

Finnbogi had been going to let it go without saying anything because he was a coward, but Wulf the Fat had intervened because he was a hero, and demanded she return it. It had looked nasty for a moment, until the warlock Yoki Choppa had asked Wulf to take a short walk with him.

The Wootah leader had returned a minute later, looking glum. "Keep the sword, Sofi Tornado. Sorry, Finn."

Sofi Tornado had glanced at Wulf as if to say *whatever, I don't need your permission*, and that had been that.

And now Finnbogi couldn't stop looking at Sofi. Like all the Owsla, she wore what looked like leather socks up to her knees, a short breechcloth and a jerkin that left her arms and midriff bare. He wasn't looking lustfully, he told himself, as he eyed her again from head to toe. Thyri Treelegs was the only woman for him. He simply contemplated the Owsla women's figures in the same detached but appreciative manner that he might regard a healthy-looking lion or a sunset reflecting in a lake, that was all. He loved Thyri. He admired the Owsla simply as peaks of physical perfection and there was nothing wrong with that, he told himself again and again.

Behind Finnbogi, Sassa Lipchewer and Paloma Pronghorn were chatting away like gossipy sisters who hadn't seen each other for a year. He was glad that Sassa was getting on with the Owsla, of course, but surely she could ask him to join her conversation? He wanted to talk to Paloma Pronghorn even more than he wanted to talk to the other warrior goddesses. Because she looked the most interesting, that was all. He could objectively observe that she was the most beautiful too, but that wasn't why he wanted to talk to her so much.

A dozen yards behind Sassa and Paloma Pronghorn, his newly discovered father Erik the Angry walked along next to the giantess Chogolisa Earthquake. Erik had Ottar the Moaner on his shoulders and Chogolisa was carrying Freydis the Annoying. Erik was tallest and broadest of the generally tall and broad Wootah tribe, but he looked tiny next to the colossal woman. Despite her size, Chogolisa wore a sweet smile on her incongruously pretty, girlish face and was jigging lightly to the song that Freydis was making up as they walked along. Most of the time Finnbogi couldn't see Ottar's two young racoons, Hugin and Munin, because of the long grass, but he could hear their yickering and see their tails every now and then.

The four humans and two racoons looked happy and bonded, like a family to which Finnbogi did not belong.

He looked back to try to catch Thyri Treelegs' eye. She was walking on her own, too. She nodded at him in a way that wasn't necessarily unfriendly, but did manage to convey the message "keep walking, Boggy, I do not want to chat."

They'd resumed their evening training sessions, but Thyri had been frosty. She still thought he'd caused Garth Anvilchin's death. Finnbogi was aching to tell her that Sassa had shot Garth when the evil lunk had tried to murder him, so

she'd see that her former lover was a bellend and then fall into
Finnbogi's arms. But he couldn't. Telling tales was a serious
taboo for Hardworkers, or Wootah as they were now called,
possibly worse than murder itself. It was so unfair!

Thyri hadn't spoken to the Owsla either, as far as he knew.
While he yearned to talk to them and didn't because he was
spineless, he knew that she wasn't talking to them because
she didn't want to. Thyri was two years younger than him
and about fifty times as cool.

Finnbogi walked on, along the track worn into the plain by
centuries of people walking the same route. Or possibly animals. He didn't know who'd made the path and he didn't care.
All of the rest of it, animals and people, all fitted together,
uniting in some greater pattern that he wasn't part of.

Sitsi Kestrel and Morningstar were on watch that evening,
standing back to back on a hummock some hundred paces
from the Wootah and Calnian camp, looking out over the
endless plain. Washed with a golden fringe by the low sun,
the wind-swished Ocean of Grass became ever hazier until it
blended into the pale horizon.

It was nine days since Sitsi had last eaten her personal
power animal, the chuckwalla lizard, but she could still see
a good deal further than any other human they were likely
to meet. There was nothing threatening on the plain, only
innumerable buffalo, eagles, cranes, wolves, coyotes, a few
bears, a lion or two, a variety of deer and other plain-dwelling
birds and beasts. There'd be several dozen types of smaller
animal going about their business hidden by the long grass,
and countless more if you started worrying about the smaller
scurrying and buzzing creatures.

A long way off was a cloud that she suspected was a
millions-strong flock of crowd pigeons, milling near what she
guessed was an unusually straight-sided outcrop of rock. Had
she had her chuckwalla that morning, she would have been

able to see the individual birds and cracks in the rock. The loss of her ability filled her with fear. She'd always known that she was the least brave of the Owsla, with the possible exception of Luby Zephyr, but the limb-weakening dread caused by the decline in her power was new to her. Was this how old people felt as their strength waned, she wondered? That would explain why so many of them looked so miserable.

Yoki Choppa, the cause of her angst, was nearby, searching for burrowing owls or tarantula hawk wasps that may have strayed eastward from their traditional territory. There was no chance of a chuckwalla this far from its home in the Desert You Don't Walk Out Of.

"What do you think about our new friends?" Sitsi asked Morningstar, without turning. She took guard duty seriously.

"The Mushroom Men?"

"Who else?"

"I'm looking forward to punching them to death. I cannot believe that Sofi Tornado agreed to nursemaid them. They look bad, they smell worse. We should have killed them when we met them."

"They don't smell bad, do they?"

"They look like they smell bad. They're not from this land. They're not meant to be here. They're disgusting. Don't you think?"

Sitsi thought. "Not really. Obviously, I don't like them... well, I do like the children, especially the little boy."

"Only because he's fucked in the head and that reminds you of your brothers."

"Maybe that's true, although not perhaps how I'd put it, but I think I'd like him anyway. And his sister. They're so innocent it's difficult to dislike them."

"I find it very easy," said Morningstar.

"Really? Those little children?"

"*Maybe* the kids aresn't so awful. But the adults are vile."

"Keef the Berserker was brave when Talisa cut off his ear

and took his eye," Sitsi protested, "and Wulf the Fat stood up to Sofi when she took the sulky one's sword. What's his name? Thinsoggy?"

"Don't know, don't care. He's not fit to lick goat shit off the sandals of the person who licks goat shit off my sandals, let alone have me remember his name. They don't belong. The sooner we kill them all the better."

Morningstar was the daughter of Zaltan, who, as well as being emperor of Calnia before Ayanna, had been a torturer, mass murderer and pervert. Given her background, Sitsi Kestrel thought Morningstar had turned out pretty well. Buried below her snobbish exterior was a good and kind soul, Sitsi was almost certain. It was just buried quite deep.

Keef the Berserker, the one whose ear and eye they'd removed, ran into view, sweeping his long-handled axe around and seeing off imaginary foes. He spent most of his days fighting invisible enemies.

"Do you think we really will kill them when we've done whatever we've got to do at The Meadows?" Sitsi asked.

"I'm amazed we haven't slaughtered them already, and eaten them to prevent them coming back. I cannot believe that Sofi is disobeying Ayanna's orders on that grubby little warlock's say-so."

"That grubby little warlock who gave us our powers..."

"Who was one of three people who gave us our powers, and very much the junior according to my source."

"Would that source be the warlock Pakanda?"

"Yup."

Pakanda had been chief warlock before Yoki Choppa, exiled by Emperor Zaltan for abusing his daughter, Morningstar. Everyone who knew Morningstar suspected that the abuse, which had entailed Morningstar tossing off the old man in return for information, was at least ninety-nine per cent instigated and driven by Morningstar. She wasn't one for doing anything she didn't want to do. But many also suspected that Pakanda had had his way with younger, more vulnerable girls who weren't emperors' daughters and hadn't been alchemically empowered to protect themselves. All in all, no one missed him.

"I don't know," said Sitsi. "There's something about Yoki Choppa that makes you believe him."

"Not me."

"You only believe men when you've got their spuff on your hands."

Morningstar laughed. "Yuck! And, my dear innocent, you ask the questions *before* you get spuff on your hands. They don't tell you anything afterwards, they just mumble and scuttle away. And it's easy not to get any on your hands."

The young archer pictured the elderly Pakanda and shuddered. "Really? How?"

"You make a firm seal with your lips and swallow it all."

Sitsi Kestrel's huge eyes goggled. She turned to look at Morningstar, which she wasn't meant to do because she was on watch. Morningstar was already looking at her. She didn't care about rules as much as Sitsi did. She wrinkled her large nose and grinned.

"No . . . You . . . Arrgh! Tell me you didn't!" Sitsi thought she might be sick.

"*Of course* I didn't. I'd sooner swallow a diseased porcupine's diarrhoea. Actually, it *is* difficult not to get it on your hands. But it's easy enough to wash off. Not, of course, that you're in any danger of having any spuff anywhere near you anytime soon."

Sitsi looked over at Keef. He threw his axe aside as if it had been whacked out of his hands, fell, did a roll and came up punching.

Morningstar followed her gaze then looked back to her. "Innowak's big balls!" The ex-emperor's daughter's eyes were almost as wide as Sitsi Kestrel's. "You can't. It's wrong! It's disgusting." She sounded more excited than disgusted, though.

Gleeful even. "It'd be like a lioness shagging a pig! When are you going to make a move? He will *love* it! What a lucky man, getting to root an Owsla. You must tell me all about it. I bet they've got curly dicks."

"I don't fancy him."

"You do, you sick little—"

"I just think he's brave. And funny."

"I think *you're* brave and funny in the head. What if you had a baby with your big eyes and his little round skull? People would think it was a demon owl. You'd better find some blueball if you really are going to shag him and—"

"I am not going to shag him." Sitsi shook her head, "I think he likes Bodil Gooseface, anyway."

"Only because he doesn't know he's got a chance with you. Show him a sign and he'll be on you like a starving dog on buffalo liver. Like an old pervert onto a girl with—"

"That's enough. I don't like him, okay?"

"You must tell me whether their curly dicks go straight when they're hard. Might be nice, a curly—"

"That's enough!" Sitsi shook her head and looked back over the land. Far away, the huge flock of crowd pigeons settling down for the evening.

Finnbogi the Boggy sat down next to Bjarni Chickenhead, who'd been sitting on his own by the fire, opposite Sassa Lip-chewer and Wulf the Fat.

"What's up, Bjarni?" he asked. When Garth Anvilchin had got it on with Thyri Treelegs and Finnbogi had been distraught, Bjarni had promised him tobacco whenever he wanted it, but had so far given him very little.

"I've only got a tiny bit of tobacco left. I'd like to save it for times of trouble."

"That's not why I sat down here."

"Right."

Bjarni had changed of late, Finnbogi thought, and it

coincided with when Bjarni and Keef the Berserker had cut their hair off to escape the Owsla. With a big ball of curly black hair, Bjarni had looked clownish and been a relaxed joker. Now he had the hair of a sensible man who thought the best thing to do with hair was keep it short and out of the way, he seemed a lot more sensible. Could hairstyle control character?

The two of them sat in fairly awkward silence watching Wulf and Sassa play. Wulf was holding out an arrow and whipping it away before Sassa could clap her hands on it. Both were laughing like the happiest people in the world.

"Having said that," said Finnbogi after what he thought was a tasteful gap, "I'm still upset about getting knocked back by Thyri. Do you think we could call unrequited love a time of trouble?"

Bjarni turned to look at him, his eyes red-rimmed. "What the fuck would you know about unrequited love?" He stood and strode away into the darkness.

Finnbogi blinked after him. *What the Hel?* he thought.

Much closer than the Owsla or Wootah would have liked across the Ocean of Grass, Tansy Burna patted the flank of her dagger-tooth cat and watched the crowd pigeons settle. Several million beaks pecked through the spider silk threads which tied the birds to the gigantic Plains Strider. They waited until all of them were ready to go, then rose as one and flapped away to forage. Their desire to stay together was greater than their craving for food, even after a long day hauling the Plains Strider across the Ocean of Grass.

All around Tansy, her fellow Badlanders prepared the camp. Dagger-tooth cats were cantering out to hunt, moose were spreading to graze and their riders were walking towards the already smoking cook fires and half-erected conical tents. Buffalo unleashed from the Plains Strider were following the moose and the cats, and other burden-bearing buffalo were standing about as minions unloaded them. The Empty Children were mounted on their bighorn sheep in small groups, overseeing all the animal activity.

Did she feel as strongly about her community of Badlanders as the crowd pigeons felt about each other, Tansy asked herself? No. She wasn't a Badlander by birth. Like almost all the men and women who comprised the Badlander tribe she'd had the choice of joining the Badland raiders or living meekly in their shadow, keeping out of their way lest they killed her, or worse. It hadn't been a difficult choice, and, after a couple of miserable years, she'd thrived. Now she wouldn't have swapped her life as a dagger-tooth squad leader for anything.

Rappa Hoga emerged from behind the Plains Strider on his dagger-tooth cat, tearing along at full gallop. He turned hard and headed for Tansy. She heard herself gasp. He looked splendid, the sun casting wonderful shadows on his dark, muscular frame. He seldom wore more than a breechcloth, whatever the weather, which Tansy approved of. She longed for the day he'd take her into his tent again. From the tips of his strong toes to the ends of his long, shining black hair, he was superb.

She both dreaded him talking to her and was desperate for his attention. It always left her feeling thrilled, but shaky and unable to eat for hours afterwards.

"Tansy," he said, his deep voice vibrating the hairs that were already standing up on her arms.

"Hi," she managed.

"We'll take the Calnians and their friends tomorrow. Make sure your squad are ready and rested." The scout Nya Muka had reported seventeen walkers a few days before. It seemed they were now in range.

"Is it just my squab taking them? I mean my squad?" asked Tansy, reddening.

"No. All the dagger-tooths and all the moose cavalry will go."

"Okay..."

Rappa Hoga smiled his big warm smile. "You're wondering why we're taking such a large force to tackle so few?"

"I am."

"From what the Empty Children have reported via Nya Muka, I believe that some of them are Calnian Owsla."

"*Really?* Wow."

"Indeed."

"Will you fight them?" The idea of Rappa Hoga fighting other alchemically powered warriors was simply too thrilling. Surely they couldn't be his match? But the things she'd heard . . .

"I hope to dart them before there's any fighting."

"Maybe you should leave one of them undarted and—"

"We're out here to collect people and animals for Beaver Man, Tansy, not for our entertainment. Make sure your people are ready for tomorrow."

He pulled on his cat's rein and was off.

"Sure," she said, watching his back as he rode away. She'd be lucky to get any sleep. She'd be lying awake, picturing Rappa Hoga fighting Calnian Owsla.

Chapter 3

An Inconvenient River

The problem with Calnia attacking the Badlanders, observed Luby Zephyr, is that the first thing the mighty army had to do was cross the Water Mother. If there's anything to make an army look less mighty, it's crossing a river so old and mighty itself that it's going to show up any group of humans, no matter the size, as a momentary mess of ants muddling across the magnificent magnitude of the earth.

On the positive side, any other rivers on the journey west would be a doddle in comparison.

It was the second day of crossings. Higher-up people like her were waiting around in Calnia until the army and supplies had crossed. On the first day Luby had been to see her parents. They were surprised and unwelcoming when she appeared and the atmosphere had not improved. She wasn't upset. They'd disowned her once when she'd needed them most, so she didn't expect much from them.

She'd tried to see Empress Ayanna twice more, but the warlock Chippaminka had prevented her both times, with plausible reasons for the Swan Empress's indisposition. Luby liked Chippaminka. She seemed like an intelligent and decent young woman who had the empress's best interests at heart.

With little else to do, Luby had indulged her new joy for walking. She'd been all around the dwellings of the Low. She'd wandered the avenues of larger huts that housed the middle classes, which was when she'd popped in on her parents. She'd walked around the pyramids that housed the elite, having a good look at the coiffed women, preening men and golden statues. She'd thought about Innowak, by whose design everything happened. Why, she wondered, had he spilt people into these groups? Why did the ones who had the most seem to deserve it the least?

On that second day, she'd ended up on a bluff overlooking the Water Mother, and stood to watch the crossing. Captains and quartermasters were trying to marshal the thousands of troops, workers and beasts of burden into an orderly procession, but the Water Mother had other ideas.

Luby was about to turn back for Calnia when a boat a quarter of the way across the broad river capsized. All the buffalo which had been on board made it back to the bank, and most of the men and women managed to clamber onto other boats, but a few people sank below the muddy churn and didn't resurface.

Thus was the indiscriminate hand of fate. A few days before those men and women had been living their lives, then they'd heard that they had to go off to war, which was probably frightening and exciting, and then, before they'd even—

It was as if the sadness of seeing those people die so randomly ruptured a dam in Luby Zephyr's head. A tumult of previously constrained thoughts flooded her mind. Why *were* they going to war? How had the girl Chippaminka risen from nowhere to chief warlock and the empress's right hand in a matter of days? *Who was she?*

Luby shook her head. She tried to remember meeting Chippaminka. She'd wanted to see Ayanna and she'd found the girl in the empress's hot bathing pool. Luby had got in with her. Why had she done that? It was all hazy. The girl had taken her feet and caressed them, and after that . . . she couldn't remember a thing. Oh Innowak, what had she done! Had the warlock bewitched her?

It seemed outlandish. She'd seen warlocks influence people's decisions and fool them, but she'd never heard of them controlling someone's mind to this degree. But whether it was the herbs or some other alchemy, Chippaminka had definitely done something to convince Luby that all was well; that there was nothing odd about her being kept from Ayanna and that invading the notorious Badlands was a perfectly sensible thing to do. It had been so subtle!

Could Chippaminka have bewitched the empress? Was there any other explanation?

Luby ran back to Calnia, into the citadel and halfway up the log steps of the Pyramid of the Sun. There she stopped.

If Chippaminka had bewitched the empress enough to make her go to war, and Luby ran in there shouting about it, then Chippaminka should find it easy to bewitch Luby again, or convince Ayanna to, at best, ignore her.

No, Luby would have to play this carefully and...what could she do? She'd be able to sneak into the empress's palace at night, wake her and talk to her...but if Ayanna was bewitched, that would have exactly the same effect as running in there shouting. She'd be able to escape the guards, but she'd have to flee and Calnia would still be marching to war on the Badlands.

Perhaps she could talk to the guards, but she knew none of them well and chances were Chippaminka had got to them, too. There was nobody she could trust.

Luby Zephyr trudged away from the pyramid, sweaty with stress, wracking her brains and wishing that Sofi Tornado was there.

Chapter 4
An Unwelcome Surprise

"Fuck. A. Woodchuck. No way. You *eat* people?" Sassa Lipchewer stared at Paloma Pronghorn. After a peaceful sleep they'd resumed their walk, following their long early morning shadows westward across the seemingly endless Ocean of Grass.

"We eat bits of bad people. It has a double benefit. It's punishment for them since it kills their soul, and we're reborn as something more fun or interesting in the next life. And the right sort of person, cooked well, tastes great. Triple benefit."

"Right sort of person?"

"Young, fit and a bit plump. You'd be nice."

Sassa was flattered, disgusted and annoyed to be called plump. She was only plump compared to women who spent all day every day training to be warriors. But there was no point arguing. "What do you mean by next life?" she asked instead.

"We're all reincarnated, unless any of your flesh is cooked in a fire that's been lit by an Innowak crystal, and someone eats it. Then you've smoked your last pipe and it's soul death for you."

"Innowak crystal?"

"Innowak's our chief god. There he is." Paloma pointed at the sun. "He's a burning swan."

"Of course he is. Don't his feathers—"

"Fireproof wings."

"And the crystal?"

"He drops crystals that can focus his power and start a fire. People find them the whole time."

Sassa looked about, half expecting to see shiny stones falling from the sky. All she saw were the various flitting and soaring birds of the plain. It might be nice to be a bird for a lifetime, she thought.

"Can you be reborn as another person?"

"Maybe. It's basically a points system. When you cut the rope by the Water Mother and saved your tribe, you would have gained points, for example. Unless Innowak wanted us to catch you and kill you, of course, in which case you would have lost points. It's not always clear what's deemed as good." Paloma paused to steer Sassa clear of a heap of fresh buffalo dung, then continued. "If you eat part of someone you get their soul's points, or a share of them if anybody else eats them, too. I'm Owsla, so I've eaten loads of people. I'll probably come back as a bear or a lion or a warlock, or maybe even Owsla again. Something good. Maybe a pronghorn, but that's probably too obvious. Innowak likes to be contrary, or at least interesting. Another god accused him of being boring once, since he flies across the sky the same way every day, and ever since he's been trying to prove that he's actually complicated and intriguing. That's why so many odd things happen, like...well, like the events that led me to be talking to you now, for example, rather than wiping your blood off my killing stick."

Sassa shivered. Sometimes she forgot that the chatty and achingly beautiful Paloma had been alchemically twisted into a monster who could have slaughtered all the Wootah in a heartbeat, and had been intending to do just that until Yoki Choppa had intervened.

"So you must have eaten plenty of people in your previous life to be Owsla in this one?"

"I guess, but it's not that simple. There's a chance element, too, so that a lowly person or animal isn't stuck being shit for ever. Some people can remember their past lives and tell you what they were. When I was small I told people I could remember being a pronghorn—that's how I got my name—but—"

Paloma looked around. Sofi Tornado was a good way ahead with Bodil Gooseface tagging along behind her. Erik the Angry and Chogolisa Earthquake and the children were far enough behind. Fifty paces away to the north, as if to embellish her story, a black-nosed pronghorn was watching them, head poking up from the long grass like a voyeur.

"—I was lying. I don't remember any previous lives. I just liked running and pronghorns are the fastest animal. And they all believed me. Who believes a five-year-old?"

They both laughed.

"So the Wootah don't eat people?" asked Paloma.

"We don't need to because we don't get reincarnated."

"Your souls die? That's no fun."

"No, we go to live with the gods."

"That sounds better. Which gods?"

"There are loads. My top god is Fraya, because—" it was Sassa's turn to look around and make sure nobody overheard "—I'm keen, desperate if I'm honest, to have a baby, and Fraya will be more help with that than a god like Tor, who most people follow. He only cares about fighting and shagging."

"Shagging'll help."

"Yes, but Wulf has Tor as his main god, so that covers us. Believe me, my failure to conceive is not through lack of trying."

"I do believe you. If he were mine I'd be jumping up and down on him morning, noon and night."

"Why, thank you, what a sweet compliment. But what about the afternoons?"

"You're very welcome. He'd need to rest in the afternoons. How long have you been trying?"

"Anything between two shakes of a lamb's tail round the back of my parents' farm to a couple of hours."

Paloma Pronghorn laughed melodiously and Sassa smiled. It was a joy to talk to a woman who got her jokes.

"We've been trying for five years, since we married. I used to eat blueball before that."

"You should talk to Yoki Choppa. The empress was having trouble conceiving and—"

"Hang on, shouldn't you be scouting ahead?" interrupted Sassa.

"Arguably. But I ran ten miles ahead first thing and there's nothing dangerous approaching, unless it's coming at us faster than anything we've faced before. So, Yoki Choppa went to the empress and . . ."

"I'll take Ottar for you." Chogolisa Earthquake reached out a gigantic hand.

"You've already got Freydis." Erik the Angry was keen to be rid of the increasingly heavy boy, but unwilling to look like a wimp.

"Yes, but I can fit a child on each shoulder."

"That's not fair."

"We've discussed this. It's not fair that I have endless stamina and the strength of a tribe because I'm powered by alchemy."

"Wap," said Ottar.

"He wants to ride with me on Chogolisa Earthquake," said Freydis.

"Well, if he wants to." Erik reached up to lift the boy off, but Chogolisa plucked him up with one hand and swung him onto the broad ledge of her left shoulder, a good foot higher up than he'd been on Erik's.

"Woooooo-tah!" shouted Ottar. He giggled madly and gripped Chogolisa's ear. She gritted her teeth but smiled.

Hugin and Munin, Ottar's racoons, yipped at the giant's feet, outraged by the boy's change in mount. They probably wanted attention, thought Erik. He bent to stroke one of them but it ran a few paces, turned and gave him the stinkeye. Ottar said something which appeased the animals and they strutted away, swishing their long stripy tails.

"Where did you pick up the racoons?" Chogolisa asked.

"They've been with this lot longer than me," answered Erik.

"Ah! You must be the exiled Wootah, who lived with the Lakchans."

"That's me."

"Why on earth haven't you mentioned that before?"

Erik and Chogolisa had been walking together and chatting more and more every day, almost entirely about her, the Owsla and Calnia. Erik was happy with that. He was fascinated by her tales. He liked her voice and her gentle but wry take on life. It was difficult to reconcile this pretty, intelligent, sweet, albeit colossal young woman with the tales that people told about Chogolisa Earthquake, the monster who crushed heads and pulled spines from the backs of living victims.

"You never asked me."

"I never asked 'were you exiled from your tribe,' but that's hardly a standard question."

"I guess it didn't come up."

"So why were you exiled? Don't tell me if you don't want to."

"No, it's all right. But it is a long story."

"Better start then."

Erik the Angry began the tale of his life. Freydis sang and Ottar chirped away about who knew what on Chogolisa Earthquake's shoulders while the animals of the plains watched them pass.

*   *   *

"So none of us *knew* that Erik was with the Lakchans. Well, Gunnhild did and I suppose Garth did, too. And maybe Wulf as well. I don't know. Garth was killed. It was very sad. We were camping on the top of the highest cliff ever and—"

Sofi Tornado took a deep breath as Bodil prattled on. It was her fault. Gunnhild had sewn the small bags for their power animals the night before and given them to Sofi in the morning, and Sofi had taken them without thanking her. Now Gunnhild wasn't keeping Bodil away from Sofi as she'd said she would.

She should have thanked her.

And then she heard it.

Something coming at them from up ahead, hidden by a gentle rise in the plain.

"Shush!" she commanded Bodil.

"You want me to be quiet? What is it, have you heard a bird or something? Sometimes, back in Hardwork, when we were—"

Sofi swept the garrulous woman's legs out from under her, pushed her down in the long grass, straddled her chest, whacked her protesting arms aside and pressed a hand over her mouth. Bodil writhed and grunted muffled outrage. Sofi Tornado pinched her nostrils shut and squeezed the air from her lungs with her legs.

Finally the fool was silent and she could hear.

She'd been right.

There were dozens of animals galloping towards them. The animals were large deer—moose perhaps—and what sounded like many smaller versions of the monstrous dagger-tooth cat that had attacked them days before. The beasts were running heavily, as if every animal was bearing a burden. A burden about the same weight as a human rider.

The approaching stampede was hidden for now behind the low rise, but they'd appear any moment. Sofi Tornado looked around. The nearest cover in the shifting green sea was a stand of trees maybe a mile away.

As she opened her mouth to shout "Owsla, to me!", Freydis the Mushroom Man girl yelled: "Baddies coming, lots of them!"

The girl, perched high on Chogolisa Earthquake's shoulders, had spotted the attackers first.

"Owsla, to me!" shouted Sofi Tornado.

"Wootah to me!" yelled Wulf the Fat.

"Drums!" called Rappa Hoga, digging his heels into his dagger-tooth cat and pulling ahead.

The twelve moose-mounted drummers struck up, initially mingling quietly with the reverberations of hooves and paws, but swiftly crescendoing into their own pulsating, thundering serenade.

The squads of dagger-tooth cat cavalry accelerated, the herd of mounted moose stretched their canter into a gallop.

Tansy Burna felt the familiar mixed rush of battle fear and battle joy spread along her limbs. She yelled *"Come on!"* to her squad as she squeezed her heels into her mount. The cat lurched and Tansy thundered across the plain, faster than most humans ever travelled, surrounded by other cavalry all urging their beasts ever faster. Immediately beside her were the five other riders in her squad, holding wooden staffs, bows with blunt arrows and catch nets. Varying degrees of smile played on their lips.

Behind them came the hundred moose cavalry, some carrying bows and blunt arrows, some with catch poles, and others holding nets between two. Following them were six Empty Children riding bighorn sheep; the surprisingly speedy animals were very nearly keeping pace with the galloping cats and moose. The Empty Children were there in the unlikely event that a dagger-tooth cat lost its shit and attacked its rider or any other Badlander.

Tansy wiped away wind-whipped tears. Birds flew and beasts scattered as they charged up the rise. The scout Nya Muka had reported seventeen walkers, including two children. The seventeen were going to get an almighty shock when over a hundred mounted warriors sprung out of the Ocean of Grass.

The brow of the hill was nearer and nearer. They'd be on their quarry any moment. Tansy squeezed her legs all the harder. She wanted to see the surprise on their faces.

"Shoot their archers only!" called Rappa Hoga, dodging the first of the enemy's arrows.

Tansy Burna shuddered. Battle was on!

The Wootah looked at each other, some excited, some terrified. Invisible beyond the grassy rise ahead, drums and hooves and gods knew what else beat louder and louder, closer and closer. The ground shook. The very air shook.

"*What the fucking fuck is this shit?*" said Erik the Angry, fear and wonder causing him to slip into the Lakchan dialect.

"Language, Erik the Angry!" scolded Freydis the Annoying.

"Buffalo stampede," declared Keef, as nonchalant as a man identifying a butterfly.

"No, Keef the Berserker, not buffalo," corrected Freydis. "Baddies."

"Thyri, Keef, Bjarni, Erik, five-man swine formation on me," said Wulf. Like Keef, he was about as ruffled as a patriarch allocating seats at a family supper. Erik was impressed. During his time with the more passionate Lakchans, he had forgotten just how important it was for Hardworker warriors to be absolutely cool in all circumstances, or at least look as if they were.

Thyri Treelegs ran up and took her position, long-bladed sax and shield already in her hands, grinning. Erik hadn't seen her grin before.

"Sassa," Wulf continued, "ten paces to the south, bow ready, Finnbogi and Gunnhild, either side of her. Bodil, you and the children hide in the grass, ten paces back from Sassa."

Erik strode through the long grass to take his place next to Thyri Treelegs in the triangular swine formation. Fifty paces to the north, the Owsla were grouped around Sofi Tornado. They were going to fight their own battle. They clearly had no respect for the Wootah tribe's fighting prowess, and, frankly, given who they were, you couldn't blame them. But might whoever or whatever was coming be a match for the Calnian Owsla? It certainly sounded like there were an awful lot of them.

Behind the warriors, Yoki Choppa was squatting in the grass, hunched over his smoking alchemical bowl. From where he was standing, Erik couldn't see the warlock's scant breechcloth and it looked like he was naked.

Erik respected magic; he'd seen what it could do in the form of the Owsla, and he was grateful for his own mystical ability to commune with animals in his limited way, but medicine-powered magic needed an agent like the women of the Owsla and it needed time—years—to have any effect. One couldn't just conjure magic out of a bowl and use it to kill a sparrow, let alone take on the amount of gods knew what that was charging at them. Unless, of course, there was something about Yoki Choppa that Erik didn't know. There'd been so many surprises recently. Maybe Yoki Choppa was going to conjure up a thousand dragons to fight for them.

That would be good. From the noise of the approaching force, they'd need about a thousand.

Erik stood his ground, his heavy war club Turkey Friend light in his hand, half dreading, half fascinated to see what was coming over the hill.

*   *   *

Sitsi Kestrel loosed an arrow the instant the first head poked over. As she'd expected, the man dodged, but she'd already shot four more of her stone-headed missiles into the space where his mount would come into view a moment later. Animals were not so good at avoiding arrows. She'd heard that Badlanders rode animals into battle and never quite believed it, but Sofi Tornado had told her that mounted warriors were coming and she was never wrong.

The rider, a giant of a man, wrenched his ride to the side and avoided Sitsi's arrows. She was almost put off shooting more when she saw that he was riding a *dagger-tooth cat*, and that there were more like him coming over the hill. She was distracted from the awesome sight by a salvo of arrows coming for her.

Difficult thing to avoid, a salvo, was her last thought before something struck her head and she went down.

Finnbogi the Boggy stood with Sofi Tornado's stone axe in his hand, slack-jawed. He saw the man on the dagger-tooth cat bound over the brow, followed by more giant cat riders. Back in Hardwork, well before they'd become the Wootah tribe, he'd fantasised about killing a dagger-tooth cat to prove himself to Thyri. Now he was faced by dozens of the creatures, he understood that killing even one had never been a viable proposition.

They weren't much smaller than buffalo, yellow-furred with brown spots and, bizarrely, great dagger teeth maybe a foot long hanging from their upper jaw over their lower lip. Those teeth didn't look very practical. How do they chew? Finnbogi wondered and—

One of the Owsla fell: the big-eyed archer, Sitsi Kestrel.

An Owsla down! They were fucked.

While he was gawping, Sassa Lipchewer loosed three arrows.

Many more than three came back at her. Sassa fell.

Finnbogi dropped to the ground next to her. Her head was bleeding, but it wasn't gushing. He swept her hair clear of the wound. She blinked her startlingly blue eyes and skewed her mouth back into its normal lip-twisted state.

"I'm all right," she said, sitting. She lifted a hand to her injury. "Whoa. Rear a deer, maybe I'm not." She slumped back down.

"Blunts," said Gunnhild, holding up one of the arrows that the enemy had shot at them.

Blunt arrows. And some of the mounted warriors were carrying nets. You didn't have to be Ketil the Wise to devine the attackers' game, thought Finnbogi. They weren't trying to kill them, they were trying to catch them. But why? It was hard to think of a good reason. He gulped. It was easy to think of a lot of bad ones.

"Right," said Gunnhild, looking at him, leaning on her jewelled clothes beater, rechristened Scrayling Beater, "*let others' terror lend bravery to the fearful.*"

"I'm not terrif—" started Finnbogi, but she was off, beetling towards the charging riders at a surprisingly spry pace for a woman in her late forties. Or was it fifties now? Finnbogi wondered. *What could it possibly be like to be as old as fifty?*

It was weird how trivial thoughts came to him in times of crisis, he thought; thoughts like the thought that trivial thoughts came to him.

The little stone axe that Sofi Tornado had swapped for his sword wouldn't be much use against the beasts and their warriors. Sassa's bow was by his feet, though. He wasn't a great archer by any means, but if he waited until they were close . . . who was he kidding?

There were hundreds of warriors mounted on moose following the dagger-tooth cats over the brow of the hill. These had bigger nets.

Gunnhild reached a dagger-tooth cat and swung her club. The rider bonked her on the head with a staff and she went down.

They didn't have a chance, outnumbered with nowhere to hide, and Finnbogi would take being wrapped in a net over a nasty head injury any day. He stood and waited to be captured.

Sofi Tornado watched Gunnhild run out to meet the attackers, club swinging. She went down immediately. She really should have thanked the old woman for those bags.

"Hold," she commanded her own women.

As the drums had boomed louder while the enemy was still out of sight, Sofi Tornado's overriding emotion had been rage mixed with a dash of frustration and a large measure of lust for vengeance. Had Yoki Choppa not deliberately destroyed his supply of her power animal, she would have heard the army coming in enough time either to evade them or to find a favourable place to fight. The stand of trees a mile away, for example, would have been about a thousand times better suited than the open prairie to a small number of skilled warriors fighting a much larger number of mounted troops.

On top of that, if Bodil hadn't been gabbling nonsense without taking a breath, she would have heard the approaching army a good deal earlier. When this was over, people would pay.

As soon as she saw the foe, however, anger and frustration were washed aside by a flood of elation. She'd heard of the concept of riding moose, but she'd never seen it. She'd never considered for a moment that people might ride dagger-tooth cats, but, by Innowak's burning arse, what a great idea.

And what a wonderful opponent. The attackers were Badlanders, she knew, and clearly they intended to capture rather than kill them. That would be their undoing. Possibly. There were an awful lot of them, and they were only five Owsla.

An arrow struck Sitsi Kestrel and she fell.

Four Owsla.

Over with the Wootah, an arrow took out Sassa Lipchewer, then no more came. They'd targeted the archers as they were the only immediate threat. She did not like their confidence.

The dagger-tooth cats were nearly on them. The riders raised their weapons.

"Owsla," she said, "free-form attack, now."

Paloma Pronghorn sprinted full-tilt at the six dagger-tooth cat riders heading for the Wootah. She was off to help the Wootah, not because she was kind, but because helping them would help them all. Their new allies were not as shit as Sofi believed. Compared to the Owsla, yes, the Mushroom Men were about as useful in a battle as a bag of tadpoles, but the people who made up their Hird were superior to the average warrior. While they'd be no match for riders on dagger-tooth cats, Paloma reckoned they'd at least hold their own against the cats themselves and Badlanders on foot, especially if those Badlanders were used to fighting on catback.

So, as nets flailed and spears jabbed, she set about dismounting the riders.

She grabbed the heel of the first and flipped him backwards. Dodging a paw swipe from a dagger-tooth, she leapt and whacked her killing stick into the head of the next fellow, pirouetting as he fell, launching herself off the haunches of his cat, somersaulting and dropping two-footed into the chest of the next rider. Ramming him off his mount and launching herself at the same time, she flew backwards, twisting in the air. She cracked her killing stick into the head of a dagger-tooth and landed as it crashed down next to her. A backhanded flick with her stick dealt with its rider.

As the Badlander collapsed, she heard Wulf the Fat shout "Charge!" He'd realised what she was doing and reacted. It was a satisfying start.

Might things have turned out differently, she wondered later, if that moment's smuggery hadn't made her pause?

She looked for her next victim and saw a yellow-eyed woman mounted on a dagger-tooth. She had her fist to her mouth. The fist was clutching a short blowpipe which she'd just blown. The dart from the pipe was inches from Paloma's exposed midriff. There was no time to dodge. The dart pierced her flesh and stuck, short feathers juddering.

"I wonder if it's pois—" she had time to think before the world whirled itself into a nauseating spin and she went down.

"Phew," thought Tansy Burna, wheeling her own cat away as the one other remaining cat in her squad was joined by the next pack of six. She wondered what the Calnian woman's power animal was to give her such incredible speed. All of the Badland Owsla were preternaturally fast, but this woman was faster. Tansy stifled the rush of excitement that she'd taken down an alchemically charged warrior—it wasn't often an uncharged person like her managed that—and focused on the matter at hand.

Her squad was beaten. There was no shame in that, not against a powered warrior. The gang of pale fighters were competent enough, but they were not powered. They were weird-looking, though—several of them had dyed their hair yellow. The female, stocky but fit and not as pale as the rest, was particularly effective. She'd knocked a cat unconscious with the pommel of her impossibly long iron knife, opened up several wounds in its rider and was winding up for the killing slash. Tansy Burna per-chooed a dart into her neck and she collapsed. The injured rider raised a hand in thanks.

Another of the enemy—a strikingly ugly man with a bandaged head—had dodged their nets, taken down two riders with a long-handled, large-headed axe and was looking for a third. Tansy darted him in the neck.

The other three, none much smaller than Rappa Hoga, had been netted and subdued. The rest of them—a couple of children and a woman who was clearly not the fighting type— looked useless.

Tansy looked across at the other group of enemies, the Calnians, and saw a giant woman pluck a rider from his moose and toss him away, pick up the moose by its back legs, swing it around her head and charge the group of dagger-tooth riders who were fighting her sisters-in-arms.

Tansy was glad she'd taken the right flank.

Near the giant she saw another woman punch a cat, and almost guffawed at her ballsiness. As if punching a dagger-tooth would achieve anything! But the cat went down. Then the Calnian warrior knocked the rider unconscious with an effortless jab.

Meanwhile, the third remaining Calnian was leaping and slashing with a knife even longer than the pale woman's— so long and thin that surely it would break the moment you struck anything with it. It seemed pretty effective in slashing great gashes in cats and riders, however.

Moose cavalry galloped up with nets and darts. The giant and the puncher went down. The remaining fighter dodged darts and dealt horrible injuries with her long knife. Riders surrounded her. She was doing well, even for a powered warrior, but it would be only a matter of moments before she was taken down.

The battle was all but over.

Tansy Burna trotted her cat around the edge of the fighters. She'd done her piece, she'd taken down a power-animal warrior and two more enemies. She'd guard the pale-skinned woman and children until the fighting was done.

Sofi Tornado leapt and spun, mistimed it *again*, and took another whack from a staff. She heard a *per-choo!* and dived to avoid the dart. She sprang onto her hands and over onto her feet and looked for her next target.

The Badlander leader had dismounted and stood facing her. The other dagger-tooth riders were pulling their mounts clear. Chogolisa Earthquake was prone, taken down by several sleep darts. Presumably, because it seemed they were trying to capture and not kill them, they were sleep darts and not death darts. Morningstar was trying to punch her way out of four or five large nets tossed over her by the moose riders. Yoki Choppa had been taken out by a staff blow at the start of the fight.

"I am Rappa Hoga of the Badlands, chief of the Plains Strider and the Badlands catch squad," said the huge man.

"I am Sofi Tornado of Calnia."

"You fought well."

She narrowed her eyes, thought, *Not nearly as well as I should have done*, but said, "I haven't finished yet."

Rappa Hoga held a large axe with great obsidian twin blades which shone like a woodland pond on a starry night. She had Finnbogi's sword.

They circled, weapons raised.

He was taller and heavier than Erik, the biggest Mushroom Man, but maybe ten years younger and not fat. His black eyes were deep-set but they sparkled like his axe head. His features were strong and symmetric, his skin darker than most but clear and smooth, his lips full and his jaw strong. He was distractingly beautiful.

He looked capable, too, but there was more than that. There was confidence in his eyes, and not the unfounded confidence of the idiots she'd destroyed in the Plaza of Innowak. He'd seen what she could do—a long way from her best but superior to any fighter she'd met—and yet he chose to take her on in single combat. He knew something that she didn't. She preferred the normal situation when it was the other way round. *Curse the loss of her power animal!*

She closed her eyes and strained to hear his movements.

His left foot shifted, then his right. It didn't help that he was more or less naked, but she heard muscles move against the leather of his breechcloth and knew what was coming.

He lunged.

She ducked, spun and swung her sword and...he caught her wrist. She jabbed a punch and he caught her other hand. He smiled. She kicked for his balls. He held her out at arm's length and her leg swished harmlessly. She felt like a child.

"Dart," he ordered calmly, still holding her at arm's length. She kicked frantically, tried to twist clear. Something struck her lower back. His face rushed away, then back towards her. Then she was gone.

Finnbogi peered over the grass tips.

The Hird were down! Thyri was down! He almost leapt up to avenge her, but there were simply too many Badlanders. And he was meant to be protecting the children.

And suddenly he had more pressing problems.

A Scrayling woman was walking her dagger-tooth cat around the captured Hird and the other riders, heading for him, Bodil and the children.

She looked aggressively healthy and ready for a fight, a few years older than Finnbogi and dressed in leather battle trousers and a white cotton shirt. It was pretty much the same outfit as he himself was wearing. She was smiling and had what could only be described as a saucy look in her darting, yellow eyes. The look reminded Finnbogi of Hrolf the Girlchaser's eyes when he'd ogled Sassa or Thyri, but on this woman the effect was appealing rather than vomit-inducing.

Ottar squeaked, staring at the oncoming beast. Freydis, also looking terrified for once, took his hand. Bodil stood up out of the grass in front of them, her knife held aloft in a shaking hand.

Finnbogi leapt up and ran at the rider.

Her mount saw him coming. *I'm going to slash you with my claws*, it seemed to say to him.

The cat reared and swiped a paw. Finnbogi dodged, leapt and grabbed the rider around her waist. She whacked at him and he fell back, pulling her off the big cat.

He whumped onto the ground and her torso crashed onto his head. He considered biting her back, dismissed that as glaringly unheroic, and tried to grapple her so that he might get on top. But she drove a fist into the side of his head and twisted like a snake, so that in a couple of heartbeats it was her sitting on him, pinning him with her legs.

She smiled, yellow eyes flashing even more saucily than before, and swung her fist into his chin. He blinked stars and she raised her fist again. *Was she planning to punch him into unconsciousness?* It looked a lot like it. That was not the painless wrapped-in-a-net capture he'd been hoping for.

He wrenched his left arm free from under her leg, blocked her punch and carried on the movement to jab her on the chin. She dodged, which freed his other arm. He swung it at her, surprised to find that his hand was still clutching Sofi Tornado's stone axe. The weapon's head whunked into the Badlander's temple. Her yellow eyes widened and she fell sideways with a sigh.

Finnbogi ran to the children and crouched next to them, trying to gather them into his arms for protection.

Nearby the dagger-tooth riders were trussing Keef, Wulf, Bjarni, Thyri and Erik. They were all either dead or unconscious. Further away other warriors were doing the same to the Owsla. A mighty looking man was holding a lifeless Sofi Tornado aloft by one of her wrists and examining her like a fisherman might examine a fine catch.

The Owsla were beaten!

Approaching them were six bald children, riding animals that looked like giant goats. In all the weirdness, these strange little people were the weirdest and the most frightening.

"It's okay," Finnbogi said to Bodil and the children, "it's going to be fine. We've been in worse scrapes than this."

One of the dagger-tooth riders spotted them, yelled a command, and a group of six cat cavalry padded in their direction.

"Have we?" asked Freydis.

Chapter 5

Beeba Spiders

Morningstar woke but kept her eyes shut. She was upright and bound. She tested the constraints. No give whatsoever. Her fault. She should have realised that capture was inevitable, so resisted punching the crap out of that daggertooth and showing them how strong she was.

She could hear and smell people and beasts—specifically Mushroom Man, dagger-tooth cat, moose, buffalo and... pigeon, if she wasn't mistaken.

She tilted her head back and lifted her eyelids just a little, like she'd done when she was a girl and hadn't wanted the servants to know she was awake.

What the...?

She forgot stealth and opened both eyes wide.

She was strapped upright to a wooden frame. The endless Ocean of Grass stretched around her, golden-green and hazy in the dawn light. Ahead was an area of buffalo-clipped grass, then the conical buffalo skin tents of nomadic people. Badlanders and their beasts busied about. So far, so what she might expect. But looming behind and over the Badlander camp was a vast wooden structure. At first she thought it was a high wall, but then she saw it wasn't solid; it was made up of beams and struts and what looked like cages—yes, she could see animals in some of them. Was that a white bear?

It looked like a giant sledge but it couldn't be, because you'd need an animal as strong as a thousand buffalo to pull

such a weight across the grass, and that animal would have
to be tall as the Mountain of the Sun to lift something that
height. Although if you combined the strength of a multitude
of animals, and if those animals could fly... No, the structure
couldn't be mobile. She'd find out what it was sooner or later.

To her left and right were two Mushroom Men, bound
like she was. The frames they were strapped to were normal-
sized sledges, leant against a chest-high pole. So they'd been
dragged here on sledges, probably behind the moose. But why
were they propped up?

She tried to crane to see who was beyond the two men.
There were more sledges, but she couldn't see who was on
them. Hopefully the rest of the Owsla were there and they'd
propped her up between two Mushroom Men just to piss
her off.

"Hello, I was hoping you'd wake up soon. Are you feeling
okay?" asked the tall, dark-haired one to her right—Bjarni
Cockhead if she remembered correctly.

To her left was the sulky one. Mercifully he was still out
cold, so she only had to listen to one Mushroom Man's nonsense. She was not going to dignify it with a reply.

"I've been awake since the middle of the night, although I
did have a bit of a kip just now," explained Cockhead, unbidden. "I guess I've got a tolerance for whatever they had in
those blowpipes. Funny, I woke feeling pretty clean, which
you wouldn't expect after a whack like that. How do you
feel?"

"Can any Owsla hear me?" called Morningstar.

"I think you're the first one to wake," said Bjarni. "Paloma
Pronghorn's on my right and... Paloma Pronghorn?... yup,
still asleep. She looks fine, though. Very fine."

"Pissflaps..." Morningstar muttered.

"I don't suppose you know what these boxes on our necks
are for?"

There was a wooden box attached by a thick leather strap

to the Mushroom Man's neck. The sulky one to her left also had one. She could feel hers now, too. The box was half the size of a clenched fist, with an open side against her neck. She could feel something spiky resting against her skin. It was not pleasant.

"Whatever's in mine moved a while back," said Cockhead. "It was about the most horrible thing I've ever felt."

So they had animals strapped to their necks. That would explain the two little breathing holes on each box. She narrowed her eyes. Someone had strapped animals to her neck without asking her permission. She did not like being fucked around like this.

"Can you feel yours?"

She didn't answer. A multitude of birds—the pigeons she could smell—rose into the air at the westerly end of the gigantic wooden structure, then fluttered back down.

Bjarni Cockhead attempted to talk to her and she watched the camp, trying to gather any information that might aid their escape. She saw more pigeons—many more—fly up and down near one end of the colossal structure. Moose riders herded large numbers of buffalo towards the other end.

Finnbogi the Boggy woke and blinked, then blinked again. The extraordinary scene wouldn't go away.

Had the rest survived? he wondered. *Had Thyri survived?* He could see other frames like the one he was strapped to. He strained to see who was on them, but could spot only Gunnhild and Morningstar.

"Morningstar," he asked, "can you see anybody else?"

She ignored him.

She actually, straight up, ignored him. So rude!

"Morningstar, can you hear me?"

Nothing.

"I can hear you!" It was Bjarni Chickenhead. "I'm on Morningstar's other side. She won't talk to me either. I'm sure she has her reasons. Paloma Pronghorn's still whacked out beside me and I can't see anybody else."

Bjarni sounded happier than he'd been for a while.

"Anybody else awake?" he shouted. Silence.

Finnbogi and Bjarni talked about their predicament, Bjarni's cheery mood prevailing. It was odd, Finnbogi thought, what cheered people. For example, despite the trouble they were in, he could see by the pulsing veins on Morningstar's neck and hear by the occasional angry exhalation that their chat was annoying her, so it pleased him to carry on and make it as inane as possible. *Ignore us*, he thought, *and we will retaliate by irritating you to Hel and back.*

Gunnhild woke. Finnbogi asked her if she was okay, didn't really listen to her reply and carried on chatting to Bjarni, discussing everything they could see.

They decided that the huge wooden structure was a fortification of some kind, possibly around a town. The millions of pigeons—which had to be crowd pigeons grouped in such a large number—could be there as pets, perhaps as a display, or maybe as a labour-intensive sacrifice. And what were the buffalo up to? And those bizarre bald children riding big goats? And the boxes on their necks? They discussed it all, their explanations becoming zanier and zanier while, by her pulsing veins and stifled snorting, Morningstar became angier and angrier between them.

After a while, Gunnhild ruined it. "*The bore is the man who says everything*," she said.

"We're doing it to annoy Morningstar," whispered Finnbogi out of the corner of his mouth, "because she won't talk to us."

"You're annoying her and proving yourself a bore. Who's the winner?"

Finnbogi carried on his chat with Bjarni for a while, but the joy had gone. *Thanks, Aunt Gunnhild*, he thought.

Paloma and Sitsi woke, then the Badlanders came, led by

a smiley fellow. So broad was the Badlander's grin that Finnbogi thought he was some kindly chap come to untie them, explain that it had all been a big mistake and lead them to a delicious breakfast.

He was about as wrong as he'd ever been about anyone.

Morningstar was so keen for the Mushroom Men's ignorant, inane chatter to end, and to find out what was going on, that she was pleased when a Badlander marched towards them purposefully, flanked by a group of warriors and other people who she guessed were captives by their lack of armament, meek demeanour and the wooden boxes strapped to their necks. The captives weren't bound, but they seemed totally compliant. She didn't like that.

Behind the lot of them came a bald, big-headed child riding a bighorn sheep.

The warrior's face was split by a huge grin, but it wasn't a happy one. It was the grin of a demon who'd crawled out of the ground with plans to eviscerate every man, woman and child and bathe in their guts.

"Hello!" said the grinner, looking up and down the line with small, black eyes. The cold-blooded smile stretched across a broad, acne-scarred jaw. "I am Chapa Wangwa. Do sit down all of you. Oh, you can't. Ha ha ha!"

"How many times have you made that pathetic joke?" asked Morningstar.

Chapa Wangwa's smile broadened all the more as he walked over to her. He peered into her eyes, his own flashing murderously, then looked her up and down. He trailed his fingers across her bare stomach, smiling and nodding. She strained at her bonds, willing them to break. She wanted to punch that smile into a pulp.

"This one is a masochist!" he cried, standing back. "Good! She will enjoy what is to come. For those of you who didn't hear, this fine woman suggested that I have made that quip about sitting down before. And she's right, I have, every time I talk to new captives. Every time! I always find it funny." He laughed.

"Do you want to hear what I find even funnier? Barring our most recent haul on the Plains Strider behind me, all the people who have heard that joke before—hundreds, maybe thousands of people—all are dead. *All* of them! Isn't that amazing! And there's more. None of them died well. Not one. Their last days were oh, so bad," he shook his head but the grin remained. "They died in agony. I killed many of them myself. One man, I slit open his legs and let him watch for days as insects, worms and other small beasts ate his feet, calves, thighs and further up, too. Quite often I will break spines so that people can watch without interfering as I torture their friends and their families. The fun I have had!"

Morningstar shivered. She hadn't felt fear since she was a child, but here it came, nudging its way back into her brain. Curse Yoki Choppa for losing the tarantula hawk wasp that made them unafraid.

"Now I'd chat and joke with you all day," the vile man continued, "but you'll be itching to know about your new necklaces. Your new *itchy* necklaces. Ha ha ha! That joke too, I have made many times!"

As if on command, the creatures in the box on Morningstar's neck moved. She couldn't stop herself shouting out. By the noise around her, the same thing had happened to everyone else.

Chapa Wangwa's grin widened even further. "You think the animals *feel* bad on your neck? You should see them! Oh no, they are not nice looking. We call them *beeba spiders*. Think of the nastiest, ugliest spider you know, give it bigger teeth and make it orange, and you might be getting close."

Behind him the largest group of pigeons yet rose into the air at the westward end of the huge wooden structure, then settled. Morningstar was certain that the whole vast frame had lifted that time. Chapa Wangwa had mentioned a "Plains Strider." Surely, that vast wooden structure couldn't move.

"And if the beeba spiders bite you, oh! It's so *so* bad." The Badlander shook his head. "They are, of course, under our control. When you all cried out like babies just now, that was the Empty Child waking them." He pointed to the bald kid on the bighorn sheep. "Now, here is the fun part. If you misbehave—if you attack me or any other Badlander, if you stray more than a short way from the nearest Empty Child, if you try to undo the leather strap around your neck—both the spiders will bite you. One would be enough, but each of you has two spiders in case one of them dies. Clever, no?"

Morningstar shivered again.

"*How bad can the bite be?* you're wondering. *Is it perhaps like a bee sting?* That wouldn't be so bad, would it? Hardly makes you break a sweat, a bee sting. It would not impede escape at all. But, I am sorry my new friends, it's worse than a bee sting. It's worse than a million bees' stings. Even though I'm sure you're all very clever people, it's worse than anything you can imagine. I will show you. Well, *I* won't show you. Maybe you will show us, masochist. Would you like to?"

He cocked his head, his eyes boring into Morningstar's, his jaw rolling and pulsing as if his grin were a separate creature performing its own sultry dance.

Morningstar held his gaze. The creatures strapped to her neck bristled against her skin.

"Just say *no thank you, Chapa Wangwa*, if you don't want the beeba spiders to bite you. And, believe me, you don't want them to bite you."

He beckoned with one hand, and the child on the sheep trotted forward. "It would be a shame to lose such a beautiful captive, but if your arrogance prevents you from speaking to me..."

Morningstar was fucked if she was going to do what she

was told by this ugly lowlife, even if she was afraid. Fuck him and fuck fear.

"I will count to three, then the spiders will bite you. One. Two."

Morningstar may have blanked him, but only Finnbogi's most vindictive and blindly curious depths wanted to see her bitten by the beeba spiders.

It looked a lot like her pride was going make it happen, though.

"*Often the better yields when the worse strikes!*" blurted Gunnhild.

"Thr—" said Chapa Wangwa.

"No thank you, Chapa Wangwa," Morningstar interrupted, in a voice that could have frozen Olaf's Fresh Sea.

"What *wise* words from the crone. Although she did call me worse than you, which I do not like." He grinned malevolently at Gunnhild.

"*Insulting words only gain meaning when the recipient opens his door and welcomes them in,*" she said.

Finnbogi braced himself. What was Gunnhild thinking? This unhinged horror was not a man to goad.

"*Insulting words . . .*" Chapa Wangwa looked confused, although still grinning. Slowly his eyes widened with happy realisation. "Oh, I see! that's *marvellous*! I like that. A person can make you feel bad about yourself only if you allow it! If you're upset by mockery, it's *your fault*! That's *good*. I wish I'd known that as a child, but from now I will keep your words with me as a shield. And I will keep you for now. Later, you will tell me more wise words."

Finnbogi almost felt sorry for the man.

Chapa Wangwa turned to the four people with boxes on their necks that he'd brought with him. "We'll use . . . you." He pointed to a medium-sized fellow, about Erik's age, balding and with an unusually large head.

"Not me!" the man fell to his knees. "I'll do anything! And you need me to identify animals!"

Chapa Wangwa smiled at the Wootah and the Owsla. "We picked this one up near the start of this hunt. He had no obvious value and we don't keep creatures who have no value, so I was going to open up that big head to see what's inside, but he convinced Rappa Hoga that he was an expert on animals and would be helpful on our round of collections."

Chapa Wangwa shook his head. "He wasn't helpful! He lied! He knew no more about animals than I do. So this is going to happen."

He nodded at the bald child on the sheep.

"Noooo! I—" The big-headed man jerked. He reached one clawed hand to the box on his neck, and shook the other hand as if he were reaching the climax of an elaborate dance. He screamed so horribly and loudly that Finnbogi's very insides vibrated, then drew in a horrendous sucking breath. His face went red, then purple. There was a loud snap.

Chapa Wangwa was bouncing on his toes, rubbing his palms together. "That was his jaw breaking! *Amazing*, isn't it?"

The man's broken jaw fell lose and his eyes bulged with agonised terror. He jerked and twisted as a series of cracks wracked his body, then collapsed like dropped laundry. One leg was straight out behind him at a nasty angle, the other was broken in several places, coiled like a fat rope.

Chapa Wangwa was ecstatic. "And that was his *back*! His spine *actually breaking*! It always happens, but I love it every time as if it were the first."

The spider-bitten man was now curled in a weird ball, legs, arms and head twitching. Chapa Wangwa squatted next to him. He eyed the line of Wootah and Owsla like a rug hawker about to demonstrate his wares, then rolled the stricken man over, straightened him out, gripped his hair and lifted his head.

"See his eyes?" Finnbogi could see his eyes. He had to look

away. "We cannot imagine his agonies but his eyes tell the story. He will stay like this for a long time, then he will die. He cannot move, of course; his spine is broken all the way up and down. It's a tightening, I think, of muscles and the cords that link them that snap the bones. I don't know, I'm no medicine man. But I have seen the insides of a lot of people!"

He dropped the man's head and stood. "In a moment, we'll untie your bonds. You'll follow me to the Plains Strider— that's the big wooden wonder you've all been wondering about."

"Where are you taking us?" asked Sofi.

Chapa Wangwa's eyes rolled around in his ugly face. "Let's keep that as a surprise, shall we? Try to enjoy the journey. I *will* tell you that it will take a few days to get there, because when we arrive . . . well, let's just say you should try your best to enjoy the journey.

"And, just to be clear," he continued, grinning, "if you attack me or any other Badlander, if you disobey any Badlander, if you try to escape, if you try to remove your box, the spiders will bite and this," he gestured to the shivering wreck of a man at his feet, "will be you."

Chapter 6

The Plains Strider

Chapa Wangwa's henchpeople untied Sofi Tornado's wrists and ankles from the wooden frame. She could have killed them both. A man rode by on a dagger-tooth cat. She could have killed him, too, and ridden away on the creature.

Instead she stood meekly, then followed with the rest of them through the Badlander camp, towards the Plains Strider. The spiders were a clever trap. Perhaps she might be able to rip the box off her neck before they bit her. Perhaps the changes in her physiology brought about by Owsla training and power-animal conditioning might make her resistant to their venom. Or perhaps, if she tried anything, she'd end up on the ground with her jaw, legs and back broken.

The Badlander warriors, cooks, servants and others hardly gave any of them, even Chogolisa Earthquake, a second glance. Up ahead, in the Plains Strider, Sofi could see a caged white bear and other large animals she didn't recognise.

You didn't have to be a genius to piece it together. The Badlanders, or at least this group of them, toured the Ocean of Grass and perhaps further, looking for interesting people and animals to take back to the Badlands. They'd caught the Owsla and the Wootah tribe not because they'd been after them specifically, but because they'd come across them and they were interesting. It was as if the Badlanders were on a deer hunt and the Owsla were any old group of deer. It was belittling.

She would show them that they weren't deer. She'd show them that the Owsla weren't to be captured and transported against their will. But how? She caught Yoki Choppa's eye, raised her eyebrows and cocked her head as if to say, "should I rip the trap off and risk the spider bite?"

He shook his head, just a little, very slowly, about as expressive as he ever was. She trusted his judgement. She would bide her time.

"Come here! You at the back, come here!" called Chapa Wangwa when they reached the side of the Plains Strider. "You're the one who fought Rappa Hoga, or at least tried to. Ha! Ha! Oh, it was funny!" He raised his voice so that anyone within a hundred paces could hear. "Most of you missed it! Rappa Hoga beat her as if she were a little child. Come to the front, child-warrior. What's your name?"

Owsla and Wootah parted to give her passage, but Sofi Tornado wasn't going to follow the orders of a grinning psychopath, unless, of course, he was her emperor (and Zaltan may have been a psychopath, but he'd never grinned). She stood, holding his eye.

Chapa Wangwa's smile only widened. "Oh, you look angry, poor little girl. You!" he pointed at Gunnhild Kristlover. "You must have something to say about anger?"

"*Anger is the mother of bravery*," said Gunnhild, loud and clear.

"No! Not what I was after. Give me a phrase that says anger is bad, not good."

Gunnhild shrugged. "Sorry, that's all I've got."

"Never mind. You—fighting child woman—come here."

"Sofi," whispered Sitsi Kestrel. "Please do as he asks. Our time will come and we'll need you when it does. *Anger is a snake. If you hold onto it, it will bite you.*"

Sofi walked to Chapa Wangwa, almost smiling because competitive Sitsi just had to show the Mushroom Woman that she wasn't the only one who could trot out a relevant maxim.

"Good, good! Now, what is your name?"

"Sofi Tornado."

"*Sofi Tornado*. Wonderful. Now, Sofi Tornado, you can be the first to climb onto the Plains Strider."

Sofi sighed and leapt onto the ladder. With the spiders on her neck, what else could she do?

Sassa Lipchewer followed the Owsla and Wootah, including Ottar's racoons, up the side of the Plains Strider. Wulf the Fat came last. The captain of the Owsla had been first up, so it was the role of the chief Wootah to take the rear. It wasn't a big thing or particularly important. It was just another example of Wulf knowing what to do and doing it.

She was proud and pleased that she'd be having his baby. Or so she hoped. She'd vomited that morning, and the morning before. The first time she'd put it down to dodgy fish; Bjarni had caught a very odd-looking thing which Sitsi Kestrel had insisted was good eating. However, nobody else had been ill and then Sassa had been sick again that morning.

So, she was pregnant.

She was elated and terrified. It had been bad enough when they were only heading into the unknown, but now they had been captured by these frightening people and she had a pair of deadly spiders strapped to her neck that might bite her at any moment . . . what was the future for the tiny person fighting to grow inside her? One thing was for sure. She was going to do her very best to stay alive until she'd given birth to him or her.

She followed Thyri Treelegs' stocky bottom up the ladder. The first level was cages of animals—bears and lions and various others. She stopped when she spotted a white bear, an animal she'd never seen before but which popped up a lot in the story of her ancestors' journey from the old world.

"Hurry on there!" shouted Chapa Wangwa from below. "We're about to leave!"

The ladder led onto a broad wooden platform as high as the highest roof in Hardwork. She climbed through a gap in the side rail and stopped again, amazed.

Sassa had never seen a ship, but she'd seen boats and knew enough from tales that this was a similar construction to a large boat—or ship—and that she was on its upper deck. It was a plank-floored, tapered rectangle, over seventy paces long, fifteen paces broad at its wide end, three paces across at the point. A navel-high rail ran around the outer edge, and Badlanders were encouraging Calnians and Wootah to find places to sit along it.

Sitting cross-legged at the pointy end, facing away from her, were six of the bald children. Nearer were four other people, all looking wide-eyed at the newcomers. Wide-eyed and bug-eyed, now that she looked at them. They all had protruding irises. They looked weird, but neither they nor the bald children were the weirdest thing on the top deck of the Plains Strider.

Sitting against the rail at the blunt end was a new monster. It was the shape of a person, but covered entirely in reddish-black fur and larger even than Chogolisa Earthquake. Picking at its toes, its brow furrowed, it seemed oblivious to everything around it.

"Hurry, sit down by the rail!" shouted a Badlander. "We're about to leave!"

Did he really mean that this vast structure was going to move? *Surely not.*

"Come on! Sit! Anywhere but near the squatch!"

"The squatch?" asked Wulf.

"Hairy giant at the end. Stay out of the reach of those long arms unless you're looking for a swift death."

Wulf guided Sassa to a space next to the four strangers, three men and a woman, who nodded greetings as they sat. They didn't look too happy, as well they might not. They also had spider boxes on their necks.

"So," said Sassa, trying not to stare at their bulging, fishy eyes, "where are you lot—"

She was interrupted by Wulf placing a hand on her arm and nodding westwards.

A vast flock of crowd pigeons was rising and blocking out a good portion of the sky. She remembered when a crowd pigeon flock had flown over Hardwork and left the whole place coated in pigeon shit. She guessed that this lot must be clearing out of the way, if the Plains Strider really was going to move.

Then the deck lurched. Sassa grabbed the rail. She felt a wave of nausea and visceral fear as, creaking like a forest in a storm, the whole deck of the Plains Strider lifted. She looked at Wulf.

He winked. "Here we go, I guess."

More creaking, more raising of the nose, another lurch and it felt like they were moving along. She looked down to the plain. The whole structure had set off across the grassland, following the flock of crowd pigeons.

"How . . . ?" she wondered

"Amazing, isn't it!" said one of the strangers, his eyes bulging all the more. "It's a big sledge, nothing more, but still amazing."

"Are the pigeons . . . ?"

"They're towing us, that's right. Every one of them is attached to the Plains Strider by a strand of silk from a beeba spider, the same nasty little bastards we've got attached to out necks. Every evening, the pigeons bite through their threads and head out to feed. When they come back, a shitload of beeba spiders spend the night reattaching the pigeons to the Plains Strider."

"They're very compliant spiders," said Wulf.

"It's the Empty Children, those bald kids," said the stranger. "They control the animals. I don't know how. It's not just the spiders and the pigeons. The back end's supported by a load of buffalo. I'm no fan of the Badlanders, but it really is an extraordinary creation."

"How does it cross rivers?" asked Sassa, looking out over the plain. They were clipping along now at about, she guessed, the pace of a running buffalo. In spite of Chapa Wangwa's threats, this already seemed like a far better way of crossing the Ocean of Grass than walking.

"Inflated bladders, attached to the buffalo and the base of the craft," continued the stranger. "Buffalo swim, pigeons fly and the whole thing floats across. But that's enough about the Plains Strider. Who are you lot and where were you headed when these bastards caught you?"

"I was about to ask the same of you," said Wulf.

"I asked first!" the man smiled affably.

"Okay, tell me your names and I'll tell you our story."

"You've got a deal. I'm Ovets. He's Walex, she's Sandea and that's Clogan." Each of his bulge-eyed friends smiled and nodded as they were introduced. "We're all from the Popeye tribe."

"Of course you are."

"What do you mean?"

"Popeye, because of..." Sassa was enjoying Wulf's discomfort.

"We're named after a god. What else would it be?"

"I..."

"I know what you're doing. You're trying to get our story before you tell us yours!" Ovets chuckled. "Come on, your story first. Deal's a deal."

"You can see right through me." Wulf chuckled, too. "Around a hundred years ago, our ancestors arrived from across the Wild Salt Sea..."

Wulf and Sassa told the Popeyes the tale of the Hardworkers and how they'd become Wootah. When they got to the part about The Meadows, Ovets interrupted.

"The Meadows in the Desert You Don't Walk Out Of?"

"Yes, across the Shining Mountains, apparently, and—"

"Don't go there." For the first time Ovets looked serious, afraid even. His tribesmates looked the same.

"Why?" asked Sassa.

"Popeye tribe territory was west of the Shining Mountains, in the Desert You Don't Walk Out Of," said Ovets.

"Was?" asked Sassa, feeling a wave of dread.

"We're the only four Popeyes left. The rest are dead."

"How?"

"It began with a flash flood in winter before the snow melted, when you don't get flash floods. Then there was a rockslide, several tornadoes, another rockslide, more flash floods," he shook his head and his protruding eyes filled with tears. "We learnt to live with the disasters, to avoid dangerous locations and find shelter. Then the monsters came."

"Monsters?"

"Giant wasps and screaming, flying beasts with claws like dagger-tooth cats. They're everywhere on the far side of the Shining Mountains, and I've heard of much worse—bigger, wilder monsters, greater disasters and more. We were in the lee of the mountains, a long, long way from The Meadows. The nearer The Meadows you go, they say, the worse it is."

"How far was the Popeye territory from The Meadows?" Wulf asked.

"About five hundred miles."

Wulf looked at Sassa.

"In the end though, it was another tribe that finished us off. Pushed east themselves, they took our land and told us to leave. There were more of them and they were better armed. We left our shelters and headed east. We are the only four that made it across the Shining Mountains. The rest were killed by squatches." He pointed at the hairy hominid at the back of the Plains Strider. "That's a squatch, but it must be freakishly weak or have a damaged mind for the Badlanders to catch it. The rest of them are the most awful, evil, powerful...they're too intelligent to be called animals. They're monsters."

Ovets took Sassa's hands in his and looked bulgingly from her to Wulf. "Please, if the Badlanders let you go or you manage to get away, promise me that you'll head back eastwards and won't try to go to The Meadows. If, by some miracle, you get past the squatches in the Shining Mountains, you'll be killed the day you arrive in the Desert You Don't Walk Out Of."

"You don't need worry about the Desert You Don't Walk Out Of," said a Badlander voice.

Sassa looked up. The grinning Chapa Wangwa was standing there, hands on hips.

"Why not?" asked Wulf.

"Because you are all going to die in the Badlands! Ha ha ha!"

Chapter 7

Calnians Do Cross the Water Mother

The Swan Empress Ayanna crossed the Water Mother in her golden swan canoe, paddled by twenty strong men. Two boatloads of drummers and trumpeters followed beating and blaring out a tune to tell the world that one goddess was crossing another.

Her army was arranged on the far bank: ten thousand warriors, plus all the chefs, tailors, weapons makers and all the others needed to march an army several hundred miles across the Ocean of Grass to crush the Badlanders. Every time the boat-borne orchestra reached the end of a phrase, the assembed men and women of her army would shout out a great "Hoo!"

Calnians didn't cross the Water Mother, so the saying went, but if one had to, thought Ayanna, one should do it in style.

Chippaminka was at her side. Further back in her canoe were her fan men, her tiny son and his own three nursemaid retinue.

The six-day-old boy could vaguely waggle his weedy limbs, moan, squeak, scream like an army of demons and suckle so hard it felt like he was trying to suck her insides out through her nipple. Objectively, he was little more than a noisy maggot. And yet, to Ayanna's surprise, she already loved him more than she loved herself. She had not expected to, at least not to the degree that she'd die for him without a quibble. Well, maybe a quick quibble—she'd explore other options—but if she really did have to die for him then she'd have been happy to.

She'd called him Calnian and everyone had told her what a great name it was. Of course, she could have called him Cockmuncher and they would have told her that it was a simply marvellous name, but she thought they were sincere about Calnian. It *was* a good name. His full title, Swan Prince Calnian, sounded rather fine.

Some had suggested that she leave the little boy behind, but she hadn't considered it for a moment. Chippaminka had consulted her alchemical bowl and agreed that he should come.

Chippaminka was the other person she'd fallen for recently. The girl was a gifted warlock, at least as powerful as Yoki Choppa, but she was also skilled in the sensual arts. Chippaminka's physical ministrations had begun with oiled massages to Ayanna's pregnant belly and progressed into more. The girl could do amazing things with her hands.

The excellent Chippaminka had also taken on more than the chief warlock role. She wasn't the slain Chamberlain Hatho's official replacement, but she'd assumed his duties, advising the empress and dealing with the boring aspects of rule, such as the logistics of assembling this huge army. Ayanna hardly needed to speak to anyone these days, other than Chippaminka and Calnian.

Yes, things were very well with Ayanna. She had a lovely new son, an excellent and humble new adviser and lover, and they were off to crush the Badlanders and take the Ocean of Grass for Calnia and Calnian.

The only major cloud was the fate of her Owsla. Chippaminka's alchemical bowl said that Yoki Choppa had tricked them into joining the Badlanders. It was hard to fathom, but she had no reason to disbelieve Chippaminka, and her bowl's claims had been backed up by the disappearance of the Owsla, apart from Luby Zephyr, of course.

Apparently Luby had been injured and left by the rest of

them well before they'd even reached Goachica territory, so was not involved in the treachery. Ayanna had asked to see Luby, but Chippaminka had saved her the bother and given Luby the prefect role. The one remaining Owsla was to train and lead the division of the army that was preparing to fight the rest of their own Owsla, should that prove necessary.

It was a sensible allocation of resources, and, once again, Ayanna had thanked Chippaminka for seeing the right path and acting on it without troubling the empress.

Ayanna looked back and spotted Luby Zephyr on the prow of one of the following boats of dignitaries and generals. She nodded to Luby, who waved rather frantically in reply. Probably trying to convey congratulations on Calnian's birth, thought the empress. Along with the rest of the Owsla, Luby was as close to a friend as the ruler of an empire could have.

"Chippaminka," she said, turning to her warlock.

"My empress?" the girl smiled subserviently and salaciously.

"Arrange a private audience with Luby Zephyr as soon as possible."

"Of course."

The paddlers paddled on, pulling her boat ever closer to the western bank and the empire of the Badlanders.

Chapter 8
Easy Riding

Around noon the following day, Sitsi Kestrel and Finnbogi the Boggy were kneeling on the deck of the Plains Strider, leaning on the rail.

"If you'd told me a while back," said Finnbogi, "that I'd be sitting on a sledge the size of a village carried by a herd of buffalo and pulled by several million pigeons, with a couple of deadly spiders strapped to my neck, talking to one of the Calian Owsla, hundreds of miles from Hardwork, heading west and watching a bunch of bald kids trot by on goats while another load of people rode by on dagger-tooth cats, I might not have believed you."

"They're not goats," said Sitsi, "they're bighorn sheep."

"Bighorn sheep? Why have I never seen them before?"

Sitsi told Finnbogi what she knew about bighorns; that they lived in the mountains, could walk up and down cliffs, that the males fought by charging headfirst at each other, and more. This led to further explanation. She had to explain what mountains were, that cliffs got quite a bit higher than the little rock walls he'd seen at Heartberry Canyon and the Water Mother, how different animals lived in different places depending on the habitat to which the animal was suited, and on and on.

They were actually okay, the Wootah tribe, Sitsi thought, but by Innowak's warm rays, were they stupid. Well, maybe not stupid: *Stupidity isn't lack of knowledge, it's lack of inquiry* one of her teachers had told her. By that measure, the Wootah were not stupid. They were, however, forehead slappingly uneducated.

Growing up, Sitsi had been on countless informative field trips. Any animals and plants that she hadn't seen in their natural habitats, she's seen in Calnia's gardens, menageries and markets, or her teachers had described them.

She knew she'd been lucky. The Wootah had never been anywhere nor had anything brought to them and knew almost nothing about the world outside the Goachica confinement. So it was odd that most of them were inquisitive. Finnbogi was like a bright child who'd been confined for life on the Mountain of the Sun in Calnia, told nothing, then let out for the first time when he became an adult. Which, she supposed, wasn't far from the actual situation.

The Plains Strider rolled along across the Ocean of Grass below a blue sky and a sparse fleet of high, white clouds gliding from south to north. They'd travelled all the previous day, stopped for the night, then set off again, always westward.

For all her education, Sitsi had never heard of the Plains Strider, or even the notion that such a vehicle could exist. She'd had no idea either that the Badlanders were touring the world collecting people and animals. She guessed the Badlanders kept quiet about it and anybody who saw their giant sledge was either captured or killed.

So, if you could forget the spiders strapped to their necks, and that the unbeatable Owsla had been beaten, and that Chapa Wangwa kept reminding them that a gruesome death awaited them at their destination, they were in a fascinating situation.

Endless prairie stretched all around. There was plenty to marvel at on the Ocean of Grass, but most striking of all were the buffalo. She'd seen herds of buffalo before, but from this elevated position she fully understood just how numerous they were. They'd passed a herd the previous day that must have been a million-strong, walking northwards in a parade ten animals wide, away from a prairie fire that blazed in the south.

As she stared at the sights, seeking out new information and devising new theories, Sitsi asked Finnbogi about the Wootah.

"Our ancestors came across Olaf's Salt Sea."

"That must be what we call the Wild Salt Sea."

"Maybe."

"Why did they come?"

"They didn't like the way they were being ruled, so the story goes, and they left."

"How were they being ruled?"

"Most people lived shitty lives, working hard and often going hungry or cold—even starving or freezing to death— so that a small but powerful gang could muck about raiding other tribes, feasting and getting pissed. The rulers could kill your kid or shag your cattle or whatever whenever the mood took them."

"They could shag your cattle?"

"That may be an exaggeration, but I think they could have done if they'd wanted to, yes. I don't really know. I never paid much attention to the elders' tales."

Sitsi wrung everything she could about Wootah history from the young man, which did not take long, then decided she might as well educate him if he couldn't educate her.

"I'll tell you something I worked out about the buffalo yesterday, if you're interested," she said.

"I'm interested!" said Finnbogi, genuinely it seemed.

This was great. In the Owsla, only Luby Zephyr had listened properly to Sitsi's animal theories, and she was gone. That wasn't quite true. Chogolisa Earthquake always pretended to be interested but Sitsi could tell that she wasn't really.

"You see that herd there?" she asked.

Finnobogi peered at the horizon. "Uh, no?"

That was heartening. Her eyesight might be diminishing, but it seemed she could still see a good deal further than normal people, or him at least. "Are your eyes normal?"

"What?"

"Do you have any problems with your eyesight?"

"No. But I can't see anything but green and blue where you're pointing."

"Good."

"What?"

"Never mind. Can you see *that* herd?" She pointed.

"Yes."

"Good, now can you see in front of them, on the path they're headed along, that the land is a different colour?"

"Yes."

"In a strip pretty much exactly as wide as the buffalo herd?"

"It's the same width."

"Which means...?"

"They're following a path?"

"*Exactly!* And who made the path?"

He looked confused for a moment, then said: "They must have done."

"That's it!"

"Uh, okay...but so what?"

"Here's the clever bit. It you have a good look at all their paths, you'll see that they pass through the lowest parts of the land and the lushest areas of grass."

"So the buffalo have planned the best routes! I get it."

Sitsi smiled at his enthusiasm. "And look ahead—the Plains Strider is following one of their paths. Can you see the track sweeping to the left to avoid the higher ground ahead?"

"I can."

"Any moment we'll turn left to follow it."

Satisfyingly, the huge cloud of draught pigeons immediately swung over to the left and the nose of the craft followed.

"Amazing," said Finnbogi. "My dad Erik—that guy over there," Finnbogi pointed to where the largest and thickest-bearded of the Wootah tribe was sitting against the opposite side rail, talking to Chogolisa Earthquake, "reckons that animals are just as intelligent as humans but they don't bother with all the dressing up and talking about pointless crap like we do."

"He was the exile who lived with the Lakchans?"

"Yes."

"That figures."

"What, why?"

"He's learned a bit."

"Oh."

"Don't be disappointed, you'll learn, too. You've been sheltered. You worked out the buffalo paths without much prompting, and as far as I know, you and I are the only people from east of the Water Mother who've done that."

Finally, one the Owsla was talking to him! They'd ignored Finnbogi the entire first day aboard the Plains Strider, then, on the second, after they'd been fed a really very decent wild rice and buffalo dish for breakfast, the shortest of them had come on over, leant on the rail next to him, told him her name was Sitsi Kestrel and quizzed him about Hardwork and its history.

Finnbogi was delighted to discover that she was no goddess, despite her astonishingly large eyes. She was just like a Hardworker woman, and yet also completely different. Like a Hardworker woman in that she was a normal person, and different because she was her own character, as different as Thyri Treelegs was from Sassa Lipchewer, or Bodil Gooseface was from Gunnhild Kristlover.

Sitsi was fascinated by everything, especially where Olaf the Worldfinder and the rest had come from, and he'd been happy to fill her in on all the details. If she had a fault, it was that she was a bit too proud of her own knowledge and a bit too keen to point out the gaps in his, but that was only if he was being picky, and he'd resolved to try to be less picky.

Thyri Treelegs, sitting across the deck next to Bodil Goose-face, hadn't looked at them once, but, by the way she was sitting, Finnbogi knew that she knew he'd been chatting away for an absolute age to the young, good-looking, famous warrior woman.

It was also simply magnificent, despite the spiders on their necks, despite the threats of the vile Chapa Wangwa, not to be walking for once. Finnbogi had thought he'd got used to walking all day, that he was even enjoying it. But a day on the Plains Strider, almost entirely free from insects, with nothing to do but sit and stare at the scenery, had shown him that he was best suited to indolence, or at least indolence with a view.

He'd seen a great storm form and sail away who knew how many miles to the south, a tornado a long way off to the south-west, millions of buffalo and other animals, and a prairie fire. And he'd talked to a beautiful warrior goddess straight out of a saga who was proving to be, if not entirely down to earth, then certainly prepared to spend time with someone who was.

The other thing making Finnbogi happy, which he thought was downright odd, was that because they'd been caught, he was no longer scared of being caught.

Yes, the Owsla were their friends now officially, but he'd seen how Sofi Tornado looked at the Wootah and he trusted her about as far as he could have thrown Chogolisa Earthquake. So, even after the Owsla had stopped pursuing then, the terror of pursuit had sat heavy in his gut. Now that they'd been captured good and proper, that fear had gone.

He knew it was dumb. If they tried to escape the beeba spiders would bite them and they'd die horribly, and Chapa Wangwa had promised them a horrible death when they arrived at the Badlands in a few days, but at least there was nothing chasing him any more.

Then, as if to prove him wrong, or perhaps because the

gods didn't want him to relax, or maybe just because Loakie would find it amusing, a shrill scream ripped through the air; then another, then another.

He put his hands to his ears. Sitsi Kestrel was on her feet in an action-ready stance, scanning the deck of the Plains Strider for the source of the terrifying noise.

"You can talk to animals?" asked Chogolisa Earthquake.

"Shhhh. The others don't know." Erik wasn't sure why he was telling Chogolisa. "I can't exactly converse with them. I can hear their thoughts sometimes. I can ask some of them to do things for me and they might. But most animals are paranoid, reactionary and selfish and it's pretty much impossible to persuade them to do something that they weren't going to do anyway."

"Can you hear all animals?"

"Most of them. But often it's not much and sometimes it's downright unpleasant. Just because you can touch everything doesn't mean you want to know what everything feels like."

"Like dog turds."

"The perfect analogy. Try to talk to a chipmunk, for example, and you'll wish you could scrub your mind clean. They're twisted little fuckers."

"Can you get our spiders not to bite us?"

The flock of crowd pigeons swung to the left and the deck creaked and moved. Chogolisa shifted to steady herself and her knee came to rest on Erik's.

"I'm already trying," he replied, leaving his knee where it was, "but I can't find anything. It's like trying to carve a stone by looking at it. And the pigeons are even odder. They just shout at me to go away lest I divide the flock. I think that whatever I can do, those Empty Children can do a lot better. Maybe they're stopping me from talking to their animals."

"What about the squatch?" she nodded at the hairy giant sitting on its own at the rear of the deck.

"I had a go yesterday. I get nothing from that either, but in a different way. I can't use my mind to communicate with people in any way. I get the same sort of feeling of nothing from her."

"Her?"

"I guess I get a little. I know she's a she, and I know she's unhappy, but that's about it. What do you—"

A shrill scream ripped the very air asunder, then another and another.

"What the..." Erik put a hand on Chogolisa's mighty, smooth arm.

"It's the spiders," he said, then, because he could see all the Owsla and Wootah on the deck were panicking, he shouted: "It's the spiders! Relax!"

"What's happening?" yelled Chogolisa over the clamour of spider screams.

"I don't know, but I don't think it's bad."

"Are you communicating with them now? Is that how you know it's them?

"No, but look at the other people." Erik nodded at the four Popeyes who'd already been aboard. They looked unconcerned.

"He's right!" shouted one of them, the man called Ovets. "It's just the spiders calling out."

"What for?" asked Wulf.

"Watch," said Ovets.

Erik did. Two flies landed on Chogolisa's neck box. They crawled through what Erik had taken to be air holes. Her spiders stopped screaming, then his did, too, then everybody else's were silent.

Owsla and Wootah looked about, some confused, some afraid. Erik was about to tell them what had happen when Sofi Tornado said: "The spiders were calling out for food. They have that food now." She sat back down, on her own, as she'd been since they set off the day before.

"Does she always sit on her own?" Erik asked Chogolisa.

"No. But when she does, we leave her alone."

Sassa Lipchewer sat quietly with Wulf the Fat and Yoki Choppa, shaken by the spider screams. The warlock Yoki Choppa was good company since he could go a whole day without speaking, which suited her mood.

Sassa did not like the spiders.

As a girl she'd fed squirrels on the edge of the woods. One squirrel had lost most of its fur and pustules had grown on its bare skin. After a few days, she'd found the squirrel dead. She'd picked it up and watched, horror-struck, as breathtakingly long and fat maggots had pushed their way out of the pustules. She felt like that squirrel now, hosting animals that were going to kill her.

"In theory," she said, as a lone bear stood out of the grass nearby to watch the Plains Strider thunder by, "the way to get these spiders off our necks is not to try."

"Right . . . ?" asked Wulf.

"If we try to take them off, they'll bite. So we have to take them off without trying."

"How do we do that?"

"I haven't worked that out yet. Any ideas, Yoki Choppa?"

Yoki Choppa nodded at Freydis and Ottar. They were walking towards the monster at the back of the deck.

"Not a good idea," he said.

"Freydis!" Sassa called. "What are you doing?"

"We're going to talk to the hairy woman. It's okay, Ottar says it's fine."

"Um. Okay!" She turned to Yoki Choppa. "He's always right," she explained apologetically.

The warlock shrugged.

Sofi Tornado could feel her power leaching from her pores. When she'd woken from the dart drug, she could hear the spiders on their necks. Now, at noon the following day, she could not.

Paloma Pronghorn walked up, legs wide to counter the rolling of the Plains Strider, and sat next to her.

"Maybe spending the day looking at your own feet is a worthwhile activity," said the speedy warrior, "but you are missing some extraordinary animal life. Lot of Pronghorns."

"Right."

"You do know we are approaching burrowing owl and tarantula hawk wasp territory?"

"I do."

"And the spider confinement thing may be clever, but it does mean we can walk around in the evening, so you should have your animal very soon?"

"Yes."

"Good, okay. Um, do you want to see the biggest herd of buffalo you've ever seen? Or a type of bear that I've never seen before? Because I can see both of those things right now and you could, too, if you'd just look around."

Sofi looked her friend in the eye. "Thing is, Paloma, I don't give the tiniest of fucks about wildlife. How about you piss off and find someone who does?"

"I will piss off almost immediately, but Yoki Choppa gave me this for you to eat." She dropped a morsel of dried caribou into Sofi's hand, "Now, off I piss! See ya!"

Sofi Tornado sat and tried to scheme but her mind kept returning to the feeling of being held aloft and impotent like a caught fish. A small fish at that. She kept hearing the swishing of her inept flailing, the sound of the blown dart, the soft smack as it punctured her flesh.

She had lost a fight.

She sat on her own until she felt the craft bump to a stop. She heard Paloma tell the others to leave her alone, then heard them climb down. She heard the squatch roar as it was encouraged to leave the Plains Strider. So a squatch could be controlled by the spiders in the same way that the people could. That was almost interesting enough to break her out of her funk. Almost.

The Empty Children walked past and climbed down from the deck. Perhaps enough distance would open up between her and them for the spiders to bite? If not, they were bound to come and get her soon, and she would kill anyone who touched her. Then they'd make the spiders bite.

Death would be a release.

She sat and listened to the noises of others busying about, settling the Plains Strider for the night and preparing the camp. It reminded her of being ill as a child, confined to her bed as the noisy industry of the day went on outside, the world somehow still functioning perfectly well without her in it.

She heard Badlanders by the side of the Plains Strider discussing what to do with her. They were interrupted by Rappa Hoga on his dagger-tooth. He asked what was going on, leapt off his cat and shinned up the wooden ladder.

The leader of the Badlander catch squad and the only person in the world who'd ever beaten her in a fight walked across the deck. His gait was wide because, she guessed, he was used to walking across this deck when the Plains Strider was moving, or possibly because he'd been straddling a giant cat all day.

"You were diminished when we fought," he said.

She opened her eyes.

The broad, tall man was wearing a pocketed leather robe over his breechcloth. It was a garment intended for practicality, not concealment. She could still see the inner curves of his large chest, the humps of his powerful abdomen and the swollen muscles of his calves and thighs.

Early in the days of the Owsla, before Sofi had been made its captain, they'd paid a punitive visit to a tribe that had its own herd of buffalo. The tribe followed the herd's migrations and managed its population, killing any stupid, weak or infirm animals. The herd, shaped by centuries of husbandry, was the finest collection of animals she'd ever seen. Even among those excellent animals, one animal stood out: a gigantic bull with smooth skin, shining wool, muscles on top of muscles. He was a busy animal, since the tribe encouraged him to shag as many of the females as possible in the hope that his sons might be equally superb.

Rappa Hoga reminded Sofi of that bull.

"It would have been a longer fight, had you been at your peak. You might have won." He squatted to bring his face level with hers. "I, too, am enhanced by power animals. Were I not, you would have beaten me as easily as you beat the rest of them. If I hadn't had my power animals for a few days, as you hadn't, then we cannot know what would have happened."

How did he know this? Had Yoki Choppa betrayed them further?

"What is your power animal?" she asked, despite herself.

"I don't know. I'm a warrior, not a cook. Now come, we have stopped in a special place. Let me show you."

Sofi Tornado considered launching herself at him. She might be able to crush his windpipe before he reacted, or her spiders bit.

Instead she stood. "All right then, let's go."

Chapter 9

By the Lake

The Plains Strider was settled on grassland to the north of a wood. People and beasts passed hither and thither, cookfires were stoked and food prepared. The crowd pigeons ascended in such a number that they created a breeze in the still evening.

Sofi Tornado followed Rappa Hoga through the camp. They passed Sitsi Kestrel showing Sassa Lipchewer how to improve her bow grip. Nearby, Keef the Berserker was sparring with Paloma Pronghorn, long axe against killing stick. Given the loss of his eye and ear, and the fact he wasn't Owsla, the Mushroom Man's moves were fluid and effective. Nevertheless, Sofi did not like to see her women fraternising with the enemy. It would not help when the time came to kill them. At least Morningstar had the right idea, off on her own, stretching after the long day of inactivity.

Bjarni Chickenhead walked by, yawning, and Sofi had to stifle her own reactive yawn. A moment later she was startled by screams. Freydis and Ottar were running around a tent, pursued by Wulf the Fat, Bjarni Chickenhead and a giggling Chogolisa Earthquake. Sofi sighed.

"The joy of the beeba spiders," said Rappa Hoga, "is that we can allow our captives freedom, even to keep their weapons. The sensible captive will use that freedom to have a few last joyful days as he or she crosses the Ocean of Grass. The less sensible ones will sulk."

At the edge of the camp Rappa Hoga called an Empty Child to follow him. The boy or girl leapt onto a bighorn sheep and trotted behind as they walked into the woods.

"How far can one get from a bighorn kid before the spiders bite?" Sofi asked.

"Not far."

Here could be a chance, thought Sofi Tornado, while there was only one child monitoring her spiders. She just had to kill the kid, rip the collar off before the spiders bit her, then defeat the man who'd beaten her so easily two days before. Then she could rush back to the camp, slice the boxes off everyone's necks in the blink of an eye, then defeat all the dagger-tooth and moose-mounted warriors.

Not a great plan.

The path led through sparse woods to a broader track that skirted the north shore of a lake. A startled deer bucked and bolted gracelessly off along the path. Geese, ducks and other waterfowl guided flotillas of fledglings across the calm water. Fish broke the surface, flashing wet backs. At the west end of the lake a herd of buffalo were drinking and grazing in the soft evening light.

They walked around the eastern end of the lake in silence, disturbing opossums, muskrats, otters and one disgruntled skunk. The woods ended at a regular man-made bank, with the lake lapping on one side and a drop of around ten paces on the other. They walked across the bank and came to a spill-way dam built of logs. Rappa Hoga stopped, hands on hips.

"We made this," he said, "with wood carried here on the Plains Strider."

"Well done."

"The industry was ours but the idea came from beavers."

"Makes sense."

"The Plains Strider follows buffalo paths."

"Wow."

"My point is that we learn from animals."

"Marvellous."

"Another thing we have learned is that if you remove the predators from an area, then the prey, unchecked, will multiply in such numbers that it spoils the land, for every animal including itself. It sounds paradoxical, yet if an animal that is meant to be preyed upon is not preyed upon, then that animal will suffer."

"Got it."

"Humans are prey animals."

She looked into his dark eyes. He appeared to be serious.

"Many years ago," he said, holding her gaze, "large predators like dagger-tooth cats were much more numerous, and there were other creatures that also ate humans. The beleaguered humans learned to create and use weapons, to cooperate to defeat animals more powerful than any man, and to build defended settlements. They fought back against the predators. They did well. Too well. They extinguished entire species, and limited the others so effectively that today it is unusual for any man or woman to be killed by an animal."

Sofi thought about the three Hardworkers killed by bears, but said nothing. Calnia's historians also believed that predatory animals had been a problem for their ancestors.

"The removal of predators may seem good for humans," Rappa Hoga continued, "but in terms of natural balance and the health of the world, it's about as desirable as deer teaming up and using spears against us. With no predators, humans have multiplied to unhealthy levels."

"So humans must be culled, and the Badlanders have taken the job?" A goose honked angrily.

"Yes."

"So why bother capturing people? Why not simply kill them?"

"Two reasons. Some of you, the better warriors and more interesting animals, will serve as entertainment for our people. We are bloodthirsty. The less capable captives will be used for research into the mundane and the magical. There is a third option."

"You want me to join the Badlanders."

"Good guess."

"The colour of your skin, the shape of your face, the size of you. You're no Badlander. You were captured on a raid and given the same option that you're planning to give me. Die with your fellows honourably, or live on as a Badlander."

"And you choose honour."

Sofi nodded.

"Of course you do. I did at first. My apologies for being too obvious. I didn't want you to know about that choice until you'd seen more of us, understood our goals and our power and, most importantly, met our chief, Beaver Man."

"Beaver Man is a very strange name."

"It's a play on words, sounds like—"

"Be the man. But that's—"

"Shit? Yes, I know. So does he. He had strange parents, but he respects their memory and will not change his name even though it does cause him some anguish."

"The great chief of the Badlanders suffers from anguish?"

"He is a complicated man. Those parents whose memory he respects so much, for example, he killed. Let us head back."

As they reached the path through the woods, she said: "Just in theory, because there are no imaginable circumstances under which I would join the Badlanders, but I assume the offer extends to my women?"

"Indeed. All of the Calnian Owsla could become Badlanders."

"Yoki Choppa?"

"He would also be useful to us."

"Any of the Mushroom Men?"

"None. I'd be surprised if Beaver Man kills them quickly, since they are interesting, but he will kill them."

Sofi nodded.

*   *   *

Finnbogi the Boggy walked past Sassa Lipchewer and Sitsi Kestrel to the edge of the wood, where he found Thyri Treelegs sprinting between two trees, resting, then sprinting again.

"You could get just as far by staying in the same place," Finnbogi suggested.

"And you could get punched in the face for saying shit things that don't even deserve to be called jokes." Thyri set off between the trees again.

"Aren't you worried you might set off your spiders?" he shouted when she'd reached the far tree.

"Not...if it means never hearing your voice again," she panted.

"Ha! Ha! I don't suppose you're up for teaching me more about fighting, then?"

"You've lost your sword."

"I meant with this." He held up Sofi Tornado's axe.

"No, I don't think so."

She still thought he'd killed Garth.

"How about I exercise next to you?"

"I can't stop you."

"We both know you could."

"I won't stop you."

That was a softening. Finnbogi suppressed his urge to jump in the air and clap. That wouldn't be very warrior-like. He jogged to join her at the tree.

Later, Finnbogi turned over in his sleeping sack, not sure whether it was Bjarni's snoring or his inability to stop fantasising about Thyri and the Owsla women that was keeping him awake.

Then he was flying, high above the land. It was the Ocean of Grass, but the grass was gone and the only trees were clustered around scatterings of oversized huts and huge, silver, phallic towers. The bare earth stank, which was no surprise as huge, gleaming insects crawled across it, spraying shit.

He soared higher and saw that the land was cut by straight, black tracks. Smaller insects zoomed along these tracks at silly speeds, as fast as Paloma. A huge, stiff-winged bird soared overhead, roaring.

The bare earth became green, and Finnbogi spotted the Plains Strider. He zoomed down to look. It wasn't the Strider, it was another giant gleaming insect, cutting the grass and spewing it into a cart. And the grass wasn't grass, it was crazily regular corn, all the same height, in fields that stretched to the horizon in every direction. There wasn't a deer, racoon, fox or any other beast to be seen.

He flew on, and on and on. It was all the same. Long corn, giant crawling insects chewing up the corn. He passed over more straight tracks where insects zoomed. Finally, he saw some life, a woman walking with two dogs. He flew down to her.

"What's happened?" he asked her. "What has happened to the Ocean of Grass? Where are all the buffalo?"

"We have killed the Ocean of Grass and all the animals," she replied, "to feed the Mushroom Men."

Chapter 10

Chippaminka Must Be Stopped

Luby Zephyr nipped between conical buffalo-skin tents, slipped past guards and skipped through dancing shadows on the fringes of buffalo dung fires.

Since they'd crossed the Water Mother the day before, Luby had been through the motions. She'd walked with her division, discussed Owsla-beating tactics and trained them hard when they stopped for the evening. She didn't know whether her two hundred warriors would be capable of defeating the Owsla—certainly a lot of them would die in the process—but she very much didn't want ever to find out.

Of course, the Owsla hadn't betrayed Calnia. Why would they? The Calnian army was marching on the Badlands under false pretences at the behest of the warlock Chippaminka. What was Chippaminka's game? Luby had tried to persuade herself that the young warlock was acting in Ayanna's and Calnian's best interests. But why all the subterfuge and mind control? The only realistic conclusion was that she was leading the Calnians to their doom. So Luby had to prise the empress away from Chippaminka's clutches and show her the error of her ways.

Arguably, there was no big rush. It would take many days to cross Badlander territory and reach the Badlands themselves. However, Luby would not be happy until she'd ended this insanity and the army was safely back in Calnia. The Ocean of Grass looked flat, but it was scored by valleys that could easily hold an ambushing army. Every moment in Badlander territory was a moment that something might go disastrously and empire-endingly wrong.

So she melted past the empress's guards, slipped round to the back of Ayanna's expansive deer-hide tent and squeezed under its leather side.

The interior was lit only by a glowing fire which wafted the aroma of some exotic wood. There was no buffalo dung on the empress's fire.

Luby waited while her eyes adjusted to the gloom. Soft snores came from the large bed in the centre of the tent. The Swan Prince Calnian, in a cot next to the bed, snuffled in his sleep.

Ayanna and Chippaminka were on the bed, naked, limbs entwined, Chippaminka's cheek resting against Ayanna's milk-swollen breast.

Luby paused. She'd expected the empress to be alone. Now another opportunity had presented itself; a better one. Her obsidian moon blades hung from her belt, freshly sharpened. Surely Chippaminka's death would break her spell?

She padded towards the bed. Chippaminka's neck was exposed. It would be the work of moments. She raised a moon blade.

Chippaminka's eyes flashed open. Luby gasped.

"I think you'd better go," said the warlock in a horrible whisper.

Horror filled Luby's mind, as suddenly and shockingly as fire bursting in a pool of pitch lit by a lobbed torch.

She didn't think. She ran. She didn't stop until she was back in her tent, wrapped in her poncho, shivering, her mind a turmoil of terror.

Chapter 11
Buffalo Soldiers

"I've decided that the collective noun for buffalo," said Paloma Pronghorn the following morning as they passed yet another huge herd of the animals, "is a fuckload."

"So what's the collective noun for crowd pigeons?" Sassa Lipchewer looked up at the great flock towing them along.

"A fuckload of fuckloads?"

"Doesn't really work."

"No." Paloma scratched her head. "What's bigger than a fuck?"

"A cuntload doesn't sound right."

"No."

"How about we scale buffalos back to a shitload, and make crowd pigeons a fuckload?"

"That will have to do for now, I suppose...Hey, look, they're at it again."

At the back of the deck, Freydis the Annoying and Ottar the Moaner were sitting cross-legged in front of the squatch. Ottar was chattering away incomprehensibly at the monster, waving his arms. The squatch was looking back at him, a mildly interested expression on its fleshy lipped, small-eyed face.

"You sure they're all right?" asked Paloma. "The squatch could punch them into a pulp before even I could rescue them."

Sassa shrugged. "I'm sure they're fine. Ottar's never wrong and Freydis has more sense than a longhouse full of jarls."

"A what full of what?"

"She's very sensible. And besides, you die—"

"When you die, yes you explained that yesterday and I cannot refute it. You certainly do die when you die... Talking about cutting things short, you see that crest on the squatch's head?"

"Yup."

"You'd look good with your hair like that, but longer."

"Really?"

"Yes, I can picture it perfectly: a long crest of hair running from nape to forehead."

"Ha ha!"

"No, seriously, let me look at you." Paloma took Sassa's chin in one hand and tilted her head from side to side. "Yup, really, I'm not kidding. You want to be an archer warrior, but that yellow hair is too frivolous. Shave the sides, leave a long bit down the middle, stiffen it with fat and you'll look a lot more formidable than Sitsi Kestrel ever will, even if you'll never be as good with the bow."

"Formidable and minging."

"No. It'll be sexy. Your face is feminine enough to carry it off. You'll look great—a woman with a yellow crest of hair in a land of black-haired people. I'll want to shag you. I wish I could cut my own hair like that."

"Why can't you?"

"If I shaved off my hair and left a big crest, Sofi Tornado would rip the crest off and make me eat it. She's no fan of extreme hairstyles and she comes down pretty hard on breaches in discipline. Will your husband punish you if you mess with your hair? Is that why you're scared of doing it?"

"Have you got a knife?"

"You want me to do it now?"

"No time like the present."

"You get a haircut when you get a haircut, that's what I've always said." Paloma whisked a knife from her belt.

"Krist died so that our sins could be forgiven, and so all who believe in him can go to his father's haven when they die," Gunnhild Kristlover explained to Sitsi Kestrel while they watched Paloma chopping off Sassa's hair on the other side of the Plains Strider.

"Like a spoilt child promising access to his father's pyramid palace," Sitsi replied.

"A spoilt child would not die for others."

Sitsi enjoyed talking to the older woman. She was by far the richest source for information about the Mushroom Men, even if some of it didn't entirely add up. And her god! What a boring one. Generally, it was not done to take the piss out of another tribe's deities, but Krist sounded so pompous and dreary that Sitsi couldn't help it.

"But you said before that Krist didn't die?"

"He died then came back."

"Which isn't dying."

"He went through the process of death."

"Which isn't quite so impressive if you know you're going to be on your feet a couple of days later."

"He didn't know that."

"I suppose that's better . . . And he forgives all sins?"

"Yes."

"And if you believe in him and his dad, you go to this wonderful haven place when you die?"

"Yes."

"But you don't if you don't believe in him?"

"That's right."

"So it's a sin to not believe in him?"

"Yes."

"So surely he forgives that sin, and everyone gets into haven?"

"Some sins cannot be forgiven."

"I bet this fellow's committed most of those." Sitsi nodded at Chapa Wangwa. The Badlander was walking towards them across the deck, grinning from ear to ear.

"Gunnhild Kristlover, Sitsi Kestrel," he smiled. "I'm glad you are together, as it is you two I was hoping to find. Of all your fellows I think you will appreciate the spectacle we are about to see more than the others." He bent his knees and spread his arms to allow for the slowing of the Plains Strider. "In a moment we will come to a stop at Wangwa Ridge. It is not named after me, as you may be thinking, and I am not named after it. No, both the ridge and I are named after the Badlander god Wangwa."

"You mean the Badlander devil Wangwa," said Sitsi, "alternatively known as the Chief of Evil and the Big Shit." She wasn't joking. This was actually true.

"One man's evil is another man's fun," Chapa Wangwa replied.

"*Never rejoice at evil; let good give you pleasure.*" Gunnhild waggled a finger.

"Is it good to strip the flesh from a man's arms? Is it good to see how many millipedes you can force into a woman's stomach before she dies? These are things that give me pleasure, so they must be good, no?"

"*The truly evil believe their actions are good,*" said Sitsi. She'd made up the aphorism while Chapa Wangwa was talking, but reckoned it was as good as any of Gunnhild's.

"You *see!*" said the Badlander. "There will never be a dull moment when we three are together. Although you will both die soon, and horribly, it makes me happy to know that your last few days will be brightened by my acquaintance."

The Plains Strider slowed and bumped down to a stop. "Come with me, come now and I will show you a marvel." He walked away, beckoning.

Sitsi looked at Gunnhild and shrugged. They both followed,

and he led them from the catch wagon, down a hill and along the eastern edge of a marsh. The marsh was a circle of brown reeds in the green prairie, busy with a variety of birds, most of which were long-legged and long-billed. On the western edge of the marsh, perhaps two hundred paces away, the land rose sharply in a crescent-shaped grassy bluff some fifty paces high. It was the most dramatic feature in the gentle plains that Sitsi had seen since the cliffs by the Water Mother over three hundred miles to the east.

"Now stand here," said Chapa Wangwa, "and shortly you will see something very amazing."

"Something that you consider amazing," said Sitsi.

"Yes!"

Sitsi looked at Gunnhild and Gunnhild looked at Sitsi. Gunnhild looked about as uneasy as Sitsi felt.

Tansy Burna whooped and dug her heels all the harder into the flanks of her dagger-tooth cat. The beast roared. The cluster of buffalo around her pressed forward in a new burst of speed, bellowing and butting aside their herd mates in their panic to escape the predator. Her cat lengthened its stride and kept pace.

Tansy loved a buffalo drive. She liked the teamwork, the speed and the killing, but what she actually *loved* was getting one over on the buffalo. She hated buffalo. For a long while she'd been sucked in like everybody else. *Oh the buffalo is so noble*, people said. *Look at its sad eyes, so ancient so wise*, they bleated. Tansy knew different. Buffalo were patronising bastards who thought themselves superior to every other creature for the same reasons that humans thought buffalo were so amazing. They looked good and they were big. But that was all they had. They had broad heads and stout horns and curly brown hair and they thought that made them special, but they were herbivores, for the love of Spider Woman. They were no better than rabbits.

Yet everyone else thought buffalo were the bee's bollocks. These drives were a useful reminder for the buffalo that they were chicken-hearted vegetarians, so scared of dagger-tooth cats and a few howling humans that they'd run to their deaths over a cliff rather than square up to them, even if they did have broad heads, stout horns and curly brown hair.

Not that Wangwa Ridge could be called a cliff. It wasn't even a hill. It was, as the name implied, no more than a steepish ridge. Still, it was high and steep enough.

Hooves thundered around her. Buffalo snorted and screamed. Her cat surged smoothly through their ranks like a sleek orange canoe through hairy rapids.

Ahead, to the west and east, one rider after another slowed their cats to pull back, out of the stampede. They were close to Wangwa Ridge. It was not always the simplest manoeuvre to extricate oneself from the running herd, so you had to pull out good and early to avoid going over the edge. Riding on was pointless anyway, since buffalo this frenzied would carry on over the ridge perfectly well on their own.

Tansy rode on, farther than she was meant to, almost breathless with excitement at her own bravery. All other cats had fallen back. She'd never been last woman riding before. One of her squad was standing on her cat, waving at her to stop. Tansy whooped with glee, leant further forward and clamped her legs all the more tightly on her sinuously sprinting cat.

There was a tornado-smashed tree a couple of hundred paces from the top of the ridge that riders called the point of no return. If you rode your cat past that tree during a stampede over Wangwa Ridge, they said, you'd have no chance of pulling out and your fate would be the same as the buffalos'.

The broken tree rushed closer and closer. Tansy Burna sat up, ready to slow her cat.

But then she thought *fuck it, no.* She pivoted forward at the hips, squeezed her legs, pressed her groin into her mount, dug her fingers into its coat and bit the fur on the back of its neck. She'd overheard one of the weird new captives say something that had stuck with her and she meant to give it a go. What were the exact words again? Oh yes, that was it—

You die when you die.

The Badlanders gathered around Sitsi Kestrel, Gunnhild Kristlover and Chapa Wangwa, all looking expectantly westward across the marsh at the ridge. Chapa Wangwa told the other Badlanders that anyone who spoiled the surprise by mentioning what was about to happen would be lowered upside down into boiling buffalo oil.

The rest of the Wootah, interested as ever to see what was going on, walked up along with Chogolisa Earthquake, Paloma Pronghorn and a few other captives. There was no sign of Yoki Choppa, Morningstar or Sofi Tornado. No surprise about Morningstar and Yoki Choppa; they'd never exactly been the mingling, let's-follow-the-crowd types, but Sitsi was not at all happy with Sofi's self-imposed solitude. The women of the Owsla were used to being led, and they needed their leader all the more in this odd situation. She also suspected that a bit of strategic thinking and ordering people about would shake Sofi Tornado from her funk. The Owsla captain had spent the entire day on her own again, talking to no one. Sitsi couldn't think of a way to be free of the beeba spiders, but surely Sofi would be able to? The Tornado had never let them down before.

Sitsi had guessed what was coming over the ridge. The Calnians themselves were not buffalo drivers. They abhorred the practice and had banned it in their empire. There was nothing wrong with killing a buffalo if you were going to use it, but stampedes killed many, many more than could be used by all but the largest cities, so almost all the dead buffalo were left to rot.

Innowak considered a buffalo drive to be an abomination and so did Sitsi.

Erik the Angry stood with Finnbogi the Boggy, Chogolisa Earthquake, Paloma Pronghorn, the two children and the racoons. All of them were looking across the marsh at the top of the ridge.

"What's this about then?" Finnobgi asked.

"I have no idea," Chogolisa shook her head.

"I think I know," said Paloma, "but our happy friend Wangwa over there has promised that anyone spilling the secret will be lowered upside down into boiling buffalo oil. On balance, I don't think it's worth telling you. Just watch."

"Are we going to like it?" Finnbogi asked

"I shouldn't think so. It might give you nightmares, but you should probably see it. It'll help you understand the Bad-landers. Maybe the children shouldn't see it, though."

"We should," said Freydis.

All was quiet. Nobody spoke. They jumped as a multitude of birds took off from the marsh and flapped away. A moment later Erik felt a rumbling, followed by a giant wave of terror washing towards them. He staggered.

Finnbogi put an hand on his arm. "Are you okay, Erik? Do you want to . . . whoaaah what was *that*!?" Finnbogi collapsed but Erik caught him.

"Finn! Finn!"

"Yes, wow. I lost my legs. Sorry."

"Picture Thyri Treelegs' tits," Erik whispered.

"*What?*"

"Picture Thyri's tits. Just try it."

Whenever Erik was overwhelmed by thoughts that didn't belong to him, he pictured the breasts of a woman whom he considered attractive. Just now, he'd told himself to imagine Morningstar's boobs, but instead he'd found himself thinking about Chogolisa Earthquake's. His choice had surprised him enough to clear the plight of the buffalo from his mind.

"Okay . . ." Finnbogi's face took on a look of concentration. "And . . . done it. Thanks. I felt terrified. What the Hel was it?"

"That, I suspect, was an old family trait that you seem to have inherited."

Buffalo appeared at the top of the ridge. Half a heartbeat later they were over it. Most lost their footing immediately and cartwheeled. Some managed to run part of the way down, but their fellows whacked into them from behind and they tumbled, too. The hefty herbivores hit the ground at the base of the ridge with crunches and cracks and screams. More and more appeared at the top, more and more cascaded down into the pile of dead and dying buffalo below.

Erik shook his head. He'd blocked the brunt of the buffalos' anguish, but he could still feel their horror and pain. He looked at Finnbogi. The boy seemed fine. If he did share Erik's ability to communicate with animals, it would make sense that he wasn't overly affected. It had been mild at first with Erik.

A human scream cut through the buffalo bellows. A figure on a dagger-tooth cat appeared at the top of the bluff. The cat leapt, rider gripping onto it, out over the tumbling buffalo.

"But Scraylings live at one with the land." Gunnhild's mouth hung open. "They respect nature . . ."

"Scraylings?" asked Sitsi Kestrel.

"You lot."

"Calnians?"

"Calnians, Badlanders, Lakchans, Goachica."

"But not the Wootah?"

"Scraylings are what we call everyone who's originally from this land; everyone but ourselves."

"What a silly thing to do. You might as well put snails, chipmunks and eagles in the same group of animals."

"But we came across Olaf's Salt Sea. The rest of you didn't."

"So?"

"We look different."

"There are black squirrels and blond squirrels. Do we group the former with buffalo and the latter with lions?" Sitsi was quite annoyed that the Wootah thought she was the same as a Badlander. "And another thing—"

"You two are fascinating as always," interrupted Chapa Wangwa, "but please can you save your chat for later and enjoy the spectacle?"

More and more buffalo hurtled over the ridge to their doom. If this was one of the larger herds, it was going to go on for a while, thought Sitsi.

"Spectacle?" Gunnhild spat. "You mean mass murder."

"Oh, come come," said Chapa Wangwa, "there are so *many* buffalo."

"Is that a reason to kill them in such a cruel and wasteful manner? There are a lot of people. Would you do this to people?"

"I *have* done this to people." His grin was chilling. "And much worse."

"*What?*"

"Never mind that now. Enjoy the sight and the sounds."

Across the marsh, buffalo screamed and struggled. Some tried to limp away on broken legs but collapsed. A couple had made the drop without injury and these ran. For a moment Sitsi thought the Badlanders were going to let them go as a reward for surviving the fall, but dagger-tooth riders galloped in and finished them with spears. It was wanton, disgusting slaughter.

"Even if you were killing the animals for food and materials, the ridge is simply not high enough for the task," said Gunnhild, her voice not far off a whine.

"I think it is exactly the right height," said Chapa Wangwa. "It's so much more interesting when creatures die slowly."

Sitsi couldn't stop watching. At the height of the stampede, to her surprise, a Badlander rider on a dagger-tooth cat appeared at the top of the ridge and leapt off.

Tansy Burna lifted her head from the neck of her galloping mount. Ahead, buffalo were disappearing. She could hear the screams of the falling and fallen beasts. Beyond them was the sky. She'd seen this buffalo drive from the other side. She knew what was coming. The river of buffalo had reached its waterfall.

She had no idea why she was doing it. It was pure instinct. She felt a rush of joy. She screamed, took a breath and screamed some more.

Tansy's cat reached the top. Time froze. She saw the marsh. She saw Badlanders and captives gawping up at her. She sat straight, drove the hard leather heels of her riding boots into her cat's flanks and pulled its fur. The cat's front paws were in the air. Its back legs bent for the spring.

They were flying for a moment, then they were falling. Her cat landed on the back of a tumbling buffalo, claws out. A paw slipped as claws tore through flesh and scraped bone. The cat fell, twisting slowly. Tansy felt herself lifting clear, towards the falling nightmare of flesh and flashing hooves. The cat managed to jab a pawful of claws into another buffalo and push herself upright, forcing Tansy back into her seat.

Cats always land on their feet.

Her mount sprung onto one buffalo's back, then another, then they were down, leaping over the dying and the dead at the base of the ridge, and splashing into the marsh.

Tansy guided her cat out of the reeds to safe ground. She was panting, her face a mess of tears and snot. Her cat roared; whether to say "that was incredible" or "if you ever do anything like that again I will eat you" Tansy didn't know. She fell forwards into the beast's hot fur and sobbed happy tears.

*   *   *

Sassa Lipchewer stood next to Wulf the Fat and watched the crazy Badlander on the dagger-tooth cat walk her mount clear of the thrashing, dying buffalo. Whatever one thought of the Badlanders, or the morals of killing so many animals purely for the sport of it, riding a cat down a cascade of buffalo had shown skill and courage.

Finally, the cascade of buffalo was over. More came to the edge, but they stopped and looked down at their dead and dying herd mates. Two small light brown calves appeared. One lifted its head in a long, sad moo. The other buffalo joined in one by one, looking down at their tragedy and lowing plaintively. It was the saddest music Sassa had ever heard. Tears spilled down her cheeks.

"On the bright side, it looks like it'll be buffalo for dinner again," said Wulf.

Sassa wiped a tear. She rubbed the shaved side of her head. More tears came. It was the calves, who'd presumably lost their mothers, that had got to her.

Wulf put an arm around her shoulder. She reached around his waist and gripped his sturdy torso.

She'd been sick again that morning, for the fourth morning in a row. She prayed to Fraya and Tor and Oaden once again that she lived long enough to have her baby. This time she added the plea that he or she wouldn't see their mother die, at least until they were old enough to deal with it.

That night, next to a campfire, Erik tried to explain his talking to animals gift, or whatever it was. However, he didn't have much to say about the nebulous skill, so he told his son about some of the animals he'd known. He'd only got as far as the first Red Fox Four, who'd been killed by the Lakchans after eating a sacred turkey called Fucks In The Rain, when Chapa Wangwa appeared, carrying a single arrow and followed by a bald child on a bighorn sheep.

"Don't mind me, do carry on your conversation." The Badlander sat and wiggled the tip of his arrow into the fire. The bighorn sheep stood behind him, munching vegetation. Flames flickered orange on the Empty Child's expressionless face.

Erik didn't want to go on about the animals he'd known in front of Chapa Wangwa, so instead he told Finnbogi about the time that Chief Kobosh of the Lakchans had tried to ban swearing.

"Excuse me, excuse me," said Chapa Wangwa after a while, holding his arrow aloft.

"Yes?" asked Erik.

"The tip of this arrow is hot, hot hot. Do you know what would happen if I pressed it into your eye?"

"It would hurt?"

"Your eye would *burst*! Not just leak, like you might imagine, but pop, like squeezing a great spot. I've done it many times, but I never tire of it."

"Who could?" asked Erik.

"Anyway, you'll be wondering about the relevance."

"I'm happy in my ignorance."

"Ha ha. The relevance is, Erik the Angry, that if you try to communicate with the pigeons again, or the spiders, or the buffalo, or any Badlander animals, I will burst not just one, but both your eyes. For good measure, I will also burst the little girl Freydis's eyes. Now, big Erik, do we have an understanding?"

Erik felt a rising urge to leap across, jam the hot arrow up the man's arse and then throttle him. His spiders shifted, tickling his neck, and he supressed his rage. He looked at the bald kid, but he or she was as expressionless as ever.

"We have an understanding," said Erik, holding the Badlander's gaze.

"Oh dear," sighed Chapa Wangwa, "I don't think you believe I'll do it. It is a problem of mine. Sometimes I have difficulty trusting people. I am sorry, but we're going to have to do this." He put the arrow back in the fire. "Now remember, the Empty Child controls your spiders. If either of you attacks me, or tries to stop me, you will die. Now, Erik, hold out your hand, please. No, palm upwards. That's right. You can stay sitting there, I'll move. I like to be accommodating."

Chapa Wangwa plucked the arrow from the fire, squatted by Erik, took his wrist in one hand and pressed the arrow head into the pad of flesh below his thumb.

There'd been a period in Erik's childhood when one of the older boys back in Hardwork had bullied him. Actually, it wasn't so much bullying as experiments with pain, with Erik as the semi-willing test subject. As an upshot, given fair warning, Erik had learned to reduce pain in one part of his body by focusing on another. So, while Chapa Wangwa pressed the hot arrowhead into the flesh of Erik's right palm, Erik caressed the grass with his left hand, focusing on the feel of the blades, their temperature, the way they slipped over each other and so on. It wasn't particularly effective, especially after he could smell his own burning flesh, but he did manage not to scream.

"You are brave!" said Chapa Wangwa, lifting the arrow. "I am glad. I like breaking brave men. Now I must go. Tomorrow, if we make good miles, we will have the most marvellous entertainment. Even better than the buffalo!"

Sassa was sitting by another campfire next to Wulf, Bjarni and Keef. The men were discussing ways to be rid of the beeba spiders. They were all either terrible ideas, or methods that Sassa had already thought of herself and discounted, so she was silently going through baby names. She was musing about Olaf for a boy or perhaps Gunnhild Pronghorn for a girl, when Thyri Treelegs appeared out of the darkness and squatted next to her.

"Sassa, can I have a word?"

"Of course."

They walked off. There were campfires all along the ridge, so they headed eastwards, onto the dark prairie. The grass was shorter here, Sassa noticed, than it had been further east, not even reaching her knee.

Thyri walked in silence. When they'd gone about fifty paces, Sassa said, "I don't think we should go much further. I don't want test the spiders' range."

Thyri stopped. "I like your new hair," she said.

"Thanks." Sassa wasn't sure about her new crest hairstyle. It needed more maintenance every day than her old hair had needed in a moon.

"What happened to Garth, Sassa?" Thyri was earnest. "I want you to tell me exactly what you know."

Sassa remembered that afternoon. She pictured Garth holding Finnbogi above his head, about to throw him off the cliff.

"There's nothing you don't know, Thyri. After we were ambushed at the camp on the far side of the Water Mother and Garth saved us, Wulf asked me to follow him and Finnbogi when they chased after the four surviving Scraylings."

"Why?"

"I guess he thought I could help. I had my bow. You were down, he was injured and Keef, Bjarni and Erik weren't there."

"All right, go on."

"I arrived in a clearing as the last surviving Scrayling charged Garth, tackled him round the waist and sent them both flying off a cliff. Neither survived the fall."

"What about the other three Scraylings?"

"Two were dead, one was fatally injured and dying. Garth and Finnbogi—actually, just Garth, I think—had already killed them."

"And what was Finnbogi doing when Garth was knocked off the cliff?"

"I didn't see that. Finnbogi told me afterwards that he'd been fighting one Scrayling and Garth another. As Garth dispatched his, the Scrayling that Finnbogi had been fighting broke off and charged Garth."

"And this is what really happened?"

Sassa remembered aiming and shooting the arrow. She remembered the mix of satisfaction and shame as it had struck the back of Garth's head. She remembered his face afterwards, cross-eyed, looking at the arrow sticking out of his mouth, like a grotesque carved frog.

"I've told you what I saw, Thyri. Garth died a hero."

"Hmmm," said Thyri.

Chapter 12

Wet Heads

As the Plains Strider resumed its westward journey the following day, Sitsi Kestrel decided it was time to break Sofi Tornado out of her bad mood. She walked on over.

"Hey, Sofi!" she chirped.

Sofi's look was so dark that Sitsi scuttled back without a word to the other side of the deck, to resume her watch over the plains with Paloma Pronghorn, Sassa Lipchewer, Thyri Treelegs, Bodil Gooseface and Keef the Berserker.

A mother, father and bear cub lumbered clear of the Plains Strider's path. Keef told a story about a girl in the woods stealing food from a family of bears.

They might be headed to their deaths, but the spider trap was so effective that they might as well enjoy it, thought Sitsi Kestrel. She wasn't exactly carefree, and she'd devoted hours to trying to think of a way to defeat the spiders on her neck, but she simply couldn't come up with anything. And she could hardly plot with Sofi if Sofi wouldn't talk to her. So why not sit back and listen to a one-eared, one-eyed man tell a story from the far side of the Wild Salt Sea?

Yoki Choppa had reduced Keef's bandages to a band that covered his missing eye and ear, split to allow him to see and hear from the remaining ones. Apparently the wounds were healing marvellously well. His blond hair, which he'd cut off to trick the Owlsa, had grown thin and spikey under his bandages, like the hair on a baby bird, and his scalp was an ill-looking white.

In spite of looking so awful, the Wootah man seemed to hold no resentment towards the Owsla for removing his eye and ear. Talisa White-tail had actually done the deed and she was gone, but Sofi Tornado had ordered it and the rest of them had been complicit. Sitsi guessed that Keef saw it for what it was—reasonable behaviour by a group of people against someone who was, at that time, their enemy. His lack of rancour showed, thought Sitsi, great strength of character. At first she'd thought the Wootah men were juvenile because they mucked about so much, but now she saw that they were tough and decent, and they liked to have fun. It seemed like a pretty happy way to go about things. A pity it would soon end.

The day passed with little new to note, other than the ongoing vastness and regularity of the Ocean of Grass. They crossed rivers with hardly a pause. The land wasn't flat, but neither was it hilly. Feature-wise, it was about as interesting as a blanket laid over a slightly untidy floor. Sitsi decided the gods had given up building interesting landscape west of the Water Mother.

She tried to remain enthusiastic about the scenery, but she didn't see anything that she hadn't seen the day before and the day before that. At one point she saw a lion chasing two pronghorns, but the lion gave up almost as soon as it had started. There was nothing new to analyse. So she sat down next to Bodil Gooseface.

Morningstar sat on her own and watched Sitsi Kestrel listen to the blathering Mushroom Woman. Seeing polite little Sitsi trying to maintain an interested expression as Bodil went on and on and on about absolutely nothing was about the most entertaining thing Morningstar had seen since they'd been captured.

Chogolisa, Paloma and Sitsi all seemed happy to mingle

with the Mushroom Men. Morningstar didn't get it. To a degree, she envied their ability to talk to their inferiors, but not as much as she was amazed and a little disgusted by it. Calnians were so far above Mushroom Men, and Owsla were so far above Calnians. The social chasm was simply too wide for Morningstar to cross. On what subject could she possibly find common ground with the likes of that thick oaf Wulf the Fat or the fluffed-up fool Gunnhild Kristlover?

Yoki Choppa never talked to anyone and Sofi Tornado was in some boring sulk that nobody could break her out of. She felt the same about the four captives from the Popeye tribe as she did about the Mushroom Men—not even slightly interested. So Morningstar spent the day looking out across the dreary, dreary prairie and trying to think of a way of getting the fucking spiders off her neck.

When they screamed for food, it took all her self-control not to rip the box off and screw the consequences.

Late that afternoon, as the Plains Strider came to rest and the crowd pigeons settled to chew through their spider leashes, Morningstar heard a rumbling roar. She thought it might be animals for a moment—perhaps a herd of lions or some other new surprise—but it was too regular.

She followed the rest of them down the ladders off the deck, almost interested to see what was making the rumble. They all walked westward and uphill, following Chapa Wangwa towards the source of the ever louder roaring.

Coming towards them were half a dozen people riding buffalo, followed by a couple of bald children on bighorn sheep. Did nobody on the Ocean of Grass walk any more? Sitsi Kestrel fell back from hobnobbing with the Mushroom fools to join her.

"So who are these lot, then?" Morningstar asked.

"Going by that noise, they must be the Cuguai tribe."

"And what is the noise, my clever friend?"

"It's a waterfall. Or, more accurately, a series of falls."

"Are you sure? It's very loud. And a waterfall seems far too interesting a feature for the Ocean of Grass."

"If it's the one I think it is, it's big enough to be a god."

"In the middle of all this bloody grass, a small tree could be a god. What do you know about this lot?"

"The falls are called Cuguai, and the tribe are named after them. Their chief is a woman called Clembur, who's been chief since she was eleven years old. The thing that's confusing me is the buffalo riding. I didn't know they did that."

"Maybe they only started recently?"

"Maybe. Perhaps the Badlanders are—"

"Greetings! Greetings!" shouted Chapa Wangwa. "Great Chief Clembur, these are our guests. Guests, this is Chief Clembur of the Cuguai tribe!"

Out of the corner of her eye, Morningstar saw Sitsi Kestrel nod and smile, congratulating herself on her knowledge.

Chief Clembur looked down at them from her mount. She was perhaps thirty-five years old with large eyes and a chin so prominent and heavy that it pulled her mouth open a little. Instead of speaking, she pulled a wooden flute from a pocket on her sleeveless leather jerkin, put it to her lips and played a complicated yet mournful tune. Although it was an entirely inappropriate way to greet people, Morningstar had to admit that she was a skilled player and it was a good tune. It was wonderful, in fact, harmonising with the thunder of the as yet unseen waterfall, and lifting that noise to the clouds, as if to explain the link between clouds and water and confirm the waterfall's status as a god.

"Greetings, Chapa Wangwa," said Clembur when the tune was done. She looked very pleased with herself, thought Morningstar. "Have you brought gifts for Cuguai?"

As she spoke, Morningstar noticed that Clembur had a spider box on her neck, as did the five buffalo riders surrounding her. Ah, there you go, thought Morningstar. This was a vassal tribe to the Badlanders. Chief Clembur's flaunting of her musical ability was an attempt to show that she was more than a slave. Morningstar wasn't fooled.

"How many gifts would Cuguai like?" Chapa Wangwa asked.

"Three?"

"I will give you two."

"Cuguai may be appeased with such a—"

"Cuguai will get two. He will be pleased. I will give you one of these," Chapa Wangwa pointed at the Popeye. They looked back at him, probably fearfully, it was hard to tell; those bulging eyes gave them a permanently skittish look. "And one of our valuable aliens." He pointed at the Mushroom Men.

Morningstar stifled a smile. This would be interesting. Being a gift for a god could mean many things, but it always meant being killed, usually in quite an entertaining way.

Clembur's eyes skimmed over the Popeye then settled on the Mushroom Men for a good while.

"They *are* horrible looking," she said. "Cuguai will be pleased!"

Finnbogi the Boggy looked at Erik the Angry. His father raised his eyebrows in return, which pretty much summed it up. What, by Loakie's pointed cock, did it mean that one of them was to be a gift for a god? The only gifts the Hardworkers had given the gods were a couple of buffalo for Tor at the quarterly Things. Those, they burned and ate. It did not bode well. And what was that roaring noise, and the steam rising from the ground up ahead? The familiar feeling of sick dread returned to his stomach.

They followed Chapa Wangwa, Clembur and the other buffalo riders. Finnbogi looked at Erik's bandaged hand. He swore it didn't hurt, but it was a nasty burn. Watching Chapa Wangwa hurt his father like that had made Finnbogi hate him more that he thought it was possible to hate another person. After Garth Anvilchin, that was really saying something.

The Cuguai people dismounted and led them onto a rocky promontory, overlooking a strange river. The prairie grass gave way to an area of bare, pink-brown, stepped rock. The river didn't so much flow through this rocky terrain as charge through it, careering down the stone steps in a series of water-falls. Finnbogi had seen waterfalls. This was another level. It was several more levels. The two largest falls were mighty indeed, maybe ten paces high, raging down with a force that would surely pulverise the bones of any creature that was unlucky enough to fall in.

On both sides of the river were more of the Cuguai tribe, dressed like Clembur in sleeveless leather jerkins, watching the newcomers expectantly.

"Wow," said Finnbogi.

"Actually, I'm a bit disappointed," said Sitsi Kestrel at his shoulder. "There's a waterfall in the north-east that's seventy paces high."

"This one's still big enough to kill anyone who tried to swim down it. Or anyone who got thrown in..."

Realisation hit Finnbogi like wet blanked dropped from a tree.

"This is Cuguai, isn't it?" he asked.

"It is," Sitsi nodded.

"So if someone's going to be a gift for Cuguai..."

"*The most obvious answer is usually the correct one,*" said Gunnhild, on his other side. "Look."

She pointed to Chapa Wangwa, who was corralling the Popeye four. He produced a bunch of grass and gestured at them to take a piece each. They did so reluctantly.

"Congratulations! You pulled the short grass!" the Bad-lander shouted on the third draw.

It was Clogan, the oldest and possibly the buggiest eyed of the Popeyes. He stared at the short blade of grass in his hand. Finnbogi looked at the roaring, churning river and the ball of fear in his stomach became all the heavier. What a horrible way to go.

"Kneel!" Chapa Wangwa shouted at the unfortunate man, pushing him down when he didn't comply immediately. He did something to him that Finnbogi couldn't see. When Clogan rose, his spider box was dangling from Chapa Wangwa's hand.

"Don't try anything," said Chapa Wangwa, pointing at the others. "Your friends still have theirs."

The man nodded meekly.

"Now, follow Chief Clembur."

Clogan followed the chief and other Cuguai upstream. Ovets and the other two Popeyes tried to follow but Chapa Wangwa pushed them back with ease. The scrawny man was a good deal stronger than he looked.

Meanwhile, more Badlanders were running up from the Plains Strider. Finnbogi guessed their tasks were done and they didn't want to miss the entertainment.

The chief strode out onto a wooden platform that protruded over the river. Further upstream was a wooden bridge, swiftly filling with Badlander and Cuguai onlookers.

Clembur stood on her own on the platform, playing a tune on her flute. Finnbogi could hear only the odd snatch of phrasing above the roar of the river. He didn't mind missing it. He hadn't cared much for her warbling.

The chief pocketed her flute and stood back.

Four Cuguai lifted the captive by his feet and hands, swung him back and forth chanting words of which Finnbogi only understood "Cuguai," then hurled him into the rushing river.

He went under, popped up and struck for shore with a competent overarm stroke. The man could swim. Finnbogi wagered that the bastards hadn't counted on that! Would he make it?

He nearly did, very nearly, but he tired, paused for a heartbeat, and the current snatched him. He flowed over a moderately sized fall, then surfaced a little way upstream of the first of the two large falls. This first drop split into four waterfalls, stout crags of wet-dark rock in between each.

Clogan went over the nearest chute backwards and cracked headfirst onto a rocky outcrop at its base.

His fellow Popeyes wailed and shouted. Along with Badlanders, Cuguai, Calnians and Wootah, they craned their necks and scanned the churning water at the base of the falls. Finnbogi found himself praying to Oaden that he'd surface. There was no point praying to Loakie. He'd probably find it more amusing to let the man drown.

Clogan didn't surface. A short time passed—a short time for the onlookers, but a very long time to be underwater. Ovets, Walex and Sandea hugged each other. Finnbogi looked away.

"He went the wrong way," said Keef the Berserker, striding up.

"What?"

"He swam towards us, which is *exactly* what you should do if you want to get spun around like he did. You see that eddy," Keef pointed and Finnbogi did see the eddy. "That's what did for him. It spun him and dumped him on the rock that smashed his head. If he'd swum away from us, he would have made it to the next fall along, which is higher but smoother. He would have been fine."

Finnbogi looked at the second fall. "Fine" was probably putting it a bit strongly. There were no protruding rocks, admittedly, but the water still slammed down like a giant's fist into a rolling and boiling plunge pool.

If somehow a person survived that, the next falls looked even more treacherous.

"I'm sure he would have been just tickety-boo," Finnbogi told Keef.

"Yeah, and if he'd struck as hard as he could and made that third fall, I think he would have had a better line for the final fall. I'm not sure, I'd have to try it."

"You might get your chance. Here comes the smiler."

Chapa Wangwa was striding towards them, clutching a handful of grass. The Badlander captain, Rappa Hoga, rode up on his dagger-tooth cat, leapt off and walked alongside. The cat followed behind him.

"Gather round, all the Wootah, gather round," cried the grinning Chapa Wangwa, "it is time to decide who's going for a swim."

"I have something of a hum going on," Wulf lifted an arm and sniffed his armpit. "Yup, that's unacceptable. I should wash for the sake of you all. I'll go."

"Oh no no no, that's not how Cuguai likes it. You must be chosen by chance. All of you must pick a piece of grass."

"Not the children."

"Oh, you are a hard man, Wulf! And I am a kind one, so I will compromise. Your two racoons, they will not have to join the draw."

Wulf stepped forward and towered over Chapa Wangwa. "That's a start, but neither will the children be involved."

The Badlander did not flinch. "Hit me! Please please please. When the spiders have done their work and you are a lump of useless flesh with staring eyes, I will kick you into place so that you can see whoever picks the short blade going down the falls."

"You will not send the children down the falls. They will not be picking a piece of grass." Wulf smiled. If Chapa Wangwa's smile put Finnbogi in mind of a snake, Wulf's reminded him of the tornado that had killed Chnob the White and very nearly done for Finnbogi himself.

"I can't help," said Chapa Wangwa. "Is it not true that all must pick a blade, Chief Clembur?"

"The Badlander is right. Once Cuguai has chosen a group, all must draw."

"Not. The. Children."

Chapa Wangwa beckoned one of the children on bighorn

sheep forward. "Empty Child, Wulf the Fat's spiders will bite him no—"

"Hold," said Rappa Hoga. If Rappa Hoga and Wulf were having a competition for who could look most heroic, it was a close-run thing. "The children will pull blades as Cuguai has demanded."

"Then you and I—" Wulf started towards him.

"Wait. There is more. You will all pull blades. If a young one pulls a blade, one of the Wootah tribe may exchange with them."

"But—" Chief Clembur took a step towards them.

"Cuguai will find this acceptable," said Rappa Hoga. It was not a question.

The large-chinned woman hesitated then nodded.

"Thank you, Rappa Hoga," said Wulf.

There was a pause while the two men regarded each other. Finnbogi could feel the manliness crackling in the air.

"Good, good! Then we can get on!" cried Chapa Wangwa, breaking the macho spell. "Come, then, and pick your blades."

The Wootah tribe gathered round the grinning Badlander.

Gunnhild went first and pulled a long piece of grass. Then Thyri, then Sassa. Next were Freydis and Ottar. All took long blades.

Wulf nodded Finnbogi forwards. He took a piece of grass between finger and thumb. He pulled. Chapa Wangwa gripped, the blade broke and Finnbogi was left with a short piece of grass in his hand.

"You...He..." Finnbogi looked around. Nobody else had seen what the Badlander had done.

"Good!" said Chapa Wangwa happily. "I'm glad it's you. I don't like you. You sat by while I hurt your father."

"But..."

"Although I am surprised Cuguai has chosen you. But sometimes Cuguai chooses someone to remove a burden from others, rather than take someone impressive for herself."

Gunnhild looked horrified. Freydis smiled at him. Were those tears in Thyri's eyes? The Owsla were all regarding him with something that seemed an awful lot like acceptance. Even Sofi Tornado was looking him in the eye for the first ever time. The three remaining Popeye were goggling at him with pity, the Badlanders and Cuguai with varyingly disguised degrees of glee.

Finnbogi looked into the rushing, churning water and nodded. It was okay. Now it was him, he wasn't as scared as when there had just been a chance it was going to be him. He was ready. He was terrified, he was going to die, but never mind. You die when you die.

"I'll go in his place."

It was Morningstar! Looking more heroic than Wulf and Rappa Hoga combined, warrior goddess, second most beautiful of the Owsla after Paloma Pronghorn in Finnbogi's rankings at that time, and, equal with Sofi Tornado, least friendly. Had he heard correctly?

There was a moment's pause. It seemed everyone else was as surprised as Finnbogi.

"I will go in his place," she reiterated.

"No no no," Chapa Wangwa shook his smiling head. "Cuguai has chosen! The irritating boy will die."

"Rappa Hoga said that if a young one pulled the blade somebody could swap with them."

"He meant the children!"

"You yourself just called him a boy. That makes him a young one."

"But..." said Chapa Wangwa.

"Remove my spiders. I'll throw myself in."

"No," said Rappa Hoga.

"You said—"

"I decreed that if a young one pulled a short blade then one of the Wootah tribe may exchange with them. You are not Wootah."

"No, that's not right. You—"

"That is what he said," said Sofi Tornado. "Stand back, Morningstar."

Morningstar stood back.

"Kneel down, please," said Chapa Wangwa to Finnbogi. "I'll remove your spiders. We don't want them to suffer such a nasty death. Remember, though, if you attack me or try and run, then I will have spiders bite . . . let me see . . . this one." He pointed at Thyri Treelegs.

Thyri raised a hand to her neck box and treated Chapa Wangwa to the same look that she'd given her brother Chnob the White when they'd discovered he was betraying them.

Finnbogi looked at the river. He was scared again, much more so in fact than he'd been before Morningstar had offered to go for him. Hope is a terrible thing, he thought.

"Okay, Chapa Wanker!" cried Keef the Berserker. "Get my spiders off and I'll swim your stream."

He knelt in front of the Badlander.

Chapa Wangwa's grin faltered. He looked at Rappa Hoga.

The chief Badlander smiled. "It's not what I intended, but it does fit my decree. Keef the Berserker will take the place of Finnbogi the Boggy and be given to the goddess."

"It's no goddess," said Keef, "it's a bit of river that flows downhill."

Rappa Hoga raised an eyebrow. "Keef the Berserker will not push his luck. In times of lower flow, sacrifices are hamstrung to ensure that the river devours them. You will be quiet, Keef, if you'd like to die with only an eye and an ear missing. You will also note that all rivers flow downhill."

"Sure thing! Sorry, I mean." Keef nodded emphatically.

The kneeling Keef lifted his chin to allow access to his spider strap.

Finnbogi looked around. Everyone was looking at him. "No, Keef, you can't. Thanks, but I pulled the short blade," he said reluctantly.

"I can and I'm going to. Tell him, Wulf."

"Are you sure?" Wulf asked.

"Yup."

"In that case, Finnbogi, I order Keef to go in your place. The decision is nothing to do with you and nobody will hold it against you. Is that clear, everyone?"

Finnbogi looked at Thyri. She looked away.

Chapa Wangwa removed Keef's spider box. Keef stood and handed his axe Arse Splitter to Ottar. "Look after it, kid."

"It's too big for Ottar to wield," said Gunnhild.

"So? I'll be back to get it in a minute." Keef ruffled Ottar's hair and the boy beamed.

"Come then," said Chief Clembur.

Keef followed her to the launch platform.

"Swim well, Keef," said Wulf.

Clembur played her flute again. The four Cuguai picked up Keef by his feet and his hands. Keef shouted instructions about where he should be thrown.

They chanted and swung, then hurled the Wootah man into the rushing river.

Chapter 13
Bob

Sitsi Kestrel teetered on the tips of her toes. Chogolisa Earthquake stood next to Erik the Angry, holding Ottar the Moaner on one shoulder, looking grim. Paloma Pronghorn had one arm around Freydis the Annoying and was *holding hands* with Sassa Lipchewer. And Morningstar—Morningstar!—had volunteered to drown in Finnbogi's place.

Sofi Tornado shook her head. She considered heading back to the Plains Strider to fetch the sword she'd taken from Finnbogi and get some practice in with the new weapon—she'd resolved to put their extraordinarily free captivity to good use—but thought on balance that it might be more interesting to watch the Mushroom Man drown.

Keef the Berserker hung above the roiling torrent for a moment then splashed in, slapping down with his arms and legs to prevent himself dunking too deep. He flipped over immediately and started swimming in the same overarm stroke as Cuguai's previous victim. The Mushroom Man, however, swam away from the bank, towards the centre of the river.

Was he looking for a quicker death? Sofi wondered.

Cuguai ignored his pathetic paddling and swept him speedily towards the first fall, a drop of maybe two paces. On the crest of the falls Keef spun like an aquatic acrobat and went over feet first, hands shielding his head.

That, thought Sofi Tornado, *is not the dumbest move I've ever seen.*

Keef flowed on like flotsam towards the first of the two large falls, head up to see where he was going, feet out front, hands paddling to keep him on course.

The Mushroom Man was going to miss the rocks that had done for the previous swimmer. However, Clogan had never emerged at the base of the falls, presumably held under by the extraordinary weight of the cascade. This, Sofi had to admit to herself, was going to be interesting.

Keef spilled over the falls' glassy lip, shouted, "Woootah!" and disappeared in the curtain of white water.

He reappeared a heartbeat later, leaping like a salmon from the foaming tumult of the plunge pool. For a moment it seemed like he must be dragged under again, but he put his head down, swung his arms, kicked his legs and powered himself clear.

"Woootah!" shouted Wulf the Fat.

"Wootah! Wootah! Wootah!" the Mushroom Men cheered. Paloma, Chogolisa and Sitsi joined in.

Morningstar looked at Sofi, one eyebrow raised.

Sofi resolved once again to improve the Owsla's swimming skills. Keef the Berserker might have made a good teacher, if he hadn't been a Mushroom Man and therefore marked for death, and if he hadn't been about to tumble down significantly higher falls that would surely kill anyone.

Keef propelled himself across the current to the far side of the stream—to line up with a rock-free section of waterfall—and swung round again, feet forward above the rushing surface, head raised.

And then he was over.

He disappeared. Sofi almost wanted him to leap up in the same way as before. She didn't much like these Cuguai people and, if Keef survived, he'd beaten their god. The Mushroom Men might be hateful, but they were her Mushroom Men.

She watched with the rest of them, Chapa Wangwa and Rappa Hoga included.

He didn't leap from the water. He didn't surface at all.

There was silence on the shore.

Owsla, Wootah, Badlanders, Cuguai and Popeye scanned the churning pool. There was no sign of the man.

Still nobody spoke.

"There!" shouted Bjarni Chickenhead. "Woo——" Then he realised he was mistaken.

Merciless time marched towards the point that a human couldn't possibly have survived underwater, then marched on past it.

Still no Keef.

"No!" wailed Bodil Gooseface.

Sassa put an arm around the girl, tears streaming down her own face below the stupid haircut that Paloma had given her.

Sofi blinked. She didn't like the Mushroom Men, not at all, she was going to kill the lot of them when this was done, but still she didn't like to see someone die like this. She shook her head. The sooner the Owsla started eating their rattlesnake and tarantula hawk wasp the better. That would stop all this pally-pally shit. She couldn't *believe* she'd almost become misty eyed over the fate of a one-eyed, one-eared freak.

She turned to head to the Plains Strider and sword practice. She couldn't face watching her women commiserate with the enemy. They might even all hug each other. If she saw that, she'd have to kill the lot of them.

"There he is!" shouted Sitsi Kestrel.

Sofi spun round.

"Where?" said Sassa, "I can't——"

Sofi could. He'd surfaced a hundred paces downstream, but there was something odd. It looked like there were two people rushing along in the current.

"Wooooooo-taaaah!" Keef shouted, as he was swept out of sight around a tree-lined bend.

Rappa Hoga leapt onto his dagger-tooth and galloped off to

retrieve his captive. Wulf the Fat and the rest of the Mushroom Men followed at a run, but Chapa Wangwa shouted: "Your spiders will bite! Come back to me and the Empty Children!"

Wulf marshalled his people and they returned reluctantly. They didn't have long to wait. Keef the Berserker came back at a run, followed by Rappa Hoga on his cat, carrying a bundle.

Keef's bandage had gone, his missing eye and ear were puckered pink holes, but apart from that he looked as hale and chipper as you'd expect from a man who'd cheated certain death. The Mushroom Men crowded round while Rappa Hoga dismounted and took the burden from his cat. It was the drowned Clogan. For a moment Sofi thought he might be alive. Could he have been trapped in an underwater air pocket? But, no, he was paler than a Mushroom Man and quite dead.

Rappa Hoga laid the corpse on bare red rock and the Popeye crowded round.

"He'd come through so much," said Ovets. "Thank you for bringing his body back, Keef."

"No bother at all!" cried the Mushroom Man. "Sorry it took me so long to find him under there." He broke free from the circle of his congratulating tribesmates and strode up to Chief Clembur. Her attempts to hide her amazement and disappointment amused Sofi.

"Interesting course you have here," said Keef, eyeing the river, serious as a wall engineer talking walls. "But I misjudged that second big fall a little. Can I go again?"

They stayed by the falls that night. Finnbogi the Boggy sat at the fire with Sitsi Kestrel, Paloma Pronghorn and most of the Wootah, listening to Keef the Berserker's tale for the fifth or possibly sixth time. Finnbogi was glad, of course, that Keef had survived, but he had kicked himself several times for letting Keef take his place. He was a good swimmer, he could have done what Keef did and it could have been him retelling the story and being worshipped by everyone.

"But how did you know you'd found his body, and not an animal or something?" asked Bodil.

Keef, sitting on a log, leant forward, put his elbows on his knees. "You go over the falls, and you're only thinking about getting out of there and getting out of there quick." For reasons Finnbogi couldn't fathom, Keef thought his waterfall story needed to be told in the second person. "You don't know which way is up to begin with and you—oh hi, Treelegs, you're joining us at a good bit. Take a seat."

Thyri had appeared at the edge of the group. Even after this relatively short time away from Hardwork, she'd become a good deal less tree-legged. Her jaw was leaner and the muscles that had burned through their fatty coating on her arms and legs were cleanly defined. She'd always dressed like one of the Owsla, minus the knee-high Owsla leggings. Now she was beginning to look like one. Finnbogi thought that it was rather noble, perhaps heroic, that, even surrounded by the aggressively sexy women of the Owsla, he still fancied Thyri the most.

"I came to get Finn," she said.

Finnbogi started. *Finn!* "What? I mean . . . what's up?"

"You've been very slack with your training recently. You start again tonight."

"But it wasn't me. I would have trained. You—"

"Are you coming?"

If Finnbogi had expected Thyri to collapse and declare her undying love for him, he was mistaken. She remained subdued, a much quieter version of her previously sassy self. But the training hadn't changed. She made him exercise, while doing the same exercises herself, until he thought he'd vomit, then she pushed him some more.

At the end she said, "See you later" and headed off Loakie knew where, leaving Finnbogi to walk back alone to the others and his sleeping sack mate Bjarni.

* * *

The Wootah lot had moved from the fire where he'd left them, and had been replaced by Sofi Tornado and Morningstar.

Finnbogi swallowed and stepped into the light.

"Um. Morningstar?" he said.

She looked up. Her plump cheeks, flawless skin and full mouth were all the more pronounced in the golden glow of the campfire.

"Yes?"

"Thanks."

"What for?"

"For trying to step in and save me today."

Morningstar sighed. "Don't for a heartbeat think that I was trying to save you. I wanted the spiders off my neck, nothing more. I'd watch you drown as easily as I'd watch a turd sink in that river."

"I see. Do you spend a lot of time watching turds sink?"

The beautiful warrior goddess looked at him as if he was one of said turds. The glare went on long enough for Finnbogi to get a serious sweat going.

"Perhaps you'd like to fuck off?" she suggested eventually.

Finnbogi walked away, grinning. Not only had his *watching turds sink* comeback been a corker, but Morningstar had actually spoken to him.

Chapter 14

Drugs Are Bad

The Plains Strider stayed put with the Cuguai the next day. Apparently there was a tornado storm in their path to the west, even though it was a glorious sunny but breezy day where they were. Sassa Lipchewer asked a passing Badlander how they knew about the tornado storm.

"We just do."

"I see. What's a tornado storm?"

"Sorry, bighorn sheep need feeding, got to go!"

And he skedaddled.

Sassa had been sick again that morning and was sure that her stomach was beginning to bulge. She wanted to talk to someone about it; get some advice from Gunnhild Kristlover, perhaps, listen to some whooping and open-mouthed wonder from Bodil Gooseface, or even put up with sarcasm and disgusting jokes from Paloma Pronghorn. Most of all, she was itching to see the look on Wulf's face when she told him.

But Chapa Wangwa had promised them that death awaited at the Badlands, and they couldn't be far off now. Did he mean it? Was it a joke? They'd tried to drown Keef, and were certainly capable of horrible cruelty. But Rappa Hoga seemed decent, and their spider neck pieces, although weird, annoying and horrific, did allow them to feel so free that it was nigh impossible to believe that they were being transported to their deaths.

There was no point in worrying about it, anyway. You

do, after all, die when you die. However, the notion of a little human growing inside her made her almost burst with excitement, love and fear and she wanted to ensure its survival. But all she could do to protect it—as well as looking for opportunities to escape—was to eat well and avoid falling off anything.

And they did eat well with the Cuguai. Apparently Keef the Berserker was the first person who'd ever survived a trip down the falls. The Cuguai were sulky about it at first, and Keef had not helped by running around yelling at everyone that he'd defeated their god. The previous evening had been a subdued one and the Cuguai had kept clear.

However, the following morning Rappa Hoga had persuaded Clembur and the Cuguai tribe that Keef's survival must be the will of the god Cuguai, and therefore something to celebrate.

The Cuguai were happy to be convinced by this cheerier take on events and had sacrificed a bear and several dogs to honour Keef's achievement. Now, in the mid-afternoon, Cuguai, captives and captors were gathered by the falls, eating a bear and grass dish that was vomit-inducingly repulsive, and dog served hot in tubes of fluffy bread with a spicy paste. The dog was pretty delicious.

"I think Rappa Hoga might be Tor!" said Bodil, walking up to where Sassa was looking over the falls.

"Physically, maybe."

"What do you mean?"

"Tor is not a clever god. Rappa Hoga persuaded these people who seem to hate us to throw us a party, without using violence. Tor would have bopped the lot of them on the head with his hammer then called for ale."

"I suppose! They are nice, aren't they, the Badlanders?"

"You think Chapa Wangwa's *nice*?"

"He's so smiley."

"He hurt Erik. And he killed that captive in front of us,

in a really nasty way, then left him to die slowly. He smiled through all of it."

Bodil's brow knitted. "I suppose . . . But he does smile a lot. And Rappa Hoga's nice."

"When we get to their town, or city or whatever it is, they are going to kill us. I don't know how, but it probably won't be nice."

"Oh no, they're not going to do that."

"Then why have they captured us?"

"Have they really captured us, though?"

"Yes."

"But we want to go west, don't we?" Bodil's eyes were wide.

"We do."

"And they're carrying us west faster than we could walk. Erik said we go more than ten times as far in a day on the Plains Strider than we would on foot. So they're doing us a favour, aren't they?"

"I suppose so, but—"

"I told you they were good. Now, if you weren't with Wulf and you had to sleep with Keef or Rappa Hoga, which one would you sleep with?"

Sassa thought *Rappa Hoga, every time*, but said: "Is killing myself an option?"

"It is not," said Bodil. "Not until afterwards anyway."

"Which you'd have to do if you chose Keef."

The two women looked over to where Keef was demonstrating axe moves to a throng of Cuguai, and laughed.

Sofi Tornado sat on a rock with the Cuguai falls on one side and the Badlander camp on the other, stretching her legs and rolling the ache out of her shoulders. She'd exercised the Owsla all morning, as hard a training session as they'd ever had, and she was pleasantly weary. All around her was a bizarre festival atmosphere as Badlanders, Cuguai, Calnians,

Mushroom Men and Popeye japed about and chatted away as if the Badlanders weren't evil bastards who'd captured half of them and subjugated the rest.

Yoki Choppa ambled up, sat on the rock next to her and proffered a bowl of lumpy brown meat. It smelled rich and slightly rotten, like human flesh that had been hung too long.

"I've had bear before," she said. "Once was enough."

"You'll like this bear."

She looked at him. He was nearly smiling.

"What have you found?" she asked.

"Tarantula hawk wasp and burrowing owl."

Sofi could not remember ever spontaneously hugging anyone, and Yoki Choppa was possibly the least huggable person she knew, but she actually had to stop herself from hugging him. She'd get her hearing back, and all the Owsla would become stronger, tougher and braver from eating the wasp. They were still missing the diamondback rattlesnake that they all needed for ruthlessness, and Sitsi's chuckwalla, but the wasp and the owl were more than Sofi had hoped for.

"Where did you get these?"

Yoki Choppa tilted his head, as if that was an answer.

"Sitsi said we were approaching the owl's territory, so you managed to trap one," she guessed. "We shouldn't find the wasp until we're further west, so you wouldn't have found a live one, but it's the sort of thing a warlock would have. You stole it, didn't you, from the Cuguai warlock?"

Yoki Choppa's head dropped a little in his version of nodding.

"So their warlock has a venomous beast in her store." Sofi narrowed her eyes. "I've never met a warlock who wasn't a hoarder. If she has one poison animal that's commonly used in alchemy, then she has all the others, too. So she'd have diamondback rattlesnake, wouldn't she?"

Yoki Choppa began to stand but Sofi grabbed his arm. "Did she have diamondback rattlesnake?"

He nodded.

"And you didn't take any?"

"I did not."

"Because it makes us cruel and pitiless and you don't want us like that. You want us to be kind to your pet Mushroom Men."

He looked at his feet.

"Enough of this bullshit enigmatic silence, Yoki Choppa. Your meddling has already killed one of my women and I will not have it happen again. Either give me a good, clear reason for why you didn't take the rattlesnake, or go and get it right now, prepare it and feed it to me and my women."

The warlock's lower lip protruded a little further than normal and his skin darkened.

"Don't you fucking sulk at me."

Still he didn't answer. "I will kill Ottar the Moaner if you don't tell me this instant."

"The rattlesnake makes you cruel," he said.

Sofi was too surprised to speak for a moment. "Cruel? Since when does a Calnian warlock, any warlock, worry about cruelty? Surely it increases our reaction speed? We need that."

"The reaction speed increase is negligible. The reason you were conditioned to rattlesnake was to make you enjoy killing." For once, he looked her in the eye. "It was Pakanda and Zaltan's doing. It was unnecessary. You would have killed Calnia's enemies without it. The rattlesnake's sole purpose was to make you perform horrific murders in the Plaza of Innowak for the entertainment of the masses. You don't need to do that any more."

Sofi Tornado opened her mouth so say something, but Yoki Choppa spoke over her. "It was bad enough that we took girls from their families and made them our killers. We did not need to make you evil as well. You do not need rattlesnake to take the Wootah to The Meadows and save us all. You do not need to kill the Wootah when it is done, and you never need murder for others' entertainment again."

"Empress Ayanna disagrees, or she would have let you drop the rattlesnake from our diet back in Calnia. Who are you to go against her wishes? Who are you to change us?"

Yoki Choppa looked at his hands. "I helped to make you."

With that, the warlock stood to go. She didn't stop him. He'd just said more than he had in one go in the all years that she'd known him put together. She was also a little shaken by being described as "evil." She'd been called a lot worse, but only ever by people who didn't matter. And what had made him and everyone else so soppy all of a sudden?

The warlock shambled back towards the Calnians, Wootah, Popeye, Badlanders and Cuguai. They were shouting and capering even more loudly. Most of the noise was coming from a group led by Wulf and Chogolisa Earthquake. They were playing a lacrosse-like game, but each of the adults was carrying a child to catch and throw the ball instead of the traditional stick. Paloma Pronghorn and Sitsi Kestrel ran to join in.

"Wheeee! Whoooo—peee!" shouted Ottar, holding the lacrosse ball, riding on Paloma Pronghorn's shoulders as she snaked through the other players like a greased weasel. Sofi could hear Pronghorn's feet striking firm earth. Just heartbeats after eating burrowing owl again, her hearing was already improving.

She thought about Rappa Hoga's offer for the Owsla to join the Badlanders. Despite Yoki Choppa's patronising lecture, she was a long way from discarding that option. If anything, it had nudged her a little closer. The Badlanders would have warlocks capable of preparing rattlesnake.

There was a great cheer as someone scored a goal. Bjarni Chickenhead and Keef the Berserker pulled their trousers down and waggled their white arses at the other team. Wulf steamed in at a tiptoeing sprint and slapped their bare arse cheeks.

Sofi shook her head.

The game finished and Bjarni wandered away. They'd won, which was good. His arse still smarted a little from Wulf's slap, which had hurt so much that it almost wasn't funny. It had also left him feeling confused and in need of a smoke or something more.

Checking that the others were well out of earshot, and even though he saw Sassa Lipchewer watching him and knew that she knew what he was doing, he canvassed a few likely looking Cuguai for mushrooms. *Wait and see*, all of them said, annoyingly.

He ate some delicious bear meat and bided his time. Towards sunset he saw some Cuguai carrying a long pole decorated with carvings. He walked on over to see what they were up to.

By the time he reached them, they were hefting the pole into a hole. Sturdy supports were pegged into the ground to hold it upright.

"What's this?" he asked.

"Climbing pole."

Other Cuguai were carrying bundles towards the now erect mast. Intrigued, Bjarni loitered.

The larger bundles contained thin, stripped twigs with pointed ends.

A woman sat down cross-legged on the flattened grass and opened a white deer-skin bundle. Using the skin as a mat, she laid out a large pestle and mortar, three pink stone pipes with reed mouthpieces, some brown lumps that looked like dried roots or perhaps tree burls, some seeds and a dried plant that had to be tobacco.

"Hello!" said Bjarni. "What's all this?"

The woman was perhaps forty years old. She had a pinched

face, sharp nose, small eyes and she blinked constantly, putting Bjarni in mind of an opossum. Like all the Cuguai, she had a spider box strapped to her neck.

"Sit down, darling, and I'll show you. My name's Tuffbur." Her voice was deep with the underlying rattle of a dedicated tobacco smoker.

"I'm Bjarni."

She shuffled aside to let him sit down, then back so that one knee was pressing into his thigh.

"This evening, we're going to celebrate your successful journey through Cuguai."

"My journey?"

"Wasn't it you?"

"It was Keef. I'm Bjarni."

"You all look the same to me. No matter. Point is we're going to celebrate Cuguai sparing someone for the first time by getting fucked up on crazy cake and snake seeds."

"That," said Bjarni, "sounds like a very good idea."

"You can help me prepare if you like, darling."

"I like."

"Right. These little balls are crazy cake. The seeds are snake seeds. Both of them come from a desert far, far to the south where you can't go any more. I went there when I was a good deal younger than you—by Cuguai, did I have a time—and came back with a load. I have a lot left, but we have to be sparing because they're both seriously powerful, and when you mix them..." she whistled.

"What to they do? Are they like mushrooms?"

"Do you like mushrooms?"

"Love 'em."

"Then you'll adore these. These are to mushrooms what a whitecap eagle is to a swallow. Now, first thing is to grind it up in little batches, so we don't lose any, then..."

Bjarni asked Tuffbur about the spider boxes while they worked.

"Do you know we hardly notice them now? We've had them for a couple of years."

"You don't try to get them off?"

She stopped pounding the crazy cake and snake seeds and looked at him. "Of course we did, darling. We did little else but discuss how to remove them for moons. People tried the wildest schemes. All of them died, as did plenty of the people who helped them."

"What sort of schemes?"

"Neither burning them nor drowning them works, the little fuckers just bite you as soon as they realise they're in trouble. Someone did manage to shoot a spider box off someone else's neck, but the shooter was bitten immediately, and the Badlanders executed the man whose spiders were killed by the arrow, in the nastiest way they know."

"Which is?"

"Being bitten by their nasty fucking spiders, of course."

The beeba spiders on Bjarni's neck moved. He shivered. "Do they ever bite anyone by mistake?"

"Not so far. The only people they've killed are people who were trying to take their boxes off or who otherwise pissed off the Badlanders. So now we just get on with life and forget about them. We still discuss how we might remove them, of course, but nobody's come close. Actually, that's not quite true. A girl, not much older than the young girl with you, lay out in the snow all night last winter. She took her box off in the morning and the spiders were frozen."

"So there is a way!"

"She died that day herself, from having spent the night lying out in the snow."

"How far can you get from the kids on the goats?"

"The Empty Children? We don't know, strangely enough. Because finding out means dying, nobody's given it a proper try."

"Fair enough."

"We do know it's at least a hundred paces. Beyond that it's—"

She was interrupted by screaming from the spider boxes.

"They always do that at the same time!" she shouted. "Best to..."

They waited until the flies came and satiated the spiders' hunger, then carried on talking until the sun was low. Another woman, a close friend of Tuffbur's by the way they mocked and sniped at each other, built a fire and boiled water for their crazy cake and snake seed mull. Tuffbur loaded the pipes. Bjarni was very keen to try the new drug.

"No, you wait. And when it is your turn, please, Bjarni, don't take too much. A sip or a small toke is enough, I promise you. More than that has killed people."

"How long must I wait?"

"Not long. Here comes Clembur now."

The chief of the Cuguai gathered her tribe, as well as the Badlanders, Calnians, Wootah and Popeye, and walked up the gentle rise to where Bjarni and Tuffbur were sitting next to the vertical pole.

Clembur gripped the pole with her arms and legs and climbed elegantly to about a quarter of the way up, so her feet were level with Chogolisa's Earthquake's head.

Everyone crowded round, watching her expectantly.

"Welcome all," she called. "To celebrate Cuguai's generosity in sparing Keef the Berserker, we will share with you our most important ritual."

The Cuguai cheered.

"Tuffbur has prepared crazy snake. It's a mix of crazy cake and seeds from the snake plant. It is a very potent drug and you must take it seriously. I cannot stress too much just how seriously you need to take this drug. It is stronger than anything you will have encountered because it it, as far as I know, the most potent drug in the world, short of those that will kill you outright. Most people love it and have a wonderful time, but there is reasonable chance, perhaps one in about sixty, that you will take it and have a simply awful time. Death is rare, if you don't take too much, but it has happened. So don't take more than you're told and please, if you're worried, do not have any. The more worried you are, the more likely it is to go wrong."

Clembur paused and looked around at everyone. "I mean it. No children can have it, and you must only take it if you want to. I repeat, death is possible. It is impossible to overstate how important it is not to take too much. Do you all understand?"

There were sensible yeses and solemn nods. Bjarni was bouncing on his toes.

"Good! Boring bit over, let's get messed up!" She leapt nimbly down. Tuffbur handed her the smoking pipe and she took a short, sharp drag. "That is as much as you need! Form a queue on me if you'd like the pipe, over there if you want a sip of tea. Do not have both!"

Bjarni Chickenhead joined the queue for the tea. Behind him were Wulf the Fat, Thyri Treelegs and, to his mild surprise, Gunnhild Kristlover. Finnbogi the Boggy queued for the pipe.

He saw Bodil Gooseface talking to Sassa Lipchewer and Erik the Angry. He couldn't hear what they were saying above the excited chatter in the queue but Erik and Sassa were looking sincere and shaking their heads. Whatever they said worked, because Bodil did not join either queue.

Nor did Keef the Berserker. He was walking away towards the river, carrying Arse Splitter, no doubt off to practise. Given that the drugs had been mashed and mulled in Keef's honour, Bjarni thought it was rude of him not to partake.

He reached the front of the queue and knelt with Thyri and two others. The Cuguai woman who'd brewed the tea walked along before them, holding the bowl to their lips and whipping it away before they drank too much. Thyri took a bird-like sip and it was Bjarni's go.

"What's Keef doing now, the madman?" said Bjarni just before the bowl met his lips. The Cuguai woman looked around, as did the others. Bjarni thrust his head forward and managed to suck in two good swallows before the woman realised she'd been duped.

She looked down at him, one eyebrow raised. "You, son, are in trouble."

"What are you going to do?" Bjarni was suddenly nervous.

"What am I going to do? It's what you're going to do that you need to worry about. If I were you I'd make myself vomit, now."

Bjarni smiled at her. She didn't know about the famous Chickenhead constitution.

Sofi Tornado watched the fools take their drugs. She was aware of her hypocrisy, since her power animals were drugs that she took every day. But her power animals improved her. She didn't know what the crazy snake was going to do to everyone, but she doubted very much that the word "improvement" was going to be on the lips of any onlookers.

She walked over to her women.

Paloma Pronghorn was wearing half a smile. Sofi recognised the look from the days when Paloma had bunked training to chase boys.

"Perhaps," Paloma tried, "since we're captives and so not really Owsla at the moment, we could—"

"No."

"I thought not."

"We're going to spar on the rock by the falls."

"We have all the fun," said Paloma.

Sofi looked at her.

"I'm sorry, you're right. To the falls it is."

Sofi led the way, pleased to be able to hear Sitsi Kestrel whispering to Paloma: "What *were* you thinking? We're *Owsla*. Not spoiled rich children. You're lucky Sofi didn't punish you. Watch what happens to those stupid Wootah. It won't be good, mark my words. Drugs are—"

Sofi zoned out, reminded that the downside of being able to hear everyone's conversation was that you could hear everyone's conversation.

They arrived at the rocky riverbank to find Keef already there, slicing through the waterfall's mist with his axe.

"Keef the Berserker!" she said. He stopped, trying not to look surprised that she'd spoken to him.

"Yup?"

"Would you like to spar with us?"

"If you think you'll be able to keep up."

"We'll do our best," said Sofi. "Why don't you try me first?"

Sassa Lipchewer sat with Erik the Angry and watched Wulf, Bjarni, Bodil, Finnbogi, Thyri and Gunnhild dance with the other tribes. The drumbeat was rapid, a large stringed instrument ground out a mournful base and a couple of prancing flute players piped out a jaunty tune over the top of it all.

It was without a moment's doubt the best music Sassa had ever heard—melancholy yet exciting and passionate—but it seemed somewhat wasted on the dancers. Other than Bodil, who'd taken no crazy snake, none of them had much of a grip on the beat and nor did they seem aware of their fellow dancers. It didn't seem to hamper their enjoyment much, though.

Finnbogi was twirling his hands in front of his face and staring at them as if they were the most captivating jewels.

Gunnhild had her eyes closed and was spinning in circles, arms outstretched. Erik had already leapt up twice to steer her away from the large fires that lit up the dance area from each corner.

Wulf was jumping on the spot with a group of Cuguai and Badlanders, drenched in sweat.

Bjarni and Thyri were dancing with Chief Clembur in front

of one of the corner fires—if you could call it dancing. Arms bent, fists clenched, all three were jumping stiffly from one foot to another. They'd been going for an age and showed no sign of slowing.

Wulf spotted Sassa and Erik watching him. He ran over, leapt, and landed in a sitting position.

"Are you having a nice time?" Sassa asked.

"Amazing." His pupils were so large that his blue eyes were almost black. "I can feel my blood moving around my hands. I can see new colours. I've found a new way of moving. And jumping? Don't get me talking about jumping. It's the best. Why have I never spent this long jumping before? You *have* to have some crazy snake."

"I don't."

"I suppose you don't. It just seems a shame. It is really good." He was staring slightly above her head, looking confused.

"I'm glad you're enjoying yourself."

"Can I cut your hair?"

"Don't you want to dance?"

"I like the crest, but it would be better if it was the length of my little finger." He held up his little finger.

Sassa actually agreed with him. Not from a vanity point of view, it was just a pain using animal fat to stiffen her hair into its current high fin. And if he was here cutting her hair he wouldn't be getting into trouble elsewhere.

"All right," she said, "go for it. But be careful."

"Here, use this," said Erik, handing Wulf his double-bladed obsidian knife.

Now the fire was treating Bjarni to the most incredible display. Why had he never noticed that fire was full of animals and flowers all growing and shrinking and jumping somersaults and dancing and shagging each other? A red vine spread up from the base of the blaze, penetrating lions and dagger-tooth cats, then becoming a great, yellow, diamond-sided sturgeon which flipped over and sank slowly, licking the other animals with its great tongue.

He knew that Thyri on one side and Clembur on the other were seeing the same as him. He could smell them, he could feel their smells, Thyri's maple syrup and girl sweat mingled with Clembur's grassy and urine-y but in a good way odour. Warmth flowed from his stomach to his head. For a moment he thought he might vomit again, a spume of pure colour into the flames, but the feeling passed and he danced on.

Finnbogi's hands were growing and shrinking, his fingers thickening then elongating, leaving pink trails as he swung them side to side, up and down and round and round. The stars were following his fingers now. He could stir patterns in them as if he was stirring specks of light in an inverted but full bowl of water. The stars changed colour as he stirred, from red to green to blue, to better colours like smokey pink and bright black. The specks of light became lines of light,which formed cubes and triangles and rectangles which throbbed and morphed into shapes more complicated than anything in this world but which Finnbogi could see and understand perfectly. He reached his hands deeper into the star pool and the globules of light flowed over his arms and face and into his mouth and he and the stars were one, joined in the sway and the dance and the thrum thrum thrum.

He was aware of someone dancing near him. It was a woman. It was the woman he'd knocked out when they'd been captured by the Badlanders. She smiled at him and copied his hands-in-the-air dance.

"I'm Tansy Burna," she said, adding a sinuous hip wiggle to the dance.

"I'm Finnbogi." He tried the hip thing. That wouldn't work so he refocused on his hands.

"You beat me in a fight," she said, then turned round and pressed her bottom into his groin and doubled her wiggle speed. This was unexpected. He stepped away. She swung round to face him and danced in close.

"That means you can have me," she said, trailing her fingers up his thigh.

"Oh! I... There's somebody else," he managed.

"Is there?" She licked her lips. "Maybe they'd like me, too? Two's company, three's a party."

"It's kind of you, but... I'm in love with her and..."

"How very boring of you. Do let me know if you change your mind." Tansy clasped his groin with one hand, stood on tiptoes and licked his open mouth. Then she danced away.

Finnbogi stared after her for a moment, then returned to the important business of dancing.

Sitsi Kestrel walked back from the calmer river below the falls and heard someone vomiting quietly at the base of a gentle declivity. She waited and listened, in case whoever it was needed help, but there were a couple of hawking spits, a cough or two, some more spitting and Thyri Treelegs came walking up the slope. She was crying, more than just the tears of someone fresh from vomiting.

Sitsi was tempted to nip off before Thyri spotted her. She'd never consoled anyone who was as high as the moon before, but didn't think it would be any fun. However, the poor girl was clearly upset. Sitsi coughed.

"Who's that?" asked Thyri, sniffing back her tears.

"Sitsi Kestrel. Are you all right?"

"Yes. No. Oh, I don't know. I feel awful. But better now I've been sick. The ground's stopped moving and the giant rabbits made of light have hopped back to wherever the Hel they came from."

"Well, you shouldn't have..." Sitsi was about to lecture her about recreational stimulants and the stupidity thereof but changed her mind. "Don't worry, you'll feel better soon. Come with me, we'll find you some water and food. That'll help."

"Not that bear from before."

"No, that was horrible, wasn't it? The dog was okay, though."

"I miss maple sugar."

"Oh, so do *I*!" Sitsi took her arm. "And maple syrup. My mum used to make a maple syrup and wild rice pudding..."

They found some inoffensive food and water next to the tall pole. Cuguai people and Wulf the Fat climbed the pole while Sassa Lipchewer watched nervously. Nearby, others were pushing stripped white twigs *through their arms*. Sitsi hurried Thyri away before she saw that. By Innowak, she hated the stupid things people did when they took drugs.

They sat on the rocks overlooking the falls while Thyri ate.

"I'm in love with a dead man," said the Wootah woman.

"How did he die?" asked Sitsi, hoping that the Owsla hadn't killed him.

Thyri told her how she'd fallen for rugged Garth Anvilchin, and how he'd been killed by the Water Divided Tribe, after saving the rest of them.

"And we're not meant to mourn." Thyri shook her head. "You die when you die and all that, and I don't mourn my father and my brother. But I was looking forward to a future with Garth. Some people didn't like him because he was tough, but that's exactly why I did like him. The rest of our men...well, they're not really men, not like the men in the sagas. Even the good warriors—Wulf and Keef—don't take *anything* seriously. They're children."

"What about Finnbogi?"

Thyri turned to Sitsi, her eyes shining. "Do you know, there was a moment when I thought I might like Finnbogi. But he was right there when Garth was killed and he didn't help. He couldn't help because he's so weak and wet. I'm training him to fight so he might do better next time, but I don't think I could ever look at him as a potential lover again. No, I thought Garth and I would find sanctuary at The Meadows, live near the others but not with them, and raise our own children to be like our ancestors, not like the infant-men that the Wootah have become."

"You're not..."

"Pregnant? No. We never...I only kissed him for the first time a few days before he was killed."

"I'm sorry."

"Not your fault."

"It happened because the Calnians ordered it, and I'm a Calnian. Also, I was chasing you at the time, and we were planning to kill you."

"Because you were ordered to."

"That's as may be, but I want to make amends. If I can help you, let me know."

"Can you take these spiders off our necks and kill all the Badlanders?"

"Sofi's working on that and, if anyone can do it, it's her. Come on, let's turn in. We'll have a better chance of surviving all this if we're well rested."

Finnbogi had been happy until Tansy Burna had rubbed his groin with her bottom and licked his mouth. Her come-on had discombobulated him, not least because he couldn't work out why he'd knocked her back. Although his friends were all around, he felt alone. And his friends didn't help. He tried to dance with Bjarni but Bjarni was too busy dancing with himself and staring into the fire. Wulf and Sassa weren't interested in him. Erik was talking to Chogolisa, again.

For a while he lay on the ground near a fire and watched small red spiders, or possibly ticks, running around a mound of earth. He knew he was doing it because he'd heard it was the sort of thing you were meant to do after taking mind-altering drugs. He felt stupid and a bit sick.

He walked up the hill to the climbing pole, but none of the Cuguai gave him a second glance. He tried to talk to a man, but the guy giggled and ran away.

He heard a yell. A young man was pushing a bark-stripped twig into his own forearm, halfway between his elbow and hand.

Finnbogi watched, fascinated and disgusted, as the Cuguai pushed the stick through his arm. When the tip popped through the skin with a little burst of flesh and bright blood, Finnbogi coughed up a small amount of sick into his mouth.

He swallowed and decided he'd had quite enough of crazy snake. He would sleep and hope the nasty poison had worn off by the time he woke.

As he padded down the hill, Erik the Angry caught up.

"Are you all right?"

"Yeah, fine, just a bit . . . I'm turning in."

"Sure you're all right?"

"I think my crazy snake has worn off and I don't feel great, but I'm okay."

"I'm sorry, maybe I should have told you not to take it. It would have been quite a dad thing to do, I suppose. But I think you were right to take it. I didn't have any because I know I hate things that mess your thoughts around and make you see weird shit. But I found that out by trying it, and then trying it again a few more times to make sure I hated it."

"Your fatherly advice is to try everything?"

"Pretty much."

"Thanks, Dad. See you tomorrow."

Finnbogi climbed into his sack. His head was whirling, he couldn't stop grinding his teeth and he had an unsolicited, raging hard-on but couldn't do anything about it because Gunnhild and the children were right next to him.

Finally, mercifully, he fell asleep.

And he was floating above a breathtakingly beautiful valley. Bare rock red and white mountains, far higher than Finnbogi had guessed even existed, soared out of gleaming woodland. He followed a sparkling river that meandered gently along the widening valley floor to a broad clearing, where a small village of Scraylings and several dozen grazing deer lived in happy harmony.

He heard a rumble, then a roar. He turned. Erupting from the head of the valley was a deluge of rock, trees and water. He flew upwards and the flood passed below him like a monstrous ravening serpent.

The torrent subsided and trickled out. The village, the deer and the people were gone. The previously pristine valley floor was mud, rocks and smashed trees.

The fire died down and the fire animals were too small! Bjarni looked around, still dancing. The world whirled around his head. He stopped dancing. He was the only one left in the dance area and the musicians had gone. There was some kind of commotion going on up the hill—new fires up there, people chanting, a tower reaching into the sky and someone climbing the tower. That was the place to be.

"Bjarni!" said a voice.

Bjarni turned. "Who wants to know? I might be Bjarni." He was pretty sure he was Bjarni, but he didn't want to commit to anything.

"You are Bjarni Chickenhead." Erik the Angry was walking towards him, his beard enormous and crawling with crabs.

"Hee hee. But what *is* a Bjarni Chickenhead? Or a Chicken Bjarnihead? A bicken charni... Do you know you have crabs in your beard?"

"Bjarni. You've been dancing for a very long time and it's time to rest and eat some food."

Bjarni closed his eyes and thought. This did make some sense.

"Have this," Erik held out a drinking horn.

"Okay." Bjarni did as he was told and followed Erik back to the camping area. Going to sleep now would be sensible.

He joined Finnbogi in the sleeping sack. The younger man

was already snoring. Bjarni closed his eyes and a thought came to him.

"Erik, are you still there?"

"Yes."

"What were you doing alone by the dance area?"

"Keeping an eye on you."

"Thanks, man."

"Are you all right now? I'm going to hit the sack myself."

"Totally fine."

"Right." Erik padded away towards the river.

Bjarni closed his eyes again. Sparks danced in the corner of his vision, then coalesced to become dancing figures, beckoning. He could hear shouts and laughter from the climbing pole.

He clambered out of the sack and headed uphill at a jog to rejoin the party.

By the time he got there, the colours had returned, and now, ever better, here came the animals. They were dancing again, around the pole. A racoon that looked like Wulf climbed the pole and shouted "Wootah!" at the top.

"Wootah!" shouted Bjarni. A deer that looked like Sassa Lipchewer walked over and asked him if he was okay. He said he was absolutely fine, never better. She told him she had to look after Wulf and walked away.

Next to the pole some other animals were putting new bones in their body, making themselves stronger.

Bjarni wanted to be stronger, like Wulf. Maybe Wulf would like him if he was strong.

"Can I have a go?" he asked.

"Sure thing," said a squirrel.

"How do you do it?"

"I'll show you. Here's a sharp one. Press the point in there, that's right, in the gap between the bones."

Bjarni did as he was told. It was a funny feeling, the new bone going into his flesh.

"No no," said the squirrel-man, "you're pushing it along,

that'll be bad. You've got to go through, like this." He pushed a bone into his own arm, until it was poking right through it at right angles. He held his arm aloft. "See? Then you pull it out." He did so with a grimace. "And then you give the stick to Cuguai by placing it at the base of the climbing pole."

How dumb was that? Poking a bone *through* your arm and taking it out wouldn't help anybody. Obviously it had to lie *next* to the bones that were already there, and the more you put in the stronger you'd get.

"I know what I'm doing. Leave me alone!" Bjarni hadn't meant to snap, but this fellow was an idiot.

"Fine, be a dick. I don't need people like you right now." The man-squirrel walked away.

Bjarni grunted, sat next to a small pile of bones, and set about pushing as many of them as he could into his arm.

Paloma Pronghorn was galloping in a terror-frothed herd, desperately fleeing the giant orange spiders. It was no good; the spiders were faster. She knew they were getting closer, knew they'd be on them any moment but she didn't want to turn.

Something grabbed her shoulder. She tried to raise her arms but couldn't. She opened her mouth to scream—

And she was awake, looking up into the face of the squatch. The hairy beast was staring down at her, one hand on her shoulder.

This isn't much better than the spider dream, thought Paloma.

The squatch jinked her head in the direction of the hill with the climbing pole and grunted something that sounded a lot like "go." Then it loped off into the darkness.

Well, thought Paloma, *who am I to ignore the semi-coherent orders of a hairy monster who wakes me in the middle of the night?* She got up and headed for the climbing pole.

Had the squatch been part of the dream? Was this her mind's way of telling her to join the party that Sofi Tornado had told her not to go to? But she wasn't going to join in, she was going to watch, so it wasn't like she was disobeying orders. It would have been remiss of her not to check out what the squatch wanted. It could be something that affected the Owsla. She certainly wouldn't smoke or drink any crazy snake. Not unless she got into a situation when it would be really rude not to.

She loitered on the edge of the revellers. She couldn't see anyone she knew and they'd all taken a stimulant that she hadn't, so it wasn't a welcoming gang.

There was man climbing the pole, three-quarters of the way up. He was clearly no expert and a fall from that height would be serious, maybe even fatal.

There was something wrong with the climber's arm. It was swollen and dripping. She realised the climber was Bjarni Chickenhead.

"Wootah!" he shouted, as if to confirm her identification. He leant away from the pole and . . .

Paloma sprinted.

She dived and flung her arms around the falling man. They tumbled and came to a rest. She disentangled herself and jumped into a crouch. Bjarni was lying on his back, eyelids flickering. His left forearm was a mess of black blood and white sticks. *What had he done?* She pulled at one of the sticks— there must have been a dozen of them—but it wouldn't come free. Blood pulsed thickly from several of the entry points.

She looked about herself. Some people were dancing, some were pushing sticks through their arms, others were kissing and caressing. You'd think that some of them might have noticed her diving to catch a falling man and come to help. Apparently not.

"Yoki Choppa!" she shouted as loud as she could, pressing her thumb into Bjarni's armpit to slow the blood loss. "Yoki Choppa!"

Sofi Tornado arrived at a sprint, moments later.

"Yoki Choppa's coming," she said, taking in the scene. "What the...?"

"Don't know. See the sticks those twats over here are forcing through their arms? He's got a load of them jammed in his wrist."

"Idiot."

"I'm not an idiot," drawled Bjarni.

"Quiet, you. Keep that arm lifted, Paloma, let me see if I can..."

Sofi Tornado pulled at one of the sticks.

"I tried that," said Paloma. "We'll do more damage taking them out."

Yoki Choppa arrived at a run. He too gave one of the sticks a pull.

"That doesn't work," said Paloma.

The warlock nodded. "Sofi, where's your new sword?"

"Where I was sleeping."

"Paloma, run and get it."

Chapter 15

Across the Water Father

Finnbogi the Boggy couldn't stop staring at Bjarni Chicken-head. His friend was pale but sleeping soundly, trussed in blankets and lashed in a sitting position to the Plains Strider's rail. Erik the Angry sat on one side of him, Wulf the Fat on the other. Erik looked about as unhappy as a man can be. At first glance, Wulf seemed as cheery as ever, but even he was uncharacteristically slumped and pale.

The commotion in the night had woken Finnbogi from his weird dream, but he'd gone back to sleep without noticing that Bjarni wasn't in the sack with him. He felt terrible about that. He felt terrible in other ways, too. When Chief Clembur had warned them about the dangers of crazy snake, she hadn't mentioned that the next day you'd feel sick, thick and desolate.

She *had* warned that people died after taking crazy snake. Bjarni had nearly proved her right. When Finnbogi had woken, he'd heard Thyri say that Bjarni was dead. Then, as he'd fallen over trying to free himself from the sleeping sack, he heard that Bjarni had lost a leg. As Finnbogi had quizzed everyone trying to find out what had actually happened, Chogolisa Earthquake had carried Bjarni over from the Owsla area where they'd been looking after him.

She told them that Bjarni had drunk more crazy snake than advised, and gone mad; or, put another way, the large dose of crazy snake had done what it was meant to do. He'd taken the stripped white twigs which the more gung-ho Cuguai warriors pushed through their arms, and, rather than pushing them through, had tried to fit a dozen or so inside his forearm. Then he'd climbed the pole and fallen. Luckily, Paloma Pronghorn had been on hand to catch him.

To make matters worse, Bjarni had used sticks that had already gone through others' arms and been lying about bloodied in the dirt for Innowak knew how long. So, knowing that infection was more or less certain, the warlock had cut off his arm at the shoulder. It was still possible, said Chogolisa, that infection might develop in his chest, in which case he would die.

Finally, she'd looked embarrassed as she'd said: "And Sofi asked me to tell you that if you lot take such a powerful drug again, you should assign people who haven't taken it to look after those who have."

So the mood on the Plains Strider that morning was pretty sour. Finnbogi tried to convince himself that he was interested in the scenery, but he couldn't. The huge cloud of crowd pigeons pulling them along was just another thing. They crossed a broad river; the Water Father, someone said, not as impressive as the Water Mother but worth a look. Finnbogi couldn't be bothered even to turn his head.

His eyes kept returning to pale Bjarni, and to his guilt-ridden father.

In the end, Finnbogi decided that not doing anything was too awful, so he walked over to where Morningstar was sitting with Sofi Tornado. The Owsla captain had his sword Foe Slicer strapped to her hip.

"Sofi Tornado?" he asked, trying not to look at the sword. "Can I tell you something?"

"Go for it," she said. "It's Finnbogi the Boggy, isn't it?"

"You can call me Finn."

The Owsla captain's expression didn't change. Finnbogi launched in.

"Someone *was* looking after Bjarni. My dad, Erik the Angry, sat for an age and watched while Bjarni danced on his own, then walked him back, gave him food and water and put him to bed in his sleeping sack with me. Bjarni was lucid and said he was fine but still Erik waited until Bjarni was asleep before leaving him. But Bjarni woke up while Erik was down at the river, got up and went up the hill on his own."

Sofi regarded him evenly for a few moments then said, "Understood." Was there a softening in her expression or was it Finnbogi's imagination?

"So it wasn't Erik's fault, or Wulf's. Or anyone's, really. Apart from Bjarni's." Finnbogi bit his lips and squeezed them together to stop himself from crying. Crying probably wouldn't be good in front of the leader of the toughest group of warriors in the world. "And that's it. I wanted you to know." He turned to go.

"Finn," said Sofi Tornado.

"Yes?" He turned back.

"Ask Yoki Choppa if he's got anything to make you feel better. When you take drugs, you've got to take drugs."

Sassa leant on the side of the Plains Strider. The long undulations of the plain had sharpened into hills and it seemed they might finally leave the Ocean of Grass for more interesting topography. The huge vehicle swept around the side of a hill and down to a broad river, by far the broadest since the Water Mother. The Water Mother had been brown and muddy. This river was the deep blue of Olaf's Fresh Sea on the finest days.

It was the Water Father, someone shouted. Sassa thought they'd have to stop but they hardly slowed as the great vehicle plunged in.

A few snorts from the trailing edge of the Plains Strider were the only sign that a few dozen buffalo were swimming them across the river, buoyed by inflated bladders. Six-strong squads of dagger-tooth cats swam either side of the vast craft, each beast carrying a rider.

Deer and various other animals galloped away up the far valley side and into the trees. Two pronghorns watched from a hilltop. Sassa wondered what all the creatures they encountered made of the Plains Strider, and whether they'd remember it later that day when it was long gone.

Out of the river, they climbed the highest hill Sassa had ever seen, crested it and came to...more Ocean of Grass. The prairie went on and on, green, green and more green and nearly flat as far as she could see. Perhaps it sloped upwards away from her to the west, but she couldn't be sure.

Presently, in the distance, she saw outcrops of bare rock dotted about. Well that was something new.

She was studying the scenery in an effort not to think about Bjarni. She was upset about his accident, but, more, she was annoyed with him for being such a shag a stag dickhead. None of them knew that he'd drunk much more crazy snake than he should have done until they'd quizzed the Cuguai and heard that he'd distracted the woman doling it out and taken a massive gulp. Because of his stupidity they'd lost a warrior, and all the Wootah had been brought low. Wulf was pretending to be upbeat and optimistic, but Sassa knew he was as unhappy as he'd ever been. He thought he'd failed his friend.

Worst of all, Wulf was right. He *had* failed them all. They were in a dangerous situation, he was their leader, yet the great arse had knocked back a mind-altering whack of crazy snake. If Wulf had stayed straight, Sassa wouldn't have had to look after him and they both would have been free to look after the rest of them. One of them could have helped Erik keep an eye on Bjarni.

If somehow they lived long enough for him to become a father, then Wulf wasn't going to so much as look at a substance like crazy snake ever again.

Sassa noticed that the Plains Strider was slowing. There was a smattering of dead buffalo on the plain ahead. They passed over a few, but there were more and more. Eventually, the shout came to stop and the pigeons fluttered down.

The land ahead was strewn with dead buffalo; some in piles, some on their own, but all together thick enough on the ground that the buffalo supporting the Plains Strider wouldn't be able to run over them. Where there weren't buffalo, the land was churned as if it had been ploughed.

She went to join Sitsi Kestrel, looking over the other edge with Paloma Pronghorn.

"What happened here?" she asked.

"Tornado storm," said Sofi Tornado, joining them at the rail.

Sassa had never heard Sofi talk apart from to order people about. "What's a tornado storm?" she asked, not sure if she was going to get a reply.

"There was a storm here the day before yesterday." The Owsla captain sounded weary but not annoyed. "It was so powerful that it created multiple tornados which the buffalo were unable to escape. Yoki Choppa saw their suffering in his alchemical bowl. Thousands upon thousands were killed."

Sassa pictured a black sky full of spinning buffalo. It would have been a sight.

"He also saw the magic that caused it, and is sure that it was the force at The Meadows."

"But that must be more than a thousand miles away!" said Sitsi. "If it's that powerful here..."

"Indeed," said Sofi. "That's why, according to Yoki Choppa, it's vital that we get you there."

"I'm sorry about Bjarni," said Sassa.

"Don't let it happen again."

"I don't know what—"

"And don't dwell on it. We need to work together now to break these spider traps. The Badlanders have done us a favour bringing us so far west so quickly, but only if we—"

"Why so glum, why so glum!" Chapa Wangwa came bounding up. "There are plenty more buffalo where these came from. Plenty! Oh, I know what's upsetting you! Are you worried that we will take longer to get to the Badlands because all these dead buffalo are blocking the way? Well, I'm afraid you are right! We would have been there this evening, but now we will have to take the southern approach. So we will arrive tomorrow. Don't worry! There will still be plenty of excitement for you all when we get there. Excitement, and slow, horrible death! What is it that some of you say? Oh yes, Wooo-tah!"

Chapa Wangwa looked at them one by one. His permanent grin faltered when he saw the small smile playing on the Owsla captain's lips.

Chapter 16

Chippaminka Reigns

Luby Zephyr walked along at the head of her section, a good way behind the vanguard of the vast Calnian army that was marching across the Ocean of Grass to its doom.

It was four days since Luby had crept into Ayanna's tent and had the living crap scared out of her by Chippaminka. They were four days closer to the Badlands, four days nearer to Calnian destruction, and Luby had been able to do precisely nothing to stop them or even slow them.

She was seriously bewitched.

If she so much as thought about returning to Ayanna's tent, or approaching Ayanna on the walk, her stomach cramped and she struggled to breathe until she forced her mind onto something else. She'd seen Chippaminka once since the night in the tent, and an overwhelming, unnatural terror had nearly made her pass out. Even trying to think of asking someone else to talk to Ayanna on her behalf or kill Chippaminka made her mind flood with a debilitating horror and stifled all rationality and planning ability.

Unable to act otherwise, Luby had focused her energies on training her section of warriors to defeat the other members of the Calnian Owsla. The Owsla, she reckoned, could be beaten by a combination of two tactics that had never been tried before—to attack them in overwhelming numbers and to try to capture them rather than kill them. The Owsla's skin was tougher, their bones stronger and they were much faster than normal people, so the last thing you wanted to do was take them on in a fair fight.

So Luby's squad had made nets and catch poles and practised with those. If the rest of the Owsla really had joined the Badlanders, she reasoned, then they must have been bewitched like her. If she could restrain them and talk to them, she might be able to snap them out of their bewitchment. Then Sofi Tornado would know how to defeat Chippaminka.

Around noon, as always, she was walking along and trying to think of ways to capture the Owsla more efficiently, with fewer of her own warriors dying, when a woman from another division ran up.

"Luby Zephyr, can you walk ahead with me for a moment?"

"Sure," said Luby. Did she know her? She didn't think so.

The woman said she was a captain. She was on her way to confront Ayanna about the madness of the venture and wanted Luby's support.

"You have my support," Luby managed, the familiar dread storming her mind,

"Let's go then, right now."

Luby thought about running to the front of the column to confront the empress and nearly vomited. She staggered.

"...I can't," she said.

The captain stared at her for a moment, muttered "you're as bad as the rest of them" and ran off.

Luby followed the captain to apologise and explain her position. She'd run fifty paces when she realised that she was nearer to Ayanna than she'd been since she was in her tent. She immediately felt sick and scared and had to stop. *No*, she told herself, *I am not getting closer to Ayanna. I am following the captain to apologise. I was rude to her and I must apologise, that's why I'm headed this way.*

Her stomach steadied and she carried on, following the captain's run to the head of the marching column, all the while looking out for Chippaminka. She couldn't see the warlock, but when the captain reached Ayanna and Luby was about thirty paces away, a great fear clutched at her throat and stopped her very legs from moving and she could go no further.

The captain said something that she couldn't hear, and Ayanna replied. Luby stood and watched, feeling sick and wretched, theoretically ready to help but sure that she wouldn't be able to.

"Empress, I beseech you. This is a mistake and we must return to Calnia immediately."

The captain blocked her path, sweaty and panting. The Swan Empress Ayanna blinked. She couldn't remember the captain's name, but she remembered her story. She was a young, high-born woman who'd been grossly overweight. She'd accepted a bet to lose her flab and become a squad leader in the army. She'd won the bet, and more. She was now in good physical shape, if saggy-skinned, and had risen to captain, a couple of ranks above squad leader. She'd been brought to Ayanna's attention as a possible future general or even leader of the army.

The empress looked about for Chippaminka, but the girl was nowhere. She fought to calm herself. She needed Chippaminka.

"Halt!" she shouted to the twelve men carrying the swan litter. Inside it, Calnian screamed as if he were having his limbs ripped from his body. A few days before, Ayanna would have rushed to see what was wrong, but she was used to it now. The baby was outraged when the litter stopped, when it started and when it changed speed. She loved him unconditionally, which was lucky for him, because if anyone else had made as much noise as he did she would have had them executed.

"Why is it a mistake?" she asked the captain.

"Where do I start?" the woman beseeched. "We have no beef with the Badlanders, so there's no need for a punitive raid. If your intention is to expand the empire, this is not the way to go about it. We've marched far too far from Calnian territory without consolidation. It's not that our supply lines are stretched, we don't *have* supply lines. A well-marshalled force led by people who know the land could surround and annihilate our army with ease."

"We will take the Badland capital," Ayanna replied. The geographers had raised the same concerns, but Chippaminka had explained them away. "Then we will be supplied by the Badland empire."

"Any army, even one this size, would have trouble breaching Calnia's low walls. One of my men has been to the Badlands. He says that the capital, the seat of their chief, has one narrow road leading to it, up a cliff several hundred paces high. With what we have, it will be impossible to take."

Ayanna was confused. She felt a little faint. The Badlands' natural defences were something else that had troubled the geographers. What was it that Chippaminka had said to appease them? She couldn't remember. The geographers had become upset and then...no, it had gone. All she knew was that the geographers had been wrong and Chippaminka had been right.

But it did seem like a startlingly good point. How could a force armed with bows, slings, spears and clubs assault a cliff? Was the captain right? No, she couldn't be. Ayanna looked about for Chippaminka, but she was nowhere. Calnian wailed on—she would have to feed him soon.

"We have hunters and buffalo are plenty." She sounded more confident than she felt. "The army is the largest ever assembled. We will swarm up and over the Badlander defences. Calnia's empire will be doubled and in one moment become strong enough to last for ever." She needed to sit down. Where was Chippaminka?

"That makes no sense." The captain was wide-eyed and

earnest. Believable. "Perhaps if we had the Owsla they might spearhead a successful attack, but we have only Luby Zephyr.

"Worse that that, there are rumours that the rest of our Owsla are with the Badlanders. If that's the case, we are in even more trouble. Sofi Tornado and Chogolisa Earthquake alone could hold a narrow pass in a cliff until they grew old. Meanwhile, the Badlanders will be able to sally forth and pick us off. If we attack, fail and retreat, they can follow us all the way home, destroying our army warrior by warrior until there is no army left. And if we lose the army? If we lose you and Calnian? Then there is no more Calnian empire. This is not the campaign that will double the empire, it's the campaign that will lose it."

Tears sparkled in the captain's eyes. "My dear Swan Empress, I am no coward. I would die for you a thousand times over, but the situation here is clear. If we fail to penetrate the Badlands, which we will, it is the end of the Calnian empire. If we do conquer the Badlands, then we win the Ocean of Grass," she lifted her hands to indicate the endless prairie. "Why do we want it? It's enormous and sparsely populated. Its only assets are buffalo, deer and dung and we have plenty of these in the empire already. What are we doing?"

Behind them the Calnian expedition stretched back to the horizon. It was a vast army, but it was dwarfed by the everlasting grasslands and the overbearing sky.

"If we turn now," the captain continued, "we have a chance. We're six or seven days from the Badlands. If we retreat with the army intact we should make it back to Calnia. Please consider what I say, Empress. I was wrong to approach you like this, but I have been trying to talk to you since before we left Calnia, been snubbed again and again, and I was desperate. Kill me for insubordination, I don't care, but please consider what I say."

Ayanna looked at the captain's beseeching face and the enormity of what she'd done came washing over her. The captain was right. Of course she was. The weight of realisation made her feel faint. She staggered back into a guard's strong support.

"I..." she managed. "I..."

Chippaminka strode past the empress and drove her stiffened fingers into the captain's neck, then turned to Ayanna.

The captain stood behind the warlock, eyes wide, clutching her throat and gasping.

"What...?" managed Ayanna.

"I have executed a Badland infiltrator who was spreading defeatist nonsense. You are ill. Give the order to make camp here. I will tend to you and we will continue tomorrow."

Behind the young warlock, the captain fell to her knees. Nobody helped her.

Luby Zephyr saw Chippaminka marching up and tried to shout a warning, but the words stopped in her throat. She tried to run to help the captain but could not. Instead, she watched the girl kill the warrior.

Then Chippaminka saw her, and she had to run.

Luby sprinted back to her division, ashamed that the relief at getting away from Chippaminka was greater than her guilt for not helping the captain.

Ayanna *was* ill. She heard herself giving the orders to make camp as Chippaminka had bidden, her own voice echoing around in her head. Someone ushered her onto a chair, someone opened her shirt and someone delivered the wailing Calnian to her breast.

She sat with her eyes closed against the painful light, listening as the tent was erected, and was soothed to sleep by the boy's suckling.

She was woken by Chippaminka at sunset. She was fully dressed, spread like a starfish on the bed in her tent. Not her most goddess-like of poses.

The warlock stripped the empress and fetched her tub of

magic salve. Initially the girl used her hands, then her arms, and then her entire naked body, sliding over Ayanna's own nakedness, gliding, pressing, melting away all physical and mental concerns, breathing warm words of comfort into her ears. Once the empress was relaxed into a warm state of near bliss, Chippaminka morphed her manoeuvres into something altogether more thrilling, using all of her body and her mouth to stimulate and arouse.

Ayanna's breath was shortening, her climax welling, when she felt the girl's small, strong hands around her neck. This was unusual. Thumbs pressed into her windpipe.

Ayanna tried to sit. The girl slipped a little on her oiled torso but gripped strong legs about her waist and held firm. The grip about her neck tightened. She couldn't breathe. The empress panicked but couldn't break free. She stopped struggling and looked at her lover, eyes pleading. She didn't want to die. She could not leave Calnian alone.

Chippaminka leant forwards, her lips brushing the empress's. The pressure on her neck released and the girl's hands were now caressing and soothing. The salve's spicy bouquet mixed with Chippaminka's odour flooded into Ayanna's nose and filled her head, intoxicating her. She breathed in several times and kissed the girl's neck from collarbone to jaw, again and again. How she adored her!

"You are mine," said Chippaminka, sliding and pulsing her body rhythmically against the empress's. A slim, firm thigh parted the empress's softer legs and pressed into her. "Do you understand?"

"Yes," Ayanna breathed.

"You listen to nobody but me. You do what I tell you. Do you understand?"

"I will do what you tell me to do."

"Anything?"

"Anything."

"Good. That's very good."

Part Two

Spiders of the Badlands

Chapter 1

Into the Badlands

Finnbogi the Boggy stood at the rail of the Plains Strider between Ottar the Moaner and Freydis the Annoying.

The land was lumpier than it had been and there was a monumental flat-topped hill—or was it a mountain?—in the mid-distance to the south. Nearer by and all around were outcrops of bare white rock, stark against the green grass. Some of these outcrops were angular, with wall-like sides, others were domes. Some outcrops stood on their own, the size of longhouses, others were grouped into what looked like towns of lumpen white huts and sheds. The rock looked soft, as if a good kick would explode it into a cloud of powder.

Grazing here and skulking there were buffalo, elk, foxes and the other standard critters, but there were also thousands of furry creatures that looked like oversized, short-haired, fat-headed squirrels. Some of these were running around chasing each other. Some saw the Plains Strider, screamed and dived into holes. Some reacted to the colossal vehicle's approach by jumping about and squeaking weirdly. Others stood on their hind legs and watched them pass, forepaws held in front of them like meek men waiting for a Jarl to finish a conversation so they can petition him with a proposal that they know he'll reject.

"They're prairie dogs," said Sitsi Kestrel, joining them at the rail. "Black-tailed prairie dogs."

"Are they dangerous?" asked Finnbogi.

"Of course they're not dangerous!" scolded Freydis. "Do they look dangerous?"

Sitsi laughed. "They're dangerous if you're a grasshopper."

"But there are so many. If they got a leader..." Finnbogi mused.

"Then they'd take over and the world would be a better place," said Sitsi. "At least the Badlands would be. We can't be far now."

"Why do you say that?"

"The Badland capital is a great outcrop of rock into which the Badlanders have carved their dwellings. These bare rocks we can see all around must be outliers of that rocky terrain. Look," Sitsi pointed, "that one's got red stripes. It's the first one we've passed like that. The rocks of the Badlands are red, yellow and white rock, so I suspect we'll see more colour as we approach."

"Have you been here before?" asked Freydis.

"No, I learnt about it in Calnia."

"Are those the Badlands up ahead, do you think?" Finnbogi nodded to the ominous dark mass on the western horizon.

"No, those are clouds. I think the Badlands are north-west of here. We'll probably turn northwards soon. Those clouds, I think, are over the Black Mountains, further west than the Badlands."

"What do you think will happen when we get to the Badlands?" asked Finnbogi.

Sitsi looked at him and the children sadly. "I don't know," she said.

"Woo!" shouted Ottar, trailing off with a sad, "taaaaaah."

"It's not going to be good," said Freydis. "We should probably try to enjoy ourselves before we get there."

Finnbogi looked across at Bjarni, still trussed to the rail and unconscious after the large dose of Loakie-knew-what Yoki Choppa had made him drink. Erik was sitting next to Bjarni, even though the warlock had said he was going to keep him unconscious for a few days. It was his only chance, apparently, of fighting the infection which had spread to his chest. Erik's hand was bandaged over the burn that Chapa Wangwa had inflicted.

"Yes, Freydis," said Finnbogi, "you're right, you die when you die. Let's get back to the game. I think the next predator we see will be a bear."

"I think lion and Ottar thinks sturgeon."

"Sturgeon? Come on, Freydis, what did he really say?"

"Wolf."

"That's better."

The Plains Strider turned north and Sitsi nodded with satisfaction. She'd been right about the location of the Badlands. A little later, they passed two smashed huts. Next to them were the bodies of several people old and young, perhaps two extended families.

"We are nearly there!"

Finnbogi jumped. Chapa Wangwa had sneaked up behind them.

"I'm so excited!" the grinning Badlander continued. "How noble of these fine people to lie here dead and remind us what awaits in the Badlands!"

"What happened to them?"

"Perhaps they annoyed Beaver Man? He will kill people for annoying him. Perhaps they didn't annoy Nam Cigam? The chief warlock will kill people for *not* annoying him."

"Is Nam Cigam a reverser?" asked Sitsi.

"...Yes..." Chapa Wangwa's smile stayed, but his eyes narrowed. "How can you know about reversers?"

"She knows everything," said Finnbogi.

"I don't know exactly how far it is to the Badlands."

"We are so close now. Wait until we come over this rise. Wait, wait...and..."

"Wow," said Finnbogi.

The Plains Strider crested a rise and the ground fell away in front of them to a broad valley. Towers and domes of rock protruded from the valley floor like giant versions of the prairie dogs' hills. On the valley's far side, the grassland soared upwards to become an unbroken line of spiky cliffs. It was like a great barrier heaved from the depths which stretched east to west for miles and miles, horizontally banded red, yellow and white. The astonishing colours of the rock ridge shone in the sun, but the purple-black sky that loomed behind it was about as foreboding as a sky could be.

Yoki Choppa prodded the flesh where Bjarni Chickenhead's arm had once joined his shoulder as the patient slept on. Erik the Angry didn't need to ask. He knew from the smell. The wound was putrefying.

He shouldn't blame himself. He couldn't blame himself.

"Erik!" shouted Finnbogi from the other side of the deck. "You've got to see this!"

"In a moment." He held shallow-breathing, rot-stinking Bjarni while Yoki Choppa pressed a new poultice into the wound, then wrapped it with fresh bandages. The bandages had been supplied by the Cuguai. They'd been helpful, but shown no remorse or apology over Bjarni's accident. Why would they? They'd warned him and he'd been an idiot. For the same reasons, Erik knew he shouldn't blame himself but...if only he hadn't left Bjarni. If only he'd checked on him when he'd come back from the river and got into his own sack.

You die when you die, but Erik was still sad to see life taken from someone who'd been as full of it as Bjarni Chickenhead.

By the time they'd finished bandaging and dressing Bjarni, the Plains Strider had come to a rest and the crowd pigeons were flapping down. Erik could feel the birds' relief at being home, coupled with their joy of being part of such a multitude. Since Chapa Wangwa's warning, Erik hadn't attempted to communicate with the animals but, more and more, their emotions came to him unbidden. From the pigeons, he mostly felt a desperate desire to be surrounded by millions of their fellows. From the buffalo he heard bovine resentment. From the spiders, nothing. Their silence was creepy.

Erik and Yoki Choppa stood and looked over the deck rail. Erik knew from the pigeons that their odyssey across the Ocean of Grass was over, and he'd understood that the Badlanders' base was a spectacular place, but he hadn't expected anything like this.

"Wow," he said.

Around them, dagger-tooth riders were leaping from their cats and leaving them with meek-looking lackeys with spider neck boxes. Other worker types were rushing towards the Plains Strider, accompanied by a knot of Empty Children on bighorn sheep.

Off to the west, another pigeon-lifted vehicle creaked off the ground and rolled away. This one was perhaps a quarter of the length of the Plains Strider and had a less impressive flock of crowd pigeons. Instead of buffalo supporting its rear, there were perhaps fifty wolves.

To the east of where the Plains Strider had settled was a collection of buildings, tents, cages and dwellings carved into the rocky outcrops that rose from the prairie. The town was several times larger than the main Lakchan settlement.

Towering over all of this to the north was a jagged cliff hundreds of paces high, striped red, yellow and white, cutting into the sky like the lower rack of an aligator god's teeth. The Badlander leader Rappa Hoga was galloping on his dagger-tooth cat along a track that led up and into the spiky rocks. The big man and his huge cat looked like a child's toy in comparison to the domineering cliffs.

Erik the Angry stared at the wall of rock—he'd never imagined that anything like it could exist—until his gawping was interrupted by Chapa Wangwa shouting for everyone's attention. The Badlander was standing next to the six Empty Children at the prow of the Plains Strider and grinning widely, even for him.

"Our journey is over, my friends! You have reached the place of your deaths!"

Erik reached up to touch his spider box and stopped himself.

"The craft you can see yonder," Chapa Wangwa continued, "is Beaver Man's own transport, the Plains Sprinter. Can you imagine? Something so huge for just one man? It is not so big as the Plains Strider, but oh, it is fast! The wolves are bred to be quick, but even they have trouble keeping up with themselves.

"Over there you see what you think is a city. This is not a city! This is where animals and slaves and the lesser captives live. The journey of the Popeye and the smelly squatch ends here.

"The rest of you," he looked at each of the Owsla and Wootah tribe in turn, as if savouring their faces, "you will climb down and follow me, up into the Badlands. You may carry your weapons—you will need them—but remember, even looking like you're going to strike a Badlander means instant death from your beeba spiders. What is that confusion on your face, young Freydis the Annoying? Oh yes, of course, you like to be literal. It's not *instant* death. It's instant broken back, broken face, broken legs, followed by slow, slow death. Silly me."

Ottar shouted, leaping on the spot, pointing at Chapa Wangwa and shaking his head.

"What is he saying?" said the Badlander. His mouth was still smiling but his eyes were wide and his nostrils flared. He was, Erik realised with some satisfaction, scared of the little boy.

"Before I tell you," said Freydis, "remember he didn't make

it up. He hears things from other places and he won't tell me where."

"Come on, come on, little girl, tell me what he said."

"Okay! He says you are a nasty and unhappy man who nobody loves and soon you will die in a nasty way."

"He says a lot."

"He tells me what he hears."

"I see. Perhaps he's right. You will all want to know. You will want to be sure that my death is *nastier* than that from the beeba spiders, so I'll remind you exactly of how nasty a beeba spider death can be. I will have your spiders bite you now, Freydis the Annoying."

"No," said Wulf.

"Try to stop me, Wulf the Fat, and I will take your wife Sassa Lipchewer too and the little boy for good measure, why not? Will you try to stop me?"

Wulf coloured so swiftly that Erik thought he'd burst into flames. "Please do not kill the girl," he managed through a clenched jaw.

"Take me instead," said Gunnhild Kristlover, stepping forward.

"Step back, or I will take you, and Sassa Lipchewer and Ottar the Moaner. And the girl."

Keef the Berserker took a step towards the Badlander, but Wulf put a hand on his shoulder. Gunnhild backed away. Chapa Wangwa's grin broadened: "Any of you, please do try to stop me killing the girl. But know that your spiders will bite and the girl's spiders will bite and the rude little boy's spiders will bite as well."

The six Empty Children who'd been controlling the crowd pigeons and buffalo stared sightlessly ahead but Erik could feel them focusing on the creatures strapped to their necks. His own spiders shifted on tickling legs. For the first time he felt something from them, an emotion so cold and so bereft of the barest breeze of compassion that he knew there was no hope for Freydis. Perhaps he would have sacrificed himself rather than watch the girl die alone, but that meant Ottar would be killed, too. They were helpless.

"Good. You see the control I have over you. You do what Chapa Wangwa tells you. Empty Children, have the spiders bite this girl's neck on my count of three."

All of them, Wootah and Owsla—Morningstar, Sofi, Bodil, Finnbogi—all of them were on their toes, desperate to act but impotent. All apart from Ottar, who reached a finger into his mouth, picked something from his back teeth and looked at it. Freydis stood with her fists clenched, staring hatred at the Badlander. She was defiant, but she was alone.

This was it, thought Erik. They all knew it. The moment they'd been dreading since their capture.

The freedom of the spider boxes had lulled them into a false sense of security, but the truth was undeniable—they were going to die. And when Freydis died—their youngest, their most innocent—they couldn't pretend any longer. Their hope would die with her. The Badlanders would draw each of their deaths out for their own amusement and there was not a single thing any of them could do to stop it.

"One!" cried the Badlander. Sofi Tornado took a step towards him. "One more move from any of you, and that person will die, and the girl will die AND the boy will die. Got it? Good."

Ottar screamed and they all turned to him. He was screaming at whatever it was he'd picked from his teeth. He saw them all looking at him and giggled.

"Two!"

Nobody moved. Everyone was looking from Chapa Wangwa to Freydis to the Empty Children. What would happen if we all rushed them at the same time? Erik wondered.

"And Thrrr..."

Paloma Pronghorn shot at Chapa Wangwa like an arrow from a bow.

She nearly made it.

Half a pace away, she crumpled. The Badlander stepped aside. Paloma tumbled past him and hit the ground hard. She rolled and came up in a kneeling position, facing them. She lifted her hand to her neck. Her skin darkened, her neck swelled, then her face.

She stood shakily, lifting her killing stick with a wobbling hand. Chapa Wangwa took a step back, grinning in amazement. A spasm racked Paloma, but she stayed on her feet.

"You are strong!" he said.

She grunted as if she'd been punched in the stomach and took another step towards him. Her face was near black now and darkness was spreading along her arms and torso. By this stage, the other beeba spider victim they'd seen had been on the ground with a broken jaw and spine.

For a moment it looked like Paloma might manage to whack Chapa Wangwa, but then the mighty sprinter slumped. She lifted her gaping mouth to the sky, screamed, and fell onto her back, body convulsing, legs and arms flapping.

Erik and others—he couldn't see who in his urgency—ran in and grabbed her limbs in an attempt to stop them from snapping.

They held her.

The darkness faded from her skin and her breathing, although shallow, became more regular.

After what seemed like an age, Paloma lifted her head and rasped: "I'm going to..."

Chogolisa picked her up and held her so that she could vomit. She didn't, though. Instead, her eyes closed and she went floppy in Chogolisa's arms.

"Wow!" cried Chapa Wangwa. "Is she dead?"

Yoki Choppa felt her pulse. "She is not."

"Amazing! *What* a tough one! Now, where were we? Oh yes, I was about to have little Freydis the Annoying killed. But I think we will save that for later. Paloma Pronghorn's limbs may not have snapped, but I think she has admirably demonstrated that you don't want to cause any trouble. As we discussed, the beeba spider poison does not cause instant death. She will have experienced agony like few will ever know and she will die soon."

Chapter 2

Rocks That Look Like Cocks

Sassa walked with Freydis and Thyri as the two tribes followed Chapa Wangwa through the Badlanders' territory.

"Look! Look!" cried Freydis the Annoying, apparently put out not a jot by Chapa Wangwa's threat to kill her, nor by Paloma Pronghorn's near death, "white prairie dogs."

"A child's fear is like summer rain," said Gunnhild Kristlover. *"Powerful in the moment, but brief and easily forgotten."*

"And both can ruin an outdoor lunch," added Keef the Berserker.

Sassa looked to where Freydis was pointing. Dotted about the sloping grassland that skirted the craggy cliff were hundreds of pale-furred versions of the creatures they'd seen from the Plains Strider. Hugin and Munin growled.

"Did you invent that name?" asked Thyri Treelegs.

"Prairie dogs? No, Sitsi Kestrel said that's what they're called and she is very nearly as clever as my big brother."

"The Owsla put us to shame," said Thyri, kicking a stone along the dusty road.

"They don't, Thyri," said Sassa Lipchewer. "If any of us had gone for Chapa Wangwa we would have been killed; you, Erik and Wulf included. The Owsla are magically charged. They have hardened bones and Fraya knows what else. You can't compare yourself to them."

"I can though."

"You shouldn't though. Our time will come. I'm sure you will have a chance to prove yourself."

They walked on, Freydis chattering away and Ottar gambolling alongside. Ahead of them, Chogolisa Earthquake and Sofi Tornado carried the unconscious Paloma on a litter. Erik and Finnbogi were carrying Bjarni on another. One of her oldest friends and her new friend were laid low, and Sassa had a horrible thought that it was only going to get worse. *Buck up*, she told herself. You may die when you die, but both Paloma and Bjarni were still alive.

The flat, broad track cut upwards into the cliff. It looked to Sassa like the plants and soil had rotted away, leaving exposed the diseased, decaying bones of the world. Next to the road the rock looked like piles of wet earth, but up ahead it towered in great fins and spires of white, red, yellow and purple. Perhaps it would have looked beautiful in different circumstances, but Sassa found it oppressive and loathsome, as if the evil of the Badlander tribe was causing the very ground that they walked on to putrefy and shrivel.

The cliffs were pocked with little round caves a pace across and there were several holes the same size on the roadside, leading down to Fraya knew what.

Sassa put a hand on her stomach and shuddered.

"That rock there," said Wulf, catching up to them, "looks very much like a cock."

Sassa looked at the five-pace-high yellow and red pinnacle he was referring to. She wasn't in the mood for puerile joshing, but she had to admit that he was right. The stout tower even had a neatly defined purple helmet. "As does that one over there," Wulf continued, pointing at another undeniably phallic pillar. "We are entering the land of rocks that look like cocks."

"We are indeed," said Sassa, smiling for the first time since they'd arrived in the Badlands. "That one's the same colour as yours, too."

"Mine has more red stripes. And it's bigger."

"Do you mind?" said Thyri. "Freydis is right here and I am, too."

"*I* don't mind," said Freydis, "but I can't see what you mean. Which rock looks like a chicken, Wulf the Fat?"

"That one there," said Wulf.

"It's more like a man with no arms, I think . . . It's not a cock or any other kind of bird. What do you think lives down all the big holes?"

"Chipmunks," said Wulf. As if to prove his point, there was a skittering to the right as two chipmunks ran up a vertical rock face, then stood on their hind legs at the top, looking down at the newcomers.

They trudged on, up into the Badlands.

More and more animals appeared, which made the place seem a lot less oppressive to Sassa. Baby rabbits darted between clumps of grass garlanded with violet flowers and a pointy-beaked bird or a chipmunk perched on every pinnacle of rock. A pair of bighorn sheep deftly descended a nearby cliff, starting a mini rockslide with every dainty step.

"Wow, that's got to be the cock of the day," said Wulf when the largest pinnacle so far came into sight.

"What *are* you talking about?" Freydis demanded.

Despite herself, Sassa had to stifle a giggle.

This was one reason, perhaps the main reason, that Sassa Lipchewer loved Wulf the Fat as much as she did. He always cheered things up. It was as if his happiness had drawn the animals and flowers from their hiding places to brighten the day. Despite their desperate situation, Sassa felt a spark of optimism.

Then they turned a corner.

The land narrowed and the track passed through a steep-sided gully fifteen paces wide. Hanging from the gully walls, nailed by their hands into the rock, were the bodies of men and women. Below each, the rock was stained red and black with blood. Dotted like decorations all around the pinned people were hundreds of severed hands, nailed in pairs a pace apart. Some looked fresh, recently parted from their owners, some had been picked clean to leave white bones and others were in various stages of decay.

An assortment of birds and insects, including huge red-winged, black-bodied wasps, was feasting on the corpses and the fleshier of the severed hands.

Then Sassa saw one of the corpses kicking at a couple of nibbling chipmunks and she realised. The hanging people, bleeding and feasted on by animals, were all alive.

The road reached the top of the cliff and the land flattened out into a grassy plain dotted all around with outcrops of rock, varying in size from pillars the height of a person, to craggy white, red and yellow mountains, some flat-topped, others spiky. The islands of bare rock were bright in the sun, but the sky to the north remained the mauve-tinted blue of a serious storm.

There were dozens more people hanging from rock faces, and hundreds more severed hands nailed around them. It was as busy with birds and beasts as the most bountiful woodlands in springtime, but all the cute critters had gathered not to eat fruit and fornicate, but to feast off the flesh of the living.

Some Badlanders were walking about carrying long spears with knapped quartz heads, shooing animals away and gouging their weapons into the buttocks of the hanging people to let the blood flow. One pair of Badlanders put two ladders up next to a hanging man who looked dead. They hacked with quartz-headed axes at his wrists and he fell, leaving his hands behind.

Well, that explains all the hands, thought Sitsi Kestrel.

Aware of her hypocrisy—the Owsla had done things to their victims in the Plaza of the Sun which were, objectively,

sickening—Sitsi Kestrel was horrified by the hanging people. She was walking along beside Paloma Pronghorn's litter,
holding the unconscious woman's hand. Was she dying? Perhaps Paloma's alchemically enhanced body made her immune
to the spider bites? Sitsi could only hope. The spider-bitten
Owsla had not regained her normal colour, though her breathing had normalised.

Sitsi had offered to take over the carrying from Sofi Tornado or Chogolisa Earthquake, but they'd shaken their heads,
grim-faced and smouldering.

Beneath their impressively vengeful demeanours, the wooden
boxes on their necks were like decorations reminding the world
of their impotence.

Owsla and Wootah—two unconscious, the rest as surly
as captured rebels being led to execution through a jubilant,
sneering crowd—followed Chapa Wangwa towards the highest pinnacle of rock.

Lining the approach was a variety of smart, light-framed
huts with woven grass walls and roofs, and a host of dark-
doored dwellings carved into the rock walls. Families of Badlanders watched them pass. There were no spider boxes on the
spectators' necks.

Finally, they came to a large, flat area of bare white rock,
stained dark in many places. Seats were cut into the rock
ridges all around, and there were tiers of wooden benches filling the gaps. It was a sports arena like the Plaza of the Sun.
The stains were blood. There were plenty of them. Towards
the centre, the stains joined into one dark patch a couple of
dozen paces across.

Sitsi groaned. It would be poetic for the Owsla to meet their
ends surrounded by baying crowds in an arena like the one
where they'd slaughtered so many. Objectively poetic, anyway. Subjectively, it would be seriously annoying.

"And here comes Nam Cigam!" chimed Chapa Wangwa.

A man was walking on his hands, backwards, towards

them. He had a large eye painted on each buttock, and an over-sized, hairy shoe on each foot. He was otherwise unadorned and naked.

He flipped over and stood, panting. He was hairless apart from a strip of beard running along his jawline. His frame was slight but wiry and leanly muscled, with a longish, slender penis and, although Sitsi was no expert in this field, he didn't seem to have any balls. He was also filthy, as if he'd rubbed himself with dirt. That was normal practice for a reverser, in place of washing.

"Badbye, goodbastards!" he cried, his voice high-pitched. He danced from foot to foot. "Here is a place where you'll have a lovely time and definitely not die. I am not Nam Cigam and I am delighted to sing this sad farewell."

Sitsi had met a reverser before, in a village the Owsla had been sent to punish. Chogolisa had shut that one up by turning his head so it was facing the wrong way. Even though she was now free from rattlesnake cruelty, Sitsi couldn't regret that slaying. Sitsi despised reversers. They were contrary for the sake of being contrary and they thought that it made them wonderfully clever. It did not; any idiot could know what was expected of them and do or say the reverse, but whole tribes were sucked in by their backward antics and revered them as hilarious geniuses.

All the Owsla and Wootah, she was glad to see, were looking at the reverser with the contempt he deserved, apart from Bodil Gooseface who was staring at him in open-mouthed wonder. Ottar the Moaner had turned round and was wag-gling his arse at the reverser, which Sitsi considered an appo-site response.

Nam Cigam walked around them, sniffing. He squatted next to Bjarni Chickenhead's litter and addressed the uncon-scious man.

"You smell like the clouds on a clear day!" he cried. "You make my nose run like a buffalo with no legs."

Utter, utter twat, thought Sitsi.

"You're funny!" Bodil laughed.

Nam Cigam hopped up to her, smiling smugly as if hopping was the inspired antic of a comedic virtuoso. "I see you like a snake with no eyes can see the moon on a moonless night! You are disgustingly ugly and I would hate to make hate to you!"

With that, he sprang back onto his hands and went back the way he came, shouting, "Hello, hello!"

"Nice guy," said Keef the Berserker.

"He's a reverser," explain Sitsi.

"He's certainly something," said Keef.

"Isn't he wonderful?" cried Chapa Wangwa. "But I brought you here to meet our chief, Beaver Man. I wonder where he is? While we wait for him I will show you a sight. Leave the two on the litters—we'll be back this way and the Empty Children can watch over them."

Finnbogi the Boggy, along with four Owsla warriors, one warlock, nine other Wootah and two racoons followed the grinning Badlander across the arena to a gap in the eastern rock wall.

"Be careful!" advised Chapa Wangwa, "we wouldn't want anybody falling."

The gap was wide enough for them all with room to spare. Over its lip, the land fell vertiginously a couple of hundred paces into a gully. Beyond, as far as they could see in all directions, was an impassable landscape of gorges, pinnacles, crinkled towers and ridges all carved from yellow, red-striped, crumbly looking rock. The tallest summit was topped with a series of horizontal bands of harder looking rock, between which were small, black caves. Finnbogi had a vision of giant insects returning to the caves with human prey to feed their fat but sharp-toothed maggots. He shuddered.

Such a place should not exist in the world of men and

women. It was breathtaking, undeniably beautiful, but also frightening and oppressively barren. You could see why the place was called the Badlands. Nothing good, thought Finnbogi, could live here. Actually, there were a couple of sprays of grass which didn't look too evil bursting from crevices, but these only served to highlight how the rest of the landscape was too steep and serious for soil, let alone vegetation.

He looked back down to the drop at his feet, falling away hundreds of paces to the dry, narrow canyon floor. He was taken back to when Garth had held him above the cliff by the Water Mother. This was higher, and somehow—

Chapa Wangwa pushed him and he lurched forwards.

The Badlander grabbed his arms and pulled him back, laughing.

Finnbogi breathed hard and thanked Tor he'd already voided his bowels that morning. He turned to Chapa Wangwa, panting, blood pulsing in his temples, fists clenched.

His spiders tickled his neck. He looked back over the huge view and tried to calm his breathing.

Then he saw them.

The deepest looking canyon in the spiky, incised landscape meandered sharply towards them from the east, so narrow and steep that he couldn't begin to see its base.

Coming along that gorge were the tiny figures of what looked like people, but who couldn't be people because they were bouncing back and forth across the ravine like insects, gripping onto one steep rock face, then flipping to the other side, holding for a moment, then leaping back across.

They disappeared out of sight behind a ridge a good fifty paces high, then a moment later they were leaping over it, still coming towards the watching Wootah.

They leapt down the near side of the ridge, bounded across the tops of crumbling rock towers and Finnbogi saw that they were indeed humans, displaying an inhuman athleticism that perhaps even Paloma Pronghorn couldn't have matched. As they neared, he saw that they were all men; lean, muscled and naked. Most had long hair which swished dramatically as they leapt from rock to rock.

"I bet they're all really thick; terrible conversationalists, I wouldn't wonder," he said to Thyri Treelegs. She was standing next to him, gawping with less reserve than might have been elegant at the naked, god-bodied men. Either she didn't hear Finnbogi or she ignored him.

The acrobats reached the twenty-paces-wide gully below the Calnians and Wootah. Finnbogi thought they must stop there, but they leapt across and scrabbled like chipmunks up the sheer wall.

"Make way!" called Chapa Wangwa.

Wootah and Calnians stepped aside to let the men flash by. Finnbogi had time only to notice that one had horns like a bighorn sheep, and then they were past, sprinting away, such marvellous examples of slender musculature and small, hard-looking buttocks that Finnbogi felt his jaw hang open.

One of them skidded to a stop, and walked back towards them. He was a little older than Finnbogi, a little shorter, but a good deal broader across the shoulders and trimmer in the waist. He had short hair, large, dark but shining eyes, a thin beard and a penis and balls that hung heavily like ripe and flawless vegetables. There was something odd about his skin. He was sweaty, but even so he was shinier that he should have been, like a varnished bowl.

Finnbogi didn't like the look of him at all.

"Hi there," he said. "I've been expecting you. I saw you coming in my alchemical bowl. I'm Beaver Man." He had a soft lisp, possibly caused by the gap where his two central upper teeth should have been.

"This is our great chief!" cried Chapa Wangwa, "All of you, get on the ground and..."

"Easy, Chapa Wangwa, easy. I asked these to be separated from the other guests for a reason. They are not my inferiors. These are the famous Calnian Owsla and the Hardworkers, whose ancestors travelled with Olaf the Worldfinder in ships from the far side of the Wild Salt Sea."

"We're called the Wootah now," said Wulf, satisfyingly unflustered by Beaver Man's knowledge.

"Wootah, Wootah...I like it! Wooooo-tah! Much less smug than Hardworker. And you are the leader?"

"I am. Wulf the Fat."

"But you're not...oh, I see. Ha ha ha! Overweight as a child, were you?"

"...yes." It was the first time Finnbogi had heard Wulf introduce himself without using his "fat cock" joke. Given what the naked Beaver Man was sporting, it would have just been awkward.

He told himself to stop looking at the man's genitals, and found himself instead looking at broad chest muscles, thick but well-shaped biceps, extraordinary stomach muscles, tucked like two racks of small loaves above... *Eyes*, Finnbogi told himself, *just look in his eyes.*

"And you," Beaver Man turned to Sofi Tornado, "are the head of the Calnian Owsla; the unbeatable Sofi Tornado."

Sofi held his gaze.

"But your Owsla is depleted, just four of you. I knew you'd had your troubles, but I thought five were coming?"

"One was spider bit this morning," said Chapa Wangwa.

"No. What a shame." Beaver Man looked around them all, Calnians and Wootah, his bright eyes bulging with sadness and sincerity. "You must avoid that happening to any more of you. Please, please do what you're told by Chapa Wangwa and my other excellent people. And, Chapa Wangwa, I'd like you to hold back from goading them into attacking you. I saw what you did to this excellent man as we were approaching,"

he indicated Finnbogi with a hand. "That false push trick is
frightening. A less relaxed fellow would have hit you and that
would have been that for him. I'd hate to lose another Calnian
or Wootah to their spiders. We will honour the body of the
woman who died."

"She didn't die," said Sofi Tornado.

"*What?*" said Beaver Man, looking as if he'd been told that
badgers could fly if they put their minds to it.

"She's not dead *yet*," grinned Chapa Wangwa.

"I hope she recovers," the Badlander chief looked like
he meant it. "Do call on any of my healers or warlocks
if you need, but I daresay the excellent Yoki Choppa has
done everything that can be done. Now, I know who the
Owsla are—by your bearing you are Sofi Tornado, your size
makes you Chogolisa Earthquake, by your punching clubs
you must be Morningstar, and you, with the stunning eyes,
must be Sitsi Kestrel the archer—but I don't know any of
the Wootah's names, other than Wulf the Fat, so let's rem-
edy that."

He walked round all of them, taking each of their hands in
turn, asking them their names and saying to each: "I'm Beaver Man, welcome to the Badlands." He greeted everyone, the
children included, with something that looked exactly like
warm sincerity and respect.

Introductions over—and Finnbogi just knew Beaver Man
was the sort of arsehole who was going to remember everybody's name—the Badlander chief leapt onto a small outcrop
to address them all again.

"Before you see where you will be staying and settle in,
I'd like to show you something. You will, of course, have
wondered why we have people hanging by their hands all
over the place, their blood flowing into the rock beneath
them. Follow me. I'll explain on the way, so please don't
stray too far, and, much more importantly, don't go too far

from the Empty Children. I'll say it again: *please* don't get bitten by your beeba spiders. I have other plans for all of you."

They followed Beaver Man back across the empty arena, to where Paloma and Bjarni were lying still. The chief examined them, asking questions and looking particularly concerned about Bjarni Chickenhead.

"Well done, Yoki Choppa," he said eventually, "you have treated them both exactly as I would have done. Your reputation is not exaggerated. Now, those of you who can, follow me."

He led them through a gap in the northern arena wall. The bizarre land split into two narrow, grassy valleys, each flanked by bare rock walls and pinnacles. There were more hapless victims attached to the rock by their hands, and many more animals, particularly chipmunks, rabbits, riderless bighorn sheep and a variety of small, brightly coloured birds. Many of the animals were feeding on the hanging people.

"We're headed up this other way." He pointed along the rightmost track and they followed a pale rock path through the grass past a couple of squat, dark-leaved fir trees.

It was very different from the wooded glades that Finnbogi had known back east, and not just because of the moaning, bleeding, animal-nibbled captives and pairs of ownerless hands. Above the hanging captives, the higher parts of the rock towers had been hollowed into homes with wooden walkways between them. Badlanders, mostly children and the old, looked down.

As Beaver Man walked, he talked.

"Are you horrified by our captives?"

Nobody answered.

"You, Finn, are you horrified?"

Finnbogi was flattered to be picked out by the young chief.

"Um...I don't think it's great?" was all he could think of to say on the subject of the hundreds of tortured unfortunates.

"Most people, I know, don't like it much. I get that. However, all of you eat animals, right? You ate buffalo on the way here. We Badlanders know the great truth that humans are no better—or worse, mark you—than animals. All living creatures have equal value. Bear that in mind, then consider that most tribes kill as many animals as they want, and this"—he waved his fingers to indicate the surrounding misery—"is all fine."

"I don't think it's fine," said Gunnhild, "on the buffalo drive on the way here—"

"You thought too many buffalo were killed because they were not eaten or used in any way?" Beaver Man interrupted.

"Yes."

"And what did you do about it?"

"I had spiders attached—"

"Without the spiders you wouldn't have acted. You might have complained a little, but you wouldn't have acted. You would have been hampered by hypocrisy, because the Goachica gave you two buffalo for your Things four times a year. You didn't need to eat those animals, but you were happy to have them killed for you."

Gunnhild grunted, but had no clever reply.

How does he know this stuff? thought Finnbogi.

"We kill animals as we want," explained Beaver Man, "and humans are animals. With most of the predators killed off by our ancestors, there are too many humans. They need to be culled for the good of the world."

Up ahead, in a departure from the normal hanging from hands, a man was pinned by his hands and feet to a large boulder, which was in turn balanced precariously on a tower of crumbly rock five paces above the valley floor. He was watching their approach, eyes wide and neck sinews taut.

"So," said Beaver Man, "there is nothing wrong with doing this."

The Badlander chief ran up the side of the rock tower and powered a two-footed kick into the boulder that held the captive. He came down headfirst, and Finnbogi thought for a thrilling moment that he might be seriously hurt, but he sprang on his hands, launched himself back onto his feet and leapt nimbly away as the rock with the man attached to it wobbled then tottered over and rolled off the tower onto the valley floor with a crunching bang.

The man screamed and screamed some more, as well he might. The rock had come to rest so that he was uppermost, but while rolling from its perch, the weighty boulder had mulched one arm and shoulder into a flapping pulp. Beaver Man danced up to the boulder and looked into the screaming man's eyes with all the interest and compassion of a child investigating a hole in a log. Then, with a strength that matched Chogolisa Earthquake's, he rolled the large stone over to crush the hapless captive's head.

The screaming stopped.

"The point being," Beaver Man continued, walking on as if he'd paused to sniff a flower, "is that we don't just do the world a service by killing people. We do ourselves a service, in two ways. The first, as with that fellow just now, is entertainment. Humans have always enjoyed killing each other in a variety of horrible ways, haven't we, Sofi Tornado?"

The Owsla captain said nothing.

"Do you agree, Sofi Tornado?" said Chapa Wangwa, following along behind. "Answer, or spider."

"I agree."

"Good. So. In Calnia and the Badlands, people like killing people and we're unashamed about it. We're going to kill most or all of you for our entertainment, for example, because you're so interesting. Our less interesting guests don't get to die in a fun way. They die slowly. That brings us to the second service we're doing for ourselves, although this one benefits the greater world, too. You'll see it soon."

They walked on, through the semi-verdant valley. The tortured, bleeding, hanging people were again a galling juxtaposition to the singing, chirruping, gambolling, albeit bloody-muzzled animals.

The canyon narrowed into a winding, rock-walled corridor, perhaps two paces wide and mercifully free of hanging people, then opened into a deep cliff-sided bowl around two hundred paces across. They followed Beaver Man out onto a wooden platform. The sides of the bowl were the normal pale powdery Badlands rock until about halfway down, then they were dark and glistening, as if liquid was oozing from the rock and flowing into the bowl. Far below, the base of the hole was filled with a lake that shone like dark, polished metal. A dozen little islands protruded from the lake, each about fifteen paces long.

Sitsi Kestrel gasped. As Finnbogi's eyes adjusted to the gloom, he understood why. The shapes were moving. The lumps, far too large to be animals, looked alive. He could now see that the dark and glistening substance was blood, seeping from the walls of the rock bowl and pooling at its base.

"Badlanders and Calnians are proud of their alchemical abilities," Beaver Man announced, his voice matter-of-fact. "But, as with all proud humans in every age, our hubris is misplaced. There is a more ancient, more powerful magic fuelled by life or, as the men and women hanging from our hills might argue, death. It depends on perspective. Their lives are reclaimed by the land and channelled into the animals you see below you."

"What are they?" asked Sitsi Kestrel. "Whales?"

"You're right to guess whales, since those are the only animals alive today that can come close to matching these in size, but, no, they are not whales. Many many years ago, more years ago than you can comprehend, large animals walked this land for a great, great deal longer than humans have scratched about on its surface."

Finnbogi saw Sitsi bristle. Beaver Man had no idea how many years she could comprehend.

"The large animals died out, as all life will," Beaver Man continued. "Still an unimaginably long time later, the sea flooded the land and the bodies of the animals were covered in mud and sand. Mud and sand, trees and weed, beasts and birds sank in that sea and lay on top of each other in layer after layer, over millions of years, being pressed by so much weight that they became rock. Then, still longer ago than your minds can even begin to imagine, the seas flowed away, leaving behind these layers of new rock that you can see." He pointed at a cliff side, which was indeed made up of clear bands.

"Which god told you all this?" asked Sitsi.

"No god. I learned from elders and have observed it myself. Look around, perhaps you will see it, too."

Sitsi did look.

"You are clever. I can see that you are beginning to think I am right." Beaver Man nodded, a smile in his eyes.

"I'd always thought," said Erik, "that the land was formed by rivers and streams cutting down over innumerable years."

"That comes next. The rock is left behind by the sea in bands, as we can see, then the rain collects into streams and rivers and erodes the rock. Forebears with more patience than me discovered that rivers cut downwards about a pace every thirty years here in the Badlands, but here the rock is soft. Usually it is slower."

Finnbogi was lost and bored by this bollocks, but Erik, Sitsi and a few others—Wulf, Sofi Tornado, Sassa, Thyri— were lapping it up. Finnbogi suspected that Thyri was faking her interest.

"I'll end the lecture, and get to the point of it, as I can see poor Finn is flagging."

"I'm not."

Beaver Man gave Finnbogi a look that he might have given to a son with sodden trousers who's claiming not to have wet himself, then continued. "As Erik said, down, down cuts the river. Eventually it exposes the bones of the beasts that died all that time ago. The bones have become rock, but they still hold the essence of life. Now, we take a current life, filter the magic of that life through the deep magic of the rocks themselves, pour that on top of the ancient bones, flesh grows back and life returns. This is a simplification, there's a lot more going on, but it's all you need to know. The result is that the most fearsome beast you can imagine walks the earth again. We call them lizard kings. We control them through the Empty Children and we could use them to, for example, rip a Calnian army to pieces."

Finnbogi looked down at the lumps. They were moving, they did look alive, but they were just lumps. They were still a long way from being a squad of monsters that could destroy an army.

"You are sceptical, Finn?"

Thyri narrowed her eyes at Finnbogi, no doubt disapproving that he'd introduced himself to the enemy by his shortened name.

"No..."

"Look over here." He darted to the edge of the wooden platform. Finnbogi and the others followed. Beaver Man pointed at a rock that looked like a tortoise shell.

"We didn't carve this," said the young Badland chief. "It wasn't here when my father was born. It was revealed as the rock washed away."

"Is it some sort of burrowing tortoise?" asked Erik.

"No, you're missing the point. Look, it has fins, not legs. This isn't a tortoise. It's a turtle, from the ocean that used to cover this land. Over millions of years it has turned to stone."

"Fuck me," said Erik.

Beaver Man was mildly taken aback by his phrasing, but continued. "So there's proof that these stone animals are the petrified remains of ancient creatures. As for proof that magic can pump life into them? Don't worry, the lizard kings are not the first creatures we have made. We know it works. These should be up and walking soon. Some of you may live long enough to see them."

Chapter 3

March to Glory

The Calnian army stopped for a midday break and Luby took the opportunity to squeeze in some training. She'd been given a mixture of the less capable warriors, ranging from the keen but inexperienced down to some serious lackwits who didn't know their axes from their arseholes. She was training the former to attack as a team and the latter to stay out of the way. It was physically and mentally demanding work that mercifully kept her mind from Chippaminka and the dead captain.

She'd seen Ayanna waver. Until Chippaminka had steamed in and killed the captain, Ayanna had listened. It had shown Luby that the empress's enchantment could be broken by persuasion. All she had to do was convince herself that she was visiting the empress for some other reason, in order to get around her own enchantment, then find a time when Chippaminka was away from Ayanna. They were five or six days' march from the Badlands, so she needed to act soon. The idea filled her with fear, but seeing the captain get so close had given her a dash of confidence.

She was demonstrating how a team of two could use leather collars on poles to hold a stronger opponent when a voice said: "Luby Zephyr, might I have a moment?"

She turned. Icy terror gripped at her throat as Chippaminka's eyes flashed coldly at her.

"I..." She heard herself saying, feeling as if the prairie had opened under her feet and she was falling to her death.

She followed the young warlock through the long grass unwillingly, as if pulled along by an invisible, irresistible tether. They'd gone perhaps two hundred paces when her legs gave way.

She lay on her back. Blue sky and white clouds were framed by blades of green. Chippaminka appeared above her, offering a hand. Luby took it. Chippaminka didn't help her up. Instead, all the misery in the world flowed through the warlock's hand into Luby and she was overwhelmed by a tsunami of desperate sorrow. She sobbed and sobbed, for Innowak knew how long.

Finally, the torture eased.

"You'll keep away from Ayanna," said Chippaminka, matter-of-factly.

"I don't want to go near her!" Luby wailed. She didn't.

"What *do* you want to do?" The girl raised an inquisitive eyebrow.

"Train my troops. Attack the Badlands. And anything else you want me to."

"Good. Recover your composure, return to your warriors and tell them what an asset I am to the army, the empress and Calnia."

"I will."

Chippaminka left Luby sitting up in the grass, wiping away snot and tears. Chippaminka had told her to recover her composure, so she would. Pleasing Chippaminka was the most important thing; the only important thing. She couldn't remember ever thinking anything else.

Calnian sucked and Ayanna rocked. Walking all day tired her, so she was glad of the excuse to sit and suckle the little boy. Now that it was painless—thanks to Chippaminka's magic salve—breastfeeding was when she loved her son the most. He was quiet, he was happy and he needed her. She could stroke his soft head and look out over the plains, herds and birds that would soon be her domain. Ayanna would be remembered for ever for adding these vast tracts to the empire, and Calnian would rule over them wisely and justly, as would his children and their children and so on. All would remember the Swan Empress Ayanna as the founder of the greatest empire and the greatest dynasty in the world. Given the amount of souls Ayanna had consumed, it was more or less certain that she'd return as one of her own descendants. Would Innowak bless her with a memory of her time as Ayanna? She didn't see why not. She'd earned it.

The captain from yesterday popped unbidden into her mind. What had she been thinking, listening to her nonsense? There would always be detractors. If everyone is pleased with what you're doing, then you're not trying hard enough. She was so grateful for Chippaminka's love and support. When the army returned to the Mountain of the Sun, she would make Chippaminka her queen. It was unprecedented. Some people wouldn't like it, but, as with all the best plans, there would always be detractors.

She looked ahead, to the north-west. Tiny white clouds embroidered the horizon. Could those clouds be over the Badlands, she wondered, marking out her target and her place of glory?

Chapter 4

The Pretty Prison

Beaver Man left them by scaling the cliff next to the monster pit like a spider. The Badlander chief was, thought Sassa Lipchewer as they headed back with Chapa Wangwa to the arena, a show-off. But he was a remarkably athletic and undeniably interesting show-off.

Bjarni was breathing shallowly on his litter but Paloma Pronghorn was gone, as was one of the Empty Children. The child's bighorn sheep was still there, standing obediently next to the bighorn that still had its rider.

Sassa looked around worriedly but was almost immediately relieved to see her new friend tearing around an outcrop of rock towards them. She was carrying the missing Empty Child on her shoulders.

"Wanted a run," Paloma explained to the Calnians and Wootah, "I didn't want to get bitten by one of those bastard spiders again and this little fellow didn't seem to mind me taking him with me, so..."

"Put him back on his bighorn sheep, now," said Chapa Wangwa.

"Sure thing, Chapa Wanka!"

"What did you say?"

"Sure thing, Chapa Wangwa!"

"Careful," the Badlander smiled horribly. "You are exuberant after surviving when you should have died, but insult me

again and you will be bitten again. You will probably not survive a second attack. Would you like to try it?"

"Not especially."

"Good. Let us go."

Chapa Wangwa turned and Paloma made a wanker gesture
behind his back.

Sassa smiled, but then noticed that Paloma's eyes were
bloodshot, her usually shining skin was sallow and hair was
sweat-pasted to her forehead in ringlets. She was seriously
unwell. The running and the cockiness was all bravado. Sassa
couldn't decide if that made her more or less confident that
they'd escape this horrible land.

Their captor led them westward, across the path they'd
ascended and beyond. The otherworldly scenery of domes,
mini mountains and spires of pale rock banded with horizontal red stripes stretched on, but the ground was grassier,
there were even more animals and, mercifully, no bleeding
unfortunates hanging from their arms. The path was busy
with well-camouflaged yellow crickets which showed themselves when they leapt clear of the human approach. Where
the track crossed a broad stretch of bare rock, the ground was
strewn with boulders and pebbles of all colours, including
much shiny quartz.

Sassa thought it was as if they'd left the world controlled
by the gods of nature and entered some lawless fringe zone
where people and landscape could do whatever the Hel they
wanted.

They stopped at a meadow half encircled by a towering
crescent of white-pink rock. The crescent was topped with
the typical fins and pinnacles of the Badlands and maybe
sixty paces high at its highest point. Spaced evenly about the
meadow were half a dozen unadorned, conical buffalo-skin
tents which looked newly made. Pale rock paths ran from the
tents to a cleared area which held an assembled but unlit dung

fire, a pile of buffalo dung, cooking equipment and several sitting logs.

"This is where you will stay," said Chapa Wangwa. "Provisions will be brought to you. You see this line?" he toed the ground where a line had been scored. "This is your boundary. It gives you around two hundred paces to roam from the fire, which is enough. Cross that line and . . . well, you know what will happen. So this is your pretty prison. We will come to get you when we require you."

"Sofi Tornado, Wulf the Fat!" Sofi looked up from her breakfast the following morning to see Chapa Wangwa walking up with a small group of warriors and a couple of Empty Children. "Come with me!" he grinned.

"After breakfast," said Wulf without looking up from his bowl.

Sofi felt her spiders stir and she guessed, by the cries of surprise, that the others did, too.

"No," said Chapa Wangwa. "Now."

Sofi was used to fighting in the Plaza of the Sun and she treated this arena no differently. She looked around the several hundred Badland spectators, analysed their sounds and their composition then pushed that information to one side. She would need to focus on whatever was coming.

She closed her eyes and listened. Concealed to the south of the arena were two very large bears, white ones from the far north if she wasn't mistaken. She tapped the hilt of the sword she'd taken from Finnbogi. White bears were a good deal larger than humped bears, and they were supposed to be more ferocious. She strained her ears. There were other odd things going on. She could hear large animals deep underground, which was a little unsettling, and the breathing of the monsters the Badlanders were creating reverberated through the rock, but there were no other immediate threats.

She opened her eyes and looked at Wulf. He was lost for words for once, staring round at the gawping Badlanders on their benches. He would never, she realised, have seen this many people in one place before. She hoped it didn't faze him.

He was tall, he was well-built, his padded jacket would deflect a normal person's knife blow, and that great hammer he held would be a ferocious weapon if well wielded. Sofi fancied his chances against most unenhanced warriors she could think of.

But against a white bear? He'd be dead in moments. Armed with a spear he might have a hope, but that hammer might as well be a turkey's tail feather for all it was going to trouble the bear.

For Wulf's sake, she hoped that they were going to let them fight together.

"What do you think—" started Wulf, but he was interrupted by a roar from the crowd as the two white bears were led in on catch poles.

"That's what I was going to ask!" the Wootah leader shouted above the spectators' noise. "You keep back, Sofi, I'll deal with them."

She raised her eyebrows at him and he smiled back at her.

"Although they are quite big." He tapped his chin thoughtfully. "Perhaps if you distract them, I'll be able to—"

"Shush."

He shushed.

The Badlanders' cheering became a murmur as Rappa Hoga strode across the bloodstained arena floor towards them, his dark skin shining. Sofi was surprised to realise that she was glad to see him.

"Good morning. Beaver Man sends apologies that he has to be elsewhere but hopes you enjoy his challenge."

"Hello," said Wulf, "do you have a spear I could borrow?"

"Let them loose," said Sofi.

"We'll let one loose, and Sofi Tornado will fight it. Wulf

will fight the second one. So, Wulf, please will you head over to the western edge of the arena until it's your turn?"

Wulf touched his spider box, said: "Sure thing. Good luck, Tornado!" and jogged away.

"Have you considered my offer?" asked Rappa Hoga.

"I have," said Sofi.

"Well?"

"I continue to consider it."

Tansy Burna bounced on her seat as the bear keepers freed the first beast, then realised that people were watching her bouncing. She had the section of bench to herself, which left her exposed and self-conscious. She carried on bouncing. She wasn't going to stop for the kind of po-faced dicks who didn't like bouncing. But all of the glee had gone from it.

Tansy loved the shows in the arena, but few of her friends did. Warriors were meant to sneer at arena fighting. Real warriors only liked real war. Tansy didn't care what she was and wasn't meant to like, but it was annoying that she hadn't been able to persuade any of the other dagger-tooth riders to come with her. Surrounded by her comrades, she could have bounced, whooped and waved her arms without worrying that people were staring.

I can't believe I'm friends with someone who enjoys those shows, one of the other cat captains had even said to her when she'd canvassed for co-spectators. *I can't believe I'm friends with someone who judges others by the entertainment they enjoy*, was the clever reply Tansy had come up with the following morning, on the way to the arena on her own.

Down on the stone, Nam Cigam danced up to the freed white bear, waving three small inflated bladders on the end of his goading stick. The reverser warlock was naked apart from a large hat made of honeycomb, the type that mothers of the bride wore on their daughter's wedding day. The animal raised a surly paw but Nam Cigam kissed the bear's nose and it shambled away, towards the centre of the arena and Sofi Tornado.

Tansy licked her lips. The Calnian Owsla captain looked good. Her mostly exposed limbs and torso shone with health and power and, if anything, she looked even stronger and more vital than she had during her journey across the Ocean of Grass. Tansy hated to admit it, but Sofi would be a great love match for her crush, Rappa Hoga. It would probably happen. The best warriors that the Plains Strider missions captured were always asked to become Badlanders, and, so far, every warrior who'd been asked to join had done so eventually. It made sense, given the horrific alternative.

Down in the arena, the bear reared onto two legs to stand more than twice Sofi's height, and lunged at her. The Calnian dodged one paw swipe, rolled under another, and chopped her long blade into the back of the beast's leg. The bear fell, Sofi jumped onto its back, leapt again and swung the blade two-handed to sever its head.

Tansy had expected the noble Owsla captain to spare the bear's life. She was a little disappointed that she hadn't.

The Calnian lifted the huge carnivore's head above her own and turned, showing it to the crowd as blood showered down, splashing off her face and shoulders and running down her body.

Tansy was one of the few who whooped her appreciation. A lot of people clapped politely but most looked on in various expressions of surprised disappointment. They didn't like to see the captives win. Tansy didn't mind. She was there to see stylish fighting, not Badland-boosting victories.

Wulf the Fat, the Wootah man, walked towards the middle to take Sofi's place. This time, Tansy thought, it was a dead cert for the bear, which was a shame. Tansy might like a stylish kill, but she also liked to see the hot men win. The Wootah man, in his weird way, was almost as gorgeous as Rappa Hoga.

The two captives met. Sofi spoke while Wulf nodded.

Whatever advice she was giving him, surely it couldn't help? Sofi tried to hand the big man her extraordinary blade, but he hefted his hammer and shook his head. It, too, was a fascinating weapon, by far the largest lump of iron Tansy had ever seen, but what use could it be against a white bear?

Wulf reached the centre and stood.

The second white bear was released.

This time Nam Cigam followed, tugging at the bear's tail. The giant animal turned its head a few times to roar at the warlock, but, for reasons that Tansy couldn't fathom, didn't maul him to death.

The bear reached Wulf. Nam Cigam danced away.

The bear reared, towering above the comparatively tiny human.

Wulf charged, swinging his hammer for the bear's knee. A sensible tactic, thought Tansy, but the bear countered by falling forwards and pinning the man under its great weight, one paw on each of his shoulders. It wasn't the most sophisticated move, but it looked like a winner.

Wulf roared and tried to pull free, but it was no use. The bear sniffed his face, licked it, then opened its mouth wide, dripping saliva onto its victim.

Finnbogi the Boggy and everyone else waited for Sofi and Wulf's safe return. Everyone else apart from Yoki Choppa, Ottar the Moaner and Freydis the Annoying, that was. The warlock was over by the fire, teaching the children how to cook.

At first Finnbogi snorted dismissively at their lack of respect, doing something so mundane at a time of great worry, but then he realised that diverting one's mind made a lot more sense than standing around, especially for the children. He wished people would get around to coming up with an escape plan, though. Maybe they already had, and he just wasn't Hird enough to be part of it?

"Boo!" said a voice. Finnbogi jumped and turned. Erik the Angry was grinning at him.

"Wow!" Finnbogi marvelled. "How did you creep up on me like that?"

"I don't really know how I do it, to be honest," said Erik. "I picked it up after spending far too much time hanging out with Red Fox Three."

"Who?"

"A fox I used to know."

"Right." How could such a strange man be his dad, Finnbogi wondered.

"Maybe I can teach you. Let's start with hiding in plain sight. I'll see if I can work out how I do it." Erik took a couple of paces away, stood by the tent and seemed to settle into himself, then settle into the scenery.

Finnbogi looked away, then looked back. He could see Erik, but only because he knew he was there. It was extraordinary. He had blended into the background exactly as the coyotes on the Ocean of Grass had done, only visible when they moved.

"You come over here and watch," said Finnbogi. "I'll try it."

Erik nodded and Finnbogi stood by the tent. He pulled his shoulders back and tilted his head, feeling a little silly but somehow knowing it was the right thing to do.

"Can you still see me?" he asked.

"If anything, you're drawing more attention to yourself by standing like such a wonk," said Erik.

"Oh. I guess I'll never get it."

"*We become experts in what we repeatedly do,*" said Gunnhild Kristlover, emerging from the tent that Finnbogi had been trying to blend into. "*Demonstration is the salt but practice is the—*"

"They're back!" Bodil Gooseface shouted from the other side of the camp.

Gunnhild, Erik and Finn ran over. Sofi and Wulf were walking back along the track from the east, escorted by a solitary Empty Child on a bighorn sheep. Wulf's face was bloodied, but he seemed unharmed.

"Are you all right?" asked Sassa.

"Never mind that!"cried Keef the Berserker. "What did you fight?"

"White bear," said Wulf.

"Wootah!" Keef spun around and jabbed his axe, presumably at an imaginary white bear. "How did you beat it?"

"I didn't."

"What?"

"Sofi killed hers in moments. Then I had to face one alone. Things weren't going well—it was about to bite my head off—when Nam Cigam saved me."

"The reverser? Why?"

"Reversers do what they're not meant to do," said Sitsi Kestrel.

Everyone seemed to accept this but Finnbogi was sceptical. Why would a Badlander have saved Wulf's life? Was it out of kindness, or was it to preserve him for some greater horror?

Chapter 5

Rattleconda

"We're going to join the Badlanders, aren't we?" asked Morningstar.

It was the day after Sofi's fight with the white bear. Morningstar had been trying to get her alone ever since. Sofi had been avoiding her because she knew what she was going to ask.

"Not the Wootah, obviously. Us," Morningstar added.

Sofi could hear two Empty Children on bighorn sheep coming along the track towards the camp, out of sight for now. "We're not joining anyone," she said.

"Rappa Hoga asked you when he took you off on your own that first night, didn't he?"

"It doesn't matter. We're taking the Wootah to The Meadows."

"Why?"

"Yoki Choppa says we should."

Morningstar turned around. The nearest person was Ottar the Moaner, twenty paces away, throwing stones in the air and trying to catch them in his mouth. A pebble bounced off his forehead and he yelped, then threw another stone. His two young racoons were yickering and trying to bite his feet.

"There's no doubt," said Morningstar, "that he's the guy to take on a force that's destroying the world. He'll be much more useful than Beaver Man and his Owsla, his cat cavalry, his giant sledges, his vast army and his blood-fuelled monsters, right?"

"Yoki Choppa says the boy is required."

"And you believe that?"

"He believes it and that will do."

"So what are we going to do? Walk out of here?"

"We'll escape."

"How?"

Sofi shrugged. The actual method of escape was a serious flaw in her plan. She'd gone over the possibilities again and again, and all seemed to end in failure. Being shipped a few hundred miles nearer their goal by the Plains Strider had been useful, but she didn't, unfortunately, know how they were going to get away.

Morningstar pointed at the beeba spider box on her neck. "They have us very neatly trapped, Sofi. Paloma may have survived her bites, but she still hasn't recovered fully and we might not be so resilient. We can join the Badlanders or we can die in their arena. They've got things that could kill us, Sofi, even *us*. What if they'd sent you in against the squatch? *Maybe* you or Chogolisa could take a squatch, but Paloma, Sitsi or I would be fucked. And they've got worse. Yoki Choppa's meddling has already killed Talisa White-tail. What are you going to do? Wait until another of us dies?"

Sofi shook her head.

"They've got us. There's no shame. We've been beaten. It happens. We have to make the most of the stones that we've thrown. We have to join them."

"We don't have to."

"It's that or death. Please just promise me you'll think about it."

"What do you think they're talking about?" Finnbogi the Boggy asked Erik the Angry.

With Chapa Wangwa's burn on his hand still smarting as a reminder not to communicate with any animals, Erik was still trying to teach animal stealth to his son. Finnbogi was not getting it, at all. Either he was a bad pupil or Erik was a bad teacher, or both. All they'd managed to do so far was irritate each other.

"They're probably building up the courage to ask you for a threesome," said Erik.

Finnbogi was torn between laughing and thinking that that was disgusting, coming from his dad. "Look at how they're looking at Ottar," he said, trying not to picture a threesome with Sofi and Morningstar, for the moment anyway. "They're going to desert us."

"They've come this far. Morningstar tried to step in for you at the waterfall."

"She explained that. She said I wasn't to think for a second that she cared about me. She was looking for a chance to escape."

"They act meaner than they are. And, anyway, Morningstar isn't in charge. Sofi would never leave us."

"They'd be much better off without us. Surely they know that?"

"We're not completely useless," said Erik. "We'll contribute to the escape and we'll all go together."

"Really, how? How's Bjarni going to get away?"

Both men looked over to where Bjarni was lying in the sun. Finnbogi still believed he was going to get better, but Yoki Choppa had said he should already be dead.

"I haven't quite got that part sorted out yet, son. You're meant to be clever, Finnbogi, why don't you think about it and see if you can come up with something?"

Finnbogi thought and thought about defeating the beeba spiders and escaping the Badlands. He kept thinking he'd got it, but then always realised that his plans had fatal flaws; literally fatal.

He was mulling over the problem the following morning over a breakfast of buffalo and duck eggs when Chapa

Wangwa reappeared with his warrior and Empty Child retinue.

"Finnbogi the Boggy and Freydis the Annoying! Follow me," he said.

"You can call me Finn . . ." was all that Finnbogi could think of saying as a sudden tornado in his gut threatened to return his buffalo and eggs to the outside world. *Him and Freydis?*

"Where are you taking them?" demanded Wulf the Fat.

"Back to the arena, where they will fight for their lives. They are unlikely to be as lucky as you because Nam Cigam won't be there this time."

Now Finnbogi was certain it was a dream. He looked round. Sassa looked stunned, Gunnhild was aghast. The Wootah men plus Thyri and most of the Owsla were advancing on Chapa Wangwa. Only Morningstar seemed unconcerned, perched on a rock spur, daintily eating a roast bird's leg and watching calmly.

"Keep back everyone," Finnbogi heard himself say, "I'm sure we'll be fine. Don't get yourselves killed."

"The boy is right. Stand back or the beeba spiders will bite," threatened Chapa Wangwa.

"Why don't you take warriors?" asked Sofi Tornado.

"You and Wulf were interesting in the arena. However, Badlanders like a Badlander victory, so that is what they will see today."

"You will not take them," Gunnhild Kristlover stepped up.

"It's okay, Gunnhild," Finnbogi had no idea where this bravery was coming from. "Don't get yourself bitten. Where there's life there's hope. I'll look after Freydis and we'll be fine. Thyri's trained me."

"Don't tell them that, you dope," said Thyri. "And don't die."

"We're going now," said Chapa Wangwa, but he waited— smiling as though the entertainment had already begun— while Finnbogi and Freydis hugged all the Wootah, plus Sitsi Kestrel, Paloma Pronghorn and Chogolisa Earthquake. When he hugged Thyri, Finnbogi went in too hard, their neck boxes banged and the two spiders in Finnbogi's went wild. Thyri's must have done the same because she jumped away as if she'd been stung.

It wasn't the perfect final parting from the girl who should have been his true love.

Morningstar paused between bites of bird and looked at them. Finnbogi thought she might bid them well in the fight to come, but he was wrong. She looked away and got on with her breakfast.

Sofi Tornado wasn't much more effusive.

"Good luck," she said.

Finally, he and Freydis approached Bjarni Chickenhead.

"Goodbye, Bjarni."

Finnbogi thought for a moment that he had died, but, without opening his eyes, he said, "Kick their arses until their arses fall off. Then stamp on their arses." It was the most he'd said since their arrival.

The last person they tried to bid farewell to was Ottar the Moaner. He was sitting on a patch of bare rock, using a stick to annoy a colony of ants trotting in and out of a hole.

The boy looked up blankly, then looked down and didn't look up again, even though Freydis said his name a dozen times.

Finnbogi took Freydis's hand and they followed the Badlanders east, towards the arena. Finnbogi turned to wave goodbye, but their people were already out of sight.

The path led along the main rock wall that comprised the edge of the Badlands massif. They walked up tight gullies and through narrow gaps in the rock wall itself and across open grassland. Animals, as usual, abounded. From one yellow outcrop a pair of coyotes watched them pass.

They reached the zone where unfortunates hung from red-banded, blood-stained rock faces, bleeding into the ground.

There were more of them than before. He recognised the three men and one woman from the Popeye tribe who'd been on the Plains Strider. They were hung in a row. Finnbogi wondered if it was better to be with your friends in such a situation. The woman, Sandea, moaned and moved as they approached. Freydis hadn't noticed them. Finnbogi thought about drawing her attention to them, and considered yelling hello. But what would that achieve? He walked on. He had his own problems.

Finnbogi had expected this, he'd known it was coming, but he really, really had not expected it to be him. He was, however, ready. He'd been training regularly, he felt leaner and stronger, and he'd bested a warrior when the Badlanders had snatched them. Okay, so she'd been winning and maybe he'd been lucky with that axe blow, but maybe he'd be lucky again? Was it possible that he'd been chosen because they'd seen him fight and liked his skills?

Although that didn't explain Freydis. He certainly hadn't expected her to be chosen. He guessed it didn't matter. It would have happened sooner or later and, of course, you died when you died . . .

"Do you think I should ask for a weapon?" asked Freydis, as if she was asking whether there might be maple sugar for tea. It was the first time she'd ever asked Finnbogi for advice. "Only if I *don't* have one I'll go into a children's Hall, but if I *do*, I might go to Valhalla or another Hall."

"I think you should ask for a weapon. Then we'll end up in the same place."

"I'd like that, Finnbogi the Boggy, but how will Ottar know we're there?"

"You know him. He'll find us."

"Yes. I suppose he will."

Finnbogi had imagined a cheering crowd of thousands, perhaps with a large gang of attractive women in the front row who would jeer him at first, then cheer maniacally as he began to win against the odds, perhaps ripping their clothes off in a lustful frenzy of hero-worship when he finally triumphed.

Instead, there were nine warrior types at the far end of the arena sitting next to Beaver Man, and perhaps thirty other men and women dotted about the arena seats, talking among themselves and paying very little attention to the two Wootah.

When Finnbogi had been about ten, Gunnhild had forced him to join the younger children in a play about Tor and Loakie's journey to the land of the giants. She'd wanted someone larger than the rest of the cast to play the main giant. They'd learned all the words and practised for weeks. On the night of the performance, they'd expected every Hardworker to come and watch, so they'd filled half of Olaf's Square with benches, seats and even logs from all over Hardwork. Finnbogi had been terrified that he would fluff the whole thing, but also excited that he might be sensational, seen in a new exotic and heroic light by everyone. In the end, though, only the parents of the children involved had turned up, half filling the front two rows of fifteen rows of seats.

This felt like that. He'd been nervous that there would be lots of people watching, and now he was disappointed that there weren't. If he was going to fight to the death in front of a crowd—or be tortured to death or whatever the Hel was going to happen—then Finnbogi wanted a capacity crowd of baying enthusiasts, plus the hot women, not a smattering of people who looked like they wanted to be somewhere else.

They walked towards Beaver Man. Finnbogi recognised his entourage as the men who'd come bounding across the rocks with him. They were dressed now, in leather trousers and cotton shirts. It was a relief not to have to avoid staring at their marvellously muscled torsos. The one with sheep horns was still wearing them. They actually looked like they were part of his head, and, as they got closer, Finnbogi could that the skin around them was inflamed and pus was oozing from the gap between horn and head, as if they were a part of his body that his body didn't want.

The rest of Beaver Man's Owsla were a regular-faced, strong-jawed, flinty-eyed lot. The Calnian Owsla had been picked for their looks as much as their skills. It looked like these men had been picked with the same criteria in mind. They regarded Finnbogi and Freydis with a mix of disinterest and contempt.

Beaver Man watched the Wootah approach, a weary smile on his strangely shining face.

"Greetings, Finn and Freydis. Has your stay been pleasant?"

"I made friends with a bobcat," said Freydis.

"That's good."

"Hugin and Munin didn't like it much."

"Racoons and bobcats are rarely friends. Now come over here, please, both of you. Don't be shy. Why don't you take a seat in front of me?" He gestured to a space on the bench at his feet, then to the men around him. "These are my friends, I'd introduce them but they're not a chatty lot and you won't know them for long. Ah! Here comes the next display. You're lucky, this is going to be a good one."

Finnbogi and Freydis sat on the lowest bench. *Were they here just to watch the battles with Beaver Man?* Finnbogi dared to wonder.

Walking out onto the arena floor was a man with a spider box like theirs on his neck, armed with a stone axe very much like Finnbogi's. Finnbogi nearly slapped his forehead when he realised he should have asked Sofi for his sword back. Surely she would have given it to him? He guessed he'd never know.

"Stop there!" shouted Chapa Wangwa, when the man reached the centre.

The man turned slowly, arms out, weapon ready, chin jutting, lips pouted. He had the puffed-out chest and permanent, half-nervous, half-threatening smile of a man who's managed to convince himself he's superb even though, deep down, suppressed but always niggling, he knows that he's not.

He caught sight of Beaver Man, took a few paces towards him and shouted: "I am Grunyan! Father of a murdered son, son of a murdered father and more man than any of you freaks! Send whoever you like at me, and I will send them to walk in the fields of the gods!"

"This Grunyan guy is awful," said Beaver Man quietly, leaning forward so only Finnbogi and Freydis could hear. "His tribe actually begged my catch squad to take him. He told us about his murdered son and father before his first fight, which intrigued me, so I let him live and had a word with some of the others that we took from his tribe. They took great glee in telling me how dreadful he was, and that he's never had any children, murdered or otherwise, and that both his parents were alive and apparently overjoyed to see the back of him. I've let him win a few fights since because it's amusing to see him become ever more bombastic. We gave him two elderly coyotes yesterday. After he'd dodged their worn-out claws and smashed their thin skulls, he leapt about like a bird in springtime. It's a shame you won't get to see his victory dance, since I've had enough of him and today he will lose."

Perhaps, thought Finnbogi, Beaver Man had seen that he had an interesting and enquiring mind and he wanted to talk to him, not to watch him die. That would explain why he hadn't taken an Owsla or one of the tougher Wootah. On the other hand, this was the fellow who'd cheerily crushed a man to death . . .

"Have you wondered what the holes in the ground are?" Beaver Man continued.

"I have."

"Me, too," added Freydis.

"Good. It's important to be inquisitive. Keep your eye on that one over there," Beaver Man pointed to a hole at the edge of the arena.

A moment later a head poked out. At first glance Finnbogi thought it was a buffalo calf, given its size, but it kept coming and he saw it was a snake; an abso-fucking-lutely enormous snake.

The green, black-spotted body that slithered out after the head was nearly half the girth of the hole. It stopped after five paces, with Loakie knew how much of its body still underground, and slipped a long, black, forked tongue from its lipless mouth. The tongue flicked up and down as the great head weaved from side to side. Extending towards Grunyan in the middle of the arena, the tongue flicked all the more, then the snake set off towards him, more and more of its horrible body emerging from the underworld.

Freydis pressed against Finnbogi. He put his arm round her and gripped her tight.

Grunyan turned as if to run, but then seemed to check himself. He turned back to wait for the snake, bouncing from toe to toe, a strange mix of confidence and terror twisting his face.

"Marvellous animal, isn't it?" enthused Beaver Man. "Its ancestors came from the endless forest, many miles to the south. They were docile creatures and not venomous. Armed with a stone axe in an open area, your average adult—even this idiot Grunyan—could have killed one. But this animal's predecessors had much alchemy worked on them, combining their essence with an altogether nastier and more venomous snake. We call the result a rattleconda."

The rattleconda was finally clear of its hole. Its freshly emerged tail was the least appealing part of the whole appalling animal. It was like a giant, segmented maggot. As if the snake knew just how loathsome it was, it lifted the hefty protuberance and shook it. The deep but melodious rattle made the hairs on the back of Finnbogi's neck stand and shiver. Freydis squeaked and huddled closer.

It slithered across the arena. It sounded like it was hissing, but Finnbogi realised it was the sound of the heavy body sliding along the soft, bare rock. On the other side of the arena,

Finnbogi noticed two Empty Children on bighorn sheep who had their heads tilted towards the snake as if controlling it.

Grunyan tossed his axe from hand to hand.

The rattleconda reared, towering above the man. It opened its mouth wide to reveal two long, thin fangs.

Freydis pushed her head into Finnbogi's chest and covered her eyes.

The snake struck.

Grunyan roared and swung his axe, but the snake dodged the blow and clamped its mouth around the man's head. With eye-defying speed, it coiled its strong body around him. The mud-green, black-spotted body pulsed ever tighter. The animal opened its mouth and reared above its encircled prey, revealing his head.

Grunyan was purple and panting. The snake tightened. Panting became choking, then a high-pitched groan as his skin darkened and his red eyes bulged from his head.

"That's interesting," said Beaver Man. "The snake hasn't bitten him yet. It's playing with its catch. Or perhaps it's showing off for our benefit. I like that. A show-off being killed by a show-off."

"But aren't the Empty Children over there controlling the snake?" asked Finnbogi.

"No. They encouraged him from his hole then let him go. They can control him, and will do if he attacks the crowd, but the rattlecondas seem to understand that they're meant to go for the person in the arena and not the spectators. I don't think it's any great intelligence on behalf of the snakes, simply a choice between something that looks like their natural, easy prey and something that probably seems to them like a bizarre animal with dozens of heads and limbs. As your Gunnhild might say, *nothing is as frightening as the unknown*."

Grunyan's head shook and Finnbogi thought he must be dead, but his eyes swivelled to follow the snake's head as it lowered again. The rattleconda opened its jaws. Its fangs were dripping with a clear substance that could have been saliva or poison, or both.

With a quick bob, the snake punctured the very top of Grunyan's skull with one fang. A thin but powerful jet of blood bloomed skyward then fell like red rain, spattering lightly off man and serpent.

"How can we consider ourselves superior to animals," said Beaver Man, "when they can produce something so enchanting?"

Slowly the snake lowered its head and the plume of blood splashed off its fangs and face until Grunyan's head was inside its mouth again. Coils sloughed off the victim's shoulders, the jaw opened ever wider, and moments later Grunyan's upper torso was inside the snake. The animal uncoiled completely, reared up and swallowed. Grunyan jerked headfirst down into its convulsing throat. The rattleconda's body bulged.

Slowly, convulsing to shift its meal ever further down its length, the rattleconda lay down and slithered back to its hole. The lump, perhaps a third of the way down its body, bulged as if Grunyan was trying to kick and push his way out.

"Is he..." asked Finnbogi.

"Alive? It would seem so," nodded Beaver Man, "and trying to escape. One man with a very sharp flint knife did manage to cut his way out once at this stage. He tried to charge, presumably at me with murder on his mind. However, I assume he was blinded by the snake's gut juices, because he ran the wrong way, fell over and lay screaming as his skin melted. The snake died, too, but the lesson there is that there is corrosive liquid inside the snake, so you want to beat it before it swallows you."

They watched the rattleconda disappear into its lair.

"It is over?" asked Freydis, her eyes still hidden.

"It is for Grunyan. The suffering of the people who had to put up with him is over, too," said the young leader of the Badlanders. "A glorious day so far. Now it's your turn."

"My turn?" Freydis was wide-eyed.

"And Finn's. You'll face a rattleconda, too. Not this one, obviously. It won't be hungry for weeks. There are plenty more, though."

"Can we fight an elderly coyote instead please?" asked Freydis. "I don't fancy our chances against a rattleconda."

"You might beat it. You'd be the first, but it is theoretically possible, and I have given you clues. Do you know, I almost *want* you to win?"

Beaver Man looked over their heads. "Chapa Wangwa, call a rattleconda!"

Chapter 6
Finnbogi the Brave

"Please can Freydis have a weapon?" Finnbogi the Boggy asked Beaver Man.

"Why?"

"If she's armed, she'll go to the Hall of a god called Tor when she dies. Otherwise, she'll go to a children's Hall. She'd like to be with me. And I'd like to look after her."

Beaver Man sat up a little straighter. "Tell me about this Tor," he said to Finnbogi, and, louder, to everyone listening, "and someone find a knife for the girl."

Finnbogi explained Tor as best he could and, following further probes from Beaver Man, he told him about the gods' Halls, about Oaden, Loakie, Fraya, Balder, Slepnear, Hel and the whole lot of them.

To begin with, Finnbogi was very aware that he was extending the time before being swallowed alive by a giant snake, but then he began to enjoy himself, making the tales as interesting as possible and putting on voices for the characters.

It took a while. Beaver Man's Owsla fidgeted. Chapa Wangwa interrupted several times to say that the rattleconda was ready, but each time Beaver Man held up a finger to silence him. When some of the spectators made to leave he instructed Chapa Wangwa to encourage them to stay or face a rattleconda themselves.

After a good long while, Freydis said, "This is *boring*, can we just get on with the snake?"

Beaver Man looked a little surprised, but said: "Hmmm. I like your stories, Finnbogi. I'm going to cut you a break."

"Yes?" Finnbogi was not surprised. He couldn't believe that someone as interesting, interested and, frankly, cool as Beaver Man was really going to order their deaths. The whole morning had surely been a ruse to scare them a little before Beaver Man asked Finn to be his friend.

"Freydis, will you go over there and stand next to Chapa Wangwa, please?"

Freydis did as she was told.

Beaver Man lowered his voice, so only Finnbogi could hear. "Either you and Freydis can face a rattleconda together, you with your axe and her with a knife..." Beaver Man looked at the sky, stroking his smooth chin.

Was Beaver Man going to ask Finnbogi to be his permanent storyteller? Or maybe to join him in his dwellings for a long, drunken lunch?

"Or Freydis goes back to the rest of them and you fight two rattlecondas on your own, unarmed."

"...What?"

"I said Freydis goes back to the rest of them and you take on two rattlecondas, unarmed."

"So I can die with Freydis or die alone. That's my choice?"

"The first choice—with Freydis and a weapon—gives you a chance. You may be able to strike the rattleconda while it's eating her."

"I thought you liked my stories?"

"I do, but I'm interested to see which choice you take, and I'm certain that Gunnhild Kristlover knows your tribes' tales at least as well as you do."

Finnbogi looked at the calm, confident, superbly healthy chief, then at sweet Freydis with her questioning, equally confident blue eyes. She might be a wise little thing, wiser than Finnbogi it often seemed, but she was still just a six-year-old girl.

"You're a dick," he told Beaver Man.

"Yes. I've been told that before," the chief replied.

Erik the Angry paced. He was near tears and he felt sick. They'd taken his son off to his death and there was nothing he could do about it! He wanted to pick up rocks and hurl them, and had in fact tried that for a while. It had helped a little, but he'd become self-conscious. So he stood, desperately trying to think of a way to rescue his son and to escape.

As always, the Empty Children on bighorns were watching, on a flat-topped outcrop to the north, stark before the pure blue sky. Their blank gaze somehow managed to say that they knew what he was thinking, and that he shouldn't even think about trying it.

"Easy for me to say, difficult for you to do," said Wulf the Fat, walking up, "but you shouldn't worry yourself into a hole. Finn's cannier than he makes out."

"Is he?"

The head of the Hird shrugged. "Possibly. Freydis definitely is. They'll come back. But we have to get out of here before they take any more of us."

Erik had the beginnings of a glimmer of a plan, and had started to make wooden disks that could, possibly, be pushed between spiders and skin to prevent bites. But he had no idea whether it would be possible to slot them in before the spiders bit and he hadn't yet mustered the courage to try.

He'd voiced his idea to Wulf, Sofi Tornado and Yoki Choppa the night before, hoping they might build on it. The problem was that he'd never been much good with animals like spiders. He'd once controlled bees, he told them, but it had taken him several moons to get them simply to fly from one hive to another on command. To beat the spiders, he needed greater control. Unfortunately, Chapa Wangwa knew when he was trying to communicate with the spiders, had burned him for it and threatened to pop both his and Freydis's eyes with a heated arrow if he tried it again.

He'd asked if Yoki Choppa had any way of enhancing his animal ability.

"No," the warlock had replied.

So that had been a disappointment.

He stood with Wulf, looking along the path that Freydis and Finnbogi had taken, bouncing on his toes with frustration.

"Erik, Wulf?" They turned. It was Sofi Tornado. She looked over her shoulder. There was nobody else nearby. "Working together, using your wooden plates, we may be able to beat the spiders. However, if either of you tell anyone what I'm about to tell you, I'll kill you. Understand?"

Erik and Wulf looked at each other, then nodded.

"Good. It's not much, but it might be enough." She looked around once more then said: "I can tell when the spiders are asleep."

"How?" asked Wulf.

Finnbogi the Boggy walked out to the centre of the arena alone, feeling naked without his stone axe. Some of the spectators regarded him with mild interest, others were talking to each other.

Nam Cigam had saved Wulf from the white bear, so Finnbogi scanned the crowds for the reverser warlock. He was nowhere to be seen.

The yellow-eyed woman he'd knocked unconscious when they'd been captured and who'd come on to him at the crazy snake party was, however, sitting on her own in the middle of one of the lower rock-cut benches. She waved at him as if they were friends. She wasn't good looking as such, but she was a woman between the ages of fifteen and forty and she wasn't repulsive, so nineteen-year-old Finnbogi fancied her. He'd knocked her back at the party only because he was drugged up and terrified, and because Thyri would have found out.

She was hardly the gang of cheering beauties he'd hoped for, but she would have to do. Now all he had to do was impress her by winning, unarmed, against two enormous, venomous serpents.

A snake's head emerged from a hole on the far side of the arena. The horrific creature slithered out about half its length and went through the tongue flicking routine.

"Behind you!" cried the yellow-eyed woman.

Finnbogi swung round. A second rattleconda was coming at him, mouth open, fangs dripping with poisonous saliva.

Sofi Tornado heard the Calnian warriors returning with Freydis, but not Finnbogi.

They wouldn't come into sight for a while, so there was no point in telling Erik that his son hadn't returned. It wouldn't help him, she didn't want to reveal more about her hearing than she already had and, besides, she had a conversation to finish.

As Erik and Wulf talked on, developing their far from satisfactory plan, Sofi mused on the danger and strangeness of knowledge. She knew that Erik was about to be deeply unhappy. He didn't. It was an odd one.

"The girl's coming back," she said, "without Finnbogi." She wasn't sure why, but it seemed he deserved to know.

Erik ran to the perimeter line to meet her.

"What happened?"

"A giant snake called a rattleconda ate a man called Grunyan. He was still alive when it swallowed him and I could see him moving inside."

"And Finn?"

"They sent me back here. Finnbogi the Boggy was droning on to Beaver Man about the gods. He probably still is. He was getting quite a lot of it wrong."

"He's not fighting?"

"I don't know. He might be."

"Big dog's cocks."

"Erik the Angry!"

I'm going to catch it and eat it, said a very weird voice.

What the fuck was that? thought Finnbogi as he ran from the approaching snake, which unfortunately meant heading directly towards the other one.

It's fleeing. Good. I love it when they flee.

It was the snake!

Don't kill me! he tried to think at it. *You don't want to kill me!*

I want to kill everything, came the reply.

No, you don't.

I do.

You don't. He tried to think in a snakey way.

I do.

This was going nowhere, and now the other snake was coming for him, too, and he was running straight towards it.

When he was five paces from the snake in front, and he reckoned the snake behind was about the same distance, he jumped to the right. The snake ahead adjusted its course, but Finnbogi looped around, fists and legs pumping, back the way he'd come. He heard the rattlecondas collide and then, in his mind, curse each other for getting in the way of their prey.

Finnbogi ran towards Beaver Man and his gang. He was quite powerful. After all the training with Thyri, he was fitter and stronger. Leaping about and running like this felt good, or at least much better than it would have done a moon and a life-time before. The Badlander boss brought him back down by shaking his head at Finnbogi as if he was disappointed; perhaps as if Finnbogi was meant to remember something . . .

He ran through all that Beaver Man had said to him.

Grunyan was a show-off. The serpents were a mix of a snake from the south and a rattlesnake. They were not controlled by the Empty Children. It was best to defeat one before it swallowed you. They didn't ever attack the spectators because they were on seats in a mass and nothing is more frightening than the unknown. Nothing is more frightening than the unknown . . .

The rattlecondas were big, but they were still snakes. Rattlesnakes, the normal kind, could kill you with a bite, but they fled when they heard you coming. Everyone knew that the way to avoid being bitten by a rattlesnake was to make a noise as you walked so that the buggers pissed off before you knew they'd been there.

He stopped and turned. The rattlecondas had disentangled and were slithering towards him side by side, as if racing to kill him.

I will get there first and it will be mine!

You will not! I will eat it!

Finnbogi closed his eyes and spread his arms. He pictured Garth Anvilchin kissing Thyri Treelegs; that long, lingering kiss while he and the Lakchans had looked on. He opened his mouth and screamed with all the rage, hatred and jealousy that he'd suppressed.

He opened his eyes.

The snakes had stopped. *What? What is it doing? Is it prey?* he felt them think.

Finnbogi pictured Garth punching him as the tornado bore down on them.

He *screamed* his anger at the fucker.

He balled his hands into fists and jumped up and down, shouting his hatred for Garth and frustration at his own inadequacies.

The snakes recoiled. *I do not like this. Is it an eagle? It might bite and tear flesh.*

It might carry us up then dash us down on rock!

Finnbogi pictured his mother dying while giving birth to him. He screamed all the more, shaking his hands in despair. There she was, beautiful but bleeding, opening her woozy eyes to see her newborn wailing in someone else's arms. She knew she was dying, knew she was leaving a baby to learn the terrors of the world on its own, knew she was going to miss the joys of his first laugh, his first word, his first tree climbed, his first fish caught. She was dying and he would never know her, never feel the raging power of her love. She was dying and she'd never soothe his crying with hugs, never cuddle him close and breathe in his smell and tell him how much she loved him. She was dying and it was so unfair.

Finnbogi lifted his head and shouted. He wanted his mum and his mum shouldn't have died. He screamed and screamed, roaring his raging loathing at the unjust world. He beat the air with his fists. He was crying. Snot was streaming from his nose into his mouth. There were a lot of people watching. He didn't care.

Wha . . . ? The snakes shrunk back on themselves.

"Fucking snakes!" Finnbogi shouted, out loud and with his mind. "You want to kill me! How dare you how dare you how dare you! I'm going to kill *you*! You *fucking dicks*!"

He ran at them roaring, fists flailing.

The rattlecondas fled and zipped down their holes.

Finnbogi stopped.

The rattlecondas were gone.

He could calm down now.

He wiped tears and mucus from his face then wiped his hands on his shirt.

A few spectators clapped like polite supporters of a sports team might clap impressive play by the opposition. The only person applauding with any gusto was the yellow-eyed woman. *There you go*, thought Finnbogi, *fantasies can sometimes, sort of, come true.*

"Well done," said Beaver Man, walking up, nodding. "That was good. Two rattlecondas unarmed . . . You didn't kill them but there's no way you could have done. You did your best and it worked. Now follow me."

Oh great, thought Finnbogi, *what now?*

Chapter 7

The Singer

Beaver Man led him along the path towards the blood pit with the large living lumps that were apparently called lizard kings.

Two Badlanders with a bucket of slops and a rag on a pole were feeding the unfortunates hanging from the rock walls. They held the rag above one man's head. He strained for it like a baby bird clamouring for gut-mulched worms.

"The compulsion to live is strong," observed Beaver Man.

Finnbogi felt faint, whizzy and other-worldly after his bout with the snakes. "I guess?"

"Why do our blood donors clamour for sustenance and prolong their agony when they know they're going to die?"

"Because they might not die."

Beaver Man nodded. *"Where there's life, there's desire to live."*

Somehow this sort of bollocks sounded better coming from Beaver Man than it did from Gunnhild. Finnbogi realised he might admire the psychopath who'd tried to have him killed by giant snakes more than the woman who'd taken him in and raised him like her own child. Life was odd.

They arrived at the pit of lizard kings. The living lumps were larger and more formed now, with defined necks and heads. Ominously, they'd moved around since the last time he'd seen them.

"Are they—" started Finnbogi.

"Don't worry about those. This way."

Beaver Man scrambled up the vertical rock face as he had before.

"I . . ." Finnbogi looked behind him. There was nobody there. No Empty Child on a bighorn sheep. Which presumably meant that Beaver Man had the same control over the beeba spiders as the Empty Children. Of course he did.

Now that Finnbogi looked more closely at the cliff, he saw that there were what one might call, if one was being generous, hand and footholds.

The climb was hateful, with moments of terror, but it had been that sort of day.

Eventually, he made it up to a two-pace-wide finger of rock poking out from higher ground to the south. There was a higher, obscuring ridge to the east, but to the north and west the view stretched across the landscape of pointy hills, pale rock hummocks and prairie. Finnbogi could see the crescent of rock that sheltered the Wootah and Owsla prison camp. He wished he was back there.

There was no sign of Beaver Man but there was only one way to go, so he walked along the ridge, around a precipitous path high above the lizard king pit, and into a valley. All was bare, pink-yellow, crumbly rock, neither a plant nor an animal to be seen, just ever more grotesque spikes and lumps of rock.

He followed the zigzagging valley, rounded a knobbly stack that would have had Wulf making comparisons, and found Beaver Man. The chief had taken his shirt off. His strangely shiny, lean-waisted yet muscular torso somehow juxtaposed and complemented his gentle brown eyes and childish face with its missing front teeth. Finnbogi gulped. He had no idea why he was following Beaver Man up this narrowing, remote canyon, but he hoped it wasn't going to involve him removing his own clothes. Having thought that, if Finnbogi *had* to be with a man, then this smooth-skinned, hairless, taut-bodied, strong—

"There's no vegetation up here," Beaver Man interrupted Finnbogi's confusing self-discovery, "but the valley below is relatively lush. Why would that be?"

"I don't know."

"It's a little colder up here, a little windier and the rain runs off a little more quickly so the ground's dryer. Every difference is minuscule, but it takes this environment across a line. The niceties of nature that inhabit the valley a short climb below—the flowers and the fluffier animals—cannot exist up here. There are no plants here, and the only animals are spiders and lizards.

"People are the same. You need only to tweak their environment a little and all the vegetation of civility and society falls away and they become base savages. The man we saw craning for the feeding rag was a proud warrior a few days ago."

Finnbogi nodded. He hadn't been listening. He was too worried about what might be about to happen.

They carried on along a constricted, airless gulley, climbed a couple of low ridges and arrived at a narrow gap between two high horns.

Two men sat on either side of the gap, each with what looked like a huge animal skull between his knees.

What, by Loakie's tits, thought Finnbogi, was going on?

As he ascended to the gap, he saw that they were at the edge of the Badlands massif. He could see miles south along the way they'd come on the Plains Strider, and west, across endless green prairie dotted about with bare pink-yellow rock islands and busy with shifting herds of buffalo.

The settlement where they'd left the Plains Strider came into view. The Plains Strider had gone, but Beaver Man's smaller craft, the Plains Sprinter, lay on the grass like a giant insect.

At the lip of the massif he could see that there were thousands of people standing maybe a hundred paces below their gap. They were gathered on a wide bowl of land elevated from the plain, among a sparse woodland of dark green fir trees.

The young chief turned. "Finnbogi, come and stand at the edge here."

Here we go. Finnbogi did as he was bid with a sinking sickening in his stomach. The shiny superman was going to throw him off the cliff. He'd escaped Garth's attempt to hurl him to his death, he'd beaten the snakes, only for this. In the finest seat in Tor's Hall, knowing that bastard, Garth Anvilchin was laughing.

"I got the idea for the Plains Strider and Sprinter from your people, more specifically from your ships," said Beaver Man.

"You've been to Hardwork? We didn't have—"

"Several people from this tribe have crossed the Wild Salt Sea and returned."

"Really? I thought—"

"That people from this side of the Wild Salt Sea were incapable of making the same journey as your tribe did?"

"No! no, I just . . . didn't know you had."

"We built big canoes. We went, we saw, we passed undetected, we returned. We have also been in the other direction, across a wider sea. The people over there are even stranger than you."

"When did you go? What did you—"

There was a cheer from below. The people had spotted their chief.

"They adore me," said Beaver Man, his tone the same as a depressed man reporting that the birds have shat on the drying laundry again. "Lesser people love to adore a leader. A few men and women are lifted above their peers to experience this sort of adoration, Finnbogi. In the Badlands I am that leader and I am the greater person. I am faster, stronger and more intelligent than any of these below us."

I bet you're not as fast as Paloma Pronghorn, strong as Chogolisa Earthquake or as intelligent as, well, me, thought Finnbogi.

"Yet everything I am was made by alchemy. How much of

me is *me*? Are these people worshipping me or the alchemy? Do you know what my power animal is, Finn? I have a few, but the chief one whose powers make me the best of all the power-charged warriors?"

"I don't know . . . lion? wolf?" Sycophancy didn't come naturally to Finnbogi, but it seemed prudent, standing on the edge of a cliff next to an absurdly strong murderer.

"No," Beaver Man answered with a sad smile, "No. My chief power animal is the deer tick."

"Oh." Would Beaver Man kill him if he laughed?

"I'm very strong and not far off indestructible, like a deer tick. Find one and try to kill it, you'll see what I mean. So these people aren't worshipping me, they're worshipping a tiny parasite whose favourite activity is digging its legs into the scrotum of a deer and sucking blood from his balls. You can see why I have existential concerns."

"I can." Finnbogi was pretty sure he knew what existential meant.

"Still, there is one skill I had before they began their work on me, and I still have that skill."

It's throwing people off cliffs, isn't it? thought Finnbogi.

But it wasn't.

"People need beauty as much as they need to see death in the arena." Beaver Man took a deep breath, opened his arms, and sang out a long, high, sweet note.

The crowd below whooped, then fell silent. The young chief's voice swooped down to a surprisingly low rumbling tone, then stepped higher and higher, then plunged back to that first note. His singing was loud, clear as a frosty morning and perfectly in tune.

Singing was his skill! Finnbogi would have been less surprised if Beaver Man had turned into a pink chipmunk. He didn't know whether to laugh or cry.

When Beaver Man reached the low note for the third time, the four men next to them blew deep, throaty tones on the huge skulls. Nearby, someone—or possibly something, Finnbogi couldn't see—rolled pebbles down the cliff face, adding a soft drum accompaniment that sounded like waves on a shingle beach. Voice, skull-horns and cliff percussion combined to produce a tune so mournful yet so uplifting that Finnbogi found himself swaying from side to side, every hair on his body standing in horripilation, a smile on his face and tears in his eyes.

Chapter 8
Attack of the Calnian Army

For Sassa Lipchewer, the two days after Finnbogi the Boggy's encounter with the rattlecondas passed both quickly and slowly. The days themselves went quickly, practising the bow alongside Sitsi Kestrel and vastly improving under the huge-eyed woman's tutelage. The nights dragged, as she lay awake dreading the next call to the arena.

Shamefully, she was most concerned about herself; or, more specifically, the baby growing inside her. She lay with her hands on her stomach, worried that the mite would grow up without a father or a mother, or never be born at all.

She couldn't believe nobody had worked it out yet. Wulf never suspected that she might be keeping anything from him, which was both endearing and useful, but on this occasion she wished that he'd see through her. She wanted to talk to him about the baby, but also she didn't want to talk about it. She'd heard that pregnancy messed with your mind.

Two things were certain, though. One, she didn't want to tell anybody else she was pregnant. She might jinx it. Babies were often lost in the early stages and she couldn't face everyone's pity if that happened. Two, she did not want her unborn child to die in the arena for the amusement of the Badlanders.

She woke on the third morning since Finnbogi's fight to find the Owsla gone. Beaver Man had taken them away.

The Wootah went about breakfast, trying to be normal, but

Sassa couldn't help looking about herself, wondering what was coming next. Most of the others were doing the same.

Perhaps it was her pregnancy, perhaps it was because their protectors had gone, but it seemed to Sassa that the Badland air that morning was even more oppressive, and that the usually welcome breeze was blowing clouds of terror through between the tents.

So when Chapa Wangwa strode into their prison camp, followed by a trotting trio of Empty Children, Sassa's hands shot to her stomach and she nearly vomited with the nauseating rush of morning sickness and foreboding.

The rest of the Wootah looked up with varying degrees of fear and loathing.

"Is the dying one dead yet?" was the Badlander's charming opener, standing above the unconscious Bjarni and peering into his face. "No? He's clinging on! Funny how they do." He looked around at them all, grinning. "Very funny."

"Come on then," said Wulf, "spit it out. What are you dying to tell us?"

"Don't look so sour! None of you will die today. Apart from maybe the dying one, of course, and any of the rest of you who have an accident. This is a dangerous place."

"So what do you want?" asked Thyri Treelegs.

"It's not what I want, it's what Beaver Man wants. He thinks you're special so he has a treat for you today. So, apart from the children and the dying man, follow me!"

"Someone should stay to tend to Bjarni and look after the kids," said Wulf.

Chapa Wangwa shrugged. "Why not?" He pointed at Bodil Gooseface and Gunnhild Kristlover. "You and you, stay. You, Bodil, are too stupid to appreciate anything. And you, old woman, I have become tired of you. I thought you'd be interesting with your clever phrases, but they're not that clever. You're a boring, dumpy old woman. And stop snarling at me, I don't like it. Remember that I am deputy to Beaver Man."

"Clag on a jarl's arse is still clag," spat Gunnhild, with a venom that Sassa had not known was there.

Gunnhild and Chapa Wangwa stared at each other. A tic flicked into life in the corner of the Badlander's grin. "I will not kill you now, old woman, because I have such a fine death planned for you. Stay here where you belong with the lesser Wootah and see if you can guess how I will kill you. You won't, though. It's too nasty for your little mind to imagine. The rest of you, follow!"

Chapa Wangwa led Sassa Lipchewer, Wulf the Fat, Erik the Angry, Keef the Berserker, Finnbogi the Boggy and Thyri Treelegs eastwards, back along the ridge of the Badlands massif, towards the arena where Finnbogi had defeated two snakes three days before. The three Empty Children followed.

Wulf fell back to walk alongside Sassa. He took her hand and squeezed it. He was smiling, but she could tell he was as nervous as she was. He was worried for her, obviously; he wasn't one to be troubled for his own safety. Had he guessed about the baby?

The Badlander turned north along a less well-worn track. They followed him.

"This isn't the way to the arena," said Finnbogi. "Or at least it isn't the way I went when I—"

"When you beat the snakes by frightening them away. Yeah, yeah," said Keef. "Well done you. There is nothing more heroic than shooing away reptiles. We all remember that fine saga about Tor spooking the lizard. And what about the time Loakie frightened a tortoise so much that it—"

"Mine were very big reptiles," Finnbogi complained.

"Sure they were. Very big, cowardly reptiles."

Sassa smiled. Keef was incensed that Finnbogi had been picked over him to fight in the arena. She had heard much more over the last couple of days about how Keef *would* have beaten the snakes than about how Finnbogi actually *had*. In fact, Finnbogi had been strangely unwilling to talk about his time in the arena. They only knew what they knew by asking questions which he'd answered reluctantly. Sassa wondered if his reticence meant he was maturing into a modest man, or whether more had gone on than he was admitting.

They crossed the track that they'd walked up from the Plains Strider six days before, and approached the highest part of spiky, soil-stripped hills. The day was hot and bright, but still Sassa felt a chill of deathly fear.

"They've gone!" said Thyri, and for a moment Sassa was confused, but then she saw. The rock was bloodstained, but the hanging people and hammered-up hands had disappeared.

"They have served their purpose!" cried Chapa Wangwa. Wulf squeezed Sassa's hand again.

They came to a ridge and climbed the steps hewn into it. It was hot work.

"I came this way with Beaver Man," said Finnbogi at the top. "I wish I'd known there was this easy way up. We climbed up just there and—oh."

Swan Empress Ayanna gazed at the spire-topped wall of the Badlands and shuddered. She hadn't dreamed for a moment that it might be so high and so daunting. Nor so red. It was like something from a nightmare; impossible and impenetrable.

"The rock is soft," said Chippaminka, appearing to read her mind. "It will crumble before our assault. The Badlanders know it. Look! Here they come to surrender."

A man was walking towards them holding aloft a spray of white peace feathers. He was dwarfed by the enormity of the Badlands looming up behind him, a white point against the yellow and red vastness.

Six others followed. One of the six was huge, around the same size as Chogolisa Earthquake.

They neared. The lone figure morphed into a young, strikingly handsome but oddly shiny man. He was carrying a spear with white feathers attached to its head. Perhaps two hundred paces behind him were Yoki Choppa, Sofi Tornado, Sitsi Kestrel, Paloma Pronghorn, Morningstar and Chogolisa Earthquake. Talisa White-tail and Sadzi Wolf were missing.

"Don't worry," said Chippaminka. "Luby Zephyr's Owsla killers will destroy these traitors. We will build a new Owsla."

Ayanna nodded. Chippaminka was right. They'd made one Owsla, they could make another. She might have lost Yoki Choppa, but she had Chippaminka now. Chippaminka was better. It was all going to be fine.

The spearholder stopped, as did the Owsla, a long way behind them. Ayanna stood tall, in her *I am an empress and a goddess* stance. Milk-swollen breasts and a slackened waist didn't help, but she thought that she still made a pretty good job of it.

"I am Beaver Man, chief of the Badlanders," said the attractive young man. There was no slackening in *his* waist. A shame she couldn't decree that men bear children.

"*Beaver Man*. Be The Man," Ayanna pronounced. "I'd heard that was your name. I'd assumed it was a joke."

"People usually say *my parents had a sense of humour* to explain a name like mine," sighed Beaver Man. "It's obvious that mine didn't. Perhaps it was meant to be a joke, but my parents are the only people who ever laughed at it. It's why I killed them."

"Why haven't you changed your name?"

"I need to be reminded that I'm not a god."

"My army will help with that."

He smiled, not a flicker of fear. "And you are a god?"

"Officially. But I, too, have a way of reminding myself that I'm human. If you listen carefully you may be able to hear him screaming."

"Ah, yes. Congratulations on your son."

"You are well informed. Now, you have my Owsla."

"My Owsla now."

"Come forward, Owsla!" she called to them.

Yoki Choppa and the women didn't budge.

Beaver Man shrugged, his boyish beauty at odds with his strong-shouldered warrior's frame. "Like I said . . ."

"What are those boxes on their necks?"

"A sign of fealty to me, like Calnia's strangulation cords."

"You're controlling them! What is in the boxes?"

"They simply prefer a winning side. Now, how would you like to surrender?"

"How would *I* like to surrender? You're well informed, so you know the size of my army."

"Twenty thousand warriors, give or take, plus support and followers." Beaver Man shook his head sadly. "A shame to kill so many. If you surrender now, I'll let your son live to return to Calnia with a tenth of your army."

"*A tenth?*" The young man's self-delusion was almost impressive. Or perhaps he was mad? "What do you plan for the other nine-tenths?"

"I have my hobbies."

"Beaver Man, think of your people. You haven't a hope against my numbers. Think of the Badlander children who will be orphaned today. It needn't happen. I will take the Badlands into the Calnian empire, and you will pay tribute. I'll let you live. You can come to Calnia. You will thrive there."

"It is you, Ayanna, who should surrender to save your own child. I will spare him, but not you, if you surrender now. Otherwise I'll take him from his mummy's dead body and raise him as my own. I'll talk about you a lot. I'll tell him you were a demon who tried to kill him."

A long way behind her, Calnian screamed. Ayanna felt her rage coming. She knew she should control herself, but also knew that she couldn't. Not when her son was threatened.

"You *shit*," she spat. "I've indulged you long enough. Fuck off back to your little rocks and take my traitorous Owsla with you. I'll see you again before the day is over, but I will tell my warriors to take your tongue first. I will not suffer your oily buffalo shit again."

Overhead a whitecap eagle screeched, surely a sign that the sun god Innowak was with the Calnians.

"Sure, whatever, goodbye." Beaver Man was aggravatingly unmoved by her tirade. He walked three paces then turned back. "If I were you, I'd send my fastest runners back to the Water Mother with young Calnian. It won't help. I'll send faster troops after them, but your death will be less awful if you know you've done everything you can to save your son."

Sofi Tornado watched it all with her toes clenched, every fibre fizzing with frustrated fury. She gripped the hilt of Finnbogi's wonderful but useless sword.

She heard every word. She tried to catch the empress's eye, but she was too far away. Beaver Man had promised that their spiders would bite if she or any of the Owsla took a step forwards, said anything or made any move that might be discerned as an attempt to communicate with the Calnian army. She could hear their spiders tapping their feet as if impatient to sink their fangs into Owsla necks. It was possible they were all as resistant as Paloma, so they might not die, but they would endure horrible agonies, be knocked out for a few hours and brought low for days. The only option was to stand there.

Why was the Calnian army here?

Beaver Man had known they were coming long enough ago to prepare his lizard kings, which meant he'd known the Calnians were going to invade a long time before the Calnians had known themselves.

So what the fuck had happened?

The only person at the Swan Empress's side for the powwow

with Beaver Man was a girl who didn't look far into her teens. Sofi had seen her before. During the Goachica raid that had started this whole ridiculous mission, she'd heard a girl shout: "They've killed Chamberlain Hatho!"

Goachica dispatched, Sofi Tornado had found Chamberlain Hatho's body. His alchemical bundle carrier, a new girl he'd apparently picked up on his travels, had emerged from hiding, wailing horror at his death. She'd been able to tell the girl's grief was false, but that hadn't surprised her. Sofi herself would have faked grief if the slimy but powerful man she'd been shagging had died on arrival in his home city.

Here was that girl again. Coincidence? Of course not. The girl had to be Beaver Man's warlock who'd persuaded Ayanna to invade. Persuaded? No, she must have bewitched her to lead such a foolish, empire-ending offensive.

Was Yoki Choppa part of it? The Wootah? Had the Wootah mission and all that had happened since been Beaver Man's doing?

"I'm going to kill him," said Morningstar through gritted teeth, echoing Sofi's thoughts. "I cannot stand this a moment longer."

"Hold," Sofi Tornado whispered.

"What can we do?"

"We have to hold."

"That's a shit option."

"Careful, Morningstar."

Morningstar glowered and Sofi did, too, desperate to act. Her spiders tickled, a reminder that doing anything would be suicide.

She looked from east to west, at the vast host of Calnians. She'd never seen so many gathered in one place. It was the entire Calnian army.

Sofi thought about the dagger-cat cavalry, the moose cavalry and, worst of all, the lizard kings, and felt sick to her stomach.

*   *   *

"Oh." Finnbogi was looking over the edge. Sassa and the others joined him. They were above the blood pit where Beaver Man had said they were growing something called "lizard kings."

It took her eyes a few heartbeats to adjust from the glare of the pale, bare rock to the darkness of the pit, but then she saw a dozen huge, sleeping animals. They had grown in the few days since they'd seen them. Their torsos, rising and falling with each peaceful slumbering breath, were the size of the largest of Sassa's family's farm buildings back in Hardwork. They had stout, pointed tails, each of which must have weighed twenty Sassas. Their egg-shaped heads were enormous, as big as two buffalo tied together.

"Come on, Wootah!" shouted Chapa Wangwa. "They are amazing, but soon you will see them in action!"

He led them along a terrifying path which skirted a spire high above the lizard king pit, then through a twisted, vegetation-free valley in which Wulf annoyed and cheered Sassa by pointing out penis-shaped rocks.

From the gap where Finnbogi said he'd seen Beaver Man sing, Sassa recognised the place where they'd finished their long journey on the Plains Strider. There was no sign of the Plains Strider, nor the smaller craft that had been there, and the previously thriving town of Badlander workers was not just deserted, it was gone altogether. The hundreds of huts and tents that had been there when they'd arrived had disappeared.

More amazing than the town's disappearance was the sight of an enormous army spread out across the land.

"The Calnian army!" chimed Chapa Wangwa happily. "Beaver Man wanted you to watch its destruction, so I will leave you. The Empty Children will be watching you."

He looked around at all of them, grinning. "Stop looking so glum. Enjoy! We all love watching death, all of us! Po-faced party poopers will say they do not, but they lie to us and themselves. So watch, enjoy, and, by all means leave this vantage point if you like, but your spiders will bite and you will die."

He left them looking out over the plain and the army, which, despite its numbers, suddenly looked very vulnerable.

"How many people do you think are there?" Sassa Lip-chewer asked, placing her hand back on her stomach.

"I reckon thirty thousand," said Thyri.

"Thirty thousand?"

"More like a hundred thousand," said Keef.

Although she could see them, Sassa found it hard to imagine that so many people could exist. Each would have their own cares, secrets, worries and fears. So much humanity. She wanted to weep for all of them, and she was angry. They'd live, they'd scrape by, they'd die. What was the point? How could she or her growing child be of any consequence in a world that contained so many?

"Where are the Badlanders?" asked Thyri.

"In the hills to the left and right of here, I should think," suggested Erik. "There are an absolute fuckload, sorry, I mean there are loads, of big stones and boulders up here. They're probably waiting until they get close before chucking those at them."

"Or they're going to watch while Beaver Man's monsters eat the Calnians," Keef added.

"Do you think we're safe?" asked Sassa.

"Safe?" said Keef. "Well, let's see. We have the world's most venomous spiders attached to our necks, there's a pit of monsters behind us and an army that's already tried to kill us in front of us, we're prisoners of a murderous weirdo who's told us he's going to kill us all and—"

"That's enough, Keef," said Wulf. "We're safe here."

With the Empty Children guarding them, there was nothing to do but watch the Calnians' advance.

When the first wave was perhaps three hundred paces from the massif, a long, deep cracking sound shuddered up from the very bowels of the earth. The ground beneath the Wootah's feet trembled, then lurched.

"Back from the edge!" called Wulf.

A low rumbling grew fiercer. It seemed to come from everywhere and nowhere. Everyone looked varying degrees of scared, apart from Keef who was inspecting his fingernails for dirt. The ground began to vibrate sickeningly.

"Crouch!" called Wulf. They all did, apart from Keef.

The vibrations increased. The rumbling became a roar. Pebbles and stones bounced down the peak to the west of their gap. Sassa closed her eyes and put her hands over her head. She felt two people—Wulf and Thyri—crouch over her.

The roar subsided to a rumbling, and, surprisingly, suddenly it stopped. Sassa opened her eyes and stood up. The Wootah were coated in dust and blinking. The peak to the west was unchanged, but the peak that had stood just to the east of them was gone. It had collapsed down and out onto the plain, along with a huge section of the massif stretching back towards the arena. Had the Wootah been ten paces to the east, they would have fallen with the rock and been lying in the broken rubble underneath the clouds of dust below.

Behind them, the three Empty Children sat astride their bighorn sheep, coated in dust but still regarding the Wootah with their dead eyes as if a mountain hadn't just crumbled and fallen only paces away.

"The dicks!" said Keef, coughing. Standing and watching while the others crouched, he'd sucked in more dust than the rest of them.

"What?" asked Thyri.

"That rock fall didn't just happen. I don't know whether it was alchemy or mechanics—more likely the latter and I think I know how, I'll tell you later—but the Badlanders made it happen. It was their big weapon. They meant to drop a mountain on the Calnian army. And they missed!"

Sassa crept back to the gap. The Calnians' advance had paused but it was undented, well clear of even the outlying debris from the massive rockslide.

"How do you throw a mountain at someone and miss!" Keef continued, "Dicks! I would have waited right until—"

There was a roar. For a moment Sassa thought the ground below them was about to collapse, but this noise was different. It was more animal, like a deep-pitched scream. Another rang out, and another. It sounded like several very large, very angry creatures.

"I'm not sure that the mountain was their big weapon," said Erik. "Listen."

There was bizarre, loud skittering coming from the cloud of dust where the land had collapsed. Something, some *things*, were coming towards them quickly.

The animal screams grew louder.

The Wootah turned to face the new peril. Sassa had both hands on her stomach.

An Empty Child riding a bighorn sheep galloped around the corner, followed by another and another. He or she clattered past the Wootah and up the remaining pinnacle to the west. The others followed, until there were twenty bighorn sheep, each bearing an Empty Child, standing confidently on a slope that a human would find difficult to climb.

The first of the screaming animals appeared, below them to the east, bounding across the piles of stones and great boulders that moments before had been a mountain.

"Spunk. On. A. Skunk," said Sassa.

It was a lizard king.

The great beast stopped, raised its appalling reptile face to Sassa and the Wootah, sniffed a couple of times, opened a mouth that could have swallowed a two-man canoe and the two men paddling it and scream-roared. Every hair on Sassa's body stood on end. She forgot to breathe.

The monster had grey-green skin like an everyday lizard, but the largest lizard Sassa had seen on their travels was the size of a large rabbit. This one was bigger than a kraklaws, much bigger, tall as a tall tree and stocky as Chogolisa Earthquake. It must have weighed as much as a tribe of people. Its head was disproportionately huge even for such a monstrous beast, and its gigantic mouth was filled with teeth like sax blades.

It ran on, bounding across the rocks on colossal-thighed back legs. Its three-toed feet had black claws as thick as a tree trunk sharpened into a wicked point. Its feet were exact but larger versions of, Sassa realized with surprise, a chicken's.

Incongruously, its forelimbs were tiny and undeveloped, as if its front legs had been replaced with a weedy man's arms. It ran on its hind legs, little forelegs flapping. With a mouth like that, Sassa reckoned, there probably wasn't much need for arms. That gob could have picked up Erik's giant bear and swallowed it in one gulp.

Another lizard king came charging up from its birth pit, then another and another, all scrambling desperately over the collapsed mountain. Butting aside boulders that they could have run around, shrieking all the while, they charged towards the Calnian army.

Yarg Lobster ran towards the Badlands in the front rank of the attack, tossing his spear from one hand to the other every twenty paces to prevent either arm becoming fatigued. He'd told the others to do the same, but had they listened to him? Had they bunnies. They were jogging along with their spears always in the same hand. So they were going to reach the fight with tired spear arms. Idiots. Worse, some of them had chosen hand axes instead of spears. Attacking an enemy up a hill with an axe? What the bunnies was the thinking behind that? There was no thinking, and that was the problem! For the love of Innowak, it was enough to make you weep.

The trouble with getting older, Yarg had realised a while back, was that it became clearer and ever clearer that everyone but him was an absolute moron. When Yarg saw a problem, he saw a solution. And when did he start working on that solution? Right away, of course, while everyone else stood around with their mouths open or, worse, got in his way.

His wife was the worst. Great hairy bunnies, she was such an idiot. She couldn't prepare for things, she was never ready when she was meant to be and when you got there, you could be certain she'd forgotten at least one vital thing. Like when they'd been to visit her parents—*her* parents, mind, so it wasn't like it was a treat for him even though he'd organised everything—she'd forgotten to bring enough food for the three kids. Yarg had seen the solution immediately, of course, and left her bleating about Innowak knew what while he'd made and set up snares. Then, of course, because she'd let the kids muck about near the snares, the snares hadn't worked and they'd ended up eating the berries that she'd collected. She hadn't said anything, but he could tell she was thinking that she'd solved the problem, when she hadn't, she'd just fucked up the best solution by letting the kids go near his traps and had them eating boring berries instead of delicious rabbit. Other people! They were *such tits*.

He knew she didn't like him changing his name from Yarg Loster to Yarg Lobster, either. She didn't get it. The Owsla all had clever animal names that reflected their strengths, and he was as good as the Owsla. He gripped problems like a lobster gripped its prey. It was pretty fucking simple, for the love of bunnies.

"Do you mind me changing my name?" he'd asked her once.

"What can you do?" she'd said.

"What can *I* do?" he'd replied. "I can do anything!"

It wasn't just his wife. He was gallant enough to admit that she probably wasn't any thicker than everybody else, he just spent more time with her so he saw more of her stupidy. Everybody else was at least as lack-witted. None of them had the nous to realise that his solutions were always the best. Did time move more slowly for him, or was he simply blessed with being able to see how things worked and interrelated more quickly and clearly than others? One of the few mysteries he could not fathom was the source of his own genius.

So, because he couldn't trust anybody else to get it right, he was leading the attack on the Badlands. Not *leading* leading—he wasn't a captain or anything like that—but he was one of the foremost warriors running towards the wall of rock. He had to be, because he would have to show everyone else how you got up a wall of rock and killed Badlanders. He wasn't sure himself yet how he was going to do it, but he knew he'd see the problem, analyse it in an instant, realise the solution and act. That was what he did.

He ran on, men and women all around him. He'd never been happier. By the end of the day they'd all owe their lives to Yarg Lobster. Finally, they'd all see him in action. Finally, they'd know. They'd toast him around the fires. Ayanna would ask him to be a captain. Would he accept her request? Would he bunnies. The captains were the biggest idiots of the lot of them. Yarg didn't need a title to be head of the pack. People followed him by instinct.

Closer and closer they ran and still no sign of the enemy. The Badlanders were idiots as well, surprisingly enough. A couple of sallies out from their rock wall would have put the bunnies up most of the Calnians (not Yarg, obviously), but they were staying hidden, waiting for Yarg to work out how to kill them.

They were still a couple of hundred paces from the Badland cliff when a huge section of it came tumbling down.

Did a massive rockslide faze Yarg? Did it bunnies. You'd

think it might, since he'd never seen a rockslide before. But it didn't. He'd never seen a cliff this high before either, but it was still nothing to him.

"Come on! To the breech!" he shouted. Without missing a step he altered his course to the north-east, towards the collapse.

Of course, he found himself out ahead because *he* hadn't dithered. He'd seen the problem, the cliff, and he'd seen a solution, the rockslide. Everyone else was scratching their arses thinking, *Oh, wow, a rockslide? That's unusual, why would a rockslide happen now? How does that affect us?* Yarg had had all those thoughts and more in less than an instant and now he was leading the way. It didn't *matter* why the rockslide had happened, it didn't *matter* that it was unlikely. It *mattered* that they could use it to ascend into the Badlands. The sooner they did, the more likely they were to catch the enemy before they'd reacted to it.

He got that.

By Innowak's bouncing bunnies, why was everyone else so *thick*?

A very weird roaring scream did slow him for half a moment—he wasn't perfect, he'd be the first to admit that—but he ran on (because he wasn't a long way off perfect).

He'd deal with whatever caused the noise when he came to it.

He didn't turn, but he knew they'd be faltering behind, which was good. They'd see him and know how much braver, how much more capable, he was.

There were more roaring screams. It was probably trumpets, meant to scare them, meant to slow them while the Badland defence adapted to the rockslide. That sort of bollocks wouldn't work on Yarg Lobster, no sir. Adapt quicker than Yarg? As if! Adaptation wasn't his middle name, but it should have been.

He ran on towards the cloud of dust where the cliff face had been, and, he had to admit, got a bit of a shock when a monster the height of a tall tree ran out of it.

For a moment, possibly an entire moment, he faltered. And then sped up again. He'd seen the problem—a twenty-pace-high monster with teeth like giant knives—and he'd seen the solution. *Get under it, Yarg*, he told himself, *ram your spear into its guts.*

How magnificent he must look, way out ahead of everyone, running towards a charging monster! It must have been a hundred times his weight—more—but did it scare him? Did it bunnies.

He tossed his spear from one hand to the other so as not to tire one arm—might as well teach them a lesson when he had their attention—and the beast was lowering its head, so that gaping mouth was coming at him like a tooth-lined net about to scoop up a fish, just a couple of feet off the ground.

He saw the problem, he saw the solution.

Paces away he slid, feet first on the slick grass. He watched the underside of the indubitably flummoxed beast's jaw pass overhead, then he sat and raised his spear. He aimed the stone tip into the gigantic belly and jammed the butt into the ground. The monster's own momentum and weight would do for it and Yarg would roll clear.

Spear tip met belly. The shaft snapped in an explosion of splinters. The stone point thwunked harmlessly into the ground.

Yard regretted not making his own spear, as an enormous talon tore into his leg.

His quarry ran on. Yarg looked down at his injury. Oh bunnies, how annoying. Because that fool weapons maker hadn't hardened the wood properly, the spear had snapped. Yarg had told him how to do it but the idiot must have ignored his advice. The failure of the spear had distracted him and he hadn't rolled clear as planned. And now...

His leg was a mess, but it didn't hurt. He could see his thigh bone. The parted flesh and muscle was oozing blood, not gushing, so no major bloodstreams had been severed. He'd live, and he wouldn't need the help of a healer. He could already see how the wound should best be treated.

He tried to stand. Agony lanced from his leg and he fell back into a sitting position, facing the Badlands.

Three more monsters were coming. They were the same as the first, perhaps a little larger. The foremost of them saw him sitting there and slowed.

He saw a problem. He saw the solution.

He lay and rolled over, so he was face down. This was how one survived attack from humped bears, and that was the largest carnivore he'd previously come across, so he guessed the same applied here. Black bears were a different story; you fought those, but with bigger carnivores you played dead.

He heard the beast slow. He closed his eyes. He was too brave, too certain that he'd been right about playing dead, to be scared.

He felt teeth pierce his side, and then an extraordinary strength crush his torso. *Stupid animal! It was meant to sniff him and move on!*

He was lifted. He saw swinging grass and sky. The teeth released him and he was flying for a moment, up and then down, into the beast's hot mouth. Darkness came as his chest was squeezed. There was a moment's relief, then he was crushed again. He felt his skin split, his bones snap, his innards burst and spill.

He was being chewed. *Why wasn't he dead yet?*

As Yarg Lobster became the first animal to be eaten by a lizard king in sixty-five million years, he cursed the spearmaker for his unhardened spear, he cursed Ayanna for attacking the Badlands, he cursed his fellow soldiers for holding back and he cursed his wife for letting him head off with the army. On that last thought, an image of his wife's smiling, bright-eyed face filled his mind and suddenly, overwhelmingly, he realised what a dick he'd been for all of his adult life.

Oh bunnies, he thought.

Ayanna stood atop a dome of rock to watch her men storm the Badlands. Chippaminka was the only person at her side. She was going to double the size of the Calnian empire in a morning and ensure them all a place in fireside histories for evermore. None of the useless generals had contributed to her and Chippaminka's plan, so they didn't deserve to be at her side to see it bloom.

The tactics were marvellous in their simplicity. Run into the Badlands, kill anyone who resisted. Her army outnumbered the Badlander warriors by ten to one, so any more sophisticated schemes would have been folly.

Luby Zephyr's Owsla killing squad was on hand to take on Sofi Tornado and her women if necessary, but Ayanna was nearly certain it wouldn't be. Somehow Beaver Man had cowed her Owsla, but forcing them to attack the Calnian army was a different matter. All of those women, with the possible exception of Morningstar, would kill themselves before killing Calnian troops.

She watched her warriors charge, swarming round the bizarre yellow-red outcrops that pocked the grassland. They were headed for the road that cut across and up the rockface to the Badlander stronghold.

She scanned the cliff for the enemy, and raised her eyebrows in mild surprise when a large section of the massif collapsed. An unimaginable weight of rock crashed to the ground with a rumbling roar that rolled out across the plain and shook her rocky perch.

What was this? The timing couldn't be coincidental. Somehow, Beaver Man had managed to knock down a huge section of his own defences. Surely it was why he'd been so confident. No doubt he'd been planning to wait until the majority of her force was committed and kill them in a rockslide. And the fool had gone early. Instead of crushing her warriors, he'd opened up a broad path into the heart of the Badlands.

She'd been optimistic before, now she was near-euphoric.

The Calnians charged, one warrior out ahead of the others.

As the dust cloud from the rock fall bloomed up into the blue sky, the loudest and strangest animal roars Ayanna had ever heard reverberated out from the Badlands.

Her confidence took a dip. When a monster thundered out of the dust, it took a dive. More and more of the beasts ran out of the dust cloud and raced to catch up with the first. The second of them stopped to snatch up and eat her foremost valiant but doomed Calnian.

The animals were huge, like monsters from a nightmare, but they were still animals. Stick enough stone in them and they would fall. The lone warrior hadn't had a chance against them, but grouping together to defeat animals more powerful that themselves was what humans did best of all. The Calnians would prevail.

Squads of club and axe warriors fell back, spearmen pressed forward and did not falter. She would reward the survivors and the families of the dead.

The monsters came on, charging at her army as if ordered to do so. How did one train such beasts, she wondered? It seemed almost a shame to kill them.

Captains arranged spear warriors into wide-spaced formations and sent archers onto the pinnacles and domes of rock. *Good*, thought Ayanna, exactly what she would have done.

"What are these animals, Chippaminka?" she asked. "Have you come across anything like them in your travels?"

"I have never seen anything like them. But I'm sure the spearmen and archers will bring them down." Chippaminka pointed to the track that cut through the spiked wall of the

Badlands. "I don't know what these are either." Something—
some things—were running down the path a good deal more
quickly than a person could run, kicking up a plume of dust.

Oh no, thought Ayanna. *What was this new horror?*

Tansy Burna galloped her cat downhill, leading her squad
of six dagger-tooth riders behind Rappa Hoga's. Others had
clubs, bows and knives. Rappa Hoga had his great obsidian
axe. Tansy Burna had only her blowpipe with sixty poison
darts slotted into the leather belt across her chest. She'd tried
fighting on catback with melee weapons, but found that all the
jumping about and swinging around put her cat off her stride,
plus the dagger-tooth cat was perfectly good at killing anybody within reach without the help of its rider. Besides, they
didn't want to kill the Calnians. Their orders were to dart as
many as possible for collection and captivity. The spider-box
makers had been working day and night for weeks.

To the south, the lizard kings were galloping towards the
enemy army, kicking up great clods of prairie grass and soil
with monstrous clawed feet. Tansy found it hard to tear her
eyes away from them and focus on the path ahead. The lizards
were astonishing, the finest creations so far. The way they
roared! It was an entirely new sound, like a mountain shrieking or a god shouting. What was next? Surely the lizard kings
couldn't be topped? But with the life force of so many of the
Calnian army who they were going to capture today, where
was the limit?

The track swung southwards onto its final section, down
to prairie level. Ahead, Rappa Hoga reached the grassland
and steered his cat eastwards along the base of the massif, followed by his squad. The dagger-tooth cat riders' role was to
follow after the lizard kings and hit the reeling survivors with
a flanking sweep, peppering them with darts and keeping
them terrified until the moose riders hit them head-on.

Tansy Burna grinned and dug her heels into her cat.

*   *   *

Watching the exchange between the empress and Beaver Man, Luby Zephyr had seen the expressions on her fellow Owsla women's faces. Back in Calnia, Morningstar had once been punished for leaving their training compound and shagging a couple of guys. It had been the eve of the Owsla's first ever fight against live captives, the first time they'd got to actually kill anyone. Morningstar had been barred from joining in, but allowed to watch. She'd looked the same that day as she did today—seriously pissed off and desperate to kill.

No, somehow Beaver Man was controlling them and it probably wasn't a coincidence that they all had little wooden boxes strapped to their necks.

She had to get to them.

When the huge beasts charged from the Badlands, Luby saw her chance. She left instructions with her deputy to try to keep clear of the fighting and sprinted westwards. If she could skirt the Badlander attack, she might be able to find a way up into the Badlands undetected, find the Owsla and free them from whatever enchantment or threat was binding them.

Ayanna watched. The first monster hit her waiting warriors, plucked up a hapless woman with its great mouth and threw her ruined body up into the blue. It wasn't finished there. It kicked and stomped, destroying, disembowelling and crushing. Men and women rushed to attack but it didn't seem even to notice. It must have killed sixty or seventy people before the second monster joined in. Then the third beast trampled its way over her warriors, then another, and another.

Archers loosed swarms of arrows, but the missiles bounced off. Accurately hurled spears fell to the ground without denting the foe. Men and women ran in underneath the beasts and thrust upwards with stout spears, but even they couldn't pierce the monsters' hides.

Still the brave Calnians attacked, still the monsters stamped, bit, hurled and ripped. As if discovering a new trick, the great lizards now began to swing their thick tails, sending groups of people flying to crash down dead or disabled.

Ayanna could not believe what she was seeing. Every moment was a disaster, and the moments kept coming. The only end she could see to it was the total destruction of her army.

The monsters waded on towards Ayanna, leaving scores—hundreds—slain and maimed.

Over to the west, the mysterious creatures that had torn down from the Badlands at great pace turned out to be dagger-tooth cats with people riding them, for the love of Innowak.

They galloped along the leading edge of her army, some swooping in with melee weapons to kill archers and slingers, but mostly keeping their distance. She couldn't see clearly, but the way they were holding their hands to their mouths and her warriors were falling, it looked as if they were using blowpipes and poisoned darts. *That is underhand*, she thought.

And now, coming directly from the road down the Badlands massif—the road she'd expected to walk up following her triumphant forces—came yet more monstrous mounted animals. The next wave of the Badlands sally was hundreds of moose, all carrying warriors.

The lizard monsters waded on towards her, killing and killing. She expected to see one of the beasts fall, some brave captain to shout out by what clever method he'd killed it, then the rest of the nightmare creatures to go down. But it didn't happen. They kept coming. They weren't eating people, they weren't killing for food as you'd expect from an animal. They were rampaging and slaying. The beasts were basically stamping her army to death.

She shook her head. What a grim, honourless way to die and how ignoble its perpetrators.

The nearest creature was a hundred paces away now, dripping with blood, kicking and crushing and sweeping its tail to knock down swathes of brave men and women. There was a dead Calnian impaled on its lower rack of foot-long teeth.

Behind the giant creatures came yet more mounted animals. If she wasn't mistaken, they were bald children riding goats, or possibly bighorn sheep. Suddenly, everything was just too fucked up and the urge to flee nearly overwhelmed her. But, no, she would stay and die. Calnian, however, must live.

Ayanna turned to her new young warlock. "Chippaminka, find Calnian and get him out of here."

"No."

"*No?*" She looked down at the girl.

"He'll die, too." Chippaminka grinned back at her.

Realisation hit Ayanna like a giant hand slapping her on the forehead.

How had she been so stupid?

The girl was a Badlander warlock. All of this, from the very start, was her doing. Ayanna had been her enchanted stooge.

She swung a punch at her enchantress and hit her full force on the jaw.

Pain exploded in her hand. Stars danced, tears stung her eyes as she blinked them open. The girl was still smiling, face unmarked.

"You were very proud of your Owsla, weren't you?" she said. Nearby a monster paused from killing to raise its head and scream-roar into the sky. "But where do you think the knowledge of how to make an Owsla came from? Your warlock Pakanda was a Badlander who left to pursue glory in the gold pyramid city of the tawdry, pompous Calnians. He returned when you exiled him. While you showed off your creations to the world, we kept ours under a blanket."

"Until now."

"No. They will remain secret. No Calnian will survive the

day to tell anyone about our animals, nor about the old magic that revived them."

"Revived?" Despite her burning desire to kill Chippaminka, Ayanna was interested.

"They are an ancient species that roamed the earth long, long before people. We brought them back with magic and mixed in some alchemy to make them even tougher and angrier than they were."

"Why?"

"For our amusement. And your destruction."

"Will you let my son live? I've shown kindness to you from the moment you arrived in Calnia and the only person you knew was killed."

"Who do you think killed Chamberlain Hatho? And I enchanted you. You wouldn't have done anything for me otherwise, so I owe you nothing. I'm going to kill you now, then head back for Calnian. I'll keep him for a while. I've been looking forward to giving him a real reason to cry."

"No, wait, I—"

The girl moved in a blur and swept Ayanna's feet from under her. The empress fell hard and her head cracked onto rock.

When her gaze cleared, Chippaminka was straddling her, as she'd done so often of late, but now those strong hands, once so wonderfully soothing and arousing, were clamped around her neck. They squeezed.

Fire, thought Ayanna, as consciousness slipped away, *I wonder if fire would work against the monsters?*

Tansy Burna ground her hips into the galloping cat's back, blowpipe at the ready, looking for living Calnians, lifting her pipe and per-chooing darts into them. She never held the pipe to her lips as she galloped, in case there was a bump that made her swallow the dart. The pipes were designed so that you couldn't do that, in theory, but Tansy liked to be safe as she could be while galloping around on a gigantic predator with crazily long fangs.

A Calnian woman staggered to her feet. Wap! Tansy's dart was in her neck. She'd be out for a few hours. When she came round, she'd be tied up wearing a spider box, or nailed to a rock wall in the Badlands with her blood draining into the warlocks' next project.

She looked for the next survivor, but couldn't see any nearby. Rappa Hoga had dismounted and was walking amongst the smashed Calnians, blowing darts left and right. She didn't want to do that. A cousin of hers had been killed by a knife to the groin from a man she'd thought was dead after a skirmish.

She pulled her dagger-tooth to a halt and it stood, panting gently. Screams rang from the south where the lizard kings raged, hurling limbs and blood into the blue. They hadn't slowed a jot.

Dead and dying Calnians stretched for hundreds of paces in every direction across the plain. The moose riders arrived at the Calnian lines. The proud beasts picked their way between corpses as their riders blew darts into the living.

Overtaking the moose riders came Beaver Man and his Owsla, all naked, all unarmed, sprinting and leaping to catch up to the lizard kings and find people to kill.

To the north, more people were running from the Badlands followed by large buffalo-drawn sledges and several Empty Children on bighorn sheep. The darted living would be piled onto the sledges and taken away. The dead would be piled into heaps and burned.

There were *so many dead*. The remaining dregs of Tansy's battle lust evaporated to be replaced by a feeling not far from despair. She saw a Calnian woman stagger to her feet, scream—possibly trying to put weight onto a broken leg— then fall. Another man was trying to push himself up and failing. Another did manage to get to his feet, looked about, spotted something—a fallen comrade presumably—and fell sobbing to his knees.

There were similar small scenes of misery all over the battlefield. Battlefield? Slaughterfield more like. Tansy realised that they may have looked like small moments of misery to her, sitting happily on her dagger-tooth, but to the people involved they were huge, terrible, final scenes.

She rode on and saw a doomed man sitting and staring at his own eviscerated guts. She put a dart in his neck. They were meant to dart only those who'd live—no point in knocking someone out if they weren't going to come round—but easing Calnian pain seemed to her like the right thing to do now.

Luby Zephyr nipped between the ranks of the Calnian army, sowing a row of confusion. She was headed for the Badlands massif. Flummoxed troops in her wake thought they'd seen someone, but couldn't be sure.

I am stealthy, she thought as she tripped along. For the first time in a long time, she had a plan. She was going to rescue the Owsla.

She was almost clear of the enemy lines when she made the mistake of looking back. She'd expected that the monsters would be beaten by now, at least some of them taken down, but they were all still raging deep into the army, slaying everyone in their path, apparently unscathed despite the attacks of hundreds of warriors. At this rate there would be no army for the Owsla to save.

She spotted Ayanna, standing with Chippaminka on the pink and yellow hillock. The empress punched Chippaminka in the face. The girl didn't budge. The monsters were heading directly for the hillock. If Chippaminka didn't kill Ayanna first, then the giant lizards were sure to get her.

Luby loved the empress, not because she was a brown noser, but because she believed that, prior to Chippaminka's enchantment, Ayanna had been a good, noble leader who'd improved the lives of pretty much all Calnians after the ravages of the previous emperor Zaltan. Improved the lives of all Calnians apart from the dickheads who'd colluded with Zaltan's depravity, anyway.

She had to save her.

With that thought, terror welled. The idea of taking even a step towards the empress made Luby cry out and shake her head. The monsters didn't scare her. She could avoid them. It was Chippaminka's cursed enchantment. They said that knowing you were under alchemical enchantment was the first and most important step towards breaking it. "They" had clearly been talking bollocks.

Or had they? She took a pace towards the empress. Her mind moaned, her limbs were heavy and aching. She took another step, then another. Forcing herself to take every pace was like mustering the courage to launch herself off a cliff.

After a dozen steps, however, it was easier. Suddenly, as if she'd burst out of the choking woods and into a bright clearing, she was running towards Ayanna's mound.

On the hillock, Chippaminka felled the empress and jumped on her.

Luby Zephyr sprinted. All around, injured Calnians clamoured for help. A dozen or so who'd somehow escaped the monsters were fighting a naked Badlander, and losing. The Badlander, clearly alchemically enhanced, was enjoying it. He snapped the arm of a Calnian and laughed.

It was a deviation from Luby's path, but only a few heartbeats, and she'd never forgive herself if she didn't take it.

She ran in, stealthy as her namesake zephyr. The Badlander gripped a Calnian by the neck and squeezed. Attacking from behind was not exactly noble, but then again neither was using alchemical strength against an unenhanced enemy. Luby slashed her obsidian moon blades through the backs of the Badlander's knees. His skin was tough, but she'd expected it to be and struck with all her own alchemical might. Skin opened, muscle and chords sprang apart. He fell back, arms waggling. She plunged the pointed end of her moon blade into his eye, whipped it out and was running on before he hit the ground.

Luby reached the hillock, moon blades in her hands, and bounded up it. Her mind was screaming at her, louder than the freaky roars of the monsters and the screams of eviscerated Calnians, urging her to turn back, to leave Chippaminka to her business.

"La la la!" she sang at her mind.

Chippaminka saw her, even though she shouldn't have done, and sprang off the prone empress: "You are strong to overcome your enchantment, Luby. I could make it stronger. I could make you kill yourself with those pretty weapons. Are they obsidian?"

"They are."

"Lovely. I'm not going to make you kill yourself though. I like a fight every now and then, and it's a while since I killed an alchemical warrior. I'll free you. Come at me."

Chippaminka lifted her hand and pulled something invisible. The enchantment snaked out of Luby's mind like a slimy chord being pulled through her brain and out of her nostrils. It was not a pleasant feeling, but the relief was extraordinary.

Luby faced her foe, feeling stronger and happier than she had in a long time.

The warlock was lithe and well muscled, but compared to Luby's enhanced, acrobatic warrior's frame, she was slight. Luby was twice the warlock's weight although she carried almost no fat, a head taller, and she'd spent ten years learning how to fight.

Still, she advanced cautiously, wary of tricks and traps that a warlock might use. She slashed with her right blade. Chippaminka dodged, as expected, and Luby swung in the left, killer blow.

The girl dropped to the ground, avoiding the slash, and came bouncing back up with an uppercut to Luby's jaw.

The Owsla woman staggered, world reeling.

Chippaminka followed, driving hard little fists into her stomach again and again with the speed of a woodpecker head-banging a tree and the power of a kicking buffalo.

"It's *so* annoying," said the girl as she punched, "but I've *always* been like this. I tell myself to spread the fight out, make it last, really enjoy it, but I can never make myself do it. *Every time!* I'm the same with food. It's gone before I remember to taste it."

Luby flailed at the girl, all tactics gone, desperate to stop the horrible assault on her gut. Finally, the warlock stopped punching her, but the attack was far from over. She saw Chippaminka leap. She was too winded and stunned to do anything apart from stand and watch.

A foot smashed into the side of her head, her eyes crossed, she was down and everything faded to black.

She came to and lifted herself onto her elbows, shaking her head.

Chippaminka was facing away from her on the far side of the hillock, holding the unconscious Ayanna above her head. She was a lot stronger than she looked, that girl.

A lizard monster stopped and looked down at them with a benign expression on its face. Through the fog of her recent unconsciousness, Luby imagined it looked like a dutiful son on the way to his parents' house who's spotted a flower that he knows his mother will like.

The beast opened its mouth. There was a severed leg stuck between two lower teeth.

"Come! Come!" shouted Chippaminka, straining up onto tiptoes, flipping Ayanna round so she was holding her upright by her hips, offering her headfirst to the hideous animal.

Luby jumped to her feet.

The monster's head lowered.

Luby ran, silently.

The beast opened its mouth wide, to snap shut on Ayanna.

Luby grabbed Chippaminka two-handed by the waist, so hard that her fingertips almost punctured flesh. The girl squawked, dropped the empress and half turned. Luby heaved with all her strength, hurling the girl upwards.

Ayanna fell to the rock, Chippaminka flew into the great mouth. The beast snapped its teeth shut and munched, blood squirting between its cracked lips.

Luby blinked. That last bit had been easier than expected.

The Swan Empress Ayanna was unconscious but alive. As the giant lizard lifted its head to swallow the chewed warlock, Luby bundled Ayanna to the side of the hillock and tumbled her over the edge, using her own body to cushion the fall. They landed, rolled and came to rest against the monster's foot. Luckily it wasn't the most sensitive of beasts and, as Luby dragged the empress away, it searched for them on top of the rock, snorted, looked about some more, roared, then strode away sulkily.

Right, thought Luby. Three more naked men were sprinting with unseemly alchemical pace towards them. Also coming were more monsters, a whole load of dagger-tooth cats with warriors riding them and hundreds of moose, also carrying warriors. There was no way Luby Zephyr was going to smuggle Ayanna off the battlefield.

There was a person-sized crevice at the base of the rock. The Owsla woman checked it for snakes—a snakebite in the middle of a battle against monsters and alchemically charged warriors would have been a really dumb way for the empress to die—then tucked Ayanna into it. It wasn't perfect by any means, but it was the best she could do. She was safe from the giant beasts there, and hopefully she'd be found by a Badlander who'd realise what a valuable captive she was.

Empress stowed, Luby ran, blending into the Calnian army and back on track to carry out her first plan of circling them to the west, heading into the Badlands and finding the rest of the Owsla. The only difference was that now it was infinitely harder because she had to dodge attacking monsters, avoid dagger-tooth patrols and keep clear of the moose riders, not to mention the hundreds of Badlanders on foot who were now streaming south out of the Badlands massif.

She ducked and weaved, breaking her movement and slinking about so even those that she ran right past hardly saw her.

As she got back on track she saw three more of the naked men tearing towards a pocket of the Calnian army that had managed to avoid the beasts. She faltered. She'd beaten one of them with ease, but stealth was her thing. She wasn't the greatest fighter. She'd win against anyone who wasn't enhanced, but when they knew she was coming all the rest of the Owsla, even Sitsi Kestrel, would beat her in a fight.

So her chances against three alchemically enhanced Badlanders were slim. But could she leave the Calnians to die?

She jogged stealthily towards them, unsure what she was going to do.

Calnian archers targeted the foremost of the Badlanders. He stopped and stood, arms out, chest proud, and let the salvo strike home. The stone heads bounced off his skin as if he were made of granite. He smiled. He was missing his two front teeth.

Luby stopped.

The hard-skinned man charged. Calnian axe men met him. He chopped a flat hand into the neck of the first and decapitated him as if his hand had been the sharpest blade. The head spiralled upwards, trailing an arc of blood. The two other naked men attacked and Calnians fell.

Luby turned and ran, headed for the massif.

She had to forgive herself. There was nothing to forgive herself for. It would have been pointless to fight the three men. She would certainly have been killed and there was nothing to be gained from that. This way she had a chance of freeing the Owsla and striking back at the now inescapably victorious Badlanders. She had done the right thing.

A hundred paces away a monster crushed a dozen Calnians with one swipe of its fat tail. *I've got to get out of here*, Luby told herself, *it's the only way to help.*

And so she fled the battlefield, skirting scenes of horror and misery, headed towards the foreboding red and yellow cliff.

Chapter 9

Reunion, a Story and a Death

Back at their camp hemmed by the crescent of rock, where the Owsla had been held for the entirety of the battle, Sofi Tornado and the other Calnians listened as Wulf the Fat described the destruction of their army. Sofi had heard the roars and the screams and knew what must have taken place, but it was still chilling to learn the details.

Wulf spoke calmly but watching the horrors had clearly upset him. His bronze skin had a grey tinge, the jocular spark in his eye had dimmed and even his curled golden hair seemed flatter and duller. However, he told them what they needed to know in an efficient and matter-of-fact way. He didn't know the fate of the empress. As far as he knew, the entire army had been killed or captured after being knocked out by the same type of dart that the Badlanders had used against them on the far side of the Ocean of Grass. Some of the Calnian army had fled out of sight, but they'd been pursued by faster Badlanders on cats and moose so he could only assume that they'd been killed or caught.

They listened to Wulf's report in sad silence, as the unmistakable scent of funeral pyres drifted up from the south.

That night Sofi lay awake in her tent trying to make some sense and draw some useful conclusions from the astonishing news.

Outside her tent, the creatures of the night went about their business, oblivious to the era-changing events. A hundred paces away an Empty Child's bighorn sheep's hooves scuffed on soft rock. Who were the bizarre little humans, she wondered? As far as she could work out, it was always the same group watching them, neither sleeping nor developing the agonising sores that should have crippled anybody sitting on something as bony as a bighorn sheep for so long.

Slowly, she became more and more certain that she could hear something else. It was a person, she was pretty sure, approaching with exquisite skill. He or she was blending into the night's rhythms, using the sounds of the wind and the nocturnal beasts to mask their own almost imperceptible footfalls.

The only person Sofi had met or heard of who could move like that was Luby Zephyr, but Sofi had left her badly injured with Caliska Coyote over a moon before and a thousand miles away. It couldn't be her.

Was it one of Beaver Man's Owsla, alchemically enhanced with comparable stalking skills to Luby's? If that was the case, he probably wasn't creeping up with a surpise gift of just for the fun of it.

A chink of moonlight appeared as the tent flap opened a finger's breadth. A shadow blocked the light and Sofi tensed.

"Sofi?" whispered a voice.

Sofi smiled. "Hello, Luby."

Luby Zephyr slipped silkily through the gap in the flaps, silent as a shadow. Sofi sat, smiling genuinely for the first time in ages. She was pleased that her super-hearing was working well enough to detect Luby, and that Luby was still so stealthy that it took super-hearing to hear her. But much more than both of those, she was happy to see her friend. Despite all that had happened, she felt warmth blossom in her chest as her heart filled with joy.

The women hugged, fell back onto the bed and embraced for a long while.

Finally, Luby began to tell Sofi her tale, but Sofi put her finger on her lips and whispered that they should go further from the rest of the sleeping Owsla and Wootah to talk.

They stole to the back of the camp and sat in the moon shadow of the crescent of rock.

Holding Sofi's hands, Luby told her how she'd had to kill Caliska Coyote, how Chippaminka had enchanted the empress to lead the Calnian army to its destruction, about the battle and the monsters, and how she'd killed Chippaminka and left the Empress Ayanna alive but not exactly well or safe. She told her how the monsters, the naked Owsla and the freakish cavalry hadn't stopped with warriors. They'd swept through the baggage sleds, killing or capturing all the chefs and smiths and every other Calnian who'd crossed the Water Mother.

Sofi told Luby about the chase, about the Mushroom Men killing Sadzi Wolf at the Rock River and Talisa White-tail's death on the Water Mother, why they were heading across the Ocean of Grass with the people they'd been sent to kill, how the Mushroom Men had become the Wootah, and the reason that she and the rest of the Owsla had been unable to join the battle.

"So what are you going to do?" Luby asked, nodding at the wooden box on her captain's neck.

Sofi looked up at the stars. "Paloma survived bites from the spiders, so it's possible the rest of us Owsla would, too, but we'd certainly be incapacitated for a good while. And the Wootah would be killed."

"You're set on saving the Wootah?"

"Yes. The boy Ottar the Moaner anyway and..." Sofi sighed, "...and the rest of them."

"You believe the boy will save the world?"

"I believe that Yoki Choppa believes it and that's good enough for me."

"And why save the rest of them?"

"They are . . . interesting. They have become allies. Friends, even."

"So what do we do?"

"We escape."

"But so far . . ."

"We haven't achieved much?"

"Well, yes."

Sofi shook her head. "The spider traps are weird but they're effective. We're working on a plan, but I need your help. I'd like you to mix with their Low and find out as much about the Badlanders as you can, and about Beaver Man's giant sledge, called the Plains Sprinter. I'd like you to find a route out of here westwards, towards the Black Mountains, that we could take if we stole the Plains Sprinter. *And* I'd like you to get some flesh from a lizard called a chuckwalla. The chuckwalla can be fresh, dried, alive; doesn't matter."

"Sure. Where do I find the lizard meat?"

That was one of the reasons Sofi liked Luby. No *what do you want a lizard for?*

"You should find some flesh in their warlocks' stores."

"That'll be tricky."

"Not for you."

"Can't I just find one in the wild?"

"Yes. On the far side of the Shining Mountains."

"I see. Well, if it will free everyone . . ."

Sofi Tornado sighed. "My plan won't free everyone. If it all goes perfectly, which it won't, I reckon half of us, at most, will get away."

"And the others?"

"They'll die."

"Doesn't sound like your greatest scheme."

"It's all we've got, and we have to do something. Otherwise they'll start killing us in the arena. It's just luck that we haven't lost anyone yet."

"Rats' cocks," said Luby.

"Big rats' cocks," agreed Sofi.

"There's one other thing we could do." Luby tilted her head.

"Join the Badlanders?"

"Yes."

"It's been offered; for us, not the Wootah."

"Tempted?"

"I don't want to see any more Owsla die. I am tempted. But we're not going to do it."

"Better to live a day as a lion than a lifetime as a treacherous cowardly dickhead?"

"Something like that."

Luby Zephyr returned the following evening with a whole desiccated chuckwalla, plus information on what was going on outside the camp, about the Plains Sprinter, and the route to the Black Mountains, as well as a detailed recent history of the Badlanders.

Sofi took the chuckwalla to Yoki Choppa to prepare for Sitsi Kestrel, then sat and listened to Luby on their rock in the moon shadow.

As the sky in the east lightened and a new set of animals started to bark and chirp, Sofi told Luby that she'd better go.

"Before I do, I bet you want to know what happened to Pakanda?"

The warlock Pakanda was the originator of the Owsla. He'd divined the alchemy and set it in place for Yoki Choppa to carry on his work. He'd been exiled from Calnia for letting Morningstar give him hand jobs in exchange for information, but Sofi knew that he'd had plenty of unwelcome interactions with girls younger, less exalted, more vulnerable and less willing than Morningstar. She also knew that his treatment of her and the other Owsla women when they'd been girls had been unnecessarily cruel and twisted. As soon as Yoki Choppa had taken over, the beatings and deprivations had stopped and their development into super-warriors had accelerated. Pakanda had beaten them, starved them and bullied them in all sorts of other ways, not because it was necessary as he'd claimed, but simply because he'd enjoyed it.

So she hated Pakanda because he was a sadistic child molester, but she also loathed him at a deeper, even existential level. With the rattlesnake removed from their diet, all sorts of realisations had surfaced, chief among which was that Sofi and her women were, undeniably, monsters, or at least had behaved as such. They'd killed innocents and enjoyed doing it.

Sofi loved who she was, revelled in her power, but she hated what she'd done with her ruthlessness. So while she loved her abilities, and those of her women, she also hated Pakanda for taking away her ability to care.

"Okay, tell me what happened to him," she said. "But make it quick."

"He was a Badlander originally and he returned after his exile. Beaver Man welcomed him in and used his skills to—"

"I said quick. Cut to what happened."

"He resumed his interest in young girls. The first—"

A coyote howled. It would be only moments before Thyri Treelegs, always first up after Sofi, was out of her tent.

"Save the details for another time. Is he still alive? If not, what happened?"

"Beaver Man found out about the girls. Pakanda begged, said that Beaver Man needed him and he had more alchemical secrets to share. But Beaver Man killed him, horribly and slowly—private parts-related torture mostly—and gathered all the Badlanders to watch, telling them that this would be the fate of any adult who mistreated children. It went on for days. When he died, Beaver Man cooked him and ate his flesh. They don't do that here—it's banned—but Beaver Man made an exception for Pakanda."

Sofi nodded. "You'd better go."

"I'm out of here. One more thing, though. Most of the Badlanders disagree with Pakanda's punishment. They wonder what marvels he might have created had he been allowed to live, and reckon Beaver Man should have given him all the girls he wanted to do whatever he wanted with, so long as he was creating beasts and alchemical warriors to fight for the Badlanders. It wasn't, one of them told me, like he was hurting the girls. Some of them challenged Beaver Man about it and he beat them."

"I see. Thanks. Work on that escape route today. Don't get caught."

"Caught? As if . . ." Luby Zephyr melted into the shadows.

"Thyri!" Sofi called a few moments later when Thyri Treelegs emerged from her tent.

The Wootah girl sauntered over, making quite a good job of looking aloof. "Yes?"

"Would you like to spar for a while before the others get up?"

Thyri stifled a smile. "Sure. If you like."

Finnbogi the Boggy continued his training with Thyri Treelegs, which would have made him happy as a bee in spring had the slaughter of thousands of Calnians not cast a pall of depression over the camp.

The Calnians, of course, had slaughtered all the Wootah's friends and family, so it should have been great that they'd all been killed. But it wasn't, because the Wootah were friends with the Calnian Owsla now, and the Owsla were upset, so the Wootah should be, too. Even though the Owsla had been trying to kill the Wootah, and only hadn't when they'd decided to disobey the orders of the Calnians . . .

It was far from simple.

The enemy of my enemy is my friend, Gunnhild explained to him.

"But what if that second enemy is already your enemy before you meet the first enemy? That would make the first enemy your friend in which case the second enemy has to be your enemy. So in that case, *the enemy of my enemy is my enemy.*" he'd said and walked away, very pleased with himself.

It wasn't an entirely unhappy camp. There was no real evidence, no single incident, but Finnbogi reckoned that the massacre had brought Owsla and Wootah closer. The sombre air had somehow fostered a greater sense of solidarity between the groups. Maybe it was because they'd both suffered similar losses.

They couldn't see what was happening in the rest of the Badlands due to the great fin of rock encircling the back of the camp and the generally lumpy topography, and they received no Badland visitors other than the mute Empty Children. However, on the evening of the day after the battle, Sofi Tornado gathered everyone by the cook fire and told them what was going on around them.

Finnbogi hadn't a clue how she knew it all, and it wasn't like she was going to tell him. The Calnians might be their friends now (apart from Morningstar) but they were still pretty weird, cagey friends.

She told them that while Owsla and Wootah ate, slept, trained and discussed how to break their spider traps, the Badlanders had burned the dead Calnians and hung the rest on the rock walls of the Badlands, draining their blood into the rock and feeding their next horrific project, whatever that was.

On the second evening, Sofi told them that Empress Ayanna and her baby son Calnian had survived, but were Beaver Man's captives. Finnbogi could not have cared less about this.

On the third day after the battle, they still saw no Badlanders other than their Empty Children guard. Finnbogi guessed they were all busy. Slaughtering thousands must create a lot of work, he mused. He spent the morning training with Thyri. Nearby, Sitsi Kestrel was teaching bow skills to Sassa Lipchewer and, to Finnbogi's surprise, Sofi was showing Gunnhild how to use her Scrayling Beater more effectively.

In the afternoon, Thyri told him that she'd be doing some advanced training with Sofi herself.

"Can I join in?" he asked.

"No," she told him.

So he moped about, then told himself that he wasn't sulking and set off to pace the perimeter of their confinement.

Just as he was beginning to cheer up, he heard a scuffling from behind a lump of rock. He craned his head and saw a bright blue bird pulling some hapless grub from the thin soil.

The bird saw him. Suddenly, as if a little door had opened in his mind, he knew that the bird was about to flee, leaving its meal.

Don't be frightened, he tried to tell it.

It cocked its head at him, less scared but still about to fly off.

Let's not be frightened together, he tried. *There's nothing to worry us here.*

That did it. The bird went back to its grub, appeased. Finnbogi tried to reach out to it with his mind again, but there was nothing more.

He spent the rest of that day trying to communicate with the various animals that scurried and flew near the camp, but he had no luck and began to think that he'd imagined the interaction with the blue bird.

Chapa Wangwa walked into the camp four mornings after the destruction of the Calnian army with some warriors and a couple of Empty Children on bighorn sheep. He was grinning, but it was an exhausted grin and his swagger was all but gone.

"Morningstar and Keef the Berserker," said Chapa Wangwa, "follow me."

"At last!" Keef bounded towards the Badlander, decapitating a couple of imaginary foes with Arse Splitter on his way and looking happier than any of them had for days.

"Good luck," said Wulf.

"Won't need it!" chirped Keef.

Sofi put a hand on Morningstar's arm and the two women nodded.

And before anyone could do anything else, before even Gunnhild could say something meaningful, they were on their way.

Morningstar walked ahead, proud and rangy as the lion that had walked past the camp a couple of days before. Finnbogi had heard from Sassa Lipchewer, who'd heard from Paloma Pronghorn, that Morningstar was the daughter of the previous emperor of Calnia, hence her aloofness. Sassa had reckoned this was no excuse since accident of birth gave you no right to be a twat. Finnbogi agreed. Paloma said that Morningstar would come round to the Wootah eventually and was actually a decent person, but, given the scowls she'd graced him with the several times he'd tried to talk to her, Finnbogi wasn't sure whether either of those claims were true.

Finnbogi had been lucky against the rattlecondas, but he reckoned Keef and Morningstar would make short work of them, assuming that's what they got. Whatever happened, they were lucky they didn't have Freydis with them.

He hadn't told anyone about the choice that Beaver Man had made him make in the arena. He'd pretty much sacrificed himself for Freydis, which was about as heroic as it got, and he was itching to tell everyone, but he knew he'd look like a tit if he blurted it out.

Most of all he ached to tell Thyri. He spent most waking hours training with her. It was near impossible not to but he knew he mustn't. Of all of them, she'd be the least impressed by someone telling heroic tales about themselves, possibly because that's all she'd heard growing up from Chnob the White, her bellend of a brother, and Rangvald the Wise, her thundercunt of a dad. Finnbogi was better than that, he told himself.

It was frustrating, though. What was the point of doing heroic things if nobody knew?

Maybe when Chapa Wangwa came back with Keef and Morningstar he could get the Badlander to tell the tale. Although Chapa Wangwa probably didn't know. He hadn't been close enough to hear what Beaver Man had offered him, and the Badlander chief didn't seem the type for gossiping with underlings. Then again, Finnbogi had no idea what type Beaver Man was. He was a murderer, a singer, a natural philosopher, a torturer, a charmer, a creator of monsters and slaughterer of armies. He didn't really fit into a "type."

"Stop fucking around. Walk next to me," Morningstar commanded quietly. She didn't like breaking her *don't talk to the Mushroom Men* rule, but she had no choice. Well, she had. She could let this guy die and then beat whatever they sent at her. But...well, his weapon was formidable and he did swing it about as if it was an extension of his arms. He might be useful.

"Sure, what's up?"

"In the arena, you do what I tell you. Got it?"

"Sure."

She looked at him. He was a little taller than her, with a disproportionately small head covered with thin, spikey blond hair like a baby chicken's. He still wore bandages over his eye and ear. His remaining little eye looked sincere.

"I'll do exactly what you want," he added. "One of us should be in charge. Should be you. You're younger, but you have much more experience of fighting alongside excellent warriors." He twirled his long axe. "Like me."

"Good to hear it," she said, not entirely sure whether he was taking the piss or not. "We might get giant snakes, we might get something else. Chances are it's going to be nasty."

"As nasty as my axe?"

"Yes."

"No. Way."

"Let's agree to disagree. Listen carefully."

"Right. Let's swap sides so you've got my good ear." He jinked around behind her.

Morningstar felt a pang of something very odd. Was it guilt? She remembered the Wootah man's bravery when Talisa White-tail had maimed him. Curse Yoki Choppa for taking the rattlesnake from her diet. "Do not attack. Jab, block, do whatever you need to do to keep the foe the length of your weapon away. I will kill it or them when the chance arises. You are not to strike unless you are absolutely sure of a kill. Do you understand?"

"I do."

"Why are you smirking?"

"*The length of my weapon.* It's a good bit longer than any other man's but it's still not—"

"Shut up. Grow up. You know what I mean. The point is not to rush. I can kill anything with one club strike. So if we are fighting something—by Innowak!"

She stopped because they'd turned a corner in the narrow gully and the land had opened up. Where there had been dozens of people hanging on the bare red and yellow walls of the Badlands, there were now hundreds. All Calnians, bleeding into the rock and dying. Her people.

She touched her spider box. There was nothing she could do.

"So patience is the watchword," she continued. "Hold back, let me kill everything."

"Got it!"

Had he? She wasn't sure. *Was* he taking the piss? The

Mushroom Men had a weird sense of humour that she couldn't understand had she wanted to. Even their leader was for ever pointing out rock towers that looked like penises, for the love of Innowak. Calnians grew out of that sort of juvenile japery about the same time they learned to shit in a pot.

Back in the camp, Sofi Tornado realised she was fretting, worried for Morningstar. It was a new feeling and she didn't like it.

By the terse words that people were throwing around, unfinished breakfasts and worried eastward gazes, the rest of the Calnians felt the same and the Wootah were concerned for Keef the Berserker.

"Gather round everybody!" she yelled. Everyone came quickly.

"Sit down," she gestured to the logs around the main fire. "I'm going to tell you a tale."

Sitsi and Chogolisa couldn't have looked more surprised if she'd produced a squirrel from behind her ear and bitten its head off. Paloma was equally surprised but better at hiding it.

Sofi waited for silence, which meant waiting for Wulf to quieten Bodil, then began.

"Far to the north is a little-populated land of lakes and islands. It's a shitty place to live. It's piss-freezing cold all winter. In summer it's boggy, swarming with large biting insects and busy with white bears which are so pissed off about being bitten by the insects that they attack and kill any creatures that they can catch, including people. Despite the shittiness of the land, a city not much smaller than Calnian grew. Rule of this city was passed down the male—"

"Hang on," interrupted Sitsi Kestrel, "are you sure this isn't a myth? I've never—"

"It could be a myth. I certainly thought it was, but recent events have led me to think otherwise...can I carry on, Sitsi?"

Sitsi nodded, reddening.

"The rule was passed down the male line. All officials were male and men were very much in charge. Nobody knows how or why, or at least my source didn't, and I guess it may have been to do with the male dominance, but the city became even more consumed and obsessed with sex than your average city. Their answer to every problem, their celebration of every success, their solace in the face of adversity, was fucking."

"Um?" said Wulf the Fat, nodding at Freydis the Annoying and Ottar the Moaner.

"The only taboo was that a son could not—" she glanced at the children, "—could not have relations with his mother until he was fourteen. Apart from that, anything went. Grandmothers with grandsons, sisters with sisters, great circles of men all joined by..."

"Dancing?" suggested Wulf.

Sofi nodded. "Something like that. And so, relaxed and happy, the city thrived for a couple of hundred years. Then a small but powerful group led by a couple of warlocks began to worship a celibate god. They claimed that there was no difference between men and women, and sought to prove it by lopping of their breasts and penises and shaving their heads and then, taking things a little too far as fanatics are wont to do, they used alchemy to sterilise the whole city, so that they'd stop... dancing the whole time."

"I'm confused," said Freydis.

"So they died out?" asked Gunnhild.

"The adults did, but their children didn't. Neutered and doomed, but desperate to survive, they poured alchemy into their children. These kids developed in all sorts of weird ways, including becoming deeply linked with the animals that were the base of their alchemy, but the ageing elders succeeded in their main goal. When the last generation of children reached puberty, they stopped developing. They didn't grow and their hair fell out."

"The Empty Children!" cried Bodil, smiling and clapping like a happy chipmunk.

"Indeed," said Sofi. "These children watched everybody else die, and then scraped by as their city decayed, living incredibly long lives. Some even say they're immortal. Beaver Man led an expedition north through all that shitty land, and brought them all back to the Badlands."

"To use them!" Gunnhild announced.

"Or save them," said Sassa.

"Exactly," said Sofi.

Tansy Burna had not enjoyed the last four days. As cat cavalry she wasn't involved in the drudgery of herding captives or burning bodies, but the stench of death filled the air and dying Calnians were hammered up on the walls everywhere. They were even hanging in the dagger-tooth cavalry's billet, including some poor woman nailed right next to Tansy's doorway. She moaned through the night as her life seeped into the rock. It was tempting to put her out of her misery, or even help her escape, but the penalty for doing either of those was death, which, on balance, was too great a penalty to pay for a decent night's sleep.

With a day off training, Tansy had escaped the hangers to watch the action in the arena. She guessed that the others felt the same, because when she'd made her usually fruitless rounds asking people to come with her, most of the cat cavalry had leapt at the chance. Even dreamy Rappa Hoga had deigned to join them.

It should have cheered her not to be on her mateless tod for once, but already the others' ceaseless banter was irritating. Why couldn't they shut up and enjoy the occasion? Rappa Hoga wasn't chatting. The cat captain knew how to behave.

With so many fighters at their disposal, the action in the arena had started at dawn and they'd already seen a couple of excellent matches. Three Calnians armed with clubs had done really rather well against a couple of alchemically maddened black bears, and had the good grace to die spectacularly. One of them had even used the severed arm of his own friend in a final, spirited defence, whacking away even as one animal ripped his foot off and the other buried its snout in his guts.

She felt a pang of sadness for the people who died. It was a new sensation but not a surprise after her turn of remorse on the battlefield. It wasn't too bad. She quite liked it, even. It added a new dash of poignancy to the whole viewing experience.

The match following the black bear fight promised to be even more of a cracker, since it featured two captives she sort of knew. Mercifully, her fellow cat riders quietened a little when Chapa Wangwa announced Morningstar the Calnian Owsla and Keef the Berserker, of the Wootah tribe, then left the two aliens standing in the middle of the arena.

If a god were to design a physically perfect woman, thought Tansy, then she'd look pretty much like Morningstar. The play of shadows around her stomach muscles was exquisite and her bare shoulders and limbs shone with smooth-skinned vitality. When Morningstar glared at Beaver Man and the captured Calnian empress Ayanna, the defiantly smouldering thrust of her chin made Tansy gasp.

Keef the Berserker was as ugly as Morningstar was attractive, but he had a beautiful weapon. It was a long-handled axe-cum-spear, with a great curved blade as well as a long spearhead. Tansy wondered what it was made of—polished iron perhaps? Whatever it was, chances were Beaver Man would have it soon and have his weapon smiths copying it. He would probably want it that very morning, which did not bode well for Keef.

The first animals were released; a couple of rattleconcondas. The crowd, most of whom weren't regulars like Tansy, ooo-ed. Tansy looked to her left and right, eyebrows raised, to make sure everyone knew that she'd seen plenty of rattleconda fights before and this was nothing special for her.

The snakes slithered towards their prey with a noise like sacks being dragged swiftly across sand. They were a particularly large pair, slowed by their heaviness, but probably the more formidable for it.

The Wootah man kept them at bay with his axe while the Calnian jumped clear of their strikes. This went on for a while. The cat cavalry around Tansy started chatting again. One of the snakes turned to hiss at them, as if telling them to be quiet. Morningstar saw the gap, leapt like a deer and brained the serpent with one punch of a stout double-headed club.

As one rattleconda died, the other struck at the Wootah man. He leapt to avoid it. For a moment Tansy thought he'd made a mistake, as the giant snake redirected mid-strike, but he swept his axe and lopped its head off.

That shut her fellow cat cavalry up. Some of them clapped politely.

Next they faced a huge white bear.

It lumbered at them and reared to over twice the height of its opponents. It roared skywards displaying long fangs, paws spread to show claws that could eviscerate a buffalo with a gentle swipe.

Morningstar barked something at Keef. He chucked her his weapon and she hurled it into the bear's neck, spear point first.

The bear fell, waved a paw weakly, and died.

A few people cheered, a few more booed.

Tansy looked at Beaver Man. He was wearing his usual bored expression. Beside him the Empress Ayanna sat stiff-backed and regal, her baby son on her lap. She was another good-looking woman. If you'd only seen the Owsla and the empress, thought Tansy, you could be forgiven for thinking that all the women in Calnia were ridiculously attractive. She'd seen their soldiers, though. They were mostly a ropey-looking lot.

Beaver Man made a two-fingered signal and Nam Cigam leapt up from his place a few seats down and capered towards the centre of the ring, waving a spear around his head.

Oh dear, this was a bit desperate. Clearly the white bear had been meant to last for a while. They only brought on the comedy when the next battle wasn't ready.

The reverser warlock approached Morningstar and Keef, dancing and thrusting his spear. Morningstar handed Keef's axe back to him and Keef pranced towards Nam Cigam, making similar exaggerated moves.

"Be careful, Keef," she heard Morningstar say.

The two men leapt about, sweeping their long weapons in exaggerated arcs that were never meant as strikes. Many of the crowd lost interest—the cat riders started to chat again—but Tansy thought it was rather lovely, like a new form of dance.

Morningstar stood and watched the men like an unimpressed mother watching weird children, then turned to head for Beaver Man and Ayanna.

Behind her, Nam Cigam suddenly leapt away from Keef and thrust his spear into Morningstar's lower back. He had surprising strength for such a slight man. The spear's bloodied tip protruded a forearm's length from Morningstar's beautiful stomach.

The crowd gasped. Everyone who'd been talking shut up and stared.

Keef the Berserker roared and chopped his axe through Nam Cigam's head. *Wow, that blade is sharp*, Tansy thought as half of Nam Cigam's skull fell to the ground, followed by the rest of him.

Morningstar turned, spear protruding fore and aft. She looked down at the dead reverser, then back at Keef, nodding. *Was she going to be okay?* wondered Tansy, surprised that she wanted her to be. Beaver Man had survived worse wounds. These alchemical warriors were tougher than your average.

The Wootah man dropped his blade and ran to the Calnian, but she held up a hand for him to stay back. She opened her mouth as if to speak, but instead vomited a gout of blood. She choked, shook her head as if marvelling at the stupidity of it all, and fell.

Shortly after Yoki Choppa had begun to prepare lunch, Keef returned to the Wootah camp on his own, followed by a solitary Empty Child. Finnbogi ran with everyone else to meet him.

He was carrying Arse Splitter at his side, walking, not prancing. He didn't look up when everyone crowded around. Finnbogi had never seen him like this. He noticed that the axe head was bloodied.

"Morningstar's dead," Keef said.

Chogolisa Earthquake choked out a sob and walked away.

"Tell me what happened," said Sofi Tornado, her face stone.

Chapter 10

An Escape Attempt

Erik the Angry woke from a dream about driving off giant snakes by shouting profanities at them and remembered that Morningstar had been killed the day before.

He wished he was still asleep. Despite captivity and looming horror, Erik had begun to enjoy hanging out at the camp, training like he was in the Hird again, eating Yoki Choppa's weird but excellent food and talking to interesting people. Mostly he spoke to Chogolisa Earthquake. As well as the old *how do we get these spiders off our necks?* and *what do the Badlanders want with us?* chestnuts, they told each other about their lives. Hers had been about a thousand times more interesting—the Calnian Owsla had been on some extraordinary missions—but she listened to his stories about bees, bears and the Lakchan tribe intently, asked good questions and made suitable "no way!," "oh no!" and "what a *dick*!" comments. It was a different scale, he mused, but perhaps he and Chogolisa got on because they'd always both been larger than everyone around them.

But Morningstar's death had shaken them all. They'd been lucky, if you could put it like that, that the Badlanders had been too busy planning the massacre of the Calnians and dealing with its aftermath to pay them much attention since they'd arrived. However, it was clear that if they hung around any longer, they were all going to die, either in the arena or murdered on a whim by Beaver Man.

So today they would escape. Or at least try to.

Erik felt sick.

Probably half of them were going to be killed immediately. None of the great escapes in the sagas of the Hardworkers or the Lakchans began with half the escapees writhing on the ground and being mercy-killed by their friends. He could not help looking around, wondering who was going to make it, and, much as he tried not to, trying to work out who he *wanted* to make it.

Chogolisa? Definitely. Finnbogi? Certainly. Bodil? Well... Shut *up*! he told his mind.

The Calnians and Wootah went about their normal morning business, communicating with raised eyebrows and head movements so as not to alert the Empty Children. One of Sofi's early versions of the plan had them killing the Empty Children, but Erik had put his foot down. There'd be no slaying of children, Empty or otherwise.

As he finished his breakfast, Sofi Tornado sat next to him and spoke clearly but very nearly silently. "Your spiders are asleep. So are Wulf's, Sassa's, Keef's, Finnbogi's, Thyri's, Yoki Choppa's, Sitsi's and Chogolisa's. Ottar's are drowsy and will sleep soon."

"Your spiders?"

"Awake as a pair of dancing lizards on a hot morning."

Erik tried to raise a consoling hand to her shoulder, but she raised her own hand to block it.

"We knew the chances," she said.

Erik nodded. *You die when you die*, he told himself.

He waited and watched. Others joined him, sitting on the logs in the middle of the camp, each holding the small, slim, sanded wooden breakfast plates that he'd made for all of them. They'd been eating off them for the last few days. That morning's meal had provided the final coating of grease to ease the slip behind their boxes, between spiders and neck.

He and Sofi had let the rumour spread that Yoki Choppa could use alchemy to determine which spiders were asleep. Sofi wanted her super-hearing to be kept a secret because, Erik guessed, it maintained her reputation of steely invincibility if people thought she could see a moment into the future, rather than hear their buttocks clench when they were about to leap at her.

Fair enough, thought Erik, but it didn't matter because Sofi's spiders were awake and she wasn't going to escape. Possibly, since she was alchemically strengthened like Paloma, she'd have the same resistance. However, even if she did survive, she'd be out of action long enough that she'd be unable to run with the rest of them. They'd decided that anyone who was bitten, Owsla or otherwise, should be finished off by the others, to save them from whatever horrors the Badlanders would visit upon them if they remained alive but incapacitated.

Because Sofi and Gunnhild's spiders were awake, Sofi Tornado had Ottar's plate and Gunnhild had Freydis's, to block off the children's spiders before they attempted their own. Had Erik's spiders been awake, he'd have had one of their roles.

He tried not to think about Bjarni Chickenhead, lying in his tent. The man had clung onto life like a deer tick dug onto a hairy arse. He was unconscious most of the time now and could hardly speak when he wasn't. Yoki Choppa said he actually was dead, just refusing to accept it. So they'd left him out of their plans and they were going to kill him as they left. Wulf the Fat in particular hated this part of the plan, but, after making dozens of flawed suggestions, he'd eventually conceded that it was the only thing to do and said that he would be the one to do it.

From listening to the spiders wake when they were startled, Sofi reckoned that people with sleeping spiders on their necks had about a heartbeat before the spiders woke, realised that their cages were being tampered with and bit them. Those whose spiders were awake would also try to slot the piece of wood in between the little fuckers and their skin, but all of them, even Paloma Pronghorn, had around zero chance of completing the task before the spiders bit.

Sofi held up her hand.

Sassa Lipchewer gripped her piece of wood. When Sofi's hand dropped, they were to slip Erik's wooden disks between their necks and the spider boxes.

She felt shitty about being glad that her spiders were asleep, so she apparently had more of a chance of surviving this crazy move. She already loved the little human struggling to grow inside her more than she loved herself and her husband. It was unexpected, annoying and wonderful.

She watched Sofi Tornado's hand, waiting for it to drop. She adjusted her grip on the wooden disk. She had to get it right, she had to...

"Sorry everyone," said Sofi, keeping her hand in the air, "It's off. We'll try again another time."

Sassa looked about to see what had happened, but it was a while before Chapa Wangwa ran into view around the corner, followed by a troop of Badlander warriors and some Empty Children on bighorn sheep. How had Sofi Tornado known that they were coming so long before the rest of them?

"Hello, hello, everybody!" cried Chapa Wangwa. Paloma Pronghorn peered at him through narrowed eyes. Her spiders were awake so chances were he'd just saved her life by appearing, but she wasn't overly keen to hear what he had to say.

"Big day today!" The Badlander grinned like a depraved goat. "One died yesterday! Many more will die today! Many more!"

Owsla and Wootah looked at each other. *Here we go*, thought Paloma. *Out of the about-to-be-bitten-by-spiders, into the snake arena.*

"What, nobody going to make a joke? No wise words from Granny?" He thrust his skull-smiling face at Gunnhild. She looked away. "What a shame! It is almost like your spirits have been crushed by the death of only one of you. Never mind, I'm sure you will find them again in the arena. Not that spirit will help you much...Now, to business! Wulf the Fat and Chogolisa Earthquake, you will carry Bjarni Chickenhead."

"He can't fight," Wulf said, his tone that of a hungover man asked to do one too many tasks.

"He's not going to. He's going to sit with Beaver Man. The boss likes to be near death, and Bjarni will die today."

"How do you know?"

"His spiders told the Empty Children, the Empty Children told Beaver Man and Beaver Man told me. Am I not good, answering your questions? I shall miss my duties looking after you. Although you shouldn't think that you're special. You're not! I'm sure I shall enjoy my next charges just a much. So. Wulf the Fat and Chogolisa are to carry the dead man. Sofi Tornado, Paloma Pronghorn, Erik the Angry, Keef the Berserker, Thyri Treelegs and Ottar the Moaner will also come with me. Bring your weapons. You're going to need them!"

"You missed me," said Sitsi Kestrel.

"I did not mean to include you," smiled Chapa Wangwa.

"You can swap with me if you like," Paloma offered.

"No, she cannot," said the warlock. "Sitsi will stay here. But please don't worry, Kestrel girl, your time will come. And what fun it will be, waiting here to see who, if anyone, comes back! Very exciting. Lucky little you."

Sitsi looked seriously put out not to be included in what was clearly a fighters' group.

"I'm sure he doesn't mean anything by it, Sitsi," said Paloma.

"Yeah, I'm staying behind," said Finnbogi, "and I beat two rattlecondas."

"Oh, I *do* mean something by it," said Chapa Wangwa, "I'm taking only the best fighters. You didn't beat two rattlecondas, Finnbogi Boggy, they went back down their holes because you're so *boring*. Morningstar and Keef killed two yesterday. But Morningstar fell against a reverser! How *embarrassing*."

Sitsi reddened and Finnbogi's hand went to his stone axe.

"Oh do! Come at me, *please!*" Chapa Wangwa jutted his chin at Finnbogi. "No? I thought not. You wouldn't come at me if you *didn't* have your spiders. You're glad you have them as an excuse not to attack me, coward boy. That is why you are not in this group. Today is a fight for fighters. And Sitsi, you favour the bow. The bow is a tool that women use for collecting food. It is not a weapon and you are no warrior. Come, let us go."

Paloma thought Sitsi's head might actually burst.

Chogolisa and Wulf carried Bjarni from his tent on his bed, his sword laid alongside him. Those chosen by Chapa Wangwa bade a variety of farewells. Wulf held Sassa while a solitary tear flowed down her cheek.

Then they were off. Hugin and Munin the racoons tried to follow, but Ottar shooed them back. Paloma found the boy's goodbye to his pets more moving that Wulf's farewell to Sassa.

Perched on the highest point of the spiky crescent, hidden under a cape the same colour as the crumbly rock, Luby Zephyr watched her friends and their weird new Wootah companions file from the camp. This was an annoying setback. She'd been awake all night dreading the enactment of Sofi's plans, and now that dread would be prolonged, or, even worse, they'd never get the chance to put the plans into practice.

To the south, the sky was the purple-black of the increasingly common storms. This one looked even more powerful than the last one. If it came north, it might help their escape. If enough of the warriors survived the arena to make escape possible, of course.

Chapter 11

A Battle in the Arena

The arena was packed. Paloma Pronghorn thought the Badlander citizens looked irritatingly similar to Calnians gathered to watch the Owsla slaughter captives in the Plaza of the Sun. Not so polished, perhaps—there was less quill decoration, fewer outlandish hairstyles and their clothing was generally more brown—but they were all dressed more elaborately than they needed to be and the average facial expression was the same as your standard Calnian gawper. They wanted to see blood. They wanted to goggle at muscle, sinew and brains. They wanted to grip their friend by the arm and marvel at mysterious bits of innard left lying on the arena floor.

Beaver Man watched with buffalo eyes from his arena-side seat. Next to him was the Swan Empress of Calnia, Ayanna, holding a bundle which had to be her baby son. She had a spider box, too. She didn't acknowledge her Owsla, she simply stared at them, looking about as pissed off as it's possible to be. Paloma knew the feeling.

Chapa Wangwa ushered them to the edge of the arena. "Chogolisa, sit Bjarni next to Beaver Man and the woman who was an empress. The rest of you stand over here. If you move, your spiders will bite and you will die. That would actually be the best option for most of you right now, but please stay put. I promise that one, maybe two have a reasonable chance of surviving today."

Badlanders jeered, but none of them spat. The Calnian

spectators had gone through a phase of spitting at the Owsla's victims. Sofi Tornado had put an end to it by dragging a large spitter into the ring, pulling his trousers off and spanking him so hard that she'd split an arse cheek. There'd been no spitting after that.

How Paloma missed Calnia. What larks they'd had.

Sitsi Kestrel paced the edge of their small zone of confinement, looking over the spiky and lumpy landscape that her friends had vanished into. She could see their footprints disappearing into a gully a hundred paces away. She could see ants investigating the footprints. But she couldn't *do* anything.

She pursed her lips, clenching and unclenching the grip on her bow. *A tool that women used for collecting food!* She'd show him. She'd put an arrow between his eyes from a mile away.

Eating chuckwalla again was like mud being washed from her eyes. She now saw how insects differed here, how the plumage of the birds varied, how the very air was a different shade. She felt ready to take on the world. But she was stuck, trapped by the accursed spiders.

She plucked an arrow from her quiver, one of Sassa's iron-headed beauties. Yes, she thought, this one will look very good slotted between Chapa Wangwa's eyes. *A tool for women...*

She twirled the arrow in her fingers and looked at the Empty Children. They returned her gaze, empty-eyed and watching. They were always watching. They weren't totally bald, she could see now, they had wispy white hairs all over their egg-like skulls. Their eyes were white, too, no sign of an iris. How did they see?

As they'd discussed their escape plans, Erik the Angry had insisted several times that nobody was to kill the Empty Children. She agreed. Even though they'd make her spiders bite and kill her if she took a step beyond the perimeter line, it would be wrong to shoot people who'd themselves been so cruelly treated.

A wave of sadness made Sitsi blink and lose focus on the spinning arrow. It flicked from her grip and landed in the grass a good few paces over the perimeter line. Fifteen red-brown ants and three orange and black dung beetles scurried for cover, then returned, presumably to see whether her arrow was a stricken animal, a dropped turd or anything else they could eat.

Sitsi looked from arrow to Empty Children. She could *feel* their wagging fingers in her mind, *no no no*, they said, *cross that line to retrieve your arrow and your spiders will BITE.*

"All of you wait here until I say you can move," said Chapa Wangwa. "You," he added, pointing at Ottar the Moaner, "follow me."

The Badlander marched to the far side of the arena with Ottar tripping along behind him. Sofi Tornado, Wulf the Fat, Chogolisa Earthquake, Paloma Pronghorn, Erik the Angry, Keef the Berserker and Thyri Treelegs watched them go.

Erik nearly screamed with rage. *Bide your time*, he told himself, *bide your time*. But how much time did they have to bide? What if Chapa Wangwa whipped out a knife and killed Ottar while they stood like deer watching a mountain lion eat their fawn?

"Right!" shouted Chapa Wangwa, walking away from Ottar, leaving him alone at the far side of the bare rock expanse. The boy stared up at ranks of baying spectators. "Now stay, and..." a dagger-tooth cat padded out onto the arena from a gap between two of the bench-cut rocky outcrops. It was maybe three or four times the size of the biggest lion, not much smaller than Astrid the bear.

It roared, sniffed the air and turned to Ottar as if it had been looking for him. Erik tried to reach out to the cat's mind, but was blocked by a boiling barrier of confusion and fury.

"Owsla and Wootah, you may move when the cat goes for the boy, which will be any—"

The dagger-tooth charged at Ottar.

They all ran, but compared to Paloma Pronghorn the rest of them were hardly moving.

The cat sprang. Ottar squeaked and hid under his own arms.

The cat descended, front paws raised, mouth open.

Paloma dived.

She was too late, Erik was sure. The animal landed hard, sending up a cloud of dust.

Paloma darted around the cloud, Ottar in her arms, and sprinted back towards the others. The cat followed.

Sofi Tornado was out in front, Finnbogi's sword Foe Slicer aloft. The cat, fixed on its pursuit of Paloma, didn't see Sofi. The Owsla captain raised her sword, reversed it at the last moment and cracked the cat on the head with the hilt.

The dagger-tooth stopped, dazed. Calnians and Wootah came to a halt around it. The cat lashed out half-heartedly, but Thyri Treelegs wapped its paw with the flat of her sax.

"Chogolisa, hold it," said Sofi.

Thyri shouted and waved her arms to distract the dagger-tooth. The big woman jumped onto its back. Limbs splayed and the cat crashed down, trapped under Chogolisa.

Paloma handed Ottar to Erik. Erik hugged the eight-year-old, realised he was trembling, and hugged him all the more.

"Do you want your cat back?" Sofi called to Chapa Wangwa.

The Badlander nodded.

"Then have your bald gophers calm it down and send it home."

"Empty Children, the cat will return to her lair."

Sofi looked askance at Erik. He felt for the cat's mind and found it. The fury was gone. It wanted to hide. He nodded.

"Climb off it, Chogolisa, careful as you go," said the Owsla captain.

"Well done, well done." Beaver Man strolled across the

arena, shining with vim. "I love teamwork. The only thing I prefer is sacrifice. So that will be the theme of your next challenge. Your young man Finnbogi the Boggy did well in his sacrifice challenge."

"He sacrificed his dignity by boring some snakes into giving up?" asked Keef.

Beaver Man gave Keef a long look, face melancholy as usual but eyes shining with something like joy. "He didn't tell you?"

"Didn't tell us what?"

"Good for him. There is more to that young man than perhaps anyone allows. I offered him a choice between likely death for him and Freydis the Annoying, or freedom for Freydis and certain death for him. He chose the latter."

"Certain death? How come he didn't die?" Keef sounded almost disappointed.

"He defeated two rattlecondas, unarmed. He is the first to do that."

"He sacrificed himself for Freydis?" asked Thyri Treelegs.

"He intended to. Then he used his guile to win a seemingly unwinnable fight; a greater victory than if he'd brutishly sliced their heads off with an axe."

Keef shrugged. "Yeah, right."

Thyri shook her head, smiling. "Well, you think you know someone..." Erik looked forward to telling his son about her reaction, assuming he lived to do so.

"Will any of you be as impressive, I wonder? Good luck." Beaver Man spun on his heel and jogged back to take his seat next to Empress Ayanna and Bjarni Chickenhead. The former looked resigned and unhappy. The latter looked dead.

"Sacrifice time!" Chapa Wangwa was bouncing on the spot, rubbing his hands. "This is going to be *fun*."

"What are you doing?" Bodil Gooseface asked Sitsi Kestrel.

"I'm not really sure. I'm waiting for the others to come

back. I know it makes no difference standing here but I think that if—"

"Is that your arrow?"

"Yes, but—stop!"

Bodil stepped over the line, picked up the arrow, came back and handed it to Sitsi. "There you go."

Sitsi looked at Bodil, then at the line across the path, then at the Empty Children. They looked unbothered, as always.

"How did you . . . your spiders?" she said, taking the proffered arrow.

"What spiders?" Bodil scanned the ground fearfully.

"The spiders in the box on your neck."

"I hate spiders. Where have you seen them?"

"There are two, in a box, on your neck."

"I thought those were ants?"

"They're spiders."

"I thought they were ants."

"Ants or spiders, they should have bitten you just now and they didn't. Do you know—"

"My mum was bitten by a spider on her leg. It swelled up like an egg."

"Do you know why your spiders—"

"It got better quickly, though, and—"

Sitsi grabbed the taller Wootah woman's shoulders and gripped hard. "Bodil, please shut up and listen."

"Ow!"

"Sorry, but please just listen. Do you know why the spiders attached to your neck didn't bite you just now?"

"I don't want them to bite me."

Sitsi sighed.

"But they couldn't anyway."

"Why not?"

"I don't think they can anyway. Can they bite through wood?"

"They cannot."

"I hope they can't. They were irritating me *so* much with

their scurrying, so I put one of Erik's little plates down the back of the box. Here, I'll show you."

Bodil reached to remove the plate.

"No! No. Leave it in. Please, don't touch it."

"But now the plate's a bit annoying." She gripped the plate.

Sitsi grabbed Bodil's wrist and dug her nails into the tendons to make her fingers spring open.

"Ow! *What?*"

"You have to keep that plate there or you will die. Do you understand?"

"Get off!"

The archer grabbed both Bodil's wrists and pressed her thumbs into her tendons. It was mean, but times were desperate. Bodil blinked tears but, finally, it looked as if Sitsi had her attention.

"If you touch the bit of wood by your neck again, I will break your wrists and it will hurt. Do you understand?"

Bodil nodded, looking scared.

"Even if I'm not around, I'll know, and I'll break your wrists. Got it?"

"Yes."

"Good. Now listen, then answer the question. When did you put Erik's plate behind your neck box?"

"Last night."

"But what about this morning, when we were all going to slot in our plates on Sofi's say-so?"

"I did wonder what that was about. I didn't want to make a fuss. Everyone seemed so excited and usually if I try to get involved with something like that I get it wrong. There was this time in Hardwork when Vifil the Individual had stolen Garth Anvilchin's trousers and—"

"Stop, shush. Crouch and stay still."

Bodil did as she was told. Sitsi pressed her ear to the Wootah woman's neck box. She could hear the spiders scratching maniacally at Erik's wooden plate.

So, thought Sitsi, they must have tried to bite her when she stepped over the line and were now pissed off that they couldn't. But the nearby Empty Children seemed unconcerned...So it looked like the Empty Children had given the order to the spiders to bite Bodil, but then not known or cared whether it was carried out.

They'd assumed that the Empty Children would know that the plates had been put in and spiders separated from skin, and alert Beaver Man or make the other peoples' spiders bite, or something else equally prohibative. But they'd been wrong. In fact, if Sitsi was right, they didn't need to all slot their plates in at the same time. Everyone just had to wait until their spiders were asleep. As soon as all the plates were in place—which wouldn't take more than a day, since the spiders slept at least part of every day—they'd be able to choose their time and stroll out of the Badlands.

"Don't you touch that neck plate, all right?" Sitsi waggled a finger in what she hoped was a menacing way.

Bodil nodded, looking afraid.

Sitsi ran back to tell Yoki Choppa to use his alchemy immediately to tell whose spiders were asleep.

She couldn't wait to tell the others when they got back.

If any of them got back.

The squatch, the giant beast that Sofi Tornado had last seen on the Plains Strider, loped into the arena, arms swinging. Its gait could have been that of a human: it was the same shape as a well built adult, but it was covered entirely in reddish-black hair and towered nearly twice the height of Erik the Angry.

Like them, it had a spider box strapped to its neck.

"The squatch!" shouted Chapa Wangwa. "You will like this. It is the third time we've had the squatch on show. It has ripped off fifteen legs and twenty-three arms! I have been counting! That one does not like to see a limb attached to a human body. But it hasn't met anyone as large as Chogolisa before. On the other hand, it's never fought fewer than seven people at a time, and all of them armed, so who knows what will happen! Erik, put your club down. Go with your friend Chogolisa to the other side of the arena and stand next to the squatch. Start fighting when I tell you."

Erik dropped his club and headed off with Chogolisa.

"Now, Thyri Treelegs and Keef the Berserker, can you see that man in the audience wearing buffalo horns?"

"I can," said Thyri.

"He looks like an idiot," said Keef. The Wootah man had healed enough to lose his bandage, but was now wearing a leather cap to cover his missing eye and ear. The tight cap made his small, round skull seem even smaller. It looked, Sofi thought, like a warlock had attached an ugly baby's head onto a headless man's thick neck.

"You two take Ottar and stand in front of buffalo hat. Keep your weapons. You're going to need them! The rest of you, stand here. If you move, your spiders bite. Got it?"

Sofi Tornado, Paloma Pronghorn and Wulf the Fat, left in the centre of the ring, looked at each other.

As Ottar, Thyri and Keef neared the buffalo-hatted man, a monstrous snake slipped swiftly up out of a hole on the arena floor, tongue flicking, head darting from side to side. Sofi shuddered. She'd seen snakes as large as this one when she was a child, but this was different. It was much zippier than such a large animal should be; as freaky as an adult buffalo leaping about like a skittish chipmunk.

The snake slithered onto the rock, lifted its disgusting segmented tail and rattled it. Sofi shuddered again. Not a nice noise. The beast slithered towards the three Wootah.

Another rattleconda emerged from the hole, then another, and another.

Four snakes, three Wootah, one of them a boy who was more likely to try to hug a snake than fight it.

Keef and Thyri turned to face the serpents, sax and axe held high.

Sofi listened carefully for a moment to her own, Paloma's and Wulf's spiders. Hers were asleep. So were Wulf's. Paloma's were awake. The Empty Children were watching.

"You two," she muttered. "Come in close. Ready your spider plates. Put them in when I say. Erik, yours are asleep. Yours are not, Paloma."

"Great," said Paloma.

"Do it faster than you've ever done anything before and you might be all right."

"I might. Or the second dose of the poison might kill me. I can't wait to find out."

"Hold for now. We'll do it only if we have to."

"Squatch, attack!" shouted Chapa Wangwa from the other side of the arena. "Snakes attack, too!"

"Why do you have to wait for Sofi to come back? I don't understand!"

Yoki Choppa shrugged.

Sitsi Kestrel actually stamped her foot. It was so frustrating! No matter how much she explained, the stupid warlock was refusing to find out which spiders were asleep, and he was giving her no good reason why. Right then she *hated* Yoki Choppa.

"What if Sofi doesn't come back?"

The warlock looked at her and shrugged so minutely that you needed alchemically enhanced eyesight to spot it.

"Oh for the love of Innowak!"

She stormed off. It was bad enough that the Badlanders were against them. She really did not need to battle Yoki Choppa's senseless stubbornness as well.

Luby Zephyr climbed the soft rock promontory that comprised half of the southern bank of arena seating, vaulted the top and sat on the uppermost stone-carved bench in an *I've been sitting here for ages* pose. She was just one of the hundreds of Badlanders come to watch the action below. That's what she looked like, if anybody cared to observe.

A woman with badly dyed purple and gold hair spun round angrily, opened her mouth to say something, then seemed to think better of it and turned back to the action. Nobody else paid Luby any attention.

They were focused on the impending death below.

Her Owsla comrades and their pale-skinned friends were in trouble.

The hairy monster swiped at Chogolisa and she was saved only by the surprisingly timely and skilled intervention of the big-bearded Wootah man.

The one-eyed man and thick-thighed Wootah girl were defending reasonably well against the serpents—very well for normal people—but the snakes were pushing them back, and one was flanking them to get at the boy who, according to Sofi Tornado, had to be kept alive.

On the far side of the ring, at the arena's edge, Ayanna was cradling Calnian, sitting next to Beaver Man and the terminally ill Wootah man.

Luby could see by the way she was bouncing on her toes that Sofi Tornado was about to try something. What she was going to try, given that she had two spiders that could kill her in an instant strapped to her neck, Luby could not begin to guess. But she might need help.

Luby stood up, which drew some attention to her, then climbed down the seats, which attracted a lot more. *I can see her, but she's not interesting,* she made the watchers think by the way she moved. *Sure, she's there. But I don't care.*

The squatch backhanded Erik and he staggered. Chogolisa jumped onto its back, wrapped her legs round its torso and throttled it. The beast didn't seem more than mildly put out by a grip that would have crushed a short-faced bear.

Erik gathered himself, prepared to charge again and suddenly *Click!*

There was someone in his mind.

Hello . . . ? he thought.

You want to save the boy? said an erudite voice that sounded disconcertingly similar to Astrid, Finnbogi's mother.

I do . . . he thought, hesitatingly.

Then come in close and I'll grab you to make it look like we're still fighting.

Okay . . . Erik saw no reason to disagree.

And please ask your friend if she wouldn't mind awfully releasing the pressure on my neck. She's very strong.

Erik charged. The squatch grabbed him by the neck and pulled him in, so his mouth was near Chogolisa's ear.

"The squatch is on our side," he whispered. "Pretend we're still fighting it, but loosen the grip on its neck."

Ah, that's better. Thank you. But I'm a she, not an it. My name's Ayla.

Sorry, Ayla.

Forgiven. Now, in a couple of heartbeats, I'm going to pinch both your spider boxes. In theory, I'll kill all four of your spiders and you'll be freed. In practice, who knows? Apologies in advance if it doesn't work and I kill you both.

What about your spiders?

I should think the Empty Children will feel your spiders die, work out what I've done, and make mine bite me. I may die. I may not. I'm quite tough.

You'll do this for us?

Don't flatter yourself. It's not for you. It's for the boy. Make sure you save him. Now, tell your friend what is about to happen and let us get on with it.

Got it.

One more thing.

What's that, Ayla?

The tall woman is in love with you and you feel the same way about her. You should do something about that, if you live.

Sofi Tornado saw that Thyri and Keef's battle with the snakes was all but lost. If they didn't act immediately Ottar the Moaner, the boy that Yoki Choppa claimed was saviour of the world, would die.

"Wulf, Paloma, plates ready?" she said.

They both nodded.

"Now."

All three tucked their wooden disks in between their neck boxes and flesh.

Sofi heard Paloma's beeba spiders sink their hard, sharp jaws into flesh. She heard her and Wulf's spiders wake as their plates slotted into place, then bite wood.

Paloma screamed, slapped her hand to her neck and fell to her knees.

"Not...this...bollocks...again..." she grunted through clenched teeth.

On the other side of the arena, Thyri fell as a snake whipped her feet out from under her with its tail. The animal was on her in an instant, wrapping her in muscular coils. Keef was brandishing his long axe at the other three giant reptiles, but landing no blows and being forced back to where Ottar was sitting on the arena floor, observing the action with all the emotion of someone watching the tide come in.

Sofi heard thudding footsteps and turned.

Beaver Man had leapt the arena side and was coming at them.

She looked from kneeling spider-bitten Paloma, to about-to-die Ottar, to charging Beaver Man.

"Go and save the boy, Sofi. I'll deal with this prick," said Wulf, nodding at Beaver Man.

*   *   *

Now thought Ayla the squatch.

"Now!" said Erik.

The squatch crushed the spider boxes on his and Chogolisa's necks as if they were made of snow, then roared as if she was being ripped in two.

Erik wrenched the destroyed box from his neck and hurled it away.

The squatch fell onto her back with a great thump, roaring shrilly, writhing and clutching her neck.

Sofi Tornado was running towards Keef, Thyri, Ottar and the snakes. Wulf was standing next to the kneeling Paloma, his hammer Thunderbolt ready for the charging Beaver Man.

Chogolisa set off to help Sofi. Erik ran towards Wulf.

"Spider plates in! Keef, Thyri, Ottar, now!" shouted Sofi as she ran towards them. "Now!"

Keef sprung back, did as he was told, then re-engaged the snakes.

Thyri, arms trapped by the snake that was crushing the life out of her, couldn't do a thing.

The boy just looked at her.

Sofi ran for the snake crushing Thyri, saw that Luby Zephyr had appeared out of nowhere and would get there first, and changed direction to aid Keef.

Swinging Finnbogi's sword Foe Slicer, she beheaded two snakes as she passed, leaving Keef to deal with the other. She could hear Luby mincing Thyri's serpent with her obsidian moon blades. The creature was twisted and loosened its grip on the Wootah warrior, who fell clear. As she tumbled, Thyri whipped out her disk and slipped it between her neck and the box. Thyri Treelegs might not be Owsla, but she was effective.

Sofi ran for Ottar. She had to neutralise his spiders.

She was a pace away when they bit him.

Erik was ten paces off when Beaver Man reached Wulf.

Wulf swung Thunderbolt. The Badlander chief powered a punch to meet the blow. Hammer and fist met. Both men were knocked back.

"What *is* that weapon?" asked Beaver Man, looking not exactly interested, but less bored than Erik had seen him look up until now.

"It's Thunderbolt," said Wulf. "For ever more, that will be the answer to the question *What killed Beaver Man?*"

"Nicely put. Although the actual question will be *What did Beaver Man take from the brave alien and use to smash his head into a bloody smear on the arena floor?*"

Before Erik saw that he was even moving, Beaver Man was holding Wulf's wrist. Wulf had time to look surprised before Beaver Man drove a head-butt into his face, followed by a slamming punch to his jaw. Wulf staggered, dazed. Beaver Man plucked the hammer's leather lanyard from Wulf's thick wrist and snatched the weapon away.

He tossed it from one hand to the other.

"Wonderful," he said, almost smiling.

Erik picked up his club Turkey Friend from where he'd dropped it earlier.

Beaver Man turned his head and his deep, dark eyes met Erik's.

"Come on then," said the Badland chief, lowering Thunderbolt with his arm straight, so that the great iron head pointed at Erik.

Turkey Friend was a fearsome weapon in most combat situations, against most people. Just then, facing possibly the most powerful of all the alchemically charged warriors armed with a legendary magic weapon passed down through the mists of time, Erik's club felt about as useful as a soggy reed.

*   *   *

Bjarni Chickenhead gathered all the strength he could muster to open and raise his eyes. Great big motherfuckers' nipple tips, this was the worst trip. He wanted it over. It would be over. It always cleared. It had always cleared before. But, man, this one was dragging on! Had there ever even *been* a time when the world hadn't whirled in daggers of light stabbing through the rotting mushroom of his mind? He could see snakes, for the love of Oaden, giant snakes!

The fog lifted a little. More people than he'd ever seen, all around, were shouting. No, they weren't all around. It was clear in front of him, apart from just a few dancers. He giggled. He liked a dancer. But wait a minute, that was Wulf the Fat! Wulf was dancing for him. Now there was a vision he could be happy with. He willed Wulf to dance closer.

But Wulf wasn't dancing. He was fighting. He was *beaten*! Wulf was down. A nasty shiny man had beaten him.

There was something in Bjarni's hand. He looked down. He was holding his sword Lion Slayer.

Well, it was pretty clear what he needed to do. He used both arms to push himself to his feet.

And fell hard, banging his head on cold stone.

Shitbags. Only one arm! Was this part of the trip?

He was lying on his side. Maybe a bit of a kip was called for, now that he was in the right sort of position for it.

But, no, Wulf was in trouble.

Someone was helping him up. A moment of clarity. It was a strikingly handsome older woman, cradling a baby and using her spare arm to haul Bjarni to his feet.

"Stop that a moment, Finnbogi the Boggy," ordered Freydis the Annoying. "What's Sitsi Kestrel doing?"

Finnbogi lowered his hand axe and looked up at the large-eyed archer. He'd been showing Freydis, Gunnhild Kristlover and Sassa Lipchewer his new spin and chop move, trying to take their minds of the unknowable plight of those who'd been taken to the arena.

Sitsi was standing, hands on hips, staring at them—at their necks, to be precise—her eyes flicking from one to the other.

"I *think* I can see whether your spiders are awake or asleep by the way your boxes are moving," said Sitsi. "I think yours are asleep, Gunnhild, yours, too, Sassa."

"Which means?"

Sitsi told them about Bodil, and her theory that the Empty Children wouldn't know if they put their neck plates in place.

"So you think we'd be safe to put our plates in?" smiled Gunnhild.

"Yes. But—"

"I'll do it."

"I'll go at the same time," said Sassa.

"I'm not sure, though. Yoki Choppa could tell us, but he says we have to wait for Sofi and—"

"And we don't know if Sofi's coming back," interrupted Gunnhild. "We don't know what the situation will be when she does, so the sooner we get our plates in and those spiders chomping on wood, the better. *The best time to plant a tree is fifty years ago. The second-best time is today.*"

"Wouldn't forty-nine years, three hundred and sixty-four days ago be the second-best time to plant that tree?" asked Sassa.

Gunnhild ignored her, lifted her wooden plate, took a deep breath and said, "Krist, protect me."

"Hold up." Sassa lifted her plate. "I'll go with you. On three. One, two..."

Paloma Pronghorn opened one eye. Wulf the Fat looked beaten, on his hands and knees, drooling blood. Erik the Angry was squaring up to Beaver Man with his club. The big bearded man did not look confident.

The spiders' bite had hurt like... well, it had hurt a similar amount to the previous time the cunty little animals had bitten her: one fuck of a lot. The aftermath, however, had surprised her—it had been a great deal friendlier than before. She'd felt the poison spread through her body, but then the evil venom had dissipated without doing much apart from making her want to cry and vomit, both of which she'd managed not to do; happily, given the number of people watching.

Maybe she'd been injected with a lesser dose, maybe she'd built immunity. Didn't matter. Point was her plate was in now, she was just about fine and very much ready to go.

She kept kneeling, though, with one eye open about a tenth. Sofi had told her that Beaver Man's shiny skin was impervious to arrows and stone axes. So it was going to take a cunning plan to beat him.

Erik swung his club. The chief dodged and launched Wulf's hammer in an uppercut that might have pulverised a mountain. Erik leapt back to avoid it, but Beaver Man pressed, hammer swinging.

Erik slid and jinked and blocked. Annoyingly, they'd swung round so that Beaver Man was facing Paloma and would see if she suddenly revitalised, but any moment one of his blows was going to... There you go. The hammer clunked into Erik's temple and he went down, dazed if not dead.

Beaver Man stood above the Wootah's hairiest warrior and raised the weighty iron hammer two-handed above his head, about to bring it down for the skull-crusher.

Pissflaps to plans. Paloma sprang up, sprinted at Beaver Man and put all her weight and speed into cracking her killing stick into the side of his head.

The impact jarred her arms so hard that she lost focus for a moment. When she regained it, Beaver Man was still standing and smiling at her, Erik forgotten behind him.

She could run. Paloma's best form of defence wasn't attack. It was to piss off as fast as possible.

But if she ran, Beaver Man would kill Erik and Wulf. Erik was rolling and groaning and not much use to anyone. Wulf was recovering, on his knees now but shaking his head, far from ready to join the battle.

She sighed, and attacked.

She landed several hits. Each one would have ended the fight with a normal person, but they didn't even dent Beaver Man's smile. However, she was faster than him and he didn't come close to landing a blow on her.

She twisted and danced with her killing stick, jabbing him in the kidneys, cracking him in the head and whacking him in the bollocks. But it was as if he were made of stone.

She hit him harder and harder, and then too hard, because she left her guard open for a moment too long and his fingers were round her neck, squeezing.

Wulf the Fat, still half dazed, charged.

Beaver Man slapped Wulf back into senselessness, then grabbed him too around the throat.

The crowd cheered. Paloma and Wulf struggled at the end of Beaver Man's arms, but they were like leaves trying to pull their tree down by wiggling about. Beaver Man gripped their necks all the harder, looking into their eyes like a wanton child studying the effects of torture on two trapped rabbits.

The crowd cheered all the more to see their chief besting two warriors so stylishly. Paloma had lapped up similar cheers from the Calnian crowd often and actually wondered a few times what it was like to be on the wrong end of an entertaining kill. She was not enjoying finding out.

At the far end of the arena, Sofi, Chogolisa, Thyri and Keef had beaten the snakes but were now fighting a squad of Badlander warriors. As her vision blurred and the clouds of unconsciousness bloomed in her mind, she realised she could not see the boy Ottar.

*   *   *

Gunnhild Kristlover smiled. "Well done, Sitsi Kestrel."

"You could take your boxes off now," said Finnbogi, looking at the unharmed Gunnhild and Sassa Lipchewer with a degree of envy, as his own spiders shifted nastily against his skin.

"Best leave them on," said Sitsi, "we don't want them to know we've...hang on. I think Freydis's spiders are asleep now. Bodil's, too."

"And mine?" asked Finnbogi, even though he knew they were awake.

"Yours are dancing about like squirrels in autumn."

Great, he thought.

Beaver Man looked perhaps the most surprised of all of them when the sword tip appeared out of his neck.

His grip loosened. Paloma fell onto her arse, next to Wulf, both retching for breath.

Erik the Angry climbed to his feet and staggered over.

Beaver Man flailed weakly at the sword tip. He managed to turn and Paloma saw that Bjarni Chickenhead was holding the sword's hilt. The dying man had thrust his blade into the small of Beaver Man's back, all the way through his torso and out of his neck. *What an amazing blade*, she thought, *and what amazing strength to stick it through the supposedly impervious man.*

Bjarni pushed Beaver Man and the Badlander chief fell, limbs flailing, mouth coughing out weird choking barks.

Behind him, Empress Ayanna walked up, holding a sleeping baby. Some children could sleep through anything.

"Congratulations," said Paloma, nodding at the kid.

"Thank you," replied her queen.

Bjarni distracted them both by thumping down into a kneeling position in front of Wulf.

Neither man looked at their peak, but Bjarni looked

particularly shit. The putrefaction from his amputated arm had spread. One side of his face was red and shiny with welling pus. An eye had collapsed and leaked out of the socket. But the other eye looked clear and sincere.

"I always loved you, Wulf," said Bjarni. "And I don't mean like a brother. I've always wanted you like a lover."

Well well, thought Paloma.

On the ground nearby, Beaver Man stopped his flailing and watched.

Wulf put his arm on Bjarni's shoulder. "I know."

"It's been my secret, my burden, I—"

"Shush." Wulf pivoted forward, gripped the back of Bjarni's head with one hand, leaned forward and kissed him open-mouthed on the lips and . . . was that tongues?

The kiss lasted a long time.

Finally, Wulf broke off and leaned back, still holding Bjarni's shoulders.

"I know," said Wulf. "I knew. And I loved you as well. But I never wanted to act on it. My parents, the tribe . . . you know what it was like."

Bjarni nodded.

"And then I fell for Sassa. What I have for her is real, I do love her, and it was acceptable so I . . . But please know that I didn't stop loving you."

Bjarni smiled. A huge tear formed in his good eye and rolled down his cheek. Then he fell.

Wulf fell onto him, hugged him, then knelt up. He put his fingers on his friend's neck.

His face was stone. "Goodbye, my friend."

He stood and took his hammer from the writhing Beaver Man.

Paloma looked over to the others as Sofi felled the last of the Badland warriors. The spectators, seeing that the entertainment had defeated the entertainers, were making themselves scarce. Chapa Wangwa was nowhere to be seen.

Wulf nodded to Paloma and Erik and they followed him to join the others.

"Would you two mind awfully," he asked as they walked, "never telling anybody about what just happened? I don't care what people know about me, but I don't want Sassa undermined."

About a dozen jokes sprung to Paloma's mind immediately, and, given a little time, she probably could have come up with a dozen more.

Instead she sighed. "Bjarni saved my life, and yours and Erik's. He died a hero and he'll be in your Valhalla now, looking out a good spot for the rest of you. That's all there is to tell."

"That's how I see it too," said Erik.

"Thanks."

Sofi chopped the throat out of the final Badland attacker and jumped round to help Paloma and the rest against Beaver Man, but the three of them were already coming towards her. She looked towards where Rappa Hoga and the cat cavalry had been sitting, but they'd gone. *Why?* she wondered briefly.

She turned her attention to the spider-bit boy.

Ottar the Moaner was lying on the ground, on his back, eyes closed. Thyri Treelegs knelt next to him, shakily.

"He's fine," said Sofi.

"What?" said Thyri, looking up with snot on her face.

"I said he's fine."

"How dare you? Scraylings might look at death differently, but he's just a little *boy* with his whole life—"

"Shush," said Sofi. "He's fine, as in *he's totally fine.* Ottar, stop playing now. We're off."

Ottar's eyes opened and he leapt to his feet.

Sofi had known he was fine by his heartbeat and his breathing. She'd known for a while that Ottar's spiders were a different type to everyone else's, but not that they weren't venomous. She guessed that Beaver Man knew he was special and didn't want him killed. Although that wouldn't explain why he'd risked the boy in the arena. Maybe someone else had swapped his spiders?

"What the—?" said Thyri. "How did you...?"

"Don't worry about it now. Let's get back to the others."

Chapter 12

Over the Edge

The wait was hateful. Sassa Lipchewer felt doubly ill with her usual morning sickness and a choking dread for what might be happening to Wulf and the others.

Black clouds thickened overhead and a probing, icy wind came snaking around the pinnacles. As yet, the deluge had held off, but surely it wouldn't be long. Might they halt the fighting in the arena if it rained? Or would they pause it, prolonging her agony?

She'd lost the burden of her spiders but Sitsi Kestrel, Yoki Choppa and Finnbogi the Boggy were still unprotected from the venomous buggers. Sitsi could see that Finnbogi's and Yoki Choppa's spiders were awake. She was trying to persuade Yoki Choppa to use alchemy to tell her whether hers were awake or not, but so far the warlock had refused, which was driving Sitsi almost to tears of frustration.

"I don't get it!" Sitsi was actually jumping on the spot. "Why not? Do you need herbs that you don't have? Maybe someone could—"

She was interrupted by Paloma Pronghorn returning to camp at an earth-ripping sprint.

"Bjarni died," said Paloma, skidding to stop, no more out of breath than if she'd been sitting on a chair for an hour. Sassa was not upset. It was a relief. But what about Wulf? "Nobody else died. All the Wootah lot are hurt, none too badly. They did well. We pretty much defeated Beaver Man and his animals—his Owsla wasn't there, thank Innowak—and we rescued Ayanna and her baby. Oh yeah, and Ottar was spider-bitten but he seems to be okay."

"Who's Ayanna?" asked Bodil.

"No time for that," said Sitsi, "I've discovered that we don't need to all put our spider plates in at the same time! Wait a minute, where's your spider box? Have you been bitten again? Your neck looks—"

"All of us who went to the arena have removed our boxes. No time to explain. What have you discovered?"

Sitsi shook her head. "Never mind. All of us here, apart from me, Finnbogi and Yoki Choppa are protected by spider plates. I told everyone to leave their boxes on because I thought they," she pointed at the three Empty Children watching from their rocky knoll, "would see removed spider boxes and make the rest of the spiders bite. Since they've seen yours missing and done nothing, that doesn't seem to be the case. You must have known that, though, or you wouldn't have run back in here without your spider box and risked us all."

"Uh, yes, I did know that."

"Oh, and Yoki Choppa," Sitsi continued. "Your spiders are asleep now. Shame you won't tell me about mine."

Yoki Choppa slipped his plate in without fuss, and said, "Follow me." He led her to a bowl of water. "Look in that."

Sitsi did, and, Sassa guessed, saw in her reflection that her spiders were asleep, because she slipped in her wooden plate and seemed to deflate with the relief of it.

"Why didn't I think of that?" she said. "But, good, now we've all neutralised our spiders and—"

"I haven't!" said Finnbogi. "Please tell me mine are asleep?"

"No, sorry, they're not." Sitsi looked suitably abashed to have forgotten Finnbogi.

"Do you mind awfully if we stop pissing around?" said Paloma. "The others will be back any moment and we've got to head off as soon as they get here. Sofi reckons Rappa Hoga went to get reinforecements and we don't have long."

The rest of the Wootah and Calnians ran into sight a moment later, led by Sofi Tornado and an Owsla-dressed woman whom Sassa had never seen before.

Sofi saw Sassa looking confused and, to Sassa's surprise, deigned to explain as they approached. "This is Luby Zephyr. She's Owsla. Came with the Calnian army and escaped the massacre."

"Good to meet you. I'm Sass—"

"She knows who you all are. You can chat later. We're leaving now."

Then Wulf was on Sassa and she had to tell him not to hug her so hard.

He put her down, stood back with his blue eyes shining in his bruised face, then reddened and looked at the ground.

"You die when you die, and Bjarni should have died a while back," she said.

"He saved my life. And Paloma's and Erik's. Probably all of our lives. And—"

"Shush. That's why he held on so long. He did what he stayed alive to do and he'll be waiting for us in Valhalla."

Finnbogi saw that all the returning Wootah and Owsla weren't wearing their spider boxes any more. So he was the only one left with spiders on his neck. *Just my luck*, he thought.

"Your spiders?" Sofi Tornado asked him.

"Still partying away. I've got—"

"Apart from Finnbogi," said Sitsi, speaking over him, "we all have one of Erik's wooden plates between our necks and the beeba spiders."

"Good," said Sofi. "Well done. Paloma, Sitsi, Luby, help everyone take those boxes off, careful as you go. Then we'll leave." Sofi looked at Finnbogi and cocked her head as if listening. "Finnbogi, stay here and hide. If they don't find you, try your spider plate in a while, perhaps at sunset, then track us. We're headed for the Black Mountains."

Finnbogi looked at Sofi. *What had she asked him to do?*

"I—" he started, but she was already turning to Freydis to unbuckle her spider box.

Finnbogi stood and watched, eyes flicking between people flinging spider boxes away and the Empty Children. The weird kids on sheep didn't seem to be doing anything. Were they asleep? He took out his wooden plate and reached towards his neck.

Sofi grabbed his wrist. "Hide. Now. With any luck the Empty Children will stay nearby and you'll be fine." She turned to walk away then stopped, and turned back. "All right, new plan. There's something that might work. Paloma?"

"Yes?" The speedy woman darted over.

"Hold your hand flat like this, thrust as fast as you can," Sofi demonstrated the move, "and I think you'll be able to get your fingers between Finnbogi's spider box and his neck before his spiders bite him."

"But they'll bite me."

"Yup. You've been fine so far."

Paloma opened her mouth as if she were about to disagree, but then seemed to deflate. "Yeah. Why the Wootah not? Stay still, Boggy."

"Owsla! Wootah! Remain where you are!" rang out a voice that made Sassa lurch with fear.

Rappa Hoga was galloping towards them at the head of a column of dagger-tooth cavalry. More and more riders followed, tearing between two pinnacles of red and yellow rock lit up blazingly by the sun, in stark contrast to the bruised purple storm clouds above.

"Now, Paloma!" said Sofi.

Paloma's hand jabbed up into Finnbogi's neck box, between skin and spiders.

"Ah!" cried Finnbogi.

"Arrrghhhhh!" screamed Paloma, ripping the box from Finnbogi's neck and flinging it away. She fell onto her side, clutching her bitten hand to her chest.

"Paloma!" cried Finnbogi, dropping down next to her.

"I'll... be... fine... in... a... moment. Run. I'll catch up," she managed, clenched up and shaking, like Poppo White-tooth had been that time he'd eaten too much buffalo meat at a Thing.

Finnbogi touched her shining hair. "Thank you."

She looked up, agonised and surprised, and... was that tenderness in her eyes?

"Fuck off!" she snarled. "I said I'll catch up."

"She will," said Sofi. "We need to run, now. Give me my axe back and take this." She was holding Foe Slicer out to him, hilt first.

He reached for it suspiciously.

"Quick. It's yours. I shouldn't have taken it. Sorry."

He handed her axe back, took his sword and both of them ran from the cat cavalry. The others were already a good way ahead. Finnbogi beamed as he sprinted. Sofi must respect him now! But why? Had she heard about his sacrifice in the arena? Did she simply fancy him?

She might respect him, but she was a much faster runner and she wasn't waiting. She caught up with the rest when he was still a good forty paces behind. He turned. The cat cavalry were coming fast, almost on Paloma who was still sitting, clutching her bitten hand.

Finnbogi ran on, Foe Slicer increasingly heavy in his hand. Of course, the sword was a much heavier weapon that Sofi's axe. And she'd given it back to him just before they'd had to run for their lives. Because she respected him now.

Sassa Lipchewer ran. The first chestnut-sized raindrops splatted to earth.

Up ahead, Freydis the Annoying bounced along on Erik

the Angry's shoulders and Ottar the Moaner clung to Chogolisa Earthquake's thick neck with his legs, his racoons bundled to his chest. Atop the giant, Ottar looked even smaller
than usual, vulnerable and spindly. Next to them ran Ayanna,
showing a neat turn of pace for a new mother, especially one
holding a baby.

Sassa held back with Wulf the Fat to accompany the slower
Gunnhild Kristlover.

"Speed up, Wulf and Sassa," yelled Sofi Tornado, catching up and shouting over the wind and rain, "follow Luby
Zephyr. I'll be backmarker."

Luby was already out of sight around the crescent of rock
that flanked the southern edge of their camp. Sassa and Wulf
did as they were told. They rounded the crescent's western
edge.

"Blow a crow!" Sassa cried as the gale and the rain slapped
into them like a cauldron of water hurled by the thunder
god Tor.

Moments latter Paloma appeared alongside them, apparently untroubled by the squall, grabbed a fistful of arrows
from Sassa's quiver and said, "bow please!"

Sassa handed it over without a quibble and Paloma streaked
on ahead.

Tansy Burna watched the escapees run through the rain.
Rappa Hoga had halted their chase, and was looking back the
way they'd come. He was waiting for Beaver Man.

The prisoners had left the leader for dead in the arena,
impaled by the long metal weapon which apparently came
from the far side of the Wild Salt Sea. Chapa Wangwa and
a couple of warlocks were extracting the man-spitting blade,
but it was painstaking work. The chief was only *nearly* immortal; the warlocks said that further damage to his organs might
actually kill him, or at least disable him.

Beaver Man, not too perturbed by the alien metal running

through him from lower back to throat, nor by the indelicate all-fours pose he'd adopted to ease the extraction of the weapon, had told them to go, and to stop their captives leaving.

But Tansy knew why Rappa Hoga was waiting and slightly disobeying orders. Chasing people through the gullied landscape of the Badlands massif was a far from perfect fighting situation for the dagger-cat cavalry, especially when their quarry included some superbly capable warriors, at least one of whom was an alchemically enhanced archer. Beaver Man was impervious to arrows. Rappa Hoga and the rest of them, cats included, were not. The cat cavalry captain was brave as a wolverine defending its children, but he wasn't going to risk his people or his cats by being an idiot.

Still Beaver Man didn't come, and finally Rappa Hoga had to shout, "Let's go!"

Tansy pressed her heels into furred flanks and her beast sprang forward. Danger of an arrow in the face or no, she loved the chase.

Finnbogi the Boggy caught up finally and ran along next to Thyri Treelegs, Erik the Angry and Chogolisa Earthquake, straining against the wind and rain. It was like trying to run through a swarm of wet bumblebees flying in the other direction.

He looked over his shoulders. Thank Loakie, the cat cavalry seemed to have given up the chase, at least for now.

Paloma Pronghorn streaked past, a bow in her hand, and Finnbogi felt a rush of relief that she'd recovered. He sped up to try to follow her, but she was out of sight in a trice. He fell back to run next to Thyri Treelegs, who smiled at him in what could only be called a friendly way. Weird.

"Here they come!" yelled Freydis, looking back over Erik's shoulder.

Thyri leapt round, sax ready.

"Keep going!" shouted Sofi behind them.

Finnbogi looked back. They were crossing a section of grassy prairie, between two clusters of pinnacled rocks. Gunnhild Kristlover and Sofi Tornado were ten paces behind Finnbogi. Two hundred paces behind them came the dagger-cat cavalry, gaining fast.

They rounded another corner and there, ahead of them, between two tumbledown pyramids of rock, was a gap with nothing but stormy sky behind it: the edge of the Badlands massif.

Standing on the rock wall either side of the gap were Sitsi Kestrel and Paloma Pronghorn, legs wide, feet planted, bows ready, wet hair whipping in the wind, wet limbs and torsos shining tautly. Finnbogi almost stopped to stare at Paloma. Instead, he kept looking at her as he ran, determined to remember the vision for ever. Had any woman ever looked that amazing before?

Sitsi nodded to Paloma and the archers sent arrows over their heads. The Badlander cat cavalry bounded for cover.

Luby Zephyr was waiting in the gap with Wulf, urging the Wootah over it.

As Finnbogi approached the edge, he could see more and more of the plain below. A long way below. How steep was their descent going to be? It looked a lot like the gap had a cliff on the other side of it.

He reached the edge and looked down. It was pretty much a cliff. Sassa, Bodil, Yoki Choppa and Keef were already out of sight. He wondered how they'd descended so fast. Gunnhild and Sofi caught up, the former panting like a dying sheep, the latter bouncing on her toes, looking happy for the first time since Finnbogi had met her.

"Luby Zephyr's cleared a trail, you'll be down before you know it," said Wulf, before kicking Finnbogi's feet out from under him and shoving him between the shoulder blades.

Finnbogi fell with a yelp. His arse hit rock, but he didn't so much land as carry on falling, zooming down a track etched into the rain-slick slope, trying to keep some control with his hands and feet. Very shortly he was travelling faster, he was sure, than any human had travelled before, with the possible exception of Paloma Pronghorn. He zipped around curves and flew over low rises. Had he been certain that the track went all the way down, and wasn't about to go over a cliff or whack into a boulder around the next turn, he might have enjoyed it.

Sofi Tornado stood at the edge, between the archers Sitsi Kestrel and Paloma Pronghorn. Ayanna, the baby Calnian and the rest of the Owsla were down Luby's slide, but the last of the Wootah, Wulf and Gunnhild, were not. Gunnhild was refusing to jump.

"You've got to go, now," said Sofi.

Wulf wrapped his arms around Gunnhild, lifted her, fell onto his own behind and slid down with the older woman on top of him and waving her limbs like a trapped cat.

Sofi shook her head—having people like Gunnhild and the baby Calnian along was not going to make this escape any easier—and turned to assess their pursuers.

Rappa Hoga and his dagger-tooth cavalry were creeping closer, crawling along gullies and darting between spires of rock. Every time one of them emerged from cover, Sassa and Paloma loosed an arrow. They'd hit several cats in their legs, but wounded none mortally and hit no riders, as Sofi had instructed.

The cavalry came ever closer. The dagger-tooths would be within leaping distance soon.

"I'm out of arrows!" called Paloma.

"Both of you go."

"I've got loads left," said Sitsi.

"And you'll need them. Go."

The two women jumped over the edge and disappeared.

Sofi Tornado stood, axe in hand. After Finnbogi's sword

the axe felt like a returned friend—a light, strong friend who was excellent at killing people. If she had to die, it would be with her own weapon in her hand.

Rappa Hoga rode his dagger-tooth out from a gully and towards her. He was huge-shouldered and dark-skinned, looking as powerful as the beast beneath him.

Sofi stood her ground as the rest of the cavalry saw that the archers had gone and followed their captain from cover.

"I beat you last time." His voice was deeper than she remembered.

"Then it must be my turn to win." She smiled. "Shall we?"

Rappa Hoga slipped off his dagger-tooth, obsidian-headed axe in hand.

Erik slid the last few paces with Freydis in his arms, jumped onto his feet and ran clear. Chogolisa was waiting, holding a grinning Ottar. Both of them were coated with red-yellow Badland mud, but Chogolisa's smile shone. The sky had brightened and the rain had eased from a destructive torrent to more of a pleasant shower.

Caked in rain-streaked mud, panting and colossal, Chogolisa was a vision of beauty.

They held each other's gaze for longer than was strictly necessary.

"Come on, Erik!" shouted Wulf. "You're needed! So are you, Finnbogi, come on!"

Father, son and giant woman followed Wulf and the rest of them, eastwards along the base of the massif.

"Isn't this the way back into trouble?" asked Chogolisa.

"Probably," said Erik, "but we'll never escape on foot. Your Luby Zephyr has another plan."

Sitsi Kestrel and Paloma Pronghorn jumped at the same time, took more or less the same path sliding down the steep hill, but somehow Paloma disappeared down the hill at more than

twice Sitsi's speed. She wasn't much heavier; they were both
sliding on their arses, and their leggings and breechcloths
were made from the same leather by the same tailor. So how,
marvelled Sitsi, for the love of Innowak, was Paloma so much
quicker?

The unfairness of it spoiled any joy that Sitsi might nor-
mally have taken from sliding down a mud chute.

Not only was Paloma smiling smugly when Sitsi arrived
at the bottom, she was also fresh-faced and radiant, having
somehow avoided the spattering mud that Sitsi could feel cak-
ing her own face. Innowak loved Paloma and he didn't love
Sitsi. It was the only possible answer.

Both women looked back up the hill. There was no sign
of Sofi. They looked at each other, both realising at the same
moment why Sofi had stayed behind.

"We should have—" started Sitsi.

"I'll go back up," Paloma made to set off but Sitsi grabbed
her wrist. Paloma strained uselessly. She might have been
faster in all circumstances, but Sitsi had archer's arms.

"She would have asked if she'd wanted you to stay. Come
on, the others need us more than Sofi does."

Tansy Burna saw a few other riders head into the open without being spiked by an arrow, so she gingerly urged her
mount from cover, head craned to look for the archers.

Their prey, and the archers, had gone over the edge. One
captive remained; their chief, Sofi Tornado.

Rappa Hoga had dismounted and was walking towards her,
great double-headed obsidian axe in one hand. He was wearing only a slight breechcloth, as usual, so she could see his
muscles bulging and tussling with every step. She gripped
her dagger-tooth with her thighs and it snarled.

Tansy admired the woman for making a stand and buy-
ing her people some time, but it was pointless. Rappa Hoga
had taken them from the arena to get their cats, then ordered

the pursuit with less urgency than he might have done not only because he wanted to wait for Beaver Man—of whom there was still no sign—but also because there was nowhere for the escapees to escape to. The massif stretched for miles to the west and north. To the east the spires and crevices were impassable to normal humans, and to the south there was nothing but prairie pretty much for ever. The one place they could escape to was the Black Mountains, but that was two days hard walk south, then west. They could give the Calnians and Wootah a day's head start and the cat cavalry—and whatever else Beaver Man sent—would still catch them with ease before they reached sanctuary.

"If I defeat you," called Sofi, "you and your cats will hold back from pursuing me and mine until noon."

"You won't defeat me," said Rappa Hoga, his voice deep and sure. "And you are in no position to make terms. You have to fight."

"True. But, as you said, I'm certain to lose, so what harm could possibly come in accepting my terms?" She sounded awfully confident for a woman who was about to have her arse handed to her. Could she know something they didn't? They were a capable lot, these Calnians and Wootah. Nobody, for example, had ever managed to remove their spider boxes before.

"Good point," smiled Rappa Hoga. "My terms then. If I beat you and you live, you will join my warriors."

"I accept. Do you? If I beat you, will you hold your chase until noon?"

Rappa Hoga looked at the sun. It was a long way before noon but, judging by the sky, there'd be no more rain that day. They'd be a cinch to track. The woman was brave, but she'd asked for crap terms. Not that she had a chance of winning anyway.

"There are others who will pursue you, over whom I hold no power," said Rappa Hoga.

"We'll take our chances against them."

"You will have no chance against them."

"I have no chance against you, so what have I got to lose?"

"I accept your terms."

"Good. But before you defeat me, there's one thing I want to know. Why destroy the Calnians? Do you mean to invade?"

Rappa Hoga looked at the Calnian Owsla's captain for a moment, then shrugged as if he saw no harm in telling her.

"Who is left back in the Calnian empire?" he asked.

"All the Calnians, apart from the army."

"Yes. The children, the old, administrators, scholars and those smiths, craftspeople and artists who weren't needed by your army."

"So you can invade with ease."

"So there's no need to invade. The tribes that Calnia has conquered don't like taxes. So they will stop paying them and Calnia will starve. Or, more likely, the tribes will rise and try to take the empire for themselves. None of them are powerful enough to achieve this now, so there will be war while the Calnian empire collapses, and for years afterwards."

"And untold misery and pain for tens of thousands of innocents."

"Yes."

"Why?"

"Beaver Man believes that humans are a plague that needs culling."

"You don't believe that."

"Beaver Man makes some convincing arguments."

"He's not an empire builder?"

"He does plan to invade when the Calnians have reduced their own numbers suitably. He will then control those numbers."

"And this is just the Calnian empire?"

"No. He means to expand in every direction, even across the great seas."

"I see. Tell me, Rappa Hoga, do you see the Badlanders as the force for good in this story? Or is it the Badlanders who are a plague that needs to be stopped?"

Rappa Hoga didn't answer for an uncomfortably long time. Was he wavering? Even before the massacre of the Calnians, Tansy herself had been wondering if the Badland cause was the right cause.

"I agree with everything my leader says and does." Rappa Hoga hefted his obsidian axe and walked towards Sofi.

"Hold." Sofi raised a hand.

"What now?"

"We need an executor. If I win, you may be in no state to order your troops."

Rappa Hoga nodded. "Tansy Burna?"

Thrilled, Tansy kicked her cat forwards. "Yup?"

"If Sofi Tornado wins and I am incapacitated, you are in charge. You will make no attempt to follow the Wootah and Calnian escapees until noon. Do you understand and commit?"

"As if she'd going to..." The look on Rappa Hoga's face made her change tack. "I understand."

"Good, let's go then."

Sofi Tornado stepped towards the captain of the cat cavalry, tossing her small, crappy looking stone hand axe from hand to hand.

Tansy Burna leant back on her cat. She wanted to see every single moment of Sofi's defeat, because there weren't going to be many.

"Ya! Ya!" shouted Keef the Berserker, waving Arse Splitter around his head and circling like a loon. The minions who'd been tending to the Plains Sprinter took one look at him, ran and didn't look back.

Finnbogi the Boggy couldn't help but smile.

To the north, the Badlands massif soared hundreds of feet out of the plain, darker and shiny in the sun after the rain, and beginning to steam. The road up onto the massif that they'd taken that first day was a couple of hundred paces to the east. Beyond that was the broken land where the landslide had freed the lizard kings.

Other than the fleeing minions, there were no other Badlanders in sight. Not yet, anyway.

To the south, on the open prairie, perched Beaver Man's long, sleek, land-striding craft. Its animals were attached; thousands—more than thousands—of crowd pigeons at the pointy end and a few dozen wolves at the rear.

Nearby, the baby Calnian began to cry. Sassa Lipchewer rushed to Ayanna, but the empress waved her away, smiling thanks. She sat on the ground, opened her shirt and began to nurse.

Finnbogi looked away. He'd just seen an empress's breast. He looked around for Bjarni, who'd appreciate the excitement, but of course Bjarni wasn't there.

Erik was on a pace-high rock bank, staring down at the pigeons. The birds (so many of them: were there a million?) were pecking about on a vast area of grass, all attached by spider silk to the nose of the wooden vessel.

Everyone was looking at Erik. They knew from his control of Astrid the bear that he could talk to animals. But would he be able to make the pigeons fly?

Finnbogi jumped up next to his father. "How's it going?"

"I can feel them, but I can't connect." He closed his eyes and furrowed his brow.

"I talked to a bird the other day," said Finnbogi.

"With your mind?" Erik kept his eyes shut.

"No, I just spoke to it."

"Right."

"Of *course* with my mind! Why else would I tell you?"

"Well, try these then. I'm not getting anywhere."

Finnbogi closed his eyes and willed his mind outwards, freeing and ushering his thoughts, his very being, up into the sky and then down, to spread like warm mist among the pigeons. He reduced his thoughts to everyday bird concerns. He matched the motion of his head to the rhythmic bobbing of the pigeons.

I am your friend, he told them. *I am with you, we are one. We want to fly, we have to fly. All of us, beat our wings and rise, rise, rise.*

"You getting anything?" asked Erik.

"I don't think so."

"Me neither."

Most of the birds carried on with their pecking. Some looked up at Finnbogi and Erik on their ledge in exactly the way that pigeons might look at any two men who were standing on a ledge.

"They're coming!" shouted Keef.

Finnbogi opened his eyes. Dozens of moose riders were galloping down the road from the Badlands massif, carrying catch poles and nets. Riding the largest moose, leading them, was Chapa Wangwa. They were still a good way away, but Finnbogi could see his grin shining out. Moose seemed much larger, Finnbogi mused, when they were charging towards you.

"Ottar, Freydis, Bodil, Sassa, Gunnhild, Yoki Choppa and Ayanna!" called Wulf the Fat, "onto the Plains Sprinter. Everyone else, to me!"

Sitsi Kestrel, Chogolisa Earthquake, Luby Zephyr and Paloma Pronghorn looked to Yoki Choppa, who nodded. Sitsi and Chogolisa followed Wulf, Keef and Thyri, jogging to meet the coming moose riders. Paloma shot ahead, overtaking the Wootah in the blink of an eye, tearing round the pinnacles and domes of rock that dotted the prairie, headed directly for the enemy.

Finnbogi forgot about the pigeons and watched her go, his mouth hanging open.

Meanwhile, the non-warrior Wootah and Calnians helped

each other over the rail and onto the Plains Sprinter. The craft was a smaller version of the Plains Strider, around fifty paces nose to tail with only one open deck. The fifty wolves harnessed in two ranks at the blunt stern snarled and barked at the boarders. A couple howled, as if calling for help. In front of the prow the silk-tethered pigeons milled about and pecked the ground.

"Come on, Finn!" said Erik. "We've got to get these fuckers aloft! Get the pigeons going and the wolves will have to follow!"

Finnbogi shook his head, closed his eyes and refocused on the birds. *I'm a bird, too*, he told them. *One of you. Come on, let's all go. It's time to fly.*

There! He had it. He willed the birds upwards and he felt them rise. *Higher, higher, we must go higher and then...* he opened his eyes to see which direction to tell them to take.

All the birds were still on the ground, looking about as likely to take off as a field full of buffalo.

The moose cavalry thundered ever closer.

Ayanna handed Calnian to the tall Wootah woman with golden hair and a twisted mouth, climbed the rail and held out her hands to take her baby back.

"No," said the old Wootah woman. "You will need to fight. Give the boy to Freydis, Sassa." She thrust a wooden pole at Ayanna. "Use it to keep the moose riders at bay."

Ayanna took the pole and stared at it.

Until very recently, lackeys had strewn reed mats wherever she walked. Those mats would be given to deserving Calnians who'd treasure them and pass them to their descendants as their most valuable heirloom.

Now, a pale-skinned alien freak, whom she'd ordered killed not long before, was ordering her about and taking her baby from her. She watched Sassa hand her son to Freydis. The girl took him confidently and Calnian didn't seem to mind. Part of her wanted to grab her baby back and scream at them, but another part knew that the old woman was right. She'd be more use holding a pole than a baby. For now, her only option, and the best choice for Calnian, was to accept their orders and get on with it.

Presumably the boat-shaped construction that they'd mounted could be propelled across the plains by the animals attached to it. The hairy lunk and the curly haired boy were trying to get the animals to move. The rest of them would have to fight the Badlanders until that happened.

Ayanna gripped the pole and readied herself to take on the moose cavalry.

Paloma flowed like a bolt of liquid lightning between the riders, swinging her killing stick to smash blowpipes out of mouths and hands. This, she realised, was what she should have done the first time she'd met the moose cavalry. No matter. That was then and this was now. The Badlanders would not defeat the Owsla twice.

A few Badlanders had bows and she smashed these, too. She dodged and jinked as she ran, avoiding darts, arrows, tossed nets and hurled catch poles. The world rushed around her, but she was fully focused and in control. The moose riders were her playthings. She leapt and twisted among them like a salmon. Her hand still hurt from the beeba spiders' bite but, she thought as she smashed a rider's knee, she'd basically become immune to them. Funny how that worked.

Most of the moose riders were looking at her, but none were aiming pipes or bows because they had none left. Good, she thought, mission completed. Now to see how much that grinning prick Chapa Wangwa smiled after she'd smashed his face in with her killing stick.

She landed and accelerated. Her foot slipped on wet rock, she was off her stride for only a tenth of a heartbeat but *crack!* something whacked into the side of her head.

She was down, tumbling, out of control, rolling under the pounding hooves of the mighty moose and the spears of their murderous riders.

"Sassa, with me, up here!" Sitsi Kestrel grabbed Sassa Lipchewer's hand and hoicked her up with ease onto a two pace-high, grass-topped and rocky sided platform.

"Shoot them as they come!" Sitsi ordered gleefully. The Owlsa woman certainly liked a fight.

To the east, a finger of Badlands massif stretched southwards into plain, then there was a grassy gap, then there was a broad pyramid of yellow-green rock. Wulf and the others stood in a line, twenty paces before the gap. Sassa and Sitsi were maybe thirty paces back from them.

The first rider appeared. Almost immediately, Sitsi's arrow struck him in the forehead and sent him tumbling from his mount. Sassa had time to curse that it hadn't been Chapa Wangwa, before the gap was filled with charging moose riders and she was finding her own targets.

She aimed, loosed . . . and missed. There were twenty more moose riders through the gap. She aimed and shot. Her arrow zipped into a man's neck, not his chest where she'd been aiming, and he fell. Emotions rushed her. She'd just killed, or at least horribly wounded, a man who might be a husband and father to children who adored him; a man who'd joined the Badlander army because that's what men did, just like Wulf had joined the Hird . . . On the other hand, she'd gone a step further towards saving Ottar and Freydis, Wulf and the rest of them, not to mention her own unborn child.

She told her meddlesome mind to shut up until they were safely away, and looked for another target.

Despite Sitsi shooting a good half-dozen of them, there were at least forty moose riders through the gap.

Screw a shrew. They were in trouble.

*   *   *

Paloma Pronghorn blinked. She'd stumbled clear of the galloping moose and crawled into a niche cleft into a rock dome.
By the grubby rug and the lingering odour of body, it was the
home of a Badlander minion. She sat on the rug and blinked
and finally felt that she could stand. The world swelled, con-
tracted, whirled a little, then righted.

By Innowak's great big aching bollocks, Paloma hated head
injuries.

She probed her wound with tentative fingers. It was bleeding, but not badly. Her skull was intact. It was time to stop
fannying around and get back to the battle. If there was a battle to get back to. She had no idea how long she'd been trying
to straighten her head.

She emerged from her slot. There was only one moose rider
to be seen. He was dismounted, lying on his front and looking over a rocky pinnacle fifty paces away. From the shouts,
screams and clashes of stone on stone, the fighting was in full
swing on the other side of his hiding place.

The prone Badlander sensed her and looked round.

It was Chapa Wangwa.

Paloma forgot her head wound, grinned almost as broadly
as the shithead lying on the rock, and ran at him.

Sitsi Kestrel was impressed with Sassa Lipchewer's archery, while
satisfied that it wasn't nearly as fast and accurate as her own.

But there were too many moose riders. For every one that
she and Sassa took out, five more came galloping through
the gap.

Chogolisa grabbed the first beast by the antlers and swung
it about her head, taking out the next two. This was why the
huge girl didn't carry a weapon. The world was her weapon.

Keef leapt in, jab-stabbing a rider with the pointy end of
his combined axe and spear. A moose rider he hadn't seen
came at the Wootah man, stone axe ready. Sitsi aimed, but

Luby Zephyr was suddenly there, leaping and slashing with her moon blades.

Sitsi searched for another target. It was harder now that the fighting was close.

Wulf was wrestling a dismounted rider, then another Badlander and another. He writhed and punched, but more piled in and they managed to hold him. Two more came at him with stone knives.

Sitsi lifted her bow, drew, and the string snapped.

"Sassa! Wulf!" she shouted.

Sassa spun, but Thyri Treelegs had already come to Wulf's rescue, chopping her sax through the first Badlander's neck and opening the other's face with an overhead slash. Wulf shook himself free, backhanded his hammer into one attacker's head and felled the other with a punch that Morningstar might have been proud of.

Morningstar...Sitsi had been about to ask Sassa for her bow, but thinking about Morningstar changed her mind.

"Sassa, please may I borrow your knife?"

Sassa pulled the long iron blade from its sheath and handed it to the Owsla archer.

Sitsi ran, sprang off their rock platform onto the back of a moose, sliced the rider across the back of one knee with the sharp little blade and pushed him off.

Her mount was headed for the Plains Sprinter, where Yoki Choppa, Bodil, Gunnhild and Ayanna were using poles to fight off moose cavalry. Freydis was standing on the deck, holding Calnian and watching the fight. Ottar, racoons at his heels, was at the prow, looking over the pointy end at the multitude of pigeons, which were all still on the ground and looking as if they were very happy there, thanks very much.

Sitsi's was one of many mounted moose heading for the Plains Sprinter, which was a problem. If the Badlanders managed to capture or disable Beaver Man's craft, there'd be no escape from the Badlands.

*　　*　　*

Rappa Hoga charged, obsidian axe flashing in circles like a child's wind toy in a stiff breeze. He wasn't going to muck about this time. This was going to be a quick kill.

Tansy Burna shivered.

Rappa Hoga swung and chopped, dancing like an acrobat, but Sofi Tornado weaved and dodged like an eel. Every blow looked like a finisher, but somehow the Calnian avoided them all.

Sofi wasn't getting any hits in herself. Tansy wondered if Rappa Hoga would even notice a hit from that tiny axe. It was just a matter of time before one of his blows landed.

Swipe, swish, chop. Rappa Hoga's axe was everywhere. Still he didn't hit Sofi Tornado. It was extraordinary. To miss by such tiny amounts, so many times, so quickly ... it looked like they were dramatic performers who'd been practising for moons. Was she protected by the gods? Was he missing on purpose? He couldn't be. With such a flurry of blows it would be impossible to miss her on purpose.

So she was dodging. *Was this her alchemical power*, Tansy wondered? And had it been weakened last time they met?

Back and back Sofi danced, on and on Rappa Hoga pressed. Sofi didn't know it, but soon she'd back into a pace-high, grass-fringed ridge of rock. She'd be trapped and her dodging days would be over.

They danced, closer and closer to the ridge, Rappa Hoga striking like a possessed ironsmith, Sofi Tornado evading his blows as if her spine and limbs were made of snakes. Neither showed any sign of slowing.

Sofi backed into the ridge. Tansy bit her lips. Now, surely, it was just moments until Rappa Hoga struck her down.

Finnbogi's eyes were closed. He could hear the fighting ever closer, but he trusted the others to keep the moose riders away from him and his father. He was getting somewhere. Not nearly as far as he wanted to, but he really felt like he was becoming less human and more crowd pigeon. He was beginning to understand their minds. They wanted company; not so much wanted it, they *needed it*. It wasn't about quality, it was all about quantity. *More more more.* There weren't enough pigeons around, there couldn't be enough. The sky should be full, the land should be full. Why was sky visible? There should be nothing but pigeons. It was like the desire to breathe. Finnbogi remembered that time Garth Anvilchin, the massive shit, had held him under Olaf's Fresh Sea and he'd realised just how important breathing was, and how much he craved it when it was denied.

More more more! More pigeons!

Galloping hooves were very close now, so close that he could smell moose. He lost focus and struggled to regain it.

Then he heard a yell. His father's yell.

He opened his eyes. Erik the Angry was snared in a net, on his back, struggling like an upended beetle and yowling at the pair of moose riders who were pulling him away.

The Plains Sprinter was besieged by a swarm of Badlanders. Thyri was standing on its rail, slashing her sax at the enemy.

Finnbogi drew Foe Slicer.

"No!" shouted Erik from his net. "They want to find more pigeons! They have to find more! You know where those pigeons are!"

I know what? thought Finnbogi. Then he realised what his father meant. He closed his eyes.

"Hello, Chapa Wangwa," said Paloma.

While she'd covered the fifty paces from where she'd seen him, the Badlander had only had time to roll onto his back. Grinning like a loon, he scrabbled away.

Paloma danced in, flicked her killing stick and shattered his knee.

He screamed. She smashed his jaw with a backhand. He put his hands to his face and his scream became a bubbling moan.

She cracked an elbow.

He managed to roll over and shook as if he was trying to burrow into the soft yellow rock.

"You deserve this," she told the back of his head. He couldn't hear. It was to convince herself. The man deserved the most violent death, but, thanks to her rattlesnake-free diet, she wasn't enjoying the torture. Curse Yoki Choppa! Life was more fun for the cruel.

She told herself to buck up and knuckle down to the torment. She planted a foot on her victim's arse. He writhed, but she held him in place with alchemically enhanced ease and drove one end of the killing stick into the bone between his shoulder blades.

There was a half-pleasing, half-sickening crunch. Chapa Wangwa's undamaged arm flapped on, but the rest of his body went limp.

Paloma Pronghorn broke Chapa Wangwa's next vertebra, then the next.

When his was spine was satisfyingly pulverised, she grabbed his foot and flipped him over.

He was still smiling, even with a smashed jaw. But, if eyes could scream, his would have been.

"You've watched your spiders kill a load of people just like this," she said. "I bet you never thought it would happen to you. What was it you said: *We can't imagine your agonies, but your eyes tell the story?*"

A piercing scream rang out near by and the battle was suddenly louder. She had to go.

She ran, leaving Chapa Wangwa to die or to live on with his body destroyed. And she stopped. If he did live, she had no doubt that the vile man would be paralysed for life. However, with the support of a tribe, a person could live a long and happy life without the use of their limbs. It was also just possible that the Badland warlocks, obviously an advanced lot, might be able to heal his wounds.

She ran back, leapt as high as she could, saw his eyes widen most pleasingly, then came down and stamped on his face with all her alchemically enhanced might.

His head burst like a pot of porridge dropped from a high tree.

"That should do it," she said to herself.

She ran back to the ridge.

The Plains Sprinter hadn't moved, which was a disappointment. The Wootah and Owsla were pressed from all sides by the moose riders and there was no sign of Sofi Tornado. None of her friends had been killed yet that she could see, but the moose riders were pressing hard.

Paloma looked back to the road down from the Badlands massif. No more enemies were coming, but surely it wouldn't be long. The moose riders were serious foes, but they were nothing compared to the Badland Owsla, the dagger-tooth riders, or, worst of all, the lizard kings.

If they couldn't get the Plains Sprinter moving, they were dead. Well, the rest of them were. Paloma could always run away.

She could help out there, or she could go and get Sofi Tornado, who'd be a lot more help than she would. She headed back to where they'd slid down from the massif.

Sitsi Kestrel was beginning to regret leaving her archer's perch. She'd slid off the moose when it had reached the fight at the Plains Strider and was taking out plenty of Badlander moose riders with Sassa's knife, but not enough. There were so many of them! Hooves thundered all around. For every beast and rider that Sitsi disabled, ten more appeared through the gap.

She made her way towards the Plains Strider. The Wootah and Calnians aboard were defending valiantly. Chogolisa had a pole in each hand and was whacking back Badlanders with aplomb.

However, Chogolisa couldn't do everything. The riders were right up against the side rail in several places. More and more were leaping off their mounts onto the wooden deck. They were being dealt with for now, but it was just a matter of time before the craft was overrun. One managed to get through to attack Freydis and the baby—what kind of dick would do that, Sitsi wondered—but Freydis danced clear and led him back to the others, where Wulf brained him.

Wulf stepping back to help Freydis opened a gap in the defences and riders leapt in to fill it. Was it the beginning of the end? She decided to run back to the rock where she'd left Sassa and her bow. She'd be more help there.

A fearsome animal roar stopped her mid-turn. The creature, or whatever it was, roared on, sending shivers through her limbs.

What now?

A huge furry figure—the squatch that had been on the Plains Strider—appeared in the gap. Chogolisa-style, it picked up a moose by the back legs and swung it left and right, batting riders from their mounts. Sitsi felt a little disloyal for thinking this, but the beast was even more effective than Chogolisa had been. It marched through the Badlanders like a thresher through corn, leaving a jumbled trail of injured moose and riders in its wake.

The Badlanders by the Plains Sprinter turned to meet the squatch. Keef, Wulf, Luby and the rest counter-attacked with renewed vigour.

The battle was far from over but it no longer looked like they were about to lose it.

Finnbogi felt himself being lifted. It was Chogolisa. She stuck him under one arm and ran for the Plains Sprinter, bashing moose riders out of the way as she ran. Something caught his eye, zooming by at the speed of a shooting star. It was Paloma Pronghorn, streaking past the battle. Where was she off to?

The rest of them were all on the Plains Sprinter, including Erik. It was great to see that his dad had escaped the net, but they were in serious trouble. Dozens of moose riders were pressing in from all sides, trying to climb aboard.

Thyri and Luby jumped apart and Chogolisa leapt between them. She plonked Finnbogi next to Ottar at the prow of the Sprinter, said "Get those pigeons in the air!" and left him. He turned to his father.

"They want to find more pigeons!" shouted Erik, clubbing a rider who'd leapt from his moose onto the Sprinter's deck. "I'm needed here! Go on, you can do it! Take them to look for more pigeons!"

Finnbogi closed his eyes.

He was on the ground, in among the pigeons. There was an ant! What a treat...but no, there was something more important, something much more important. He flapped up and looked around.

There weren't nearly enough of them! He felt empty and scared to be among so few. His brothers and sister pigeons were empty and scared, too. But he could help, he would help, he knew where there were more pigeons, many many more.

Follow me! Follow me! I know a flock, a much bigger flock! We can join it, we can fly into the middle of it and fly for days seeing nothing but pigeons! Come, come, let us go! Follow my lead!

The surge of hope from his fellows made him swell with joy as, along with the rest of them, he flapped his wings and took to the air.

The weight of the flock was in his mind. They wanted to go with him, they wanted to be shown the way. He didn't need to get to the front to lead them, he could share the knowledge in his mind. *Fly*, he told his fellows, *let us all fly!*

Out feet are tied! Our feet are tied! a million birds yelled at him as they reached the end of their tethers. *We will peck the tethers!*

No! Leave the tethers! Finnbogi cooed. *We can still fly, can we not? We can still find the others! Pull the tethers with your feet! You see, we can still fly! Remember the flock! Focus on the flock that we will find! Forget the tethers. Let us fly!*

He felt a million pigeon heads bob in agreement. He was the leader. No, he wasn't a leader, he was one of them. He was them, they were him. They were all the leader and they were all the led. It didn't matter. The important thing was that they were on their way to find a bigger flock.

Was there another reason to go? Something about friends being in danger? Nah. That must have been a dream. *Coo coo!* Danger? There was no danger. They were looking for the big flock and he knew where it was, that was all that mattered.

The Plains Strider lurched, then rose two paces. Luby Zephyr pushed another moose rider from the rails with her pole, then risked a look.

The Wootah man Finnbogi was standing at the prow, flapping his arms. Beyond the man who would have looked like an idiot in almost any other situation, the vast flock of crowd pigeons had risen from the plain, lifting the Plains Sprinter by barely visible strings tied to the prow and the legs of each bird.

Planks and struts creaked, squeaked and even screamed, but they held. The wolves that lifted the rear howled, walked, then trotted, then ran.

Ten heartbeats after Luby Zephyr had realised they were moving, they were heading away from the Badlands massif, at the pace of a running wolf. She held onto the rail, bending her knees with the rise and fall of the craft. It was very much like floating down easy rapids on a giant canoe.

The Owsla woman looked about. For the moment, nobody was trying to kill them, which was nice. The moose riders were still galloping alongside, but all their efforts were spent on keeping up.

The Sprinter was still accelerating, directly towards a steep-sided pinnacle of yellow-red rock.

"Left, Finn. Finn, left. LEFT!" Erik the Angry shouted at his head-bobbing, arm-flapping son.

Just when it seemed that collision was inevitable, the craft swung left, missed the pinnacle by an axe's breadth and rolled on.

The moose riders on the right all had to veer away to go around the rock. When they appeared on the other side, they were twenty paces back, and not gaining.

"Which is faster, Sitsi," Luby asked, "wolf or moose?"

"Wolf, but not by a great deal, and only over short distances, and these ones are carrying us and a lot of wood."

"But the moose are all carrying people."

"True. I guess we'll see."

"Why don't you shoot some more of the Badlanders?"

"I've only got five arrows left."

"Ah. And can you see Sofi coming?"

Sitsi scanned the massif. "I can see Pronghorn running back up the cliff that we came down, but no sign of Sofi. Don't worry, I'm sure she'll...oh crap."

"What?"

"Can you see them, on the road to the east?"

Tiny human figures were streaming down the main track into the Badlands massif.

"I can see some people, but I can't—"

"It's the Badland Owsla. Nine of them anyway, Beaver Man isn't with them. They're going a great deal faster than wolves or moose. That guy with bighorn horns is in the lead and... oh no!"

"What?"

"There are Empty Children on bighorn sheep coming down the cliff. If they take control of the pigeons, we're sunk."

"But bighorn sheep can't be as fast as wolves."

"They're not meant to be, but neither are they meant to

carry freaky bald kids who can control animals. I guess we'll see."

The Badland Owsla had already reached the base of the massif and were heading across the plain towards them. The children on bighorns were not far behind.

"Right, Finn," shouted Erik in the prow. "Right. RIGHT!"

Sofi knew the ridge was behind her. She could hear water dripping from the grass that fringed its edge.

It was a delight to be alive, with her hearing and powers of analysis restored. It was even more of a delight to have a second chance against the only person who'd ever beaten her in a fight.

Rappa Hoga tried to mask his moves. He knew how her power worked. It gave him some advantage, maybe, but, now she was back at full strength, not nearly enough. He could feint and dissemble until the buffalo came home, she could still dodge every attack as if he'd announced what he was about to do and then moved with exaggerated slowness.

He was never going to hit her and it was a joy to see his expression change as he realised it.

Now he knew he was in trouble, he wasn't toying or try-ing to wear her down, he was trying to end the fight with every blow. She jinked left, right, back, then ducked as the axe flashed over her head, and prepared to jump to the left to avoid the kick that was coming in a heartbeat.

His foot came at her knee, followed by a jab with his left fist and a downward diagonal swipe with the axe. It would have been a great move, if Sofi hadn't seen it coming as clearly as a flaming buffalo galloping towards her at night.

She heard the ridge getting closer and closer behind her. She heard Rappa Hoga's breath change. He was about to use the advantage of the ridge and swing a mighty blow that she'd have to jump backwards to avoid. But she knew he knew that's what she was listening for. He was trying to trick her into dropping to the ground to avoid it. Again, a clever move. When she'd been owl-less for a while it would have worked. But now she could hear the skin of his arm shift against his torso in preparation for a different strike.

So she leapt. As Rappa Hoga's axe swished below her, Sofi cracked her stone axe into his temple.

He was stunned for a heartbeat. Here was her chance.

Sofi landed on the ridge and leapt again, powering every muscle and loading all her weight into possibly the hardest kick that she'd ever delivered. Her foot whacked into the side of his head and he fell.

She landed and looked to the cat cavalry. They were watching open-mouthed.

"No pursuit before noon!" she shouted, then ran for the edge of the Badlands massif and freedom.

Part Three

To the Shining Mountains

Chapter 1

Chain Running

"Hello," said Sofi Tornado, as Paloma Pronghorn appeared in the gap at the edge of the massif. Paloma's eyebrows jumped like caterpillars on a flicked blanket as she squeaked and leapt lissomly backwards. Then she tried to mask her surprise. "You were taking your time, so—"

Sofi held up a finger and surveyed the plain below.

A huge flock of crowd pigeons was pulling the Plains Sprinter south, leaving behind a couple of dozen pursuing moose cavalry. Sofi almost smiled. She hadn't expected Erik to manage it.

To the east, however, there was plenty to stop her smiling.

Sprinting at an unnatural pace from the massif were nine Badlander Owsla and six Empty Children on bighorn sheep. She'd seen the Badlands' Owsla leap about the land with an athleticism that only Paloma could match. She'd heard that they'd ripped the Calnian army apart as least as effectively as her own Owsla would have done. Now they were running towards the Plains Sprinter faster, she was pretty sure, than she herself could run. And there were nine of them, against five Owsla. On the bright side, there would have been ten of them had Luby Zephyr not killed one, so they were vulnerable.

The bighorn sheep were keeping pace with the naked Badlanders with ease, which was odd, but way down in the league of odd things that she'd seen since they'd left Calnia.

Beyond them all, running away to the south-east in a great loping stride, was a large, hairy human figure, which had to be the squatch from the arena.

"Let's go, fast as we can."

"Shall we?" Paloma held out her palms and looked at her questioningly.

"Let's."

Paloma turned and reached her arms backwards. Sofi gripped the runner's wrists. Paloma gripped Sofi's wrists, then ran off the edge.

It felt like Sofi's arms must surely rip from their sockets, then she was flying. Paloma sprinted down the near-vertical slope with Sofi bouncing behind her, touching the ground once for maybe every twenty of Paloma's paces. It was faster than falling. They'd reached the bottom before Sofi remembered to breathe.

"Are you all right?" yelled Paloma as they tore across the plain.

"Never better!" shouted Sofi, and it wasn't far from the truth. Were they going at half Paloma's speed? Maybe not even that fast. But it was perhaps ten times as fast as Sofi could run herself and it felt fantastic. If Sofi could have spent a day as anyone else in the world, it would have been Paloma.

The Badland Owsla fell behind them to the east. The moose cavalry and Plains Sprinter were closer and closer. They ran through the moose cavalry, who didn't have time to do anything other than look surprised. They passed the snapping, springing wolves harnessed in a line to the Sprinter's stern, then Paloma slowed as they came alongside.

Chogolisa Earthquake grabbed Sofi by the arm and hauled her aboard. Paloma leapt and landed on the wooden deck in a crouch, one hand flat on the ground in front of her and one fanned on a straight arm behind her in an unnecessarily flamboyant display.

They'd made it.

Finnbogi stood at the prow on tiptoes, flapping his arms and nodding his head in an excellent impersonation of a crowd pigeon. Sofi staggered to her feet on the deck, and came as close to laughing out loud as she had in all her adult years. Next to Finnbogi, Erik shouted instructions. Ottar stood watching Finnbogi, laughing and clapping, as well he might.

The young Wootah man had done well.

Father and son had manoeuvred the craft into one of the broad buffalo roads, so there should be no sudden surprises like a big rock or a cliff in their path. They were currently heading slightly uphill, through a prairie dog city. Wave after wave of the little animals ran and dived into their burrows when they spotted the Sprinter bearing down on them.

The rest of the Owsla and Wootah were on the side rail, spreading their weight around the vessel. While they'd been planning the escape, Erik had spent far too long explaining why this would be necessary.

The Swan Empress Ayanna, sitting against the rail suckling her child, nodded to Sofi, who nodded back. Yoki Choppa dipped his head in greeting. Chogolisa and Luby beamed at her. The rest of her women were there, all looking pleased to see her. The only two who didn't greet her were Sitsi Kestrel and Keef the Berserker. They were standing together at the back of the craft, watching their pursuers. Sitsi's little finger was touching Keef's where they were holding the rail. Was something happening there, wondered Sofi?

She went to join them, legs wide to counter the rolling of the Sprinter.

Twenty paces back, and falling further away every heart-beat, were two dozen moose cavalry.

Two hundred paces behind them, catching slowly but surely, were the naked nine of the Badlands Owsla and six Empty Children, whose bighorn sheep were still running a lot faster than bighorn sheep were meant to run.

There was no sign of the dagger-tooth cavalry. Sofi didn't

expect to see them. She was pretty sure that Rappa Hoga would rather die than break his word and pursue them before noon. If you could judge someone in a few heartbeats—and Sofi thought you could—the woman that Rappa Hoga had deputised seemed like the honourable sort, too. So whether Rappa Hoga came round or not, she did not expect to see the dagger-tooth cat cavalry.

"How many arrows left, Sitsi?" she asked.

"Five."

"Hmmmm."

Sofi began to plan how they'd fight the Badland Owsla, but was interrupted by screaming roars ringing out from the north-east. It was a sound that she recognised from five days before.

The fearful cries reverberated from the massif again and again, louder and louder.

The lizard kings were coming.

Chapter 2

Finnbogi the Pigeon

Tansy Burna stood with Rappa Hoga on the edge of the Badlands massif, their dagger-tooth mounts pacing about behind them, pissed off that there was nowhere dry to lie down.

They watched the moose cavalry and the Owsla stream after the Plains Sprinter. Far to the east, six thunder lizards had joined the chase.

"They're doing well, the Wootah and Calnians," said Tansy.

"The lizard kings will catch them."

"They will, but they are survivors. If anyone can defeat the lizard kings, or at least escape them..."

Rappa Hoga turned to her. "It sounds like you want them to get away."

"Of course not. They're enemies of the Badlands. One of them nearly killed Beaver Man, or at least hurt him badly. I'd never..." she noticed the look on his face, "why...do *you* want them to get away?"

He looked down at her, eyes dark and deep. He held her gaze for a good long while. The wind blowing up from the plain below played with his long black hair.

"We are Badlanders," he said eventually. "We are commanded to catch them and that's what we will try to do."

"So we head now?"

"No, we wait till noon, as I agreed."

"They'll head for the Black Mountains."

"They will."

"The Plains Sprinter will have to go south a good way around the massif before it can turn west for the mountains. If we were to head due west, then..."

"No. We will follow their track."

"But we might be able to head them off. With the head start they'll have we'll never catch up if we simply—"

"I said we will follow their track."

"You really *don't* want to catch them, do you?"

"That's enough, Tansy Burna."

Sassa Lipchewer sat with her back against the left-hand rail, swaying with the rumbling pitch and yaw of the Plains Sprinter, one hand holding a wooden upright, the other on her stomach.

As she'd shot her final arrow at the moose cavalry, a sharp twinge had flared across one side of her torso. Now it was a dull ache that burst with pain when she moved. It was a muscle strain, she told herself. Just a muscle strain. The baby was fine. The baby's life *wasn't* ebbing away as she sat there, unable to do anything to help it...

No, it was no good! *She knew her baby was dead!* She'd killed it with all the stupid leaping about and all that fucking archery!

She crushed her eyes shut to squeeze back tears, then opened them and glared at the Swan Empress Ayanna, nursing her son on the other side of the Plains Sprinter.

Sassa should have been back in Hardwork, with her mother telling her that all was fine with the pregnancy, and to stop fussing. But, no, her mother was with the gods and she was adventuring across the land, her hair chopped into a silly ridge, being attacked by demons and monsters and the land itself and it was all because *that woman over there had sent people to kill them all!* And now, not only did Ayanna have the gall to carry on as if she hadn't ordered the deaths of all their loved ones, she had the temerity to be showing off her happy, healthy baby all the fuck-a-duck time.

East of the Water Mother, Sassa had killed two people— murdered them. She'd killed more since, that very morning, but it couldn't be called murder if they were trying to kill you, could it? And Garth's death had been him or Finnbogi, so the gods would probably give her some leeway there. However, she had straight up murdered Hrolf the Painter. She'd justified it a million ways to herself since, but really, if she was honest, she'd killed him because she didn't like the pervy way he looked at her, and because she was pretty certain she'd get away with it. If she'd been able to go back in time and retake the decision, she'd have killed the bastard again.

Point was, she'd murdered before and she'd forgiven her- self. She'd told herself that that was all in her old life, back on the other side of the Water Mother. It was a new life now, all transgressions to the east of the Water Mother absolved.

However, it did look an awful lot like she was going to have to transgress really quite seriously again by killing Ayanna. They were running from monsters, the baby inside her was dead, her family was dead, and it was all Ayanna's fault. Pun- ishment was due.

A stab of pain across her stomach made her jump. *Deep throat a goat. Her baby!*

She mustn't dwell, she told herself, or she'd scream and wail and everyone would know. Besides, on the slim chance that the tiny growing person was still alive, she should try to stay calm.

She decided to focus on external problems, and stood to see how their escape was progressing.

It was not the most calming of decisions.

The Badland Owsla and the Empty Children had overtaken

the moose cavalry and were maybe fifty paces behind the Plains Sprinter. A long way back, several hundred paces at least, came the gigantic thunder lizards. They were gaining slowly.

Sofi Tornado, Sitsi Kestrel, Keef and Wulf were standing at the back rail, between barrels full of the spiders that wove the pigeons' tethers. Everybody else was where Erik had told them to be, spread around to balance the bizarre land boat.

"Beaver Man is riding the lead thunder lizard!" called out Sitsi Kestrel.

Sofi nodded. "Shoot five of the Empty Children with your remaining arrows."

Sitsi strung her bow and raised it.

"No!" cried Erik, half running, half stumbling back down the rolling craft. "We do not kill the children."

Sofi sighed. "They will be in range soon to control the pigeons. When they are, the Plains Sprinter will stop and you will be stamped to death by monsters, if you're lucky enough to die that quickly."

Sassa noticed that Sofi had said "you" and not "we." Clearly the Owsla captain had no intention of sticking around to get killed herself. How bad would things have to get before the Calnians abandoned the Wootah to the Badlanders? Probably not much worse than they were...

"We cannot swap children's lives for our own," Erik insisted.

"There are six of them. There are eighteen of us. Six of them to save eighteen of us. It works for me, moral-wise."

Erik looked around the Plains Sprinter, nodding as he counted. The exact numbers weren't really the point, but Sassa slightly adored him for doing it.

"Seventeen!" he called triumphantly at the end.

"You left out Calnian."

"Calnian? Who the Hel is Calnian?"

"Ayanna's baby."

"Oh. Yes. Eighteen."

And Sassa liked Erik just a little less again. Men really did not give a flying fuck about babies.

"Still," Erik continued, "we cannot kill children. Try it, and you'll be fighting me as well."

"Me, too!" called Wulf.

Sofi sighed. "Hold for now, Sitsi. But if the pigeons lose so much as a pace in height, five of those children are dead."

"And the other one?"

"Maybe Finnbogi will be able to hold control against one. Otherwise Paloma will be able to run at it and take it out."

"I will?" Paloma asked.

"You will."

Sofi Tornado turned to survey the Plains Sprinter, eyes harder than Wulf's hammer. She was a compassion-free, battle-forged warrior to whom death and killing were as normal as breakfast.

Those warrior's eyes met Sassa's. Sassa tried to look like a warrior herself. She was ready to fight. She wasn't a paranoid pregnant woman terrified that her baby had died inside her. Sofi switched her glare to Ayanna and her child. Then she looked straight back at Sassa.

She knew. She knew she'd thought about murdering the empress.

Sofi walked towards Sassa, strong yet lithe, solid yet vital, every muscle and sinew shouting out that here was as fine a fighter as alchemy and a lifetime's training could produce. She was undeniably the most impressive looking human that Sassa had ever seen.

The wonderful warrior stood in front of her. Sassa flinched. Sofi placed a hand on her shoulder. Sassa guessed she was about to rip her head off and tried to brace her neck, but instead Sofi leant in so that her mouth was a finger's breadth from the Wootah woman's ear. She *smelled* strong.

"Your baby," she whispered, "is alive, healthy and growing exactly as it should be. The moment that changes I will let you know, but it won't. Growing babies are a lot tougher than you'd think."

Sofi returned to the back rail.

Sassa blinked. She placed a hand on her stomach. Could she feel the heartbeat? She rather thought she could. She smiled as tears pricked the edges of her eyes.

She looked across at Ayanna, nursing her son. Suddenly she felt lighter. She was looking at a mother, nursing a baby. Maybe Ayanna had ordered their deaths, but she hadn't known them... still. But if all Sassa's transgressions east of the Water Mother were forgiven, then, she reasoned, she should probably extend the same courtesy to Ayanna.

Finnbogi the Boggy was no longer Finnbogi the Boggy. He was a crowd pigeon. Not even Finnbogi the Pigeon. Just a pigeon.

He considered soaring, maybe diving, perhaps dipping a little. But, no, it wasn't about that. It was about being with them all, about beating his wings and flying with all of them, finally part of something! They flew as one, they were together, they *were* one. He could fly, and flying was okay, but it was nothing compared to the joy of being one little member of a massive community. And that community was going to get bigger, much bigger! Up ahead, to the west, was an unimaginably large flock. They just had to fly on and—

"Left, Finn, left!" a voice he recognised rang out. It was a voice of authority and he knew he should—they all should—do what it said. He agreed, they all agreed, so they all dipped a wing and turned leftwards.

"Well done!" said the voice. Finnbogi was pleased that he'd pleased it. They were all pleased. Turning had helped. They were closer to the others now, and getting ever closer.

"Can you speed up?" asked the authoritative voice.

We probably can, can't we, thought Finnbogi and all of them. They beat their wings a little harder and then . . .

No! What was this?

We want to turn! said the others.

We do? No, no no. The others are west, cooed Finnbogi. *We have to go south first, then turn west.*

But he could feel the rest of them turning the wrong way. It was no surprise that he hadn't convinced them. He was no leader. *He* wanted to turn now, even though he knew it was wrong. Or was it wrong? It wasn't wrong if everyone else thought it was right.

"Turn back, Finn! You can do it!" said the voice. But, no, the voice wasn't a pigeon. The pigeons wanted to turn and Finnbogi was a pigeon and the pigeons were him. Turning back was what it was all about now and the idea of it made his pigeon chest swell all the more.

He joined in the new communal chant. *Turn back! Turn back to the north! Turn back!*

"Sitsi, take out five Empty Children," Sofi gave the order reluctantly, knowing Erik would object. She didn't give a crap about the weird kids, she was worried only about the people she was leading out of the Badlands. The Empty Children were overriding Finnbogi and the vehicle was veering north, back towards the Badlands massif. By the way Finnbogi was turning northwards himself, arms outstretched, they were in his mind, too.

"You will not shoot them!" Erik yelled, running back from the prow. He might have sounded more commanding had the pitch of the vehicle not made him zigzag like the superbly drunk man Sofi had once seen trying to run across the Plaza of Innowak.

"Hey, Sofi," called Gunnhild Kristlover from her place on the right-hand rail. Sofi ignored her. One Wootah's disagreement was quite enough for her. She had no need to listen to whatever dreary platitudes old Mrs. Deadweight had to spout.

"It must be done, Erik."

Erik hefted his war club.

Wulf left his place at the rail to stand next to Erik, the hammer Thunderbolt in his hand.

"I'm not going to falter," explained Sofi, "I'll knock both of you out if needs be. Sitsi, shoot them."

"Sofi, listen!" shouted Gunnhild.

Sofi looked at her. "What."

"How about shooting the bighorn sheep, and not the children? We all eat meat, don't we, Erik, so you can hardly disagree with the idea of killing animals to save our lives?"

Brilliant. "Sitsi, shoot the sheep," Sofi barked.

Moments later five sheep were down and their mounts were tumbling.

Sofi nodded thanks at Gunnhild. Why hadn't she thought of shooting the sheep?

One Empty Child rode on among the naked, sprinting Owsla men, oblivious to its siblings sprawling on the plain behind.

Annoyingly, while the buffalo road turned towards the west and the Black Mountains, the Sprinter's course carried on bending around to the north, so it seemed that the single Empty Child still had the upper hand over Finnbogi. Sofi would give the young Wootah man a few moments to wrestle back control, then send Paloma to take out the remaining sheep. The Badland Owsla, as if guessing her intention, clustered round the running bighorn.

"West!" Erik shouted to Finnbogi as he ran back up the Sprinter. "We have to turn west!"

North, north, we're all turning to the north. Finnbogi liked flapping, flapping was wonderful, but this stretch and turn manoeuvre was even better. The best thing about it was that they were all doing it because they all wanted to do it. He vaguely remembered not wanting to turn. What an idiot he'd been. There were so many of them, all moving together!

West! He heard a voice shout.

Hang on. That was why he hadn't wanted to turn! This would be even better with even more or them, and more of them, many many more, were to the west, not the north. They'd gone past whatever obstacle had forced them to go south, and now they could focus on going west, towards the mega-flock. *Come on everyone, this is wrong! We have to turn west!*

A weighty body whumped into him from above, forcing him down. Another one struck, and he was out of the flock! He fought to stay airborne. He had to get back, in among his siblings. Two more pigeons were coming at him, one each side. He slowed and dodged the first, then accelerated to avoid the second, but the tether around his ankle jerked him back and a claw flashed across his face.

He fell. His wings clipped the grass but this time the tether helped, jerking him backwards and upwards. He strained to gain altitude, to get back into the warm body of the flock. Why had they attacked him? He *had* to get back into the flock!

No, you don't. You don't belong in the flock. You disagree. You don't want to turn north. You are bad for the flock. Dash yourself on that rock up ahead. Kill yourself.

Righty-ho then, he thought, readjusting his course for the rock. *Time to die.*

As he dived towards his death alone, loneliness struck him and he remembered the flock, and he remembered the greater flock to the west. He had to unite them.

I will not kill myself! He flapped upwards.

A pigeon was on him, its talons dug into the leading edge of his left wing. He flapped his right madly, but another pigeon dived in and there were talons in his right wing, too.

They forced him down.

Lower and lower they went, further and further from the other birds. The sense of loss on leaving the flock was far more powerful that the pain of talons dug into his wings.

They veered towards a pinnacle of rock, then dived at it.

He struggled but they held his wings. He tried to do something with his legs, but they were short and useless. His attackers were clear of his pecking range. He cooed with rage, but that didn't help at all.

He called the others. They didn't respond. He knew why; he could feel it, too. The desire to fly north was immense, it was almost all-encompassing, but only almost. He *knew* they had to head west. They had to find the other flock. Numbers, numbers, the more the better!

You are wrong. You must die. Kill yourself.

There were a million pigeon voices, all shouting at him, and, do you know what, they were right. How could his path be the right one, when they were a million and he was one? One had no value. And when one disagreed with the flock it was worse than worthless. It was a danger to all. They were right, he had to kill himself. It was for the good of his flock.

Let go of my wings, friends, he told them. *Return to the flock and waste no more effort on me. Thank you for showing me the way.*

Well done, they told him. *You went astray but your last act is a noble one.*

The birds released their grip.

Finnbogi folded his wings and dived headfirst towards the rock. Pigeon skulls were thin. It shouldn't be too painful.

Why did he know about pigeon skulls? How did he know he was a pigeon? Something popped in his head. *No! He* was right, the flock had to go west. Diving headfirst into a rock was the very last thing he wanted to do.

The ground hurtled up at him. He spread his wings, desperate to stop. It was far too late. He was going to hit the rock, hard.

Go west, all of you, all of us! he cooed as he fell, hoping to put the flock right before he died. *That's where the numbers are!*

The rock rushed towards him. Finnbogi flapped frantically. He was going to hit, there was no doubt about that.

He managed to turn, so that his claws were foremost, and *whump!* he crashed.

He was winded, he'd lost feathers, but nothing was broken. A couple of restorative bobs of the head and he was ready to go. Above him the flock flew on, thousands upon thousand of them, still turning to the north. He'd change that.

Cooo! Die, flock deceiver! Cooo! A single pigeon was diving directly at him, beak first. He was coming in fast, sure of his target.

But Finnbogi had learned to dodge.

He flapped aside at the last moment. There was a crunching splat as the other bird demonstrated that pigeon skulls were thin indeed.

Brothers, sisters, Finnbogi called as he flew back up to the flock. *Westwards! We will find numbers there! They will welcome us in! So vast our flock will be, that the majority of us will rarely see land or sky as we fly. We won't know whether it is day or night because there will be nothing but pigeon after pigeon after pigeon after pigeon all around us.*

You're right, said the collective mind of the flock with gleeful relief. *Come in, come among us, let us turn to the west. The west!*

"Paloma," said Sofi, "you're going to have to take out that last Empty Child."

Sofi pointed at the bighorn sheep and its rider, galloping along in the middle of all the sprinting Badlander Owsla. As if she'd shot an arrow from her finger, the child fell from his mount. The bighorn ran on. The Empty Child lay prone on the prairie.

The Plains Strider creaked as the draught pigeons shifted their course back to westward.

"When did you learn that?" asked Paloma.

Chapter 3

Naked Men and the Death of an Owsla

Sitsi Kestrel searched the Plains Sprinter for projectile weapons. She found none, other than the structure of the craft itself, which they could break up and hurl at attackers if it came to that. Not that a few chunks of wood would do much good against the Badlander Owsla, let alone the thunder lizards.

They'd changed course so that they were heading west and a little north. Sitsi was fairly certain it was the right direction.

She knew that the Black Mountains were around seventy miles west of the Badlands. She'd learned that the Green tribe inhabited the Black Mountains, that they were enemies of the Badlanders, and that the Badlanders didn't dare enter the forests of the Black Mountains.

However, her information might have been out of date or simply wrong; it wouldn't have been the first time the geographers had made mistakes after believing a mendacious traveller. The Badlanders might have killed or enslaved the Green tribe, or even become their allies. Or maybe the Greens were worse than the Badlanders and even greater horrors awaited the Calnians and the Wootah? Maybe that was why the Badlanders never went into the Green Mountains?

However, she'd told the others that the Green Mountains would be safe and they'd taken her at her word. It was something of a worry.

A far more pressing worry was the Badlander Owsla,

twenty paces behind and galloping closer with every stride. Eight of them were more or less identical; fit young men, naked and unarmed, running at the same pace, showing no signs of tiring. One was different. He was about the same size, but he had bighorn sheep horns. By the bright red skin and the pus oozing around the horn's edges, they appeared to have been grafted onto his head, not entirely successfully. Sitsi wondered how useful the horns would be in a fight. She was going to find out soon.

The change in course meant that the lizard kings were out of sight, for now at least. They still heard the odd screaming roar, but the beasts didn't seem any closer. Which was lucky, because Sitsi could only see one plan.

"We're going to have to stop and deal with their Owsla, aren't we?" she asked Sofi.

"No. I don't want to stop." Sofi looked troubled. It was not a common look for her and Sitsi did not like it.

"What are you worrying about?" Wulf the Fat was walking down the craft towards them, legs wide to keep his balance.

"Can we go any faster, Erik?" shouted Sofi.

"I don't think so," he called back.

"So." Sofi addressed Wulf. "The Badlander Owsla will catch us up within the next couple of miles. If they've got any brains, which they probably have, they'll disable the wolves carrying the back of the Sprinter. We'll grind to a halt. We might defeat the Badlanders—or maybe not, they are alchemically powered too and they outnumber us—but if they disable the Sprinter the lizard kings will catch up and then we're fucked."

"Could we hide from the lizard kings?"

"Possibly, but that would give the dagger-cat cavalry time to reach us and they'll sniff us out. We have to get to the Black Mountains today, and the only way for all of us to do that is to keep the Plains Sprinter running."

Wulf nodded. Sitsi knew that he knew that the Calnians

could desert the Wootah and run to safety. She hoped he appreciated their sacrifice, and hoped that it wouldn't come to any of the Owsla actually sacrificing themselves.

"So what do we do?" asked Wulf.

"Chogolisa, Paloma, Sitsi, Luby and I will jump out and take on the Badlanders. Finnbogi will slow the craft so that we can catch up when we're done."

"I will come with you. So will Keef, Erik and Thyri."

"No."

"I don't mean to be a dick about it, Sofi, but the Hird would sooner die than sit back while others fight for them."

"Erik's needed on board to tell Finnbogi what to do."

"Sassa can do that," called Erik from the front. "He'll listen to her. Sassa! Come up here and whisper in Finnbogi's ear to go a little to the left and then a little to the right."

She did it, and it worked.

"I don't like the way he's grinning when I tell him what to do," Sassa wrinkled her nose.

"Don't worry. He's a pigeon at the moment, enjoying pigeon thoughts." Erik walked towards the stern. "I'm coming with you."

Sofi sighed. "All right. Chogolisa and the Wootah, get ready on the north rail. Luby, Paloma, Sitsi, with me. Sassa, get Finnbogi to slow a little. Everyone jump when I say."

Sitsi jogged over to Sassa to borrow her knife again then joined the others. Wulf was telling the Wootah and Chogolisa the formation he wanted—a triangle with the giant woman at the front.

Sofi was silent. There would be no formation on her side. Owsla fought alone.

Sitsi climbed onto the rail.

The Badlanders saw what they were doing, grinned and beckoned to them. They were fit, they were young, they were alchemically enhanced. Chances were their confidence was not misplaced.

Was this the best idea, she wondered?

"Go!" Sofi shouted.

Sitsi Kestrel landed with Sofi Tornado on one side and Luby Zephyr and Paloma Pronghorn on the other. In a fight, that was about the best place one could be.

The Badlander Owsla slowed to a walk and split into two. Four of them came at Sitsi's group. The other five, including the bighorn guy, headed for the Wootah and Chogolisa.

"Spread out," said Sofi.

The Badlanders' nudity was distracting and not in a good way. It just made them look all the odder because they were all so freakishly similar, like figures carved by the same carpenter. Sitsi guessed they must be brothers, three sets of triplets perhaps or maybe even all born at the same time. They walked with a swing, smiling confidently. They looked more like cheery strangers about to spark an unwelcome conversation than warriors about to attack.

Then they sprang; one at Paloma, one at Luby, two at Sofi.

Sitsi had a millionth of a heartbeat to be offended that they'd ignored her, presumably because she was the smallest, before shock almost brought her to a standstill.

The two that attacked Sofi took her down. The Badlanders grabbed the arms of the best warrior in the world, hooked their feet under hers, and threw her to the ground.

Each attacker kept hold of one of Sofi's wrists with one hand and raised the other in a fist to drive down into her face.

Sitsi didn't have time to see how Paloma and Luby were getting on. She leapt at Sofi's nearest Badlander, iron knife flashing, and stabbed him through the back of his neck.

He stopped punching Sofi but, instead of falling to the ground and dying like any other reasonable human, he swung his arm across in a blur, grabbed Sitsi by her neck and stood, lifting her off her feet.

Sitsi flailed uselessly. She couldn't kick him, she couldn't hit him with any strength. And she couldn't breathe.

The Badlander smiled and tightened his grip.

Ayanna watched from the back rail of the Plains Sprinter alongside Gunnhild, Bodil and the two children. Yoki Choppa was over to one side, hunched over his smoking alchemical bowl. Below them the row of wolves loped along, seemingly resigned to their fate now, or at least no longer snarling and barking.

The empress gasped as Sofi was knocked down, held and punched by two Badlanders. That should have been impossible. Sitsi tried to rescue her and was taken out immediately by one of Sofi's attackers. Ah, thought Ayanna, Sofi will spring up now. But no. Her attacker kept her pinned, punching her face again and again.

Luby Zephyr was wrestling with one of them on the ground and Paloma was in a running, leaping, fist fight with another.

The Wootah and Chogolisa Earthquake were faring better. They were in a tight triangle. At the front was Chogolisa, armed with a log. On the left were Erik with his club and Thyri with her blade, and on the right were Wulf with his hammer and Keef with his long axe. The Badlanders were running at them again and again and retreating again and again.

One of the naked men tried to break the stand-off by leaping over Chogolisa's swinging log, but Keef caught him in the stomach on his axe's pointed end, then wrenched the weapon free as the Badlander fell.

The Badlander landed on his feet and kept coming, but guts flopped out of his opened stomach, tangled with his legs and he went down.

Ayanna looked back to her women, caught a glimpse of Paloma leaping into a tree followed by a Badlander, but then the Plains Strider rounded a corner and they were out of sight.

Ayanna looked about herself. Finnbogi was flapping his arms at the prow, playing pigeon. Sassa was next to him, staring ahead and telling him where to go. Bodil and Gunnhild were gawping over the back rail. Ottar and Freydis had returned to the places that Erik had assigned them on either side, halfway up the craft. The boy was fussing over his two racoon cubs. Freydis was leaning over the rail, watching the world go by, playing with her hair and singing.

Why had she wanted them dead? These were not destroyers of the world, and they certainly weren't part of some Badlands plot. If she hadn't sent her Owsla to kill these honourable innocents, then surely Chippaminka wouldn't have been able to enchant them all? Perhaps the Wootah were loved by the gods, as the Goachica had believed, and all that had gone wrong for Calnia was a punishment from those gods for attacking them? She should have stopped when her lover and Calnian's father Kimaman had been killed. That should have been sign enough.

She turned to Yoki Choppa, but Yoki Choppa had gone. Ayanna looked about the Plains Strider. The strange little warlock was nowhere to be seen.

Sofi dodged and dodged. Innowak knew how they'd taken her down, but she could hear the punches coming and she could avoid them, for now at least. Sitsi ran in, which took one attacker away, but the other had managed to pin Sofi's arms with his legs, and, annoyingly, he was stronger than she was and much, much heavier than a man his size should have been.

She writhed and convulsed but could not shift his bulk. Behind the man pinning her she could see her other attacker choking Sitsi to death. She had to get free.

In her frustration, she misjudged one of his punches and it whacked her chin. That shocked her enough to mistime the next dodge, so his punch cracked into her temple. She avoided two more, but she was slowed and out of synch. A blow landed on her forehead. The pain blinded her for a moment and another punch cracked into her chin.

Then a hand closed around her throat and began to squeeze. Her arms were pinned! She tried to buck but he was too heavy. She tried to hook him with her legs but he was too far forward.

Sparks danced in her eyes and her thoughts began to cloud. She was in trouble.

Erik looked at the grinning Badlander with his bighorn horns. *How come all these Badlander dicks grin so much?* he wondered.

"Hold the formation!" cried Wulf.

Keef had gutted one and Chogolisa had broken another's legs with her log, but there were three more and Erik did not like the look of this bighorn bastard.

As if to confirm his worries, Bighorn charged, directly at Erik. He swung his club but Bighorn dived under its arc and struck him, headfirst, in the gut.

The next moment he was lying on the ground. Bighorn had him gripped by the shirt and was pulling his head back for a butt that Erik did not want to receive. Bighorn looked him in the eye as if to savour the moment and, because he was a dreadful Badland bastard, grinned at him.

There was a crack! Bighorn's grin melted as his eyes crossed to look at the fissure that had opened up down the centre of his bighorn skull.

"Bighorn, meet my friend from the age of iron!" cried Wulf the Fat, swinging Thunderbolt for a second blow.

Luby Zephyr swung her moon blades but the Badlander avoided them, grabbed her arms, and they were down, rolling and wrestling. She drove her palm into his chin, a killer move on anyone else, but he barely noticed it. She gouged his eye but he seemed to enjoy it. He countered every attack. He was stronger and faster and slippery as a greased fish and she was fucked.

She struggled up. If she could get just a few paces away, to the trees, she'd be able to use her stealth and disappear. But he grabbed one of her feet and she was down again and then he was on her back. He took her head in his hands and there was nothing she could do. Nothing.

Fuck, she thought.

He twisted. Her neck broke.

She could still see. She knew she wasn't breathing and she knew she was going to die. One good thing about having your spine severed so high up, she thought, was that there was no pain.

She could see the Badlander punching Sofi, she could see the other one strangling Sitsi.

Was this the end of the Owsla, the death of her little gang?

All those times in the Plaza of Innowak when they'd killed other groups of warriors, all of those had seemed like a game, as if only the Owsla were real and the others had all been created purely to entertain the crowd. Never for a second had she considered the possibility that her group might be slaughtered by another.

But there you go. She guessed it had to happen to everyone eventually.

As the world slipped peacefully away, she wondered if her parents would ever learn how she died and what they would say to their friends. They'd probably be embarrassed.

Ayanna was distracted from her vigil at the back rail of the Plains Sprinter by Ottar the Moaner, speaking emphatically but unintelligibly to his sister. Freydis the Annoying's mouth was ever wider, then tears sprang in her eyes and she shook with sobs. Ottar, too, began crying.

Sassa and Finnbogi were busy controlling the craft and Bodil and Gunnhild, watching over the back rail, hadn't heard the children.

Carrying Calnian in one arm, Ayanna walked over to

Freydis. It was easier to move about now the craft was travelling more slowly.

"What's wrong, little girl?" she asked.

Freydis sniffed and looked up at her, her blue eyes shining with tears. "Something sad has happened," she said.

Ayanna felt a sob rise in her own throat. She squatted and lifted her spare arm. "Come here," she said, "both of you."

Ottar and Freydis ran in and hugged her. They were slight things; she could feel their ribs rising and falling as they sobbed with their hot little bodies pressed against her and Calnian. They weren't alien world destroyers. They were babies, not much older than her own, and they'd been through such horrors and it was all Ayanna's fault.

She wondered what the sad thing was. She didn't want to know just yet. She held the children and let her own tears fall onto Freydis's golden head.

Sofi shook her head and opened her eyes. The naked Badlander was smiling at her, one fist raised. She struggled, but to no avail. The man looked down his torso, then back to her with an even bigger smile, waggling his eyebrows as if to say *take a look at that*. Sofi looked down and saw that he had a large, twitching erection.

Oh, that was too much.

She put all her strength into bucking him off, but he only smiled all the wider. He pulled his fist back.

A shadow flashed over them. She heard a *pouf!* noise. The Badlander flailed and then he was off her, screaming and tearing bloodily at his own face.

Sofi leapt up to see Yoki Choppa reloading a blowpipe with something from his alchemical bowl, eyes and pout focused on his task like a man who's stopped in the street to refasten the fiddly clasp of a bracelet.

A Badlander came at him from behind. Sofi ran but she wasn't going to make it in time.

The warlock ducked the punch without turning or changing his expression, raised his pipe and blew powder into his attacker's face. The Badlander yelped and fell. Yoki Choppa headed for where one of Sofi's original attackers was sitting on Sitsi.

"Sofi! I'm going to do the dive and trip!" Paloma Pronghorn was running towards her, pursued by a Badlander. The speedy Owsla fell to the ground. The pursuing Badlander tripped over her and stumbled. Sofi swung her axe into his temple and he toppled.

"Make sure he's dead, Paloma!" Sofi had to check on the others.

The man who'd been on Sitsi was screaming and clawing at his face after Yoki Choppa's attentions. Sitsi was climbing to her feet.

Ten paces away, Wulf the Fat was hammering the life out of what looked like the last of the Badlander Owsla.

The Badlander who'd been on her was lying prone, still alive, judging by the bubbles coming up through the mess, but he'd clawed his own eyes out and torn off his nose.

Where was Luby Zephyr?

Sofi found her, face down in a bed of yellow and blue flowers.

"Luby?" she called softly, "Luby?"

She couldn't hear breathing or a beating heart. She gripped her friend by the shoulders and gently turned her over. Luby's head flopped to the side. Her neck was broken. Her eyes were shining but she was smiling, as if she'd died contented.

The captain of the Owsla felt a great ball of grief welling in her gut. She shook her head, pushed her grief back down, closed her friend's eyes and jumped up.

"Sitsi?" she called.

"I'm okay," the wide-eyed archer said hoarsely. "He could have killed me, but he was taking his time...It was really horrible, but I'm okay. Thank you, Yoki Choppa."

The warlock shrugged.

Sofi owed her life to him, too, but she'd thank him later. "Is anyone badly injured? Is there anyone who can't run?"

"We're fine over here," called Wulf.

"Chogolisa, carry Luby. Paloma, help the slowest. The rest of you, run after the Plains Sprinter, fast as you can but do pace yourselves." She listened for a moment, "We'll need to run for about two miles. If you become exhausted—"

She was interrupted by the screaming roar of a lizard king ripping through the air. There was another, then another. They were much closer than she would have liked.

"Let's go," she said.

Chapter 4

Lizard Kings

Two miles later, Sofi Tornado sat at the side of the Plains Strider with the dead Luby Zephyr's head on her lap, listening to the lizard kings gallop ever closer.

"We're coming for you!" It was Beaver Man, riding one of the monsters. The bastard knew she could hear him. "I was seriously considering letting all of you live. You amuse me, and so few things do these days. But you killed my boys. Why couldn't you just stop and surrender? Now my pets are going to eat you. Apart from you, Sofi. I'm going to keep you."

His goading didn't affect Sofi, other than to inform her that he was too badly injured to keep up with his monsters on foot. He wasn't the type of man who'd ride when he could run heroically out in front, and, had he been able to, he certainly would have fought with his Owsla.

Good. She looked down at Luby, beautiful and pale. Sofi was going to kill Beaver Man or die trying. His injuries should make it easier. She was not going to be noble about it.

Sitsi reckoned they were twenty miles from the Black Mountains. The lizard kings were half a mile behind, gaining, and would be on them well before they reached safety. Sofi couldn't hear the cat cavalry coming, which probably meant Rappa Hoga had kept his word. But the lizard kings were enough. She had a few plans. She hadn't decided which one to use. They all involved sacrifice.

She sighed, lowered Luby's head gently onto the deck, and stood.

The buffalo road that led towards the Black Mountains was crossing a broad valley towards a notch in a low but steep bluff. A herd of buffalo which had been following the road was galloping away southwards. To the north, dozens of geese were flying away in arrowhead formations and more prong-horns than Sofi had ever seen in one place before were bounding off up the valley.

The valley floor itself was flat, grassy and marshy in places, a break from the lumpy and wooded landscape that they'd been passing through. Fingers of low white cloud reached across the blue sky. They were past the Ocean of Grass. Despite the situation, Sofi was relieved. She'd seen enough prairie to last ten lifetimes.

Still, she'd prefer any amount of soul-sucking savannah to the sight of the six super-lizards cresting the ridge behind them. On the upside, Beaver Man had brought only six of the twelve lizards. On the downside, from what Luby had told her about their imperviousness, he'd need only one.

She walked to the prow. Erik, at the back rail now, turned and opened his mouth to say something—presumably about staying where she was to keep the trim perfect and maintain optimum speed—but he saw the look on her face and stayed quiet.

Sassa Lipchewer was still directing Finnbogi and doing a good job of it. Up ahead, the flock of pigeons flapped on. The constant thin rain of crap tumbling to the ground made them look like a low, vibrating cloud. How, Sofi wondered, did the lower birds avoid being shat on by the birds above? Maybe they didn't.

"How's he doing?" she asked Sassa.

"He's tired but I think he'll make it. I can't be sure. I don't have much experience of young men controlling millions of pigeons."

"He's doing well."

"He is. And...?" The Wootah woman's hand was on her stomach, her eyes wide. Sofi could hear the growing child's heartbeat, so fast that it would have been alarming if she hadn't heard exactly the same rapid beat in women every day in the city of Calnia. This one sounded no different. It was another life for Sofi to save.

She shook her head. How had she gone in such a short time from a taker of lives to a saver of lives? It was a lot more difficult and not nearly as much fun.

"What's wrong?" Sassa asked.

"All is fine with you. I'll tell you if that changes, but, like I said, it won't. Assuming you're not eaten by a lizard king."

"I'm sorry about Luby." The Wootah woman sounded sincere.

"So am I."

Sofi walked back down the Plains Strider, preparing herself. The plan she had which was most certain to take down the lizard kings involved all of the Owsla dying. Other, shakier plans might kill only two of three of them. Every single plan she could come up with was likely to kill herself. It was annoying. Interested as she was to see what happened in the next life, she was keen to make more of this one first.

She stood above the lolloping wolves. The animals weren't tired, according to Erik. Like everything else in the Badlands, it seemed, they'd been messed with alchemically and had unnatural stamina.

"Sofi," said Erik.

"I'll stop walking around now."

"It's not that. I've managed to communicate with the spiders in the barrels. It's easier now they're away from the Empty Children."

Erik was trying to look serious, but Sofi could see he was struggling to hide a smile. He clearly thought he'd come up with something fantastic, and wanted to draw it out as long as possible.

"They're a lot like the bees I trained back in Lakchan territory," he continued. "You just have to—"

"Get to the point, Erik." She was not in the mood for apiary.

"Sorry. Point is, I've been talking to them for a while and I can be quite persuasive. You would not believe how much the spiders hate giant lizards now. They already know they're unnatural. They say the lizard kings had their time, and now it's over."

She'd hoped for something more than this. Of course, she'd considered hurling the spiders at the monsters. But even if the spiders didn't just disperse without biting anything, which they would, the lizard kings had skin that a big man couldn't pierce with a spear when his life depended on it. The spiders couldn't bite through thin slices of wood.

"It doesn't matter how much they hate them, they can't bite them."

Erik's eyes twinkled. "Not on the outside..."

"Come on, Erik, out with it."

"The spiders know they can't bite through the skin. They also know that the lizard kings have stupidly big mouths. They know they have to leap onto its feet, run up its body, get into those big mouths, run down into the dark, look for a soft bit, and bite."

"Really, all the spiders know this?"

"...I'm not sure. I don't know if all of them are persuaded. I'm working on it."

"Can anyone help?"

"Finnbogi, I should think, but he's—"

"Anybody else?"

"No."

"Here." It was Yoki Choppa. "Eat this." He held out what looked like three plant buds.

"What is it?"

"Focuses the mind. It might help."

Erik opened his mouth, presumably to ask why Yoki Choppa hadn't given him the concoction way back in the Badlands.

"Found it when we fought the Badlander owls," Yoki Choppa said before Erik had the words.

Erik did as he was told, then sat and closed his eyes.

They reached the base of the notch in the bluff and the Plains Sprinter slowed as the crowd pigeons towed it up and out of the valley. The lizard kings were halfway across the valley behind them, splashing through a shallow lake, sending up great waves of water and birdlife.

Sofi could see Beaver Man now, clasped round the neck of the rearmost lizard.

"You shouldn't have fled, Sofi," he said sadly. "I had plans for you. With you and Chippaminka at my side, we could have so enriched the world. It's a shame that—"

Sofi stopped listening to him.

The Plains Sprinter crested a rise and accelerated. The Black Mountains were ahead, a low line of dark bumps. The scenery to the west of the valley had reverted a little to dispiriting grassland, but there were enough wooded hillocks and tree-lined ridges to promise more interesting landscape to come. It had been a while since Sofi had been in the mountains. She liked mountains. She hoped she'd get to see these ones.

The Swan Empress Ayanna watched the Wootah children watching the dinosaurs. The boy was open-mouthed, staring in wonder. Freydis, holding his hand, looked sad and sensible.

Why oh why had she fallen for Chippaminka? She'd been weak. She could produce plenty of excuses, she could blame others, but the fact was she should have been stronger. Luby Zephyr had managed to break the enchantment to save her and now Luby was dead.

Freydis said something to Ottar and the boy nodded. Ayanna simply could not bear the idea of watching the Wootah children die, let alone her own baby. She would do whatever she could to save them.

Paloma Pronghorn ran back eastwards. She'd been west to the foothills of the Black Mountains to check the path. Bar the odd herd of deer, which Paloma had scattered just for the distraction of it, the way was unimpeded. The buffalo trail led directly to a valley which cut upwards into the mountains and, apparently, safety. She didn't know why they'd be safe in the mountains, but Sitsi Kestrel said they would be and Sitsi knew everything.

She was running even faster than usual, trying to pound away the sorrow of Luby Zephyr's death, and keen to get back before the rest were eaten by the lizard kings.

Over a rise, and the flock of crowd pigeons pulling the Plains Sprinter came into view. She couldn't see the craft itself yet. The pigeons could be pulling a mangled platform of half-chewed corpses for all Paloma knew.

Finally, she saw the vehicle, with Calnians and Wootah safely aboard. The lizard kings had closed the gap to about a hundred paces, however, so it didn't look like they were going to stay safe for long.

By Innowak, the monsters were amazing, so much larger than any animal Paloma had even imagined before. Although... their enormous thighs were awesome, their huge jaws looked fearsomely powerful, but their weird little weedy arms bounced as they ran, like the limp limbs of an effete boy forced to do sport for the first time.

Paloma sprinted down the hill and leapt aboard. The Wootah and Calnians nodded grim greetings, apart from Finnbogi, who stood at the front, flapping like an exhausted bird that had been flapping far too long and was about to fall from the sky. All of them would probably die very soon. It was a shame. Paloma wasn't going to die herself if she could help it. If it all went completely to shit and there was really no chance left, she would piss off very quickly, dragging Sofi and Sitsi with her. She wouldn't be able to save Chogolisa, Yoki Choppa or any of the Wootah. Sad, but there you go.

"All good ahead, path is clear to the mountains!" she called to Sofi. "Shame about behind!"

Sofi nodded, then turned to Erik. "Now, do you think?"

The beasts were ninety paces away.

"What are you going to do?" asked Paloma.

"Let's give it a crack," said Erik. "Chogolisa?"

Chogolisa Earthquake picked up one of the spider barrels. It was big, nearly as tall as Paloma; big enough, indeed, to hold half the spiders needed to attach silk to all those crowd pigeons.

Paloma saw their plan, but didn't see its point. There was no way their little teeth were going to trouble the lizards.

"High as you can," called Erik.

"No," said Sofi, "just throw it so it smashes."

Chogolisa did as she was bid.

The barrel burst behind the craft in an explosion of shattered wood and orange spiders.

Moments later the first lizard ran over them. The rest followed.

They watched.

The lizards kept coming.

What had they expected?

"Sitsi?" asked Sofi.

"A good number of spiders are on the first lizard and one of the others. They're heading upwards."

Paloma peered. There *were* little orange things scurrying up the legs of the foremost lizard.

"Are they going to crawl up their arses?" she asked.

"Why didn't I think of that?" Erik sounded disappointed.

"But, then again, I guess their arses are clenched pretty tight. I'm not even sure where their arseholes are."

"Sitsi?" asked Sofi.

"They're only on two of them."

"Pigfuckers."

The front-running lizard king realised that it had hundreds of spiders crawling up its body. It roared and scrabbled with those funny little arms, knocking spiders from its chest. It was pretty much, Paloma realised, exactly what she would have done.

"A good number went into its mouth on that roar," said Sitsi.

The monster shook its head, opened its mouth and made an extraordinary CAAAH! sound, retching like a cat with a fur ball in an attempt to force the invaders from its mouth. Instead, more spiders rushed in.

"Throw the other barrel, Chogolisa," said Sofi. "Ten paces past the lead lizard."

The barrel sailed through the air and smashed on the ground. The foremost monster gave up trying to regurgitate the spiders and refocused all its roaring, stomping energies on chasing the Plains Sprinter. It looked like swallowing half a hundred spiders had done it no harm whatsoever at all. It ran through a tree, splintering trunk and branches without slackening its pace.

"It's possible, of course," opined Erik, "that beeba spider venom has no effect on lizard kings. Some animals are immune to venom that's harmful to humans."

The lizards thundered closer, roar-screaming the joys of a chase nearly ended. The second spider-swallowing monster went through the same process as the first; panic, hacking like a pipe addict for a few heartbeats, then resumption of the chase.

"All the other lizards have spiders on them now," said Sitsi after a while, as if it mattered, "bar the one Beaver Man is riding. His ran wide when Chogolisa threw the second barrel."

"Calnians, to me," said Sofi, "Wootah, too."

Everyone gathered round Sofi.

"Are we all agreed that our goal is for Ottar to live, to get to The Meadows?"

Most people nodded grimly. Paloma didn't. Her goal was to live a long and happy life.

"Right. The only person who can run the boy to safety in the Black Mountains and beyond is Paloma. So, when the lizards reach the Plains Sprinter, she will run westwards with him on her shoulders."

"Suits me!" Paloma smiled, "But what about the rest of you?"

"There are six lizards and Beaver Man. We have all of us, a few dozen wolves and a shitload of pigeons. Erik, start communicating with the wolves now. Tell them they hate giant lizards, got it?"

"Got it."

"Wulf, I want you, Thryri and Keef to—"

A scream tore the very air apart.

The lead lizard king yowled like a thousand tortured dogs as it tumbled. It hit the ground with a shuddering boom, then rolled, kicking huge talons skywards. One of its legs kicked harder and faster than the other, crazily fast, then shot vertical. There was a crack like the snapping of a tree trunk and the leg flapped uselessly to the ground.

"On the other hand," said Erik, "it's possible that the spiders need to get quite a long way into the beasts before they find a soft bit. Sofi? Sofi? Are you all right?"

Sofi was crouched on the deck, hands pressed to her ears.

A second thunder lizard scream rent the air, followed almost immediately by another. One by one, the lizards screamed and went down.

Paloma glanced to the prow. Sassa was watching, mouth

open, but Finnbogi was still facing west, flapping wearily for the mountains. Shame, thought Paloma, that he'd missed the death of the lizard kings. He'd have appreciated the spectacle.

Soon five huge corpses were strewn in the wake of the Plains Sprinter, carrion birds already flapping down.

Good luck pecking your way into those fuckers, thought Paloma.

One great beast still pounded after them, Beaver Man's relatively tiny head craning round its neck. They'd won five little battles, thought Paloma, but this one animal was still more than capable of winning the war.

Deviating around its falling herd mates cost it some ground, so it was now about a hundred and fifty paces back. However, it was gaining, if anything, faster than before.

Wulf the Fat tapped Sofi Tornado on the shoulder. "Screaming's over!"

Sofi rose and blinked. The death roars of the lizard kings had felt like two knives pushed into her ears and twisted.

Five monsters down, one left. A good start, but Beaver Man needed only the one thunder lizard to kill them all.

"How far to the mountains, Paloma?"

"Fourteen miles, give or take a half."

Sofi jogged to the prow.

"Can we go any faster, Sassa?"

"No."

"Could you—"

"He's giving it all he's got."

Sofi jogged back. The lizard king was a hundred paces behind.

"I don't suppose we have any more spiders?" she asked nobody in particular.

"We don't," said Wulf.

"Apart from those ones," said Paloma, pointing to where two boards met at the rear right-hand corner of the Sprinter.

Six large pale orange spiders were crushed into the darkest place they could find, writhing over each other to escape the light.

"Only six left," said Sofi.

"They're willing to help," said Erik. "But this time ALL of them need to get inside the lizard."

"Paloma, hands out." Sofi took out the leather alchemy pouch that Gunnhild had made for her and poured desiccated burrowing owl meat into Paloma's hands. Paloma made a face. "Put that somewhere safe," Sofi added.

She squatted above the spiders and flicked them into her bag with the point of her dagger-tooth knife. She worked carefully, bouncing on her heels and ready to leap aside at any moment, but the nasty little animals gave her no trouble.

She stood, a bag containing half a dozen spiders in one hand.

"Anyone got any ideas how we get this deep into a thunder lizard, then open it?" she yelled. She didn't like asking advice, but she could think of only one method that might work. It did not appeal.

"Chogolisa could toss me onto its head?" suggested Sitsi. "I could open the bag and pour the spiders down its throat?"

"That won't get them far enough down, they'll probably be crushed before they get out of the bag, and Beaver Man would kill you before you could act. Anyone else?"

She looked at all the adults in turn and they all shook their heads, apart from Bodil Gooseface who smiled nervously and said: "What is it you're after?"

Yoki Choppa came to stand next to her. The monster was fifty paces back.

"If you stop and leave my craft intact," said Beaver Man so only Sofi could hear, "I'll spare the children."

"If you head back to the Badlands now," called Sofi, "we'll spare your pet."

"No matter, another Plains Sprinter is already under construc—"

He was cut off by a scream-roar from the monster. Sofi covered her ears.

"There is one way," said Ayanna, walking over from her place by the rail when the roar was over, "but you've already thought of it."

Sofi nodded.

"You don't have to do it." The empress smiled sadly. "I will."

"No."

"It's not a request, Sofi Tornado."

"I don't take orders from anyone during a battle, even you."

"Then it is a request."

"The answer is no. Do you doubt your best warrior, Empress?"

"And you're doubting the ability of a woman driven by love for her son and desperate to atone for the disgrace of slaughtering a tribe that didn't deserve it? Not to forget leading twenty thousand of her own warriors to a senseless death, and leaving an empire weak and ripe for decades of tyranny and misery?"

The empress held Sofi's gaze.

The craft joggled along and the beast thundered ever closer. Ayanna was not nearly as physically strong as Sofi, but the job didn't require super-strength.

"Are you sure?"

"I am," nodded Ayanna. "Give me the bag and one of Luby's moon blades." Then, louder, "Chogolisa! You're needed over here."

Erik shifted from foot to foot. They were so nearly clear, they'd come through so much, but this one remaining monster could ruin it all.

Hate the lizard, hate the lizard, he told the wolves again.

We dooo hate it. We want to bite it and kill it.

And you will, but you must wait until you're released.

We will, we will, we will hooowl and run and jump and bite. We want to do it nooooooow.

Sofi's idea was that the wolves would attack the lizard. While it was distracted, Chogolisa would throw Sofi onto its head. She'd blind it with Sassa's iron knife, while dodging Beaver Man's attacks. It wasn't a great plan and Erik felt bad, persuading the wolves into attacking a beast that would kill them.

Hate the lizard, hate the lizard, he told them.

"Erik," said Sofi, pinching his arm to drag his attention away from the wolves, "We're going to try something else that doesn't need the wolves. But keep them ready. We will probably still need them."

"What are you going to do?"

Sofi sighed. "You'll see."

The Swan Empress Ayanna wasn't sure. Of course she wasn't. You'd have to be pretty thick to be certain about a decision like this one. The trick had to be to get on with it before you changed your mind, she guessed. It wasn't like people who'd made decisions like this before had been around afterwards to explain their thought processes.

She stood alone. Gunnhild held Calnian. She couldn't bear to look at him. She already knew every crinkle of his skin, his every expression, his smell. She'd try her best to take those memories to her next life. She'd eaten so many people that she was going to return as something amazing, so she shouldn't be scared of death, she told herself.

She was, however, terrified.

She hoped Calnian lived long enough to be told what she'd done and to understand it. She hoped he lived much, much longer than that, and hoped he would never forget her—or never, at least, forget the memory of what she'd done. She hoped that her son would look at his own children one day and tell them that they were alive because of Ayanna. She hoped that he'd see her looking with love out of the eyes of her descendants.

The lizard stormed ever closer. The foul Beaver Man peered around its neck like a loathsome boil.

She gripped the bag of spiders in one hand and the moon blade in the other.

"I'm ready, Chogolisa," she said to the huge woman. "Pick our moment well, please."

The lizard king reached the rear of the Plains Sprinter, towering above them like a tree over a shrub. Its enormous, three-toed feet slammed down within an arm's reach of the rear rail. There was a doggy squeal. Blood sprayed up from the rank of wolves.

The monster saw death at its feet, roared to the sky, then bent, opened its vast, gaping, tooth-fringed maw and screamed hot, stinking hatred at the Wootah and Calnians.

Chogolisa heaved and Ayanna was flying. She soared between rows of giant lizard teeth and crashed into harsh wetness. She felt the skin rasp from her face—rough tongue like a dog, she thought—then everything turned turtle and she was slithering down and down into dark, pulsing, crushing wetness.

She sucked in a gulp of putrid air, thinking *this is my final breath.*

They'd hoped that if Chogolisa tossed her far enough, the lizard would swallow her without chewing. So far so good. What Ayanna had wondered, but not discussed, was whether she'd drown or be boiled alive by the monster's stomach juices before she could act.

Its neck convulsed around her, forcing her downwards. She clutched the spider bag in her left hand, between her legs, trying to hold it lightly but securely at the same time, while gripping onto Luby Zephyr's moon blade in her right hand.

It was cooler than she'd expected inside the monster. She remembered holding her father's hand on a winter morning, watching the hunters gut a humped bear. It had steamed for an age and her father had told her that all big animals were on fire inside. This one was not.

You believe everything that adults tell you when you're a young child. Who would tell Calnian about the world? Ayanna hoped that whoever brought Calnian up would be bright, interested and informative. Sitsi Kestrel would be good. She should have stipulated that Sitsi be involved in his upbringing. Too late. But Sofi would see him right; she was a good woman, that Sofi Tornado.

She lifted Luby's moon blade and sliced into the inside of the lizard's neck, or wherever she was now. The sharp obsidian weapon slid in easily. So the skin here was soft. Ayanna pumped her fist, slicing and slicing. It was satisfying work. Would it be so bad to be reincarnated as a manual labourer? She'd heard that a day's physical work could be pleasing.

Her cutting met resistance. She put all her strength into it, and whatever had resisted gave way springily, with a gush of liquid.

The movement of the thunder lizard changed. Had it stopped? Had she done it? Had she saved them all? Or were the spiders still needed? Was she far enough down to let them go?

Her face was hot now. Was that the heat of the beast or its acid? Probably the latter. It was very hot. Not far off agonising. Suddenly she realised how much she wanted to breathe. She dropped the blade, opened the neck of the bag and pushed it inside out.

The spiders crawled out over her hands as the heat became unbearable. It felt like the skin was melting off her body, limbs and skull. She screamed. Acid rushed into her throat.

Finnbogi flew on, weary but happy in the flock, and near-euphoric about joining the much larger flock in the west.

But you made that flock up yourself. It doesn't exist. You're not really a pigeon, said some nonsense voice in his head.

He cooed chucklingly at the voice and pigeoned on.

His fellows flapped above, below, in front, behind, to the left and right. Something moved in his gut and he squeezed out guano. The birds below shifted, directed by the group mind to avoid his tumbling effluent.

The group mind noted a flock of cranes flapping towards them from the west, on collision course. It was, for cranes, a large flock, but it saw the crowd pigeons' dramatically larger group and adjusted its course southwards. Several hundred birds above Finnbogi crapped with happiness at being in so much more numerous a throng. He flicked his wingtips, jinked his head and the deluge of guano tumbled harmlessly past.

The mountains are ahead, the way is clear, but where is the other flock? asked the group mind, mildly panicked.

It's probably on the ground, feeding. We'll join it in the feast soon, said Finnbogi.

That makes sense, the million birds said to themselves.

The lizard shook its head, slowed for a moment, then kept coming. Had Ayanna died for nothing? Sitsi Kestrel's bowels churned with horror at the notion.

Erik, Chogolisa, Sofi and Wulf stood at the stern, wide-legged and ready with the poles that had been so effective at keeping the moose cavalry at bay. Sitsi reckoned they'd be about as effective against the lizard king as a few mean words, but it was all they had.

The monster closed the gap. It was not happy. It was shaking its head and was clearly in some degree of discomfort. But it hadn't slowed. By the time it reached them again, it seemed to have resolved the empress-stuck-in-the-throat complaint and got right back into killing rage mood.

It swung its head at the four at the rear of the deck and they backed away. Wulf the Fat ran straight back in and rammed his pole at the beast's eye. The pole splintered on the animal's cheek. Wulf fell forwards onto the boards. The lizard king darted its head down like a wading bird going for a fish.

Chogolisa Earthquake grabbed Wulf's foot and pulled him clear. The lizard king's mouth hit the deck where the Wootah man's head had been a tenth of a heartbeat before. Wood splintered.

Beaver Man, perched on its neck, grinned at them.

Sitsi saw Sofi Tornado run in, leap and ram her dagger-tooth knife into the monster's eye. The knife stuck, the beast seemed unharmed. It turned to Sofi, managing a "you shouldn't have done that" look despite the knife. Beaver Man kept his seat, calm and happy as an emperor waiting for his breakfast. The beast lunged at Sofi. She leapt backwards, heels over her head, and landed hard. The beast leant for her.

Sofi scrabbled back but her hands slipped on wolf blood. The monster opened its mouth. Sitsi ran for it, Sassa's knife aloft, but Keef and Thyri were there first, Keef stabbing it in the good eye with Arse Splitter and Thyri jabbing her sax into its nostril.

The beast pulled its head back and screamed.

Thyri's blade fell from its nostril and she caught it.

"When the arse is too big to split, the eye will have to do!" yelled Keef, shaking Arse Splitter above his head.

The Plains Sprinter pulled away but the beast rallied and lowered its head to carry on the chase. Closer and closer it came, if anything faster than before. The Wootah and Calnian warriors waited. Sitsi stood with them now, Sassa's knife in her hand. It was a little late to worry about the trim of the craft.

She looked at Paloma. The speedy woman lifted her killing stick and gave it a look that said *what am I meant to do with this?* Sitsi smiled despite herself.

The lizard king came level, but it was holding back now, wary of the sharp weapons. Beaver Man climbed onto the top of its head and walked along its muzzle with impressive balance.

The chief of the Badlanders was about to leap down on them when the lizard king itself leapt and flew heels over head in a full backwards summersault.

Beaver Man jumped clear and rolled away. The beast landed with a great crumpling thud. It shivered and convulsed. Both its legs stiffened, then snapped.

The Plains Sprinter rocked on. Sitsi expected Beaver Man to sprint after them, but he stood and watched them go, looking rather forlorn next to the huge body of his spider-paralysed mount.

"WOOOOO-TAAAAH!" shouted Wulf and Keef, "Woooo-tah!"

The rest of them joined in, Wootah and Calnians. Paloma, Chogolisa, Sitsi, Keef, Wulf, Thyri and Erik joined hands and jumped up and down, the Wootah chanting, "Owsla! Owsla!" and the Owsla shouting, "Wootah! Wootah!"

"Owwwwwwwslaaa!" called Sassa from her spot next to flapping Finnbogi in the prow.

Yoki Choppa didn't say anything, but he did look almost cheery. Even Sofi Tornado bent half her mouth into a smile and said, "Wootah."

Sitsi danced, Paloma's hand in one hand and Keef's in the other. She was grinning. It was the first time since they'd been picked up by the Badlanders some seven hundred miles to the east that they hadn't been in direct danger.

Bodil, Gunnhild and the children came to join the celebration. Gunnhild was holding the baby Calnian. They might not be in direct danger for the moment, but their problems were far from over. And they should remember who'd sacrificed herself to save them.

"Ayanna!" Sitsi shouted, "Ayanna!" and the rest of them, Calnians and Wootah alike, took up the chant.

"Quiet, quiet," shouted Erik after a short while. "Sorry to

poop the party, but their dagger-cat cavalry is still after us. All of you please stop jumping about and spread yourselves around the edge of the Sprinter."

Sitsi went to stand next to Sassa Lipchewer and Finnbogi the Boggy at the prow.

"Will we be safe in the Black Mountains?" Sassa asked her.

Sitsi looked at the dark line of high land to the west.

"I learned from . . . reasonable sources that there was something in the Black Mountains that the Badlanders were terrified of, so they never went into them."

"What kind of something?"

"The sources did not know."

"So maybe we should be terrified of it as well?"

Sitsi sighed. "Possibly. I hope not."

Chapter 5
So This Is Uphill

Erik the Angry tried not to goggle. Some of Hardwork's old-world tales were set in mountains so he understood the concept, and some of the Lakchans had seen mountains and told him about them, but Erik had never imagined that land could tower quite so high.

The buffalo road led up a broad valley populated by a multitude of prairie dogs. They chittered and chirred as the Plains Sprinter creaked by, some poking halfway from holes, others standing on the edge of their mounds with forelegs rested on their chests and many more diving into their holes and reappearing. These prairie dogs had white tails, whereas further east prairie dog tails had been black. Erik opened his mouth to report the observation to Chogolisa Earthquake, but decided it probably wasn't that fascinating.

"They stand a little like thunder lizards, don't you think?" he said instead.

Other than Finnbogi flapping away at the front, the rest of the Wootah and Calnians were spread around the Plains Sprinter, resting. Erik and Chogolisa were sitting facing outwards, their legs under the rail and dangling over the edge. Erik was working on some leather and bone to create a drinking skin with a fake nipple for the baby Calnian. Very tired, he was resting against Chogolisa's arm. She didn't seem to mind.

"It's a good thing they're not the size of thunder lizards," she nodded. "Passing through thousands of them like this would be a very different experience. I often thank Innowak that the smaller animals are the size they are."

A black, orange, yellow and red-striped wasp alighted briefly on the rail before buzzing off.

"Imagine if wasps were the size of buffalo," Erik mused.

"They'd take over in days."

"They'd need a leader."

"I'd do it. I'd be Chogolisa Wasp Queen."

"I like it. How about Erik Wasp King?"

"I don't know. Don't you think Erik the Wasp Shit-Shoveller sounds better?"

"Not really. I'm a terrible shoveller."

"You'd better be king then. Kings don't have to be good at anything." She put an arm around him and squeezed.

Erik's heart lurched and his cheeks reddened.

The Sprinter rolled on up the increasingly high-sided valley, much slower now that Finnbogi's flap rate had decreased to an exhausted fluttering of the hands. Erik and the Owsla woman sat at the rail and pointed out more animals to each other—a brazenly russet chipmunk, lavender butterflies, a black and white woodpecker with a red head.

Chogolisa's arm stayed around his shoulder. As he congratulated her for spotting a pair of badgers rooting about on the edge of the treeline, it seemed more than normal to put his arm some of the way around her waist.

"And have you noticed that the prairie dogs have white tails here?" she asked.

The valley narrowed and the Plains Sprinter could go no further. Sassa told Finnbogi to stop. The pigeons flapped down and the Plains Sprinter settled.

Erik looked behind, expecting to see the dagger-tooth cavalry tearing up the valley towards them. However, the valley was empty, bar half a million or so prairie dogs staring after them.

Then a figure did appear. It was Paloma Pronghorn. One moment she was a dot in the distance, then next she was right with them.

"No sign of the baddies," she said, "not for twenty miles anyway. Looks like the cat cavalry stuck to their word."

The chase, it seemed, was over. At least for now.

"Well done, lad." Erik put a hand on his son's shoulder. "You saved us all."

Finnbogi blinked, bobbed his head back and forth, said: "Coo-c-cool. Glad that's over. I'm very hungry," then passed out in his father's arms.

They left the pigeons to bite through their spider silk tethers. The wolves were harnessed so that they'd need to release only one cord to let the whole lot go. Sofi told Paloma to stay back and wait until the rest of them were well clear before freeing them. First, though, they had to build a pyre for Luby Zephyr.

"You know that letting the wolves out among all these prairie dogs is a bit like freeing fifty thunder lizards in a big village?" Erik asked Sofi.

"Would you like to leave the wolves that saved us all tethered to starve? Or would you rather kill them all before we go?"

"Well, neither."

"Then shut the fuck up." She stalked away.

Erik blinked after her.

"Don't take it personally," said Chogolisa. "She's had better days."

It took moments for the Wootah and Calnians to build a pyre. Despite Paloma's assurances, many of them had half an eye down the valley for the dagger-tooth cavalry or any other horrors appearing. The only two who didn't contribute to the pyre were Yoki Choppa, who was off in the woods gathering ingredients for an alternative to breast milk, and Finnbogi, who'd come round and was sitting against the Sprinter eating berries, moving his head about in small jerks and blinking a lot.

Sofi Tornado laid Luby on the wooden bed, kissed her forehead, stood back, picked up a burning torch and jammed it into the guts of the pyre.

Lambent flame danced up with a crackling roar and consumed the young Owsla woman. Sofi watched, stone-faced, then handed Luby's remaining obsidian moon blade to Freydis the Annoying.

The girl looked up at Sofi, wide-eyed. She opened her mouth, but Sofi shook her head and Freydis nodded, seeming to understand. The captain of the Owsla turned and strode away up the valley. The girl looked at the wickedly sharp blade in her hand.

"You must play your part in the coming fight, Freydis," said Gunnhild. "It is time you started bearing your share of the group's burden. *Rear your children as gods and they will become devils.*"

"Wouldn't a devil be better at fighting?" asked Freydis.

Everyone else gathered kit as Gunnhild used Erik's makeshift breast to feed Yoki Choppa's concoction to Calnian. The baby drank enthusiastically to begin with, but broke off after a while and cried. He started with a few coughing sobs but soon he was wailing as only a baby human can.

Erik looked about. If there were any enemies or dangerous creatures that hadn't spotted the smoke from the fire, then Calnian's screams would bring them in. How did something so small make such a loud noise? And why?

"He's drunk enough," said Gunnhild in the lull while Calnian sucked in another lungful of air, "I don't know—"

"Ottar wants to hold him," said Freydis.

"I don't think giving him the boy is going to—" Ottar pulled at her hand and nodded. Hugin and Munin yipped up at her.

Gunnhild sighed and handed the screaming baby down to the boy. Erik couldn't hear what she was saying, but she was shaking her head disapprovingly.

Calnian stopped crying the moment Ottar hugged him. Heartbeats later, he was asleep.

"*The young understand the young,*" said Gunnhild with a wise nod, as if giving the baby to Ottar had been her plan all along.

The tree-lined sides of the grassy valley closed in and the slope became steeper. Soon they were walking a well-used path uphill into the woods. The path mostly followed a tumbling brook which broadened sporadically into black, shiningly reflective ponds. Appealing birds and mammals sat on almost every branch and rock. The high-pitched, single-note barks of chipmunks, the hammering trill of woodpeckers and myriad other animal noises harmonised into joyous woodland music.

Erik walked next to Chogolisa and Finnbogi. His son insisted he was fine after his fainting—he'd simply needed some food after all the flapping—but Erik was worried. With each step Finnbogi pulsed his chin back and forth as if marching to some silent beat, and he kept cocking his head to one side and blinking in an undeniably pigeon-like manner.

"Are you sure you're all right?" Erik asked.

"Oooo yes. Oooooo," muttered Finnbogi.

Erik looked at Chogolisa. "I'm sure it will pass," she said.

Up ahead, Freydis traipsed along next to Ottar and his racoons. Ottar was carrying the slumbering and intermittently snorting Calnian in a scarf that Yoki Choppa had tied into a papoose around his shoulders.

The path led up and up. It was a steady trudge but still wearying for people who hadn't walked a long way for a few weeks and many of whom had never walked more than a few hundred paces uphill. After a short while, Ottar was stamping and puffing under the burden of the slumbering Calnian.

"Would you like me to carry you?" Chogolisa called.

Ottar stopped and turned, shaking his head and pointing at the baby and the racoons in turn.

"I'll take you both. Hugin and Munin will follow me just as easily as they follow you."

"'Kay," said Ottar.

"And I'll carry you if you like, Freydis?" asked Erik.

"No thanks, I like walking here. It's better than the grass, isn't it? Can I hold your hand, Finnbogi?"

Finnbogi strutted ahead to join the girl, chest proud, bum out and nodding to his own beat.

The vegetation was light under strange pines and stands of silver-barked deciduous trees. Mostly they walked on a carpet of soft pine needles, which went a little way towards making up for the endless uphill. Every now and then the woods opened into a clearing and they could see red rock faces a good deal higher than the Heartberry Canyon and Water Mother cliffs they'd all been so impressed by. The rock here was a deeper red than the powdery sculpted soil that had comprised the Badlands massif. It looked harder; more permanent and godly.

In the broader clearings, they could see the mountains ahead, towering higher than Erik had imagined possible. Several times he had to hastily close his mouth before Chogolisa spotted him gawping at the majesty of it all.

The oldest surviving Wootah walked along with two lovely children, two friendly racoons, his son and a woman he liked a lot. He filled his lungs with the fresh, pine-scented air. Climbing higher and higher into these marvellously fragrant, starkly impressive, animal-thronged hills made his spirits soar. This, he thought, is the sort of place that he was meant to be.

Sofi Tornado did not like the woods one little bit.

The combination of thousands of animal noises and

millions of shifting leaves reflecting all those sounds made her enhanced hearing much less effective.

To make things worse, she was sure they were being shadowed. It wasn't humans, it wasn't dagger-tooth cats, but something, some *things* to be precise, were following them up the valley while managing to stay hidden in the trees. She asked her women to investigate, but Sitsi couldn't see them and Paloma, tearing noisily about the woods, couldn't find a thing.

Maybe she was imagining it, she told herself. Maybe Luby's death had knocked her senses. But she knew that was bollocks. There was something following them through the woods and she wanted to know what it was.

They camped in a clearing a few paces uphill from the river. Sofi and Wulf took first watch, with Paloma and Freydis stationed in a tree way down the valley. The idea was that they'd take it in turns to sleep and, if the Badlanders did come, Paloma would carry Freydis on her shoulders back to the rest of them. Freydis was no wimp, but Sofi was keen to toughen her up because their journey was about to get a whole lot tougher.

After a simple supper of roast prairie dog and berries, everyone apart from Sofi and Wulf, even Yoki Choppa, fell immediately into a deep sleep.

Sofi sat on a log, watching the campfire's light dancing on the leaves, thinking about life, death and Luby Zephyr. She was still sure that something was watching from the woods, but as the night wore on she became more relaxed about it, because if it was going to attack them it probably would have done already. Could it, she wondered, be Luby's spirit following them?

Sofi told herself off for such vapid musing and watched Wulf pace around the camp. Ayanna had died for them. So had Luby. But she couldn't blame the Wootah. All of them had risked their lives in the escape and it was just bad luck that had killed Luby and not one of them. They'd done well.

They were not nearly as useless as she'd thought, and, if Yoki Choppa was right and the boy Ottar was going to save the world, then Luby hadn't died in vain.

Sofi sat and thought about all the times she'd spent with her friend until it was time to wake Sitsi and Keef for the next watch.

Sofi's dream about Luby Zephyr arguing with Wulf next to a river crossing morphed into reality as she woke and realised she was listening to Paloma Pronghorn talking to a stranger.

She opened one eye. It was a short while before sunrise and the woods were brightening. Paloma and Gunnhild were standing down the hill a little, talking quietly to a man whom Sofi didn't recognise.

The man was telling them about paths washed away in the recent storms which had been the worst that anyone could remember. "They've got it worse out west, though, much, much worse," he said.

Paloma told him that they'd seen some right old weather on their travels.

"Two of the Wootah survived being picked up by a tornado," said Gunnhild.

"Wow. Amazing you've made it this far."

"*You can't break a stick in a bundle,*" said Gunnhild.

"What?"

Sofi jumped up and walked over.

"Hello. You're Sofi Tornado," said the man. It was more or an accusation than a question. He spoke the universal tongue in the accent-free, confident tones of someone who, like Sofi, did no proper work. He was short, dressed in a light-green smock and a dark-green skirt, and his hair was receding from a big, bulbous head.

"I am," she replied.

"I've been sent to meet you. I'm Klippsta. Welcome to the

Black Mountains from the Green tribe." He sounded about as welcoming as a misanthropic hermit receiving the third surprise visitor that day.

"How did you know we were coming? How do you know my name?" Sofi asked.

"Tatinka Buffalo knew you were coming, I don't know how. I know your name because everyone's heard of Sofi Tornado of the Calnian Owsla. I was told to come and meet you and I was promised that you wouldn't kill me. Will you?"

"Let's see how it goes. Who's Tatinka Buffalo?"

"Chief of the Green tribe and head warlock. Called Buffalo because she's even more useful than they are. I can tell you about her on the way if you want. But please do come on now. Wake everyone up. We've got to get going." He looked into the trees.

Sofi followed his gaze.

"What's in the trees?" she asked.

"Nothing."

"So we can take our time here? Maybe a game or two of lacrosse before we head off?"

"No! I...I'd like to get home before dark, that's all. The path goes along cliffs, it's uneven in parts and my wife doesn't like it when I leave her alone with the children for one night, let alone two. She's managed to alienate both her and my parents, so we can't get anyone else...well, I won't bother you with my worries."

Sofi held his gaze. "And there's nothing else? Nothing in the woods?"

"Nothing that will trouble us in the day."

"But you must have come here in the dark," said Paloma.

"No. I travelled yesterday and slept nearby."

"What are you afraid of in the dark?" asked Sofi.

Klippsta looked at his feet, but said, "Nothing. Look, it's a beautiful journey, especially as we get higher. We should see some wonderful animals. I saw several bears with cubs on the way here. It makes sense to do it in the light."

Sassa Lipchewer was woken by Gunnhild Kristlover poking her shoulder. "Quick, quick. We're going now."

"Are the Badlanders coming?" Sassa asked.

"No. Apparently there's lots of lovely scenery to fit in before sunset."

Sassa smiled. "Finally, a good reason to be in a hurry."

"*Constant worry is crippling but complacency is cretinous.*"

When Wulf returned from his trip to the river, Sofi Tornado walked over, looking several degrees more immaculate than anyone who'd slept in the woods had any right to look.

"Wulf?" she said.

"Yup?"

"Klippsta is from the Green tribe," she nodded her head at the stranger. The man in green was hopping about like someone who's been ready to leave for quite some time. "They're the tribe around here. Sitsi knows no reason to fear them. There is something that might be dangerous in the woods, however. Klippsta knows what it is, but he won't tell me."

"Any idea what it might be?" Wulf yawned. Sassa knew the yawn was to show how little the prospect of danger concerned him.

Sofi shook her head. "Klippsta wants us to walk to his tribe's main settlement, a day's walk to the north-west. He's keen to get there before nightfall to avoid whatever it is in the woods. I think we should go with him. What do you think?"

Sassa thought her husband dealt very well with the surprise of Sofi Tornado asking his opinion. Once his eyebrows had returned to their usual level, he said:

"What are our options?"

"Stay here for ever, return to the Badlands, cross the Black Mountains without visiting the Green tribe or go to the Green tribe."

"Let's go to the Green tribe. I'd like to hang my hammer somewhere friendly for a couple of days and I'm sure I'm not the only one."

"And we need to find a home for Calnian," said Sassa.

Sofi nodded. "Right."

"Wootah! What could go wrong?" Wulf smiled as Sassa shivered.

Chapter 6

A Chill

Walking uphill was a lot less knackering than flapping like a pigeon. Judging by the spring in the others' steps, everyone else also felt a great deal zippier than they had the previous evening.

Finnbogi the Boggy was walking in the middle of the group, behind Bodil Gooseface and Keef the Berserker. Waterfalls splashed across the trail, stands of silver-barked trees shone in the morning sun and there were, if anything, more cheery and unafraid little birds and mammals fluttering and hopping about than ever before.

Despite the loveliness, a gnawing ball of unease was turning and growing in Finnbogi's gut. There simply weren't enough people around him. Not nearly. Who was missing? He counted everyone. They were all there, apart from Paloma Pronghorn who was off scouting. But surely there should be more; many, many more of them? He wasn't far from panicking. *There should be more of us!* his mind wailed at him.

He focused on Bodil and Keef up ahead, in an attempt to calm himself. He felt a bit bad about Bodil. He'd never had that post-shag chat with her that Sassa had made him promise to have. Having thought that, his policy of avoiding the subject of their liaison by the Rock River seemed to have worked just as well, if not better, and certainly with a lot less embarrassment for everyone. Bodil had stopped hassling Finnbogi and turned her attentions to Keef. Maybe Sassa wasn't as wise as she thought she was.

Could Bodil want to be more than friends with Keef, he wondered? Surely not. Finnbogi couldn't imagine that she found the one-eyed, one-eared, small-headed man attractive. But what if they did get together and had a child and it had his looks and her brains?

"What are you thinking about?" asked Thyri, appearing at his side.

"Um..." He looked about. Paloma Pronghorn was leaping down some boulders up ahead. With her honey smell, beautiful, inquisitive face, wasp waist and limbs that glowed with power as if cast from dark, magic gold, Paloma was the only woman in the world more attractive than Thyri. Finnbogi wasn't in love with her in the same way, of course, because a woman like Paloma would never look at a boy like him once, let alone twice, but that didn't stop him from thinking...He checked himself. He couldn't tell Thyri about his confusing lust for Paloma. He tried to clear his mind and think up something that he *could* tell her he was thinking about, but the terrible loneliness rushed back in. *Why are there so few of us?*

"Still a bit freaked after yesterday, are you?" Thyri asked kindly, rather than barking at him to answer her question.

"It wasn't easy, but I'm glad it's over." *Phew* he thought. Maybe you get a new level of respect when you're the life-saving, hero type and you don't have to answer questions? Sofi Tornado answered only about one question in five that any Wootah asked her, and everyone thought she was amazing.

Yes, he thought, saving them all had ushered in a new phase. Goodbye Finnbogi the boy, hello Finn the man.

"Do you know that you're walking like a pigeon?" asked Thyri.

"I am?"

"Yes. Like this." Thyri puffed her chest forward, stuck her

bottom out and walked heavily on her toes, poking her chin in and out as she went along. Finnbogi welcomed the invitation to look her up and down—Tor's bollocks, Paloma might be amazing but Thyri was still breathtakingly hot—but he wasn't sure that she should be taking the piss out of the man who'd saved them all.

"Oh, don't worry, I'm sure it will pass," she smiled. It was the first time she'd smiled at him since they'd crossed the Water Mother. "We're grateful for what you did, Finn. I'm grateful."

Finn! Not Finnbogi or Boggy, she'd called him Finn!

"I only pretended to be a bird for a bit."

Thyri laughed. "Agreed, you didn't exactly battle an ice giant, but you did something that nobody else could have done, and we would have all been killed or caught if you hadn't."

"I didn't save everyone." Finnbogi pictured Sofi's face at Luby's funeral pyre the day before.

"Well, yes. Ayanna and Luby made great sacrifices and we should remember them, but you played a great part, Finn, and it will not be forgotten."

"Thanks."

They walked on, listening to the sounds of the wind, the animals, and Bodil, yabbering away to Keef.

Previously, Finnbogi realised, he'd seen every moment with Thyri as a desperate opportunity to impress her with his wit and opinions. But he didn't feel the need any more. The difference was, he guessed, that he'd actually done something heroic. It wasn't just controlling the pigeons. They all knew that he'd chosen to take on two rattlecondas unarmed to save Freydis.

He no longer needed to explain what a hero he was going to be one day. He'd shown them. He wasn't smug. He was relieved. He felt like he'd been carrying a dozen logs for his whole life without knowing it and had just put them down.

You are what you do, not what you say you're going to do was one of a few of Gunnhild's phrases that had always niggled at him.

They walked on, up the sun-dappled path. It was the coolest day since they'd left Hardwork. Red bluffs reared from green woods like benevolent defenders. Bighorn sheep, normal ones without Empty Children on them, picked their way across the crags. Larger birds soared lazily overhead and little plump ones fluttered among the trees.

And Thyri Treelegs was walking next to him as if it was the most normal thing in the world. His ball of fear dissolved and he felt about as happy as he could remember feeling.

They came to a rare downhill section, where the thick, overarching branches turned the path into a softly lit tunnel.

"Finn," said Thyri.

"Um-hum?" He turned to smile at the beautiful young woman at his side.

"You're still walking like a pigeon," she said.

The walk was lovely, but it was also long and Sassa Lipchewer was just beginning to get footsore and a little tired of endless, idyllic wildlife-stuffed woodland when they arrived in the Green tribe's main settlement. It happened suddenly. One moment they were trudging downhill along a wide wooded track having seen no signs of other human life all day, the next they were walking along the broad central road of the largest and busiest village that Sassa had seen.

Colourfully dressed people nodded, smiled and bade them welcome as if they were used to strangers. Indeed, the inhabitants themselves looked like an amalgamation of tribes, with skin hues ranging from darkest brown to almost as pale as Sassa herself.

"Everybody's very brightly dressed," said Sassa to Klippsta. "I thought because you were in green, and you're called the Green tribe..."

Their guide laughed, a lot more cheerful it seemed now that
he was out of the woods. "We wear what we want. I wear
green to blend into the forest and observe animals more easily, but most do the colourful thing. About ten years ago some
people moved here from an island to the south. One of them
was a tailor who based his designs on the brightly coloured
fish that fill the sea there. It caught on. People dressed drably
when I was a boy. I prefer this."

"But you don't do it yourself?"

"Oh, I do, just not when I'm in the woods."

The village, or town as Klippsta had called it, was sprawling and sparse, with skin tents and light huts dotted here and
there a good way up steep valley sides. The central road ran
next to a river, spanned by regular wooden bridges as richly
decorated with animal carvings as the furniture back in
Hardwork. Workers' sheds were spaced along the road, and
flamboyantly clad craftspeople and artisans looked up to nod
at the newcomers.

Keef jogged up to join the lead group, leaving Bodil's side
for the first time that day. "Doesn't it get cold here in winter?" he asked Klippsta.

"Very," said Klippsta. "We're often snowed in for a moon
or two."

"You must freeze."

"We cover the huts in buffalo skins before it snows."

"I suspected as much. But how do you prevent—"

"Hello!" Sassa looked down. A girl not much more than
half her height was walking next to her. She wore a white
hat and an orange dress with a broad white stripe across its
middle.

"Where are you lot from then?" the girl asked. Like
Klippsta she was dark-skinned, and spoke slowly, drawing
out the words.

"We're from two tribes far to the east," said Sassa, "the
Wootah and the Calnians."

"What's your name?"

"Sassa Lipchewer."

The girl peered at her mouth. Sassa realised that she was chewing her lips, as ever, and stopped.

"Great name!" she smiled. "I'm Tatinka."

"Hello, Tatinka."

"So why have you come such a long way west?"

"It's a long story."

"It's half a mile to Manchinga's Plaza. Why don't you tell me as much as you can before we get there?" Tatinka beamed up at her girlishly. Despite her size and her merry smile, there was an authority about her. Sassa felt agreeably compelled to tell Tatinka everything.

"All right. It began early one morning back in Hardwork I suppose, with two columns of smoke..."

Sitsi Kestrel liked the Green tribe town. It was more spaced out and less planned than Calnia and there were no walls. That suggested both a less dictatorial ruling class and a freedom from fear of attack, which tallied satisfyingly with what Klippsta had told her earlier.

She'd quizzed Klippsta for a long while on the walk up into the Black Mountains and felt that she knew, if not as much about the town and the tribe as was possible, then certainly as much as Klippsta was happy to tell her. She'd been glad to hear that Tatinka Buffalo was still chief. Tales of the woman's intelligence and kindness had reached Calnia.

They walked up to an area a little way from any huts or tents that Sitsi guessed must be Manchinga's Plaza. Manchinga was the Green tribe's chief god, a man who'd been deified after exterminating the giant dogs that preyed on the tribe back in the mists of time. (Sitsi felt briefly guilty about the huge pack of wolves they'd unleashed on the area.) One half of the arena's boundary was wooded, the other was a grass bank, where Sitsi assumed the spectators would sit. It was intimate and peaceful, very different from the enormous, open Plaza of Innowak where the Owsla had killed so many.

The only decoration was a carving of a giant dog with a large, plain but well-made chair at its base. It was a chief's seat, if Sitsi had ever seen one, but there was no chief to be seen.

She looked around, suddenly nervous. *Why had they been brought to an arena?* She pictured Beaver Man walking from the trees, clapping sarcastically. Sofi was assessing the surroundings, too. Judging by her narrow eyes and tight lips, she was as wary as Sitsi.

The Green tribe girl who'd been talking to Sassa climbed up so she was standing on the dog throne. Sitsi was pretty sure that children shouldn't be climbing on a chief's chair and was on the verge of saying something when she noticed that the child wasn't actually a child, but a small woman.

"Hello, Wootah and Calnians! I'm Tatinka Buffalo," said the little woman. "Welcome to the Green tribe on behalf of the tribe, me and Manchinga. Sassa has told me about your escape from the Badlands. I'm sorry for your losses, but well done for escaping. You're the first of their captives to make it here since they came up with those disgraceful spider boxes around four years ago. So welcome indeed. I have heard tales about the Calnian Owsla, of course, and some snippets about the Wootah, so it's fascinating to meet you and I cannot wait to find out more. However."

Tatinka paused, looking around them all.

Here we go, thought Sitsi. *They've still got the giant dogs that Manchinga was meant to have killed and we're going to fight them.*

The small woman continued: "Although we've got a lot to discuss—not least about how you're going to reach The Meadows and what we'll do with Ayanna's baby—it can all wait until tomorrow. You've come a long way and been through some terrible times. So, when I finally stop droning on in a few heartbeats, you can relax. Klippsta will take you to some lovely huts by the river, where you'll find more food than you can eat and more booze than you can drink. So you don't have to talk to any strangers or be gawped at, the whole area will be just yours, other than for a couple of Greens who are excellent at keeping themselves to themselves and even better at roasting bighorn lambs."

Sitsi wanted to like Tatinka and believe her, she really did. However, there was something powerful simmering beneath the smiling little woman's confident friendliness. Whether it was something good or bad, Sitsi could not tell, but the last person who'd smiled at the Owsla so much had been Chapa Wangwa. She could see that Sofi was suspicious, too. Everyone else was smiling back at the chief, other than Yoki Choppa, impassive as ever, Ottar the Moaner, who was whispering nonsense to the baby strapped to his chest, and the baby himself, who was looking calmly up at Ottar.

"One more thing, then I'll let you go," Tatinka continued. "Nothing's going to make you want to post guards more than a stranger telling you that you don't need to post guards, but...you don't need to post guards. You've seen the town, you've seen that we have no walls. We're protected by something stronger than wood."

"Protected from what?" asked Sofi.

"Everything," answered Tatinka, holding Sofi's gaze. "Now go and relax. I'll see you tomorrow around lunchtime. If you want anything that's not already by the huts—drink, herbs, mushrooms, wet nurse for the baby, whatever—ask Klippsta and we'll do the best we can."

That evening, a good while after sunset, Finnbogi was urinating directly into the river, long and loud, wondering if there was any greater joy that pissing into calm waters on a starlit night.

He walked back up the path towards the flickering fire and

chatter, placing his feet carefully. When you'd drunk as much of the Greens' honey drink as he had, it was easy to walk into a bush, as he'd discovered on the way down to the river. Placing his feet diligently, he made it back to the camp without incident.

"Camp" didn't do justice to the place. It was about fifteen thousand times nicer than the best camp they'd had since leaving Hardwork. The huts that Tatinka had assigned them were like a lovely little village, and the two guys who Tatinka had sent to cook the lamb were the best hosts. Without talking to anybody, moving around with a stealth that Luby Zephyr would have been proud of, they saw to every need, or at least lots of their needs. Of the six or seven times they'd refilled Finnbogi's mug of honey drink, for example, he'd noticed them doing it only twice. It was full again now, perched on a table next to the fireside log where he'd been sitting next to Paloma.

He smiled at Freydis and Ottar asleep on bearskins near the fire, then at his newly refilled drink. Then he noticed that everybody was looking at him.

"What?" he said, looking down to check he'd put everything away. He had, thank Manchinga the dog slayer.

"You've done well recently," said Wulf the Fat. "Choosing to fight two rattlecondas to save Freydis—unarmed—was a Hel of a thing. Conducting the pigeons for that long, long journey was beyond awesome."

They were all smiling at him, Thyri included. Paloma, too. He wanted to cry.

"So I've talked to everybody and everybody agrees. You will no longer be known as Finnbogi the Boggy."

He gasped and blinked.

Wulf stood, walked over and put a hand on his shoulder. "From now on, nobody will call you by your childhood name of Finnbogi the Boggy. To recognise your sacrifice, to thank you for saving all of our lives and preserving the Wootah, you will be called Finnbogi the Pigeon Fucker."

"Oh." His heart sank. "Great. Pigeon Fucker. Okay."

"I'm joking!"

Everybody laughed, other than the non-laughers Sofi and Yoki Choppa.

"What will I be called?" asked Finnbogi.

"I don't know. It's traditional to decide when everyone's had a drink or six, so let's get on with it."

"Finnbogi the Brave?" suggested Sitsi Kestrel. Finnbogi wanted to hug her.

"No, no, no!" cried Keef the Berserker, jumping up from his spot on the log next to Bodil. "That's not how it works. Finnbogi the Brave is far too cool. Finnbogi the Pigeon Fucker works for me. Often one's first instincts are best. Let's go with Pigeon Fucker."

"Come on, Keef," said Thyri. "*The Berserker* is a pretty cool name and don't forget this is a man who made the right choice *and* talked to a bunch of pigeons."

"Yes, *the Berserker* is cool," said Keef. "Of course it is. I'm cool. Finnbogi is...Finnbogi."

"How about Finnbogi Big Bollocks?" suggested Paloma Pronghorn.

"Closer, still a bit much," said Keef.

"Finnbogi Little Bollocks?" asked Chogolisa Earthquake.

"That's better," Keef said, serious-faced. "Finnbogi Tinyk-nob might work..."

"How about Finnbogi the Constant Wanker?" laughed Gunnhild.

Finnbogi looked at her, appalled.

"Oh, don't pretend you went off into the woods on your own all those times because you were interested in insects," she added, cheeks glowing with honey drink.

Finnbogi shook his head. This was not going well.

"Finnbogi the Ogler?" said Sofi Tornado. Finnbogi wanted to crawl into a hole. Surely she hadn't seen him ogling her? He'd been very careful.

"Some magnificent suggestions," said Wulf. "But I don't think we've found it yet. Has anyone got anything a little more complimentary than 'the Boggy'?"

"I know I'm not meant to make up my own name," Finnbogi risked saying, "but can I be called Finn instead of Finnbogi?"

"No way," said Keef, "you can't change your first name."

"That's the Hardwork way," said Sassa Lipchewer, "but we're Wootah now and we make our own rules. Wulf?"

"Yeah, why not. Finn it is. So we're looking at Finn the..."

"Dim?" suggested Gunnhild. Finnbogi stared at her again and she smiled back, unabashed.

"Finn the Trim doesn't suit him," said Thyri, "how about Finn the Prim?" She took a swig of her mug, looking very pleased with herself.

"Finn the Cunt?" said Keef.

Thyri snorted honey drink out of her nose. Finnbogi was not enjoying this.

"Finn the Thyri-Fancier?" said Sassa.

Finn glared at her, ears burning. She winked. He glanced at Thyri. She was looking at her feet, not laughing any more. Was she blushing?

"Finn the Deep," said Bodil.

"Finn the Creep," suggested Paloma.

"What was that, Bodil?" said Wulf.

"Finn the Deep," repeated Bodil.

Yes yes yes, Finn pleaded silently.

Wulf nodded. "I like it. But has he done anything particularly deep..."

"He saved us all," said Bodil.

"So did I!" said Keef.

"When?" said Thyri.

"When these fuckers chopped my ear off and took my eye out and I still didn't tell them where you were." He pointed at the Owsla women. All of them, even Sofi Tornado, looked suitably chastened.

"You didn't know where we were any more than they did, or than we did, for that matter," Thyri argued, getting further from the subject of *Finn the Deep*.

"Well, I didn't tell them where you were going. And me and Arse Splitter saw off more moose riders than anybody else yesterday, and I took Finnbogi's place swimming down the waterfall at—"

"That'll do, Keef," said Gunnhild. "Let's get this done so we can get back to interesting conversations. We'll call him Finn the Deep. It may not be entirely accurate, but he'll like it. Maybe *man cannot change the name of dung and make it meat*, but Finn deserves a name that he'll like and that will remind him for ever of his selflessness and bravery. Maybe it'll even inspire him to carry on acting like a decent adult."

Finn nodded his thanks. He didn't trust himself to talk.

"Well, Wulf?" asked Gunnhild.

"Yup, sure. Goodbye for ever, Finnbogi the Boggy. Welcome to the Wootah tribe, Finn the Deep."

Finn's mouth fell open. They were all watching. Thyri looked proud. Paloma was smiling at him and nodding.

"I still prefer Finn the Cunt," muttered Keef, but he caught Finn's eye and winked.

Tears threatened. Finn's lower lip wobbled.

"I . . ." He choked out a sob. Tears came. Finn the Deep snorted and ran from the fire, the laughter of the others ringing in his ears.

Paloma Pronghorn found him sitting on a broad rock high above the camp. It was a moonless, cloudless night, with more stars than there were pebbles on Hardwork beach, some twinkling on their own, many more combining into sparkling celestial clouds.

"I..." he said.

"Expecting Treelegs?"

"Well..."

"Great girl, not a tracker. She's looking for you down by the river."

"Oh, I—"

"Shush." Paloma placed a hand delicately on his shoulder then gripped his shirt tight. For half a heartbeat he thought she was going to head-butt him, but she lowered her face and opened her lips. A heady wave of her animal, honey musk washed across him and then her mouth was on his, her tongue pushing between his teeth. He pushed back with his own tongue, then gripped her hips and leant back onto the rock, pulling her with him.

Sitsi Kestrel wasn't surprised when Paloma went after Finnbogi—sorry, Finn—even though they'd all seen Thyri Treelegs head after him, too. Sitsi had seen it several times in Calnia. When she was drunk, Paloma became unstoppably attracted to men that other women liked, and hang the feelings of the other woman.

Sitsi had watched Finn fawn over Treelegs ever since she'd met them, and seen her cold responses. If Paloma found Finn first, which she would, and little madam Thyri was thwarted, then that was probably a good thing; a lesson in humility for Thyri and the opposite for Finn.

The fire cracked and orange sparks flew up to the stars. Wulf and Sassa bade everyone goodnight and headed off together. Sitsi had seen Sassa pour every one of her drinks away in the dark without taking a single sip. There was only one reason to avoid poisoning your innards while keeping your abstinence secret. The notion made Sitsi smile, but it was also a worry. It was a very long way to The Meadows.

Keef got up to go to the river and Bodil followed him. Sitsi sighed. Sometimes she wished she was more like Paloma.

"Still good for first watch, Sitsi?" asked Sofi, standing.

"Sure."

"And you, Gunnhild?"

"I have abstained and am ready. *Be wary of drinking when work is upon you.*"

"Right."

Everyone else turned in then, apart from Erik and Chogolisa, who were sitting on the same log and chatting quietly. The big man looked like a child next to the colossal Owsla woman, but they still looked good as a couple.

The large-eyed archer left them to patrol the perimeter and gain her night vision. She met Thyri, stomping up the path from the river.

"Goodnight!" Sitsi chirped. The Wootah girl grunted a reply without looking up and would have barged her out of the way if Sitsi hadn't sprung aside.

A little while later Erik and Chogolisa headed to the river separately, then went back to their own huts.

Chogolisa could do with being a bit more like Paloma as well, thought Sitsi.

Finnbogi woke on the rock, a chill in his bones and an ache in the arm that was under Paloma Pronghorn.

Paloma Pronghorn.

He lay for a short while, watching the sky lighten, listening to the animals wake and breathing in her scent mixed with the fresh aroma of the woods. The golden moment was somewhat marred by his bursting desperation to piss, but he managed mostly to ignore that.

Finally, Paloma woke and turned. She smiled sleepily at him, then her eyes shot open like a startled deer's.

"Shall we go back to the huts?" he asked. "Or maybe stay out here for a bit and—"

"No. I like a run when I wake up. See ya!"

And she was gone.

Chapter 7

The Green Tribe

Sassa Lipchewer woke on the comfortable bed and pulled the fur against her chest. Wulf was up and gone. She told herself not to worry; he always woke before her under normal circumstances. Normal circumstances! Lever a beaver, what a joy. She wished they could stay with the Green tribe for ever but she knew that a second night was unlikely.

The time for Sassa's moon cycle had come and gone. She hadn't needed the proof. She knew she was pregnant and Sofi Tornado had confirmed it. Wulf had drunkenly spilled the beans about Sofi's secret super-hearing to her the night before. She'd already trusted that the Owsla captain wasn't lying about her baby's health, but now she knew how she knew, it was even more reassuring.

But she knew she mustn't tell Wulf yet. Too much could go wrong at this early stage. She reckoned she was thirty-two days pregnant. The Hardwork custom had been to wait ninety days before telling anyone other than your mother. She was going to try for that. Sofi, unsuited as she was, could take the mother role for now.

Reluctantly, she climbed off the warm bed and headed out. She bade good day to Sofi and Bodil and trod carefully down to the river. The morning was warm and soon filled with the sounds of splashing and shouting from Keef and Wulf playfighting.

Keef waded out as she approached and ran off into the

woods in pursuit of imaginary foes. She watched Wulf wash, as did a couple of beavers, their heads poking up from the dam downstream. A family of muskrats appeared from their cattail lodge on the far, shaded side of the river and swam right by Wulf. Swift little birds swished up and downstream, dipping for morning drinks.

"I'm pregnant," she said as Wulf walked out of the water, surprising herself almost as much as him.

His eyes widened, his face cracked into a grin and he ran to hug her. She didn't mind that she got soaked.

Back at the camp, Erik the Angry shouted "Hey Paloma!" and waggled a couple of wood and sinew paddles at her. Paloma had seen him working on them the night before and guessed that they were meant to be rackets for a ball sport, or possibly fishing equipment. "Want to come down to the river and try these out?" he asked.

Fishing equipment, then. She looked about, wracking her brains for an excuse not to go and wondering what she'd done to give him the impression that she might enjoy fishing.

"Why don't you ask Ot—" she started, then spotted Finn the Deep heading down the hill from the previous night's liaison. "Actually, that sounds like a fun thing to do, Erik. To the river!"

They passed Wulf the Fat and Sassa Lipchewer, both of them grinning like mad people.

"The river is the place to be!" said Sassa.

"It certainly is!" cried Wulf, dancing in a circle. "It certainly is!"

"Someone got theirs this morning," said Paloma when the ecstatic pair had skipped on. She regretted it immediately. As far as Erik knew she'd got hers with his son the night before. They hadn't actually shagged, they hadn't done much at all, but Erik didn't know that. What was more, as Sitsi had whispered hoarsely the moment Paloma had got back to camp that morning, Erik *hadn't* got his with Chogolisa Earthquake, even though he should have done and must surely be regretting that he hadn't had the balls to make a move.

It was a bit odd, walking along with the previous night's pull's dad, but, then again, she told herself, everything was a bit odd these days.

They arrived at the river.

"Right, strap these to your feet, please." Erik held the paddles out to her.

She didn't take them. "Why?"

Erik put his creations down on a rock. "I got the idea watching ducks take off." He carried on. His explanation was detailed, with much gesticulation and running on the spot. Paloma watched, amused and confused.

"Fine," she said at the end of his overlong lecture. "Give them here. I'll have a crack since you've put so much effort in. But it's not going to work."

She sat on the rock and lashed the rackets to her feet, feeling like an idiot. Erik told her to make sure they were straight and encouraged her to tie them as tightly as possible, all the while bouncing boyishly on his toes.

"Right," he said as she stood tentatively. "Do you want me to go through again how—"

"I got it." She set off along the bank just a little faster than a normal person could run. She leapt onto the surface of the river with her legs still going, ran for about two paces until the leading edge of one of the watershoes submerged and she tripped. She tumbled and splashed down into the roaring water. She scraped on a rock, sank, hit the riverbed arse first, waved her arms, found her feet and stood. It was hip-deep and cold as a white bear's bollocks.

A group of muskrats swam sleekly past, heading for their cattail lodge. All their noses were pointed resolutely forward, perhaps convinced that if they didn't see her, she wouldn't see them.

"Are you all right?" shouted Erik, wading into the water. "You did brilliantly!"

She coughed, flicked some sort of water slug off her arm, then belched. "Yes. Brilliantly. I have never felt more accomplished or glamorous."

His face fell. "But I thought you had it for a moment?"

"I did. You're right. I think they might work. If I run with my legs wider, maybe go faster and focus on keeping my feet tilted upwards a little...I do think they might work. You're pretty clever, Erik."

His bearded face cracked into a grin and his eyes lit up. He was actually better looking than his son, or at least a good deal sexier. "Do you need help getting back?" he asked.

The river was not fast flowing, but the current was sucking at her with some force and she was not a good swimmer.

"I'll be fine," she said, "just wait there and—"

She lifted a foot and the current caught the watershoe. Her leg pulled away. She pirouetted her arms and tried to lift the other foot, but it snagged under a rock.

She went under again, arse over head. She pulled for the surface, but she was held by an eddy and sucked along, upside down.

I will not die like this, she thought, *it's simply not fitting for the world's fastest warrior.*

Try as she might however, she could not right herself.

She was just beginning to think about panicking when two big hands gripped her under the armpits and pulled her up into the sweet air.

"Thanks!" she spluttered, as Erik jogged backwards, towing her to the bank.

The second attempt was much more successful, possibly because she believed it might work. She splash-padded all the way across to the far bank, gripped a branch and leapt out.

"Hooray!" shouted Erik.

"Well done, Wootah man!" she called back, meaning it. It

might be a simple idea, but neither Yoki Choppa nor any of the other warlocks who'd developed and trained the Owsla had thought of it. Of course Erik couldn't claim all the credit— it had still required her awesome speed and nobody but her could have done it—but she was impressed nevertheless.

Had she had these a moon or so before, they'd have caught the Wootah tribe at the Rock River and what would have happened then, she wondered?

She ran across twice more. On the third attempt, she headed upriver about three hundred paces before the left shoe fell apart and she took another spectacular tumble. This time, she angled for the bank as soon as she knew she was going down and didn't need to be rescued.

All the way back to the others, Erik talked about possible improvements to his design, and other exciting applications for it.

His excited voice must have carried to the little village, because when they arrived at the huts everyone had stopped what they were doing to see what the fuss was about.

Paloma shouldn't have found it gratifying that both Thyri Treelegs and Finn the Deep were glowering at her. She really shouldn't have done.

Sassa Lipchewer and Wulf the Fat spent the morning smiling at each other. Every now and then Wulf laughed and clapped his hands. Despite all that they'd been through and all that might lay ahead, Sassa was about as happy as she could remember being.

Chief Tatinka Buffalo came at lunchtime, as she'd promised, along with Klippsta and a man whose face looked like it had melted. One of his eyes was a ruined mess, the other clear and darting.

Klippsta was in green as before, the chief wore blue with a turquoise hat and the burned man was in a brown and cream tasselled leather smock, with a stone hand axe hanging from his belt.

It was warm but breezy, so the smoke from the cookfire in the centre of the circle of huts was annoying. The chief suggested that they all move to a clearing by the river.

The water sparkled, birds swooped and dipped, the leaves on the trees swished in the wind. Tatinka stood, confident and calm. The melted-face man looked hostile and self-conscious. Sassa tried to smile reassuringly at him. *We're not going to think less of you because you're burned,* she tried to convey. *All the dicks who would have judged you by the way you looked died on the far side of the Water Mother.*

Once they'd all gathered, the little chief climbed onto a log.

"Good morning, everybody. I hope you are well rested. This" she gestured with a palm to the newcomer, "is Weeko Fang."

Weeko Fang nodded, his good eye flicking from face to face.

"He has come from The Meadows."

There were gasps. Weeko nodded all the more.

"Weeko, please can you tell them about their destination?" said Tatinka, as breezily as if she were asking for tips on cake making.

"Sure," he said, in a voice like a sack of shingle being dragged along a shingle beach. "First, I apologise for my rough intonation," said Weeko. "I was in a fire."

"No shi—ack!" said Keef, stopped in his insensitive tracks by a backhanded fist to the groin from Wulf.

"You want to go to The Meadows."

"Yes," said Wulf.

"You don't." Weeko shook his head. "You really don't. It's the worst place in the world. You will be killed before you're even close to it."

Gunnhild put her hands on Ottar's shoulders. For once he didn't shrug her off. He was staring open-mouthed at Weeko Fang.

"There's a prophecy," said Sofi Tornado.

"You can't help."

"What's happening over there?" asked Gunnhild.

"To the west of here are the Shining Mountains. They are far higher than the Black Mountains, so high that you will find deep snow at their summits even in the hottest summer. On the far side of the Shining Mountains is the Desert You Don't Walk Out Of, stretching hundreds of miles west to the Meadows. Throughout that whole desert is destruction and death. The closer to The Meadows you go, the worse it becomes. I got this," he pointed to his face, "in a firenado."

"A *what*?" asked Keef, sounding more excited than might have been seemly.

"A tornado that's caught on fire. They roar across the desert like giant, spinning, burning snakes on their tails, setting everything ablaze and hurling it up into the sky. Sometimes there are two or three of them, travelling together like a hunting pack. They leave behind them a trail of fiery rain, burned ground and nothing—*nothing*—alive."

"Wow," said Keef, impressed.

"How did you escape it?" asked Paloma.

"I left the others. I'm not proud of that. They weren't my kin. I hardly knew them, but..." He shook his head. "I ran. The firenado picked me off my feet as I reached the river. It spat me out into the water almost immediately, but I'll never forget that agony."

Sassa flicked a bitey looking fly off Wulf's bare arm. Her near-euphoric mood had cooled considerably.

"The firenados are maybe the worst of the weather," Weeko continued, "although your standard flame-free tornados, rockslides and flash floods have killed plenty. But the weather isn't the greatest danger, not by a long shot."

"What is?" asked Wulf.

"The monsters."

"We've fought monsters," said Keef.

The two one-eyed men held each other's gaze for a moment. "Not like these," said Weeko.

"I bet we fought worse." Keef twirled Arse Splitter.

"Did any of them fly?"

"Um..."

"Did any have claws that could snip a man in half?"

"Well..."

"Were any of them five hundred, a thousand times the size of a buffalo?"

"Actually, yes, the last lot we fought—"

"Did these ones you fought swell, turn purple and burst, showering a deluge of burning poison for miles around?"

"Not exactly..."

"Then you haven't seen monsters. Not like these. Some mad god is mashing the most dangerous, toughest animals into horrific, disgusting creatures and swelling them up to bizarre sizes. Crabs as big as hills with scorpion tails instead of pincers; huge, hairless bears with tarantula fangs, millipedes as thick as your arm with—"

Weeko broke off to have a coughing fit. Tatinka handed him some water. Even Keef was silent until he'd had a few gulps and could continue.

"The best things you can say about the monsters in the Desert You Don't Walk Out Of is that they're unstable. The biggest ones don't last long. They fall apart and, like I said, they burst. But while they're alive...you just got to hide. And I think they're living for longer now. The smaller ones certainly don't die as quickly as they used to. The newest thing when I made it out of there were flocks of flying, man-sized insects with claws for hands. Their screams will melt your bones with terror. They fly down, screeching so loud that people are too scared to fight back, and slaughter a whole village; people and animals, too."

"Where do the monsters and the weather come from?" asked Wulf.

"The Meadows. There's something there distorting nature, defiling its laws to make living nightmares."

"What is it at The Meadows that's creating all this havoc?" asked Finn. Sassa thought he sounded more serious and grown up than ever before.

"I don't know. There are rumours. Many say it's a long-dead warlock queen mourning her child. There may be some truth in that. There is a massive pyramid at The Meadows, the tomb of a queen who died a long time ago. Shortly before this all started, the two largest tribes in the Desert You Don't Walk Out Of—the Warlocks and the Warriors—decided that there was something magical hidden in that tomb. They both wanted it, so they went to war. Whether either of them found it, I don't know. What I do know is that both of those once proud and numerous tribes are now all but destroyed.

"So I implore you. *Do not try to go to The Meadows.* Even if you could cross the Shining Mountains—which you can't because of the squatches—but even if you could you'd be dead within hours."

"The squatches are our friends," said Erik.

Weeko looked at Erik like a wife might look at a husband who's suggested they introduce a couple of squirrels into their love-making routine.

"You've been to the Shining Mountains?"

"No..."

"The squatches in the Shining Mountains are cruel and they're clever. They could tear you apart with their astonishing strength—even your big girl there—but they prefer to use their minds to stop your heart."

"If they're clever, can they be reasoned with?" Wulf asked.

"No. They have about as much respect for humans as we have for fish. Would you listen to a fish?"

"If it was talking to me, yes."

"Okay, bad example. But they have no respect for us. They enjoy killing us, that's it."

"How did you get through?"

Weeko sighed. "I made a deal."

"What kind of deal?"

"If they let me go, I would trick a load of people into going back there and they'd be able to kill more humans."

"Nice," said Wulf.

"I didn't intend to honour the deal when I made it, and I don't intend to now."

"I see. Still, squatches or no, we have to cross the Shining Mountains and destroy the force at The Meadows," said Wulf.

"You might as well try to destroy the sun. Flee now. Head back east and pray that the living nightmare stays west of the Shining Mountains, at least for as long as you live."

For a long moment, there was silence. The wind in the leaves now sounded like the whispering of monsters, about to burst from the trees and kill them all. Sassa looked at her friends, Wootah and Calnians.

"We should go back," said Gunnhild. She was still holding Ottar by the shoulders. Freydis was holding his hand. "We cannot take the children into a land like that. *There is no shame in knowing the line between bravery and foolishness, and staying the right side of it.*"

Wulf looked at Sassa. For once, he did not know what to say. Even Keef was lost for words. Had they come this far to turn back now?

"We have to go to The Meadows," said Yoki Choppa eventually. Everyone turned to him. "The nightmare that Weeko Fang describes is strengthening. It will cross the Shining Mountains and will spread across the world. All will be killed, human and other animals, unless we act. Ottar the Moaner can defeat the force at The Meadows. He needs us to get him there."

"But how can this little boy stop such a magic?" pleaded Gunnhild.

"I don't know," said Yoki Choppa.

"Tell us what you do know!" demanded Gunnhild.

"I already have." The warlock looked down.

"How then will we even start?" Gunnhild continued. "The squatches will kill us!" Sassa was glad Gunnhild was speaking up because it saved her from doing so. She didn't want to take her developing baby near any more monsters, but neither did she want to lose face by saying they should turn back.

"Weeko will lead us over the Shining Mountains," said Sofi Tornado.

"Did you miss the part about my deal with the squatches?" growled Weeko. "They're expecting me to return with a group of people so that they can murder them."

"So that will let us walk right into their territory."

Deep throat a goat, thought Sassa. Sofi had crossed the line between bravery and foolishness and kept going for a few miles.

"Where they will kill you," said Weeko.

"We'll work something out."

"You're insane."

"Perhaps. But you will take us," said Sofi. "We're the only chance you've heard of to stop The Meadows killing everyone, and you need to make amends for fleeing when the others died."

Weeko held her eye for a moment, then nodded. "All right."

"Er, Sofi," started Wulf.

"Yup."

"Is following Weeko the best plan?"

"You have another guide?"

"No."

"Good. We'll leave now."

"No, we won't," said Wulf.

"We won't?" Sofi turned to him. She didn't put her hand on her axe handle but Sassa could see her fingers twitching.

"We've suffered," said Wulf. "All of us. We'll have one more night's rest, then we'll go."

"People are dying right now, Wulf. The power from The Meadows is strengthening every moment."

"So we'll walk faster after a rest. We need that rest."

Sofi lifted her chin, then deflated and nodded. "Oh, why not? Tatinka, may we stay one more night?"

"Of course you may. Not least because there is another, more immediate danger that you must face."

"Oh no," said Bodil. "What?"

"Beaver Man. He will be waiting for you at the southern edge of Green tribe territory. He is already on his way there with his dagger-tooth cat cavalry."

"How does he know where we'll leave your territory?" asked Sassa.

"Probably in the same way that I know he's coming. But it's also possible that he's worked it out. There's only one good path south from the Black Mountains and you presumably told him where you were headed?"

"Hmmm. And the lizard kings?"

"They are dead. Beasts like that can never live for long, thank Manchinga. The ones you killed would have died within a day or two."

"How *do* you know all this?" asked Gunnhild.

Tatinka smiled. "Manchinga sees."

"Why doesn't Beaver Man follow us into the Black Mountains?" asked Wulf.

"He fears the mountains."

"Should we?"

"Klippsta will escort you south. As long as you are with him you are protected. Manchinga also saves."

"So you say," Klippsta muttered.

"We've been through this, Klippsta," said Tatinka. "I wouldn't send you if it was dangerous."

"Will your people help us defeat Beaver Man?" asked Sofi.

"They are not warriors. However, I will give you weapons which should help. I have five arrows that will pierce Beaver Man's skin, and you have the world's best archer."

Sitsi bristled like a happy cat.

"There's one more thing," Tatinka continued. "You have a baby with you. He will not survive your journey. Please will you leave him with us?"

"Sofi?" asked Wulf.

"It does make some sense," said Gunnhild, trying, Sassa reckoned, not to look desperate to be free from baby care.

"He's the heir to the Calnian empire," said Tatinka. "We won't use him politically, but we will tell him who he is, and perhaps one day he will regain his lands. Or perhaps you'll all come back here and you'll help him."

"He'll stay here," said Sofi.

"There are two other young who should stay here, who I will undertake to look after myself," said Tatinka.

"But Ottar is the prophesy..." said Finn.

"His racoons are not."

Ottar looked about, open-mouthed and despairing. Hugin and Munin pressed themselves into his feet, yickering. Ottar squatted down and gathered the animals to his chest.

Tatinka walked across to him.

"Ottar, your small friends are young and will not be able to cross the Shining Mountains. You or someone else could carry them, but the racoons will hate it, they may die, and the person carrying them will be dangerously burdened."

Ottar moaned and shook his head.

"If it was just the mountains, my dearest boy," Tatinka continued, "it might be worth the risk. However, on the far side of the mountains is the Desert You Don't Walk Out Of. It's a terrible place for racoons in normal times. As things stand now, they will definitely die. It would be cruel to take them with you. You understand, don't you?"

Ottar squeezed his racoons, then looked up at the chief of the Green tribe and nodded, eyes full of tears.

Sassa couldn't help her own tears springing, but neither could she help being just a little satisfied to see all of the women of the Owsla—even Sofi Tornado—walking briskly away lest, she was sure, any of the Wootah should see the world's finest warriors crying over a boy and his pets.

Chapter 8

Off We Go to Kill Beaver Man

A thin drizzle soaked them slowly but efficiently. The local deer didn't seem to mind the penetrating damp and were more numerous here than anywhere else on their odyssey so far. In the long uphill hike out of the Green tribe's town there were thousands of the buggers. A couple skittered from their direct path, but most only looked up from their grazing and chewed fearlessly at the Wootah and Calnians as Klippsta and Weeko Fang led them by.

Ottar the Moaner's wailing didn't seem to disturb the deer. Erik the Angry had never seen anyone as magnificently grief-stricken as the boy. Freydis tried to comfort him for about twenty heartbeats before declaring him a lost cause and marching on ahead, at which point the boy sat on the path and howled and wouldn't go on. So Chogolisa swung him up onto a shoulder, where he wailed all the more, kicking and punching in frenzied anguish.

Erik the Angry's emotions morphed from wet-eyed empathy via self-congratulatory tolerance to silently imploring the little fucker to shut the fuck up. He could have dropped back or walked ahead, away from the sob siren, but Chogolisa was carrying the boy and Erik felt that he should support her.

Two things cheered Erik, though, both of them footwear-related. First, Tatinka had given excellent leather boots to all the Wootah, with hard but pliant soles (she'd also offered them to the Owsla, but Sofi had said they would be hampered by such large shoes). Erik was very grateful for them. The boots looked smashing and, by the way they gripped the wet track and had so far kept his feet warm and dry, they were as good as they looked. The second was his invention of Paloma's watershoes. He'd spent the previous day making two new pairs. In both he'd used more sinew to make them tougher and he'd weaponised them by fire-hardening and sharpening the edges. One pair was roughly the same size as his proto-type, one was a great deal smaller. Erik guessed the optimal size was somewhere in between the two, but these were early days.

The image of Paloma Pronghorn running across a lake, unstrapping her shoes and laying into an unsuspecting enemy with them cheered Erik at least as much as his new boots. However, the image of Paloma sitting on the lake edge asking her foe if they wouldn't mind waiting a mo before she smote them because she had to unstrap her watershoes was a bit of a turd in the cookpot. He'd have to have a look at making those bindings easier to release.

The path flattened out and Ottar's wails, finally, quietened into a snotty snivelling. Freydis fell back to rejoin them and asked if she could go up on Erik's shoulders.

They walked along in contented silence until Chogolisa asked: "What are you thinking about?"

"How to improve Paloma's watershoes."

"Put grease on them to repel water?"

"Possibly, but no, it would be an extra hassle and she doesn't strike me as the type who likes getting grease on her hands."

"You'd be right there. How about beaver fur?"

"Difficult to attach so that it would stay on at high speed."

Chogolisa made several other suggestions, all of which weren't bad but weren't good enough. In the end she gave up and said: "What do you think is in the woods?"

"Fuckloads of deer?"

"Erik the Angry!" scolded Freydis from his shoulders.

"Many deer."

"That must be it. Beaver Man and his army of dagger-tooth cats are cowering on the plain because they're scared of deer."

"Uncle Poppo was bitten by a deer once," said Freydis, "but it was his fault."

As Freydis told the story of Poppo and the deer-bite, Erik looked into the trees. He thought he saw something bigger and a whole lot darker than a deer slinking through the undergrowth, but then it disappeared.

"What *is* in the woods?" he wondered aloud when Freydis's story was done and Chogolisa had finished laughing.

"You really want to know?" asked Klippsta, who'd nipped up silently behind them.

"Sure," said Chogolisa and Erik at the same time.

"They're ghosts," said Freydis.

"Good guess," said Klippsta. "That's pretty much right. The Badlanders have been using some weird ancient magic for years to create their freaky animals. When they do that, the essence of the animal's life—its soul if you like—leaves its body. I don't know how, I guess she uses a similar magic, but Tatinka calls those souls here to live in the woods."

"Why?" asked Erik.

"To scare me when I'm alone, I reckon. Sometimes I feel them pass right through me," he shivered.

"And to stop the Badlanders," said Freydis.

"That is the official reason. I don't know what all those souls would do to Beaver Man and his gang, but I guess he does, because no Badlanders have been into the woods for years."

"I don't think they're scary," said Freydis.

"You don't have to come back all this way on your own," complained Klippsta.

Erik guffawed.

"What's so funny?" asked Chogolisa.

"Klippsta reminded me of an old Lakchan joke."

"Go on then."

"Okay. A child and a child murderer are walking together, deep into the dark, dark woods. *These woods are scary!* says the child. *You think you've got it bad?* answers the child murderer. *I've got to come back this way on my own!*"

Erik laughed but nobody else did and they walked on in silence.

"That wasn't a very good joke," said Freydis after a while.

The drizzle dissolved into a mist which eddied in ghostly tendrils around treetops and craggy outcrops, until Innowak the sun god decided that enough was enough, blasted the mist away and beamed his dazzling rays onto the wet rocks and leaves. A multitude of tweeting birds bounced in from wherever they'd been sheltering and embroidered the fresh morning with their shrill song, serenading the passage of Wootah, Calnians, Weeko Fang and Klippsta.

It was a two-day journey to the southern edge of the Black Mountains. They camped the first night next to a broad, dark lake. The lake was made, according to Klippsta, by a multitude of beavers damming the valley.

Finn the Deep trudged south to inspect the beavers and their dam. He didn't have anything else to do. Paloma had been with Erik since they arrived, running on the lake's surface with some special shoes he'd made. He could see why it was fun, but he couldn't see why they both had to laugh so much, and why she had to fall into his arms at the end of every run. She clearly preferred being with his dad to being with him. Which was completely fine. His dad was a great guy. Finn really didn't mind. He was Finn the Deep now and such things did not trouble him. Although it wasn't like Paloma had even *tried* hanging out with him to see what it was like before getting all chummy with his dad.

He'd tried to talk to Thyri, too, but she'd been too busy sharpening her sax to even acknowledge his greeting. Again, not a worry.

The beaver dam was an amazing thing, he told himself. How *had* they got those huge logs in place and how *did* they keep them there, he tried to wonder.

He stayed as long as he could pretend to himself that he was marvelling at the beaver dam, but Erik and Paloma were still at it when he got back. Sofi Tornado had joined them now. Paloma was towing the Owsla captain behind her, along the water. The soles of Sofi's feet were slapping against the surface, jetting plumes of spray. Finn thought he heard Sofi whoop, but decided it must have been Paloma or a goose or something.

He looked about for something else to focus on. He found Ottar the Moaner, sitting on a rock by the lake, crying silently. He sat next to the boy and put his arm around him.

"Don't worry. I'll bring you back here and we'll see Hugin and Munin again."

Ottar made a face like twisted laundry and groaned like a morose moose. To Finn's surprise, he understood what the boy meant. He was saying thanks, but he knew that he'd never see his racoons again.

So spectacular was the scenery on the following day, great fins and towers of stalwart grey rock soaring out of the forest, that Finn the Deep almost cheered up about the fact that Paloma Pronghorn hadn't even fucking spoken to him since they'd kissed. Neither had Thyri Treelegs. And, for some reason that he was sure she could justify with an annoying phrase, Gunnhild was avoiding him, too.

It was mid-morning when Wulf the Fat jogged up, his face split with a grin that Chapa Wangwa would have been proud of: "Look, man, and remember this moment for ever. You will never see a rock that looks more like a cock."

"Pretty sure you've told me that before," said Finn.

Wulf pointed at a rock tower maybe six times the height of a man. It was topped with a helmet-shaped boulder. Two round boulders poked from fir trees at its base.

Wulf was bouncing with delight. "It's even got pubes! It proves my theory beyond any shadow of a doubt. There is *definitely* a Scrayling cock god who's gone around making these. This one is not a mistake, my friend. There's no way— by Tor, there's another one. It's even better! The knob of a chubbier man! Or maybe the chubbier cock of a thin man..."

The two young heroes strode along spotting cock rock after cock rock and laughing. Wulf's enthusiasm for phallic geology made Finn forget the woes that the world had yet again piled upon him. Then, in the middle of the afternoon, they descended a path that overlooked another beaver-made lake. This lake was smaller, surrounded by domes and vertical slices of grey rock on one side, and with meadow and trees running into it from the other. There were no beavers to be seen, perhaps because, standing on the far shore, was Beaver Man himself, hands on hips, looking up at them.

"And this," said Klippsta, "is the edge of Green tribe territory. I have enjoyed your company, goodbye."

And off he buggered.

"Has Beaver Man seen us?" Bodil asked.

Nobody answered.

"Got your arrows, Sitsi?" asked Sofi.

"In my quiver."

"Good. The highest of the outcrops on the west of the lake looks like a good vantage point."

Looks a lot like a cock, too, thought Finn. He glanced at Wulf. The captain of the Hird, leader of the Wootah diaspora, winked. Finn bit his lip, but a squeak of laughter peeped out.

"Chogolisa, go with Sitsi," Sofi continued, throwing so dark a look at Finn that it made him sweat.

Sitsi and Chogolisa slid away.

Finn watched Erik watch Chogolisa go. His father's blue

eyes were wide with concern above his bushy, dark blond beard. They all knew Erik liked Chogolisa and that she liked him. So why had his dad been pissing around with Paloma?

"Where are the cat cavalry?" asked Keef.

"In the trees behind Beaver Man," said Sofi. "Wulf, take Erik, Keef, Thyri and Sassa around the eastern shore. Cross the meadow quickly then stay in the trees, stay together and stay defensive. Sassa, shoot anyone who has a blowpipe. Do not hesitate. They mean to kill you and yours. If it all goes to shit, flee across the lake to the rocky end. They won't be able to swim as well as you and Sitsi can dissuade them from trying with arrows from her perch."

"The rest of you, stay here, protect the children."

Finn looked about. Weeko Fang was focusing on scraping a pattern in the dirt with his toe. So the hero of the Desert You Don't Walk Out Of didn't mind being put on nanny duties instead of fighting. But Finn the Deep did.

"I should go with the Hird," he said.

"This is a proper post, Finn. The cats are fast and could easily flank the others and run up here. You have just as good a chance of being killed as everyone else."

"Oh. Well, that's okay then."

Finn could see Paloma and Sofi intermittently as they headed down the slope, through the trees. The Hird plus Sassa ran across the meadow and into the trees on the eastern shore, as instructed. Sitsi appeared at the top of the highest outcrop at the west end of the lake.

On the far side, beyond the southern shore, the dagger-tooth cavalry padded towards Wulf and the rest of them.

Finn looked at Ottar and Freydis. Ottar was still miserable, showing no interest at all in the butterfly that his sister was pointing out to him.

Then it all happened.

Beaver Man jogged across the clearing. Paloma Pronghorn

tore across the lake on her watershoes, pulling Sofi Tornado behind her. Beaver Man stopped to watch them approach. Sitsi's arrow hit him square in the chest and penetrated deep.

That's it! Finn realised he was bouncing on his toes in excitement and stopped. But Sitsi had hit Beaver Man with the magic arrow right in the heart!

He really hadn't thought it was going to be that easy.

And, of course, it wasn't.

Beaver Man ignored the arrow protruding from his chest. He ran to meet Sofi and Paloma. Another arrow stuck in his shoulder and checked him for an instant, but only an instant.

Sofi and Paloma reached the shore. Paloma sat to unfasten her watershoes. Sofi walked to meet Beaver Man, stone axe swinging.

Sitsi's spirits sank. She'd pierced his heart! Why wasn't he dead? Tatinka had told them that the arrows would penetrate his flesh, and she'd been right. Sofi had suspected that they wouldn't have much effect on him, and she'd been right, too.

Sitsi sat, bow on her lap. The rock wobbled below her. The top of the pillar she was on was a separate boulder, which had somehow stayed on its perch through the ages. The wobble stilled and Sitsi relaxed. These were Sofi's orders. Shoot him twice, then wait in plain sight until the next cue.

"Wootah tribe!" It was Rappa Hoga.

They could see glimpses of dagger-tooths and riders through the trees and Sassa had raised her bow a couple of times, but so far she'd had no clear target to shoot.

"Yup!" answered Wulf.

"Stay where you are. Do not attack us and you may live to the end of the day. Do you understand?"

"Do you mean do I understand what you're saying, or are you asking whether I agree to it?"

"The latter."

"In which case, go fuck yourself! We're coming for you!" yelled Wulf. "Woooootah!" then, in a hoarse whisper, "all of you stay exactly where you are. Do not attack them unless I say. Don't shoot any of them, Sassa."

"I strongly recommend," called Rappa Hoga, "that you remain where you are."

Sofi accelerated into a run and launched herself at Beaver Man, all her weight and strength in an axe blow aimed for his head; at least that's what it looked like. He raised an arm to block, as she'd known he would. She diverted her axe's swing to smash his elbow and slammed her palm into his nose a moment later.

She skipped away. The Badlander's nose was ruined, there was white bone protruding from his elbow, but there was no blood.

"The deer tick," he said, "is my chief power animal. Not the most splendid of beasts, but indestructible and strong as an army. Come on, I'll let you have one more go at me without striking back before I kill you."

She danced towards him, axe flashing, and heard him prepare to punch her. Indestructible, but not as noble as he liked people to think. She ducked the blow, smashed his chin with an axe uppercut and drove her pointed fingers into his liver, hoping that his lower organs might be vulnerable.

They were not.

Beaver Man leapt at her, arms and legs flailing in a frenzied onslaught. Frenzied was Sofi's least favourite type of attack. She couldn't avoid every blow. Her upper thigh exploded with pain as he drove a knee into bunched muscle, then he caught her on the temple with a punch like a moose's kick.

She reeled. He followed, hammering fists into her midriff. A rib, possibly two, cracked. A backhanded slap blinded her for a moment.

She heard him step back, heard him wind up for a punch

that would take her head off. There was nothing she could do about it.

Then something struck her hard and she was flying.

Sitsi watched Beaver Man beat the crap out of Sofi.

Sofi had told her to hold, whatever happened. She did as she was bid but it was horrible to watch. Anyone but Owsla would have been killed long before.

Beaver Man wound up for a punch that would surely finish things, but Paloma, having finally unstrapped her watershoes, came tearing across the clearing, dived at Sofi and shot on, carrying the Owsla captain into the woods at around the same speed as a falling star.

This was Sitsi's cue.

Beaver Man turned to follow Sofi and Paloma. Sitsi Kestrel loosed an arrow. It zipped over the lake and skewered the Badlander through the back of the neck.

No matter how good an archer you were, it was difficult to shoot exactly where you wanted. Imperfections in the bow, twine, arrow shaft, head and fletching could all affect the course of an arrow, as could external factors like wind, altitude, temperature and the wetness of the air. So Sitsi was very happy when her arrow pierced Beaver Man's neck dead centre, severing his spine.

Instead of flopping to the ground and never standing again, however, as any decent man would have done, Beaver Man turned slowly, smiled at Sitsi despite his mashed face, and ran towards her. He hit the lake and Sitsi thought he was going to swim, but, no, he ran across it like Paloma, but without the watershoes.

She swallowed hard.

He reached the base of the tower and shot up it like a squirrel. He leapt onto her boulder triumphantly.

Other warriors might have fought him then and there, but

Sitsi knew her strengths. Asking Innowak to watch over her, she leapt backwards off her perch.

Tansy Burna steered her cat through the woods, her nose pressed into musky neck fur, always keeping trees between her and the Wootah woman with the bow. She found Rappa Hoga sitting on his cat at the edge of the trees, watching Beaver Man run across the lake, scale a rock tower and frighten one of the Calnian Owsla from the top of it. Beaver Man jumped after the woman and out of sight.

"We could dismount," said Tansy, "crawl through the undergrowth and take the Wootah with blowpipes."

"We could," he agreed.

"Shall I give the order?"

"No."

"We need to—" she started, but he shook his head to silence her.

Paloma looked over her shoulder. Nobody was following. She stopped.

"He's not following," said Sofi, speaking as if she had a mouthful of berries.

"Are you all right?" Paloma asked as she laid the Owsla captain on the pine needle-carpeted woodland floor.

Sofi narrowed the eye that wasn't swollen shut. Blood trickled from her mouth and several cuts. "Never better," she said, pushing herself up. "Come on let's—ahhh," she fell back down. "Seems I'll need a hand standing. Then we need to get back."

Finn the Deep noticed something amiss, beyond the fact that Sofi had been beaten and Sitsi was about to be killed.

"Where's Bodil?" he asked.

"She went off down the hill a while back," said Freydis.

"Why?"

"I think she was bored up here. I know I am."

"Oh, for the love of Loakie..."

He scanned the slope below them, but couldn't see Bodil. He was meant to be looking after her. Where had she gone? He hoped she didn't fuck things up any more than they already were.

Sitsi fell with her bow drawn, saw Beaver Man leap after her, and shot. The next moment the wind was knocked from her body as Chogolisa caught her. The big woman set her down and Sitsi looked up.

Beaver Man was pinned through the shoulder to the boulder at the top of the rock tower. Tatinka's amazing arrow had gone through him and deep into the stone. He waggled his arms and his legs like a baby on its back, then gripped the arrow shaft and pulled.

Sitsi reached for the final arrow and drew.

Her bowstring snapped.

Beaver Man yanked at the arrow.

Sitsi delved into the spare bowstring pocket on her quiver. It was empty.

"Where's my spare string?" *She'd had two in there!*

"Wait there! I'll be down in a moment to kill you!" called Beaver Man from above, with the tone of a man nipping back to the hut to grab his forgotten smock.

"Give me the arrow," said Chogolisa.

Sitsi handed it to her. Chogolisa gripped the shaft with her teeth, leapt onto the rock tower and climbed, big fingers and toes somehow finding holds.

She reached Beaver Man, ignored a kick to the face, and drove the arrow through his leg. The big woman then climbed round the rock tower and out of Sitsi's sight. Meanwhile, Beaver Man carried on yanking at the arrow in his shoulder, which would surely come out at any moment.

Chogolisa appeared above him at the top of the rock tower,

plucked the arrow from the Badlander's shoulder then drove it back in, deep into the rock underneath. He waved his arms up at her but couldn't reach.

Then Chogolisa made her mistake.

She slapped her hand down onto the arrow in his shoulder to drive it deeper into the rock. This she achieved, but she also drove the arrow through her own hand, pinning it to the Badlander.

She wrenched. Beaver Man grabbed her hand and held it.

Chogolisa grunted with pain and tried to pull her hand free.

The perched rock wobbled, then tottered, then fell.

Sitsi watched open-mouthed as the boulder tumbled away from her off the top of the stack, with Beaver Man and Chogolisa attached to it. She heard stone, man and woman hit the lake with a resounding boom.

Erik the Angry stood with Wulf on the wooded lakeside. They watched Chogolisa climb over the tower, then saw the top of the tower topple with her and Beaver Man attached to it.

Erik dropped his club, stripped in a trice, dived in and set off across the lake like a deranged turtle, wet white buttocks flashing in the sunlight.

Sitsi Kestrel clambered over the boulders, saw that someone was swimming across from the far side of the lake and realised that whoever it was would never make it in time. She took a deep breath and launched herself headfirst into the lake.

She was no swimmer.

All was noise. Water rushed up her nose. She had no idea which way was up. She caught a glimpse of movement in the dark and tried to calm herself. Then she could see Chogolisa on the bottom of the lake, her hand trapped under the boulder. Beaver Man, she realised, was under the great rock, squashed into the lake bed.

She had no idea how, but somehow she managed to swim down to Chogolisa. She gripped her friend's free wrist, braced her feet against the rock and pulled with all her might. Chogolisa heaved, too, but even her great strength couldn't free the trapped hand from under the colossal stone.

Water roared in Sitsi's ears. Kicked-up silt now obscured her vision entirely. Her strength was failing. Chogolisa's efforts were slowing. Sitsi had to surface. She pulled at Chogolisa's arm one last time, squeezed it goodbye and kicked upwards.

As she rose, something dark sank past her.

Sitsi surfaced, sucked in air, then trod water and prepared for another dive. The swimmer crossing the lake was still a good way off. She sucked in a lungful and was about to submerge when Chogolisa popped up next to her, followed by someone with dark hair who could only be Beaver Man.

She grabbed Beaver Man's head to push him under, but he squeaked and she realised it wasn't him at all. It was Bodil Gooseface.

"Hello!" said Bodil when Sitsi had released her head.

They swam back to the shore that Beaver Man had run from, looking over their shoulders for any sign of the chief of the Badlanders. Erik joined them soon after they'd set off, full of concern for Chogolisa then full of joy when he realised that she was all right.

As they waded ashore, Sofi Tornado emerged from the trees supported by Paloma Pronghorn. Sitsi was about to shout a greeting when Rappa Hoga appeared at the other end of the clearing on his enormous dagger-toothed beast. His cat cavalry followed.

"I'd hoped to fight you again," said Rappa Hoga to Sofi.

Sofi hacked and spat blood. "I ... I'll just sit down for a while. Then we'll fight." She sat.

Rappa Hoga dismounted.

"I'll fight you," said Erik striding forward, unarmed, dripping wet and naked.

The captain of the cat cavalry looked him up and down and raised a hand in a "please pause" gesture.

"Wootah and Calnians in the trees and on the hill!" he shouted. His voice was so deep and strong that Sitsi could feel her skin vibrating. It was not unpleasant. "Come out, come down, come here. You have my word that my cat cavalry will not harm you. I want to talk to you."

His dagger-tooth roared as if it disagreed.

Sitsi looked at Sofi. She nodded.

"Do as he asks!" Sitsi yelled. "Sofi says so!"

"And, for the love of all that's good," the captain of cat cavalry added, pointing at Erik "bring this man's clothes to him."

Sitsi couldn't stop staring at his cat. It wasn't as large as the monstrous dagger-tooth that the Owsla had fought on the way to Hardwork a few weeks and a million years before, but it was still a lovely, magnificent beast.

"Calnians and Wootah," said Rappa Hoga when everyone was gathered. "I apologise on behalf of the Badlanders and myself for impeding your quest, for the deaths of four of your number and for the suffering that the rest of you have undergone."

Calnians and Wootah looked at each other. This was not expected.

"Beaver Man's philosophies made great sense to me and I loved him," Rappa Hoga continued. "I'm not sure why, perhaps it was your influence, but I've recently come to see that we have gone too far. Far too far. It is not up to us to cull human numbers, and we should not have used magic and alchemy for such ill ends. I think Beaver Man had good intentions, but we became a force of evil. Still, I did not dare rise against him and his Owsla. It took people with your courage and your strength to—"

"Yeah yeah yeah, what happens now?" interrupted Keef the Berserker.

"Sorry about him," said Wulf.

Rappa Hoga chuckled. "He's right. I can be pompous. What happens now is that we go our separate ways. I return to the Badlands, proclaim myself chief and set about dismantling Beaver Man's systems. I will free all the Calnian captives, help them return to Calnia and choose a new ruler." He glanced at the lake. There was no sign of the Badlander chief. "You can continue on your journey. Sofi, you are injured and walking will be painful."

"I'll be fine."

"So I will leave you my cat. It will be your mount. Finnbogi—"

"It's Finn now."

"If you say so. Finn, you controlled the crowd pigeons, did you not?"

"I did."

"Good. Can you communicate with my cat?"

Finn closed his eyes. "I can."

"Then he will cause no trouble. Set him free when you no longer need him and he will return to me." He turned back to his troops. "Tansy Burna, may I ride behind you?"

Tansy reddened and nodded eagerly.

"Then I will be gone. Farewell and thank you, Wootah and Calnians."

The Badlander cat cavalry rode away and disappeared into the trees.

Chapter 9

A Kiss and a Monster

The lakeside was an ideal camping spot, but everyone was keen to put as many paces as possible between themselves and Beaver Man. He couldn't possibly be alive, down there on the bed of the lake. If he was, there was a rock the size of a hut on top of him and he wasn't going anywhere. But he'd walked away from an arse to neck sword-spitting, so who knew what else he could survive, and they'd seen him topple a rock not much smaller than the one he was trapped under, so if anybody was going to escape that situation, leap out of the lake and attack them, it was Beaver Man.

So Calnians and Wootah strode out of the Black Mountains, following the track south and a little east into rolling, wooded grasslands mostly populated by buffalo, turkey and pronghorn. Sofi, Ottar and Freydis led the way atop the magnificent dagger-tooth cat.

They walked hard, jogging the downhill sections. There was no arseing about and even Bodil hardly spoke. Shortly before sunset they stopped at a place that would just about do as camp. They ate foraged nuts and fruit and a buffalo calf which Yoki Choppa sliced thin, rubbed with herbs and seared on hot stones. After dinner, everybody who wasn't on guard went to sleep as soon as they lay down.

Morning came and Beaver Man hadn't appeared and killed them all, which was a relief. The rolling tree- and buffalo-filled land was gentler but at least as beautiful as the Black Mountains and everything was a great deal happier.

Following Weeko Fang's hoarsely whispered directions, they trailed Sofi and the children on the big cat south at a more sensible pace than the previous day's, and hardly looked over their shoulders at all.

Erik the Angry had resolved something the moment Chogolisa surfaced in the lake. He found several excuses to put it off, but, as they walked along a wooded valley busy with squirrels all overlooked by a cliff of red rock to the north, and everyone else was obscured by the trees ahead, he said: "I like you very much."

Her pace didn't falter and she didn't look at him.

"That's not how you do it," said Chogolisa after about twenty heartbeats that felt like an eternity to Erik.

"What?"

"You don't tell me that you like me. You wait until we're camped. When I walk away from the fire, you follow me and try to kiss me."

"I see. You're right. Sorry."

"Apology accepted."

"Hang on a moment." Erik rubbed his bearded chin. "Just so I'm clear."

They stopped. She turned and looked down at him. It was still strange to Erik that such a pretty woman was so large, and a tiny voice in his head did suggest that some people might think he liked her because he missed his giant bear, but the fact was, whatever the reason, he did like her. A lot.

"You'd have to crouch if I was going to kiss you."

She shook her head. "I spend my life crouching. I don't want to be crouching the first time I kiss you. See that boulder?"

"Yup."

"You should stand on something like that."

He jumped onto the boulder. "Like this?"

"That's it."

"Then what would I do?"

"You'd say something like: *I think I've got a fly in my eye, can you take a look, please?*"

"Well, that is odd, because I do have a fly in my eye right now."

"Oh, really? I'll take a look."

She stood by the boulder, now only a little taller than Erik. He put his hands on her waist, feeling like he might burst. She cupped his face with her uninjured hand and leant forward.

"I can't see it yet," she said. "If I just lean in a little more . . ."

They kissed for a long time. At one point, Erik opened his eyes and saw a grey-brown squirrel watching them from a hole in a tree. He winked at it, closed his eyes and carried on kissing Chogolisa.

Eventually he broke off and said, "It's going to be a challenge, trying to find a boulder every time we want to do this."

"Nobody said love was easy, and we can always lie down."

The following morning, Erik the Angry sauntered along smiling like a fat man after a large lunch. They followed a buffalo road south through undulating grassland and woods. Where there weren't buffalo, there were pronghorn and other deer. Turkeys ran amok in the woods and the plains were carpeted with prairie dog mounds and busy with the appealing little animals.

It seemed to be a predator-free zone until mid-afternoon, when a pack of sly-faced grey wolves trotted towards some buffalo calves. A few enormous bulls chased them away. The wolves slunk off, looking over their shoulders with expressions ranging from "we were going anyway" to "we'll be back."

Well before it was time for their first rest, the cat carrying

Sofi and the children stopped. The others caught up and Erik saw a figure a good mile ahead, standing on a mound and watching them approach.

"It's a girl," said Sitsi, "maybe ten years old. High forehead, big lips. Looking this way."

"Anyone else about?" asked Wulf the Fat.

"Not that I can see."

"Are you alone?" asked Sofi Tornado when they reached the child. She was wearing a simple brown dress and had white feathers in her hair. Erik had known that Sitsi Kestrel had good eyesight, but he was still surprised to see that the girl really did have a high forehead and lips like a river fish. He'd been able to see that from about forty paces. Sitsi had seen it from a mile.

"I'm Chitsa," said the girl, unfazed at being questioned by a woman riding a dagger-tooth cat. "Dead Nanda said you were coming so they're all hiding in a valley to the east. I can show you if you like?"

"Who's Dead Nanda?" asked Sofi.

"Our warlock, and my aunt. She's dead, but she still walks around and talks."

"Why did they hide?"

"Dead Nanda said magic people were coming south with a dagger-tooth cat."

"Why aren't you hiding?"

"I wanted to see the dagger-tooth cat. Can I stroke his face?"

"I wouldn't," said Sofi.

"Do you want me to show you where the others are?"

"No thanks. You should be getting back to them."

The girl shook her head. "They don't like me. Do you want me to show you something really amazing instead? It's just down in that valley over there." She pointed to the south-west.

They followed the girl to where the land curved down into

a shallow canyon busy with rabbits, rocky on one side with a steep grass verge on the other.

A heavily trodden path ran along the valley floor, but there was no other sign of activity.

"Sitsi, Paloma, up on the valley sides, eyes skinned."

"Come on, it's this way!" said the girl heading along the path as the two women leapt nimbly out of the gully.

"No. We wait here while they check it's safe."

"I wish it wasn't so safe around here," Chitsa pouted. "This valley is the most interesting bit of the most boring place in the whole world."

"Is this your homeland?" Weeko asked.

"No. We came over the mountains."

"You came from the Desert You Don't Walk Out Of?"

"Yup."

"How long ago?" asked Wulf. "How did you make it over the Shining Mountains?"

"It's a boring story and it's sad. I'll take you to my people and they can tell you, but you have to look at what I want to show you first."

"Tell us who you are, now," said Weeko Fang.

The girl looked scared.

Wulf put a hand on Weeko's arm. "Thanks, Weeko, but it's fine. It can wait until we get to her people."

Weeko shrugged.

Paloma and Sitsi reported that all was clear but stayed up on the valley sides keeping watch while the rest of them rode and walked down into the canyon.

"Here you go!" said the girl after a while, pointing to a hole in the rocky northern wall. The small cave was oval, wider at the top than the base, about a third Erik's height.

"A hole," said Keef. "Wow."

"Watch this." Chitsa plucked a feather from her hair and dropped it. It shot down the hole as if someone had pulled it on a string.

"You try." She handed Keef a feather. He let go and jumped as the feather whooshed down the hole.

"Wow," he said, in a very different tone from the previous wow. He scooped up some soil and poured it out of his hand. It flew down the hole. "You can feel it," he waved his hand. "Wind is rushing down the hole."

Moments later everyone was queuing to let things go and watch them zoom into the ground. Even Sofi dismounted wincingly, plucked some grass and watched it fly down.

"What is it?" she asked Chitsa, who was standing by the little cave mouth, smilingly smugly.

"According to Dead Nanda, it's the window to another world. There's a whole world down there that mirrors ours. Right now, on the other side, there's a girl showing people just like you the hole, apart from in the other world they're not people like us, they're demons."

"Does it always suck like this?" Keef asked, tossing more grass into the airstream.

"No. Sometimes it sucks, sometimes it blows. It depends on the weather down there."

"How do you know all this?"

"We just know."

"I'm going in!" He waved Arse Splitter around his head.

"The demons will kill you," Chitsa nodded.

"I've got to have a look. Wulf, hold my feet!"

Wulf did so, and Keef squeezed through the gap.

Everyone watched until a muffled cry came from Keef to pull him out. Once extracted, he stood and dusted himself down.

"Well?" asked Gunnhild.

"Dunno. Couldn't see a thing."

Everyone laughed, apart from Chitsa. "You were lucky," she said.

"We'll need to stay here for a while," said Keef, "widen the hole, make some rope and torches and see what's down there."

He pointed at the trees on the other side of the canyon. "These trees'll be good for what we need." He jogged backwards on tiptoes. "Yes, we can build a frame there," he pointed, "angle a couple of trunks out from it, rope up a boulder and swing it against the hole. That'll open up a passage and—"

"No," said Sofi. "We're going to Chitsa's tribe now to see what they can tell us."

"But—"

"That's what we're doing, Keef."

"Why don't you come with me down the hole, Wulf? It'll be heroic. Imagine! You, me, Arse Splitter and Thunderbolt in a world of demons. It'll be the greatest story ever told."

"Men go down hole," said Thyri. "Find all the feathers and grass that people have chucked down there and nothing else. Yeah, it'll be amazing."

"Tell you what, Keef," said Wulf, "right now I've got mountains to climb and a desert to cross, plus monsters and firenados to battle. If that gets boring, I will come with you down your hole."

"Bjarni would have been up for it..." muttered Keef as they walked on.

"Which is exactly why we shouldn't do it," said Gunnhild. *"A fool chooses excitement over duty. He finds shallow pleasure and shallower gains."*

The first thing that Paloma noticed about Chitsa's people was that they were all female and all were elderly or young; none were the traditional warrior age. Two of the older women were holding babies. They were around twenty in all, standing in front of four conical hide tents and looking wary—as they should with a bunch of warriors and a dagger-tooth cat walking up to them. It was possible that there were more of them, perhaps hiding and waiting to ambush, but Paloma didn't think so. Their tents would have slept only about twenty, for one thing.

A woman stepped forward. By her hat of grey hair, sallow skin and sunken eyes, she had to be the warlock Dead Nanda.

Sofi reassured her that no harm was meant. Dead Nanda nodded and asked who they were. She was calm and articulate, if a little shrill; not at all what Paloma would have expected from someone who was meant to be dead.

Sofi told Dead Nanda that they were the Calnians and the Wootah, heading west, then where they'd come from and how they'd got here.

"Our village was not far west of the Shining Mountains. It was destroyed in a flood, then we were attacked by monsters. That's when I was killed."

"What sort of monsters?" asked Wulf.

Paloma was glad nobody was asking why Dead Nanda thought she was dead. Her sort of pseudo-warlock affectation was annoying and not to be encouraged.

"Giant insects, mostly," she answerwed, deadpan. "That wasn't so bad, we could defend against those. When a pack of several dozen hairless wolves killed half our number, including me, the rest of us decided to leave."

"How did you get across the Shining Mountains?" asked Weeko.

"We didn't," said Dead Nanda.

"But you are here," said Wulf.

"Most of us didn't make it. The squatches killed every male, young and old, and all the women of warrior age."

"Why?"

"For pleasure, it seemed. They murdered some with their minds; knocked them down as if with an invisible hammer. The rest they tore apart with their hands. There was no fighting them. We tried. We didn't so much as scratch one of them."

"Why did they let you go?"

"They said—I say 'said' but they *thought* into our minds— that they were letting the young go to grow into adults that they might hunt."

"And they let the older women live to look after them?" asked Erik.

"No. They said that we were bad eating."

They spent the afternoon with Chitsa's people. While Wulf, Sofi and Weeko spoke to Dead Nanda and a couple of others, learning what they could about the Shining Mountains and the Desert You Don't Walk Out Of, the rest of the Wootah and Calnians hunted and foraged, not to bolster their own supplies—they'd left the Green tribe well stocked—but to add to the refugees' meagre reserves.

After a long afternoon gathering herbs and berries under Yoki Choppa's guidance, Finn finally sat a short way from the large fire they'd built, exhausted. He'd rested for only a moment when he heard Sofi shout.

"Warriors, make ready. Non-fighters, hide. There's something coming towards us. I don't know what it is, but it's large. Sitsi, it's there," she pointed westwards and upwards. "What is it?"

Finn looked where Sofi was pointing, and saw a black dot in the distance. It doubled in size even in the couple of heartbeats before Sitsi said: "It must be one of the monsters we've been hearing about. It's got oversized insect eyes, fangs like a dagger-tooth, a bulbous naked body like a shaved, pregnant cat and two, no three, pairs of wings flapping very quickly."

"How big?"

"I can't tell with any accuracy because there are no reference points. Hang on, there's an eagle passing behind it . . . no, sorry, to the front of it. A long way in front. It's very big. Wingspan maybe a hundred paces. I guess the body's the same length, hard to tell from this angle. And it is heading for us."

Finn could make out its flapping wings now.

"Weeko, Dead Nanda, any ideas?"

"I haven't seen anything like that," said Weeko. "But I think hiding would be a good idea."

"Everyone, over to the gully," shouted Sofi. "Apart from Owsla. And Wulf?"

"Yes?"

"I'd like Sassa on the edge of the gully with her bow, ready to flee but also to shoot."

"None of the Wootah are going into the gully," said Wulf, "apart from the children, and Gunnhild if she wants."

Finn gripped Foe Slicer's hilt. He didn't, he was surprised to realise, want to go to the gully.

"Bravery is being afraid but standing your ground," said Gunnhild.

Chitsa and her people ran with Ottar and Freydis to the gully. Dead Nanda stayed.

"Spread out!" called Sofi. Finn found himself on the edge, farthest from the gully.

The creature flew nearer and grew ever larger. Soon they could all see just how horrific it was. Sitsi hadn't mentioned its dangling, black, insectoid legs. Dozens of them sprouted from its grey-pink belly like hairs. Instead of a foot, each had a shining spike at the end.

The gully did have some appeal, Finn admitted to himself, but he stood his ground.

Then they could hear it, a great leathery flapping, and a strange rasping which Finn guessed must be its breathing. It rose and fell in the air, as if flying was a struggle.

"Fuck. A. Duck," said Paloma when the creature was a couple of hundred paces away and they could see it all the more clearly. Its yellow fangs dripped great globs of goo.

Sassa looked at her and Paloma smiled back.

"Sitsi, Sassa, try belly shots first, one arrow each," said Sofi. "Shoot now."

Two arrows whistled off towards the beast and disappeared into its great soft stomach.

For a moment nothing happened, then the wings stopped flapping and the huge animal fell from the sky. It hit the ground a hundred paces away with a great squelching whump.

"Well, that was easy," said Keef. "Bit of a shame I—"

He was interrupted by a loud buzzing as a swarm of insects rose from the downed monster.

"Now these I have seen before," said Dead Nanda. "They'll die soon enough, but their stings will kill you. They don't like fire, so arm yourselves accordingly." She plucked a burning ember from the fire.

Finn grabbed a burning branch then watched as the cloud of insects spread a little, then coalesced and headed for them, filling the air with their sharper buzzing.

Finn saw that they were the same kind of wasp that had terrified him back on the shore of Olaf's Fresh Sea shortly before the Calnians had come—huge black bastards with red wings.

Just as he'd done back then, he squatted, but this time he had a burning ember to ward them off with. The buzzing was all about for a moment, then it quietened as the wasps fell with a noise like muffled hail. A few of them bounced off Finn and he winced, but then it was over.

He stood, along with everyone else apart from Gunnhild, who was lying nearby, her body convulsing. He ran over to her.

His aunt's neck was swollen and purple, her face red and her tongue protruding. There were two yellow lumps on her throat with red dots in their centres. She'd been stung twice. Her hands shook with the effort of trying to suck in air. She squeaked strangely. Her eyes bulged with begging horror.

"Help!" he yelled.

In a moment, Yoki Choppa was kneeling on the other side of Gunnhild with a flint knife pressed into her neck. He grunted as he straightened his arms to press down and cut into her windpipe. Finn watched in horror as the warlock sliced left and right to enlarge the bloody hole, then jammed his blow-pipe into the slit.

Gunnhild slumped and her arms dropped to her side, but her chest rose then fell as she breathed through the warlock's blowpipe.

"You saved her!" Finn gasped.

Yoki Choppa came as close to smiling as Finn had ever seen. "Maybe."

Chapter 10

Eagle's Bluff

The Wootah and Calnians helped Chitsa's people move their camp away from the carpet of dead wasps and stinking remains of bloated monster, while Yoki Choppa picked through its weird corpse collecting samples.

The following morning Finn was woken by Wulf the Fat.

"Gunnhild is dead," he said.

"What the . . . how?"

"I don't know. Yoki Choppa says it could have been the wasp's venom, or perhaps she just died. People do. You die—"

"Yeah."

Wulf nodded and walked away.

Finn lay and blinked tears, then resolved not to cry. He got out of his sleeping sack and walked to where Gunnhild's body was wrapped in a blanket.

Erik and Chogolisa were using deer shoulder blades to dig a hole. Freydis was watching them, weeping gently. Sassa was there too, with her hand on Freydis' shoulder. Ottar was nowhere to be seen.

"Do you want to see her?" asked Erik, standing up and stretching his back.

"No," said Finn. He wanted to remember her alive. "Where's Ottar?"

"He's throwing things into the hole with Chitsa."

They buried Gunnhild, then headed off south and a little

west, walking hard in the days and sleeping well at night. They left the hills and found themselves back on vast prairie, although the grass was mercifully a great deal shorter than the hip-high stuff they'd waded through in the east. Sitsi insisted this particular prairie wasn't the Ocean of Grass. Finn didn't see why it wasn't; it looked the same to him. He didn't push it though.

Although you'd think she might have wanted to console him, Paloma Pronghorn kept her distance at all times. The few times that he managed to engineer an encounter, she was polite, but you'd never guess that they'd shared the most romantic moments of Finn's life in the Black Mountains. And Thyri seemed permanently pissed off. They trained together every evening, but Thyri hardly spoke and she whacked him even harder than before. His improvement in blocking saved him from serious injury, thank Loakie.

As Finn walked he tried to think about Gunnhild, but thoughts of Thyri and Paloma kept interrupting his attempts to mournfully muse. He'd decide that he was deeply, heroically, in love with Thyri, then resolve that, no, Paloma was simply the most exquisite person in existence and he had to be with her. It was sad, he told himself, considering nothing was ever going to happen with either of them.

He tried to be pleased for his father. Erik and Chogolisa looked as happy as post-coital rabbits. They delighted in the animals and birds. They laughed a lot; giggled even. How sweet it was, Finn told himself. Objectively, perhaps, it was a little unfair that the father that had abandoned him should find a second love when Finn was yet to find his first one, but Finn wasn't the type to feel hard done by. No, by Tor, he definitely wasn't.

It wasn't just Erik and Chogolisa that Finn wasn't jealous of. Keef the Berserker and Bodil Gooseface also seemed to have found each other. You wouldn't know it during the day. Keef was as zany as ever and Bodil as dumb, and they didn't speak to each other any more than they had before. But every night Sofi always put them on the same watch and they shared a sleeping sack. While Finn had managed to alienate both Paloma and Thyri by kissing Paloma, Bodil and Keef had gone from nothing to an established couple who might have been together for years. It was weird. But it didn't bother Finn the Deep.

A short way into the third day, Sofi climbed off the cat and limped along next to it. The children rode the beast some of the time, but they walked next to it more and more.

Walking is good for limbs and essential for the mind, Gunnhild would have said. Finn was surprised to find himelf missing her sayings.

"Shouldn't we send the dagger-tooth back to Rapa Hoga?" asked Erik.

"He said we can keep it while we need it," said Sofi, ruffling the beast's ears.

On they walked. It rained, they got wet. The rain stopped, they dried. Just like buffalo, they were, mused Finn. He spent a lot of time looking at buffalo, trying to keep his mind off the two women. Finn had thought the buffalo's melancholy eyes were looking into his soul, but when he reached out to their minds he found that they were simply sad because everything died.

On the eighth day the grassland was punctured by rocky outcrops that Sitsi Kestrel said must herald Eagle's Bluff.

"Eagle's Bluff?" asked Sassa Lipchewer.

"If I hadn't joined the Owsla, my parents would have sent me to Eagle's Bluff. That's what they'd claimed anyway, but they didn't say it until I was very much part of the Owsla, and it's easy to make statements that are never going to be tested."

"What is Eagle's Bluff?"

"A big lump of rock with a town on it, so they say. I've never seen it. The town, so they also say, is an amalgamated

tribe of the elite, a gathering of the best warlocks and bright-
est thinkers from all the tribes. However, that's obviously
flawed, because if you are a great thinker or a warlock, then
you use that. Either you stay with your tribe and help them,
or you travel and learn. What you don't do, surely, is gather in
one place to show off how clever you are to other braggarts.
They say that every single person on Eagle's Bluff thinks they
are the cleverest person there, which sums up for me what a
dreadful place it must be."

"Are you the cleverest person in the Owsla?" Sassa couldn't
resist asking.

"By some measures, perhaps," said Sitsi, colouring, "but
in terms of practical application of intelligence and knowing
what's best for the Owsla, then Sofi is cleverest. Now, if you
don't mind, I have to go and shoot our dinner."

Sitsi stormed off, leaving an amused Sassa.

Well before they saw the blunted tooth of rock that was
Eagle's Bluff, they could see a thick column of smoke.

"Is the smoke normal?" asked Sassa.

"I don't think so," said Sitsi.

They camped that night in the lee of a bare rock scarp overlooking a valley of buffalo-clipped grass. As if celebrating
the passing of the buffalo and the lack of soaring birds above,
there were tens of thousands of the little brown prairie dogs
tearing about in the last of the light, including thousands of
soft-furred, round-headed babies squeaking and leaping for
flying insects.

They'd eaten well yet again. Sassa hadn't known it was
possible to make food as delicious as Yoki Choppa's creations.

Despite what lay head, Gunnhild's death and the mystery
of the smoke from Eagle's Bluff, Sassa felt well and happy
tucked under Wulf's arm, watching the dancing fire.

"Tell them," Keef the Berserker was saying to Bodil Gooseface nearby.

"You're not meant to."

"You're not meant to go more that ten miles from Hardwork. You're not meant to cross rivers full of sharks. You're not meant to hook up with your enemy. You're not meant to be so awesome with a long axe that everyone thinks you're a god."

"So?" asked Bodil.

"So *you're not meant to* doesn't mean anything any more. There are no rules."

"Oh, all right. I'll tell them."

Bodil stood. The setting sun highlighted the red in her dark hair. "Everybody!" she said. "Everybody!"

They all gathered round apart from Paloma Pronghorn, who was out scouting. Sassa enjoyed watching Finn look around for Paloma, see she wasn't there, then try and fail to sit next to Thyri Treelegs. Sassa didn't mean to be cruel—she hoped he would find someone suitable at some point—but she did find his turmoil amusing.

"Right, everyone," said Bodil. "I'm not sure why I'm telling you all this, but Keef thinks I should. I'm pregnant."

Bodil and Keef had shagged for the first time twelve days before, Sassa calculated. So if Keef had got her pregnant, there was no way she could know it. Unless something had happened that Sassa didn't know about, and she was certain that it hadn't, then Bodil had had sex with only one other person, and that person must be the father.

Keef seemed bright, but since he never listened to anybody else, he actually knew very little about anything he wasn't directly involved in. Sassa wouldn't put it past him to be totally ignorant about the mechanisms and timescales of child creation. And Bodil was Bodil. If there was a couple who could think that a woman was already showing the signs of a child conceived just a few days before, it was them.

Judging by the heartbeat's pause before the hearty congratulations, everyone else was doing the same sums as Sassa. And, like Sassa, they were all glancing at Finn the Deep.

"Finn the Deep Red!" she whispered to Wulf.

He raised an admonishing eyebrow at her and it was her turn to blush. To be told off for taking a situation too lightly by the man whose new delight was spotting penis-shaped rocks really was something.

Eagle's Bluff was a collection of stepped, flat-topped mountains standing stark from the plain. Its slopes were bands of grassy ridge and pale rock, tinged gold by the rising sun. Less smoke than before, but still more than you'd expect from domestic fires, was snaking up into the blue from the nearest bluff.

As soon as the top of the bluff came into view, Sitsi Kestrel saw what she'd been dreading. "It's all burned," she said. "The whole town."

The wood and leather buildings of Eagle's Bluff were, Sitsi had heard, up to six storeys high, crammed into higgledy-piggledy streets and famed for their complicated designs and intricate carving. Well, they weren't any more. The only things standing now were jagged, burned timbers.

"There's a camp on the prairie," she said a little while later, when the collection of tents around the foot of the bluff came into sight. There was someone heading towards them from it. For a while Sitsi was confused because it looked like two wolves pulling a man along behind them. Then it turned out to be exactly that.

Two large, happy wolves bounded towards them, dragging a triangular sledge. The passenger was sitting high on a frame built up from the base, so that his seated bottom was the height of the wolves' backs. It meant that he could see much further than the standard sledge rider, and he didn't have to sit slanting backwards, feet up, bum down, which Sitsi had always thought looked very uncomfortable.

The sledge swung in an arc as it neared, the rider apparently directing the wolves with a rope attached to their leather collars. He wasn't bumping around as much as he should have been, because the frame was made of bowed, springy wood that absorbed some of the impact from the lumpy ground.

It was, Sitsi had to admit, quite a clever contraption.

"Hello, I am Lesta Heppul," said the rider, pulling the wolves to a halt using the rope. He was maybe ten years older than Erik. His crown was bald, his face was shaved or plucked, but a curtain of straight, black hair ran from ear to ear around the back of his head. He wore a robe of brightly coloured feathers and oversized leather shoes with pointed ends.

"I'm afraid you've come at a terrible time." He didn't sound too upset, more like a busy man announcing a vexatious inconvenience.

"What happened?" asked Sofi.

"The town burned down. Every single bit of it. Dozens killed, maybe hundreds. We'll never know. Probably not hundreds. Maybe not even dozens. I think most people got away. You've got to be pretty thick to be killed in a fire, really. Unless you were unlucky enough to be exactly where the bolts of lightning struck. Or in one of those silly towers, I suppose.

"Bolts plural?"

"Strangest thing. A storm hit, two nights ago. There was no rain, only lightning and lots of it, all focused on our proud settlement of keen minds and learned souls. I saw at least five bolts strike and heard many more. Even my little hut is gone. Very annoying."

"I'm sorry to hear it," said Sofi, "We are—"

"Oh, I know who you are," interrupted Lesta. "You five," he nodded towards Sofi, "are Calnians, part of their Owsla and one warlock. I'm afraid I don't know who you are, my dear warlock, but you," he pointed at the women, "are Sofi Tornado, Chogolisa Earthquake, Sitsi Kestrel, and..." he looked at Paloma's legs "...a runner by your thighs and calves...of course, Paloma Pronghorn. Where are the rest of you? You're meant to travel as an inseparable ten, a band of sisters whom no force could—"

"It is just us," said Sofi.

"I see." Lesta Heppul nodded. "I'm sorry. Of course it's just you. And you others... Well, you're Weeko Fang, you've been here before. The rest of you are more difficult, but when you have eliminated the likely... You are *Hardworkers*." He said "Hardworkers" as if it was a difficult word to pronounce.

"Wrong!" cried Keef. "We're the Wooooo-tah!"

Sitsi smiled.

"The Woooootah?" Lesta Heppul's brow furrowed. "I see. The Woooootah... Are you sure?"

"We used to be called Hardworkers. We're Wootah now," said Thyri Treelegs. "How could you know about Hardwork?"

"Oh, thank the gods of rationality. You changed your name! And why not? Wootah... I like it. It's better than Hardworkers, that's a horrible name. When did you change?"

"About forty days ago," said Thyri.

"Ah, good. I couldn't have known. And now I know before the rest of them do. Jolly good. You must excuse my excitement. Identifying people and collecting information on the tribes is my hobby, as is creating contraptions like the one I'm riding. My main work, however, lies in the movement of stars, specifically its effect on animal migration."

He looked at the Wootah and Clanians as if expecting someone to ask him more about his work. When nobody did, he carried on. "Now, I daresay you've come looking for hospitality. Unfortunately, that will be impossible. Our resources are entirely stretched as it is, as I'm sure you can imagine. So, with great sadness, I have to ask you to carry on your way."

Sofi shrugged. "Sure."

And that was that.

Off they walked, towards the Shining Mountains. Sitsi was disappointed that Eagle's Bluff was gone before she'd seen it, but she was more amazed that Lesta Heppul had taken almost no interest in them whatsoever. Surely someone who professed to be fascinated by people would want to know where such a strange group of people were headed, and travel with them for a while asking questions. It didn't look like he'd even noticed the dagger-tooth cat, for the love of Innowak, but he'd managed to tell them plenty about himself.

It was, she'd decided, confirmation of what she'd always suspected about Eagle's Bluff. They said they were interested in the outside world, but really their heads were lodged a long, long way up their own arses.

Finn the Deep didn't mind missing Eagle's Bluff. He had his own new worries. How could Bodil not know? It was a few days since Bodil and Keef had hooked up. It was over a moon since they'd been beside the Rock River. He caught Bodil Gooseface's eye and she smiled at him as gormlessly as she might have done before they'd left Hardwork. He tried to return the gesture.

Could she really not know?

Finn had shagged her by the Rock River; not shagged, that was too disrespectful a word for something that produced life. But it wasn't as if he'd *made love*...can you call it making love when it's from behind, he wondered? Whatever, the baby was his, not Keef's.

Should he tell Bodil? Or Keef? Or just shut the Hel up? But what if he didn't say anything and the baby looked exactly like him?

He finally managed to get Sassa Lipchewer on her own shortly after Eagle's Bluff disappeared into the haze behind them.

"What do I do about Bodil?" he asked.

"Nothing."

"What?"

"That's what you did last time, after you promised me you'd speak to her. Why should I try for anything else?"

"Sorry." Finn looked at his feet.

"You should be. You took the lazy, easy and selfish option. Luckily for you, the situation worked itself out."

"I'll talk to her this time. I'll talk to them."

"I don't think you should this time," said Sassa.

"You do understand that it's my—"

"Yes, dillard. I know exactly what we're talking about. However, the child is not *yours* just because your rutting started him or her off. Do you belong to Erik?"

"No."

"No. And, more importantly," Sassa sighed, "the chances are the baby won't make it."

"What?"

"We've been lucky. We've only lost Bjarni and Gunnhild since we crossed the Water Mother. You should have been killed by the snakes, we should all have been killed by the tornado, by the giant lizards, by the dagger-tooth-cat riding warriors, by Beaver Man, by the moose lot, by the Badlander Owsla—by the Calnian Owsla—and by any other number of animals and accidents that have plagued us."

"So we're survivors. We prevail."

"It takes only a moment to be killed by the horrors out here. Look at Luby Zephyr, or Gunnhild. And who knows what we still have to face before The Meadows, let alone when we get there. If we get there. You heard what Weeko Fang said."

"Maybe he was exaggerating?"

"You saw the monster. How can you think that?"

"Because I'm an optimist?" Even as he said the words, he regretted it. He might be Finn the Deep now, but he still couldn't talk to a beautiful woman without saying dickish things that weren't anything like what he actually thought.

"Because you're an idiot." Sassa shook her head. "More of us will die before we reach The Meadows. Maybe all of us."

"Now you're being pessimistic. I hardly think—"

"*Pole a mother-fucking vole!* If you didn't realise that most of us are going to die, you're more of an idiot than I thought."

That was a bit much, even if he was saying dickish things.

"I'm sorry," Sassa said, deflating a little. "You're not an idiot. The point is if you die and Keef and Bodil live, then they never need know that the baby is yours."

"You said it wasn't mine!"

"Finnbogi."

"Sorry. I can't believe they haven't worked it out, though."

"Some people have different talents."

"Some people don't have minds that work properly..."

"And some people are shits who get women pregnant as part of a failed scheme to make other women jealous. I'll repeat this, Finnbogi, because you really have to understand. They do not need to know that the baby is a result of you boning Bodil."

"Okay, sorry, got it. But...if it's so dangerous where we're going, why doesn't Bodil go back to the Green tribe? Surely it's reckless to carry a growing baby into a world of monsters."

"Stop, Finn."

He did. She walked round in front of him, put her hands on his shoulders and fixed him with her light-blue eyes. For perhaps the first time ever in all the years he'd been studying her to an arguably unhealthy degree, she wasn't chewing her lips.

"Can you not feel it, Finn?" she asked.

"Um...?" She wasn't going to come on to him, was she? Not her as well.

"We are on a quest," she said. "All of us. Hardworkers may have sat idle for a hundred years but this sort of shit is in our blood. This is our adventure, our story. And the Calnians',' too. We're all in it, all the way. None of us can turn back. Do you understand? We are on a quest. That's it, beginning and end. You finish the quest or you die trying. Don't you get that?"

He did. He hadn't thought about it specifically, but the

journey to The Meadows was all that he had, and all that he wanted. Well, he wanted Thyri and Paloma, together if the gods were feeling unprecedentedly magnanimous, but that was superficial. He needed the quest like he needed air.

He nodded. The realisation of his life's purpose was a relief. And if he died in service of that quest? Well, you know what they said about death.

Chapter 11

Overhanging Cliffs

They travelled south, east of a range of hills that stretched out from Eagle's Bluff, then turned south-west. Weeko Fang, complaining of exhaustion, rode the dagger-tooth, accompanied some of the time by Freydis and Ottar. There was one brief scare when a large pack of wolves closed in on them shortly after dawn one day, but the dagger-tooth cat roared, Sitsi and Sassa shot a few, Paloma spirited around and brained a couple with her killing stick, and the surviving predators dispersed.

They passed a couple of hills and the odd flat-topped outcrop of rock sticking out of the plain like a monster's molar, but mostly it was short grass and stands of scrubby trees. There were fewer animals here than there'd been in the long-grass prairie back east, but there was always a pronghorn, a deer, a lion, several hundred buffalo or some other animal watching them pass, and the sky was busy with flitting birds, hovering hawks and gliding eagles. It was hot in a weird way, as if the sun was weaker but closer, like a fighter who's about to collapse making one last effort to win the battle.

The Shining Mountains were a dark mass initially, but soon they could see that they were capped with snow. The mountains didn't look too high, but it did seem odd that they should have snow on them when it was sweltering on the plains.

Some people seemed happy: Keef and Bodil, Wulf and Sassa, Erik and Chogolisa, Ottar and Freydis. The rest of them got on with walking.

Finn still failed to talk to Paloma and Thyri. If anything, they seemed to like him a little less every day. Paloma gave up on subtlety and just ran whenever he approached. Thyri carried on training with him in the evenings, but with a permanent scowl, and she never talked to him during the day. What had he done? Could Thyri really be that angry that he'd got it on with Paloma? And could Paloma really be that embarrassed that they'd kissed? She'd been very drunk...In the Hardwork tales it was men who got shitfaced, did dumb things then regretted their actions.

On the tenth day after leaving Eagle's Bluff, the valley narrowed into a canyon with a sparkling, brilliantly clear river tumbling out of the mountains along its rocky notch. There was a path up the valley side, but it was very rough. It soon petered out. They clambered on up, over boulders the size of longhouses.

The dagger-tooth cat roared and moaned. The children and Weeko Fang dismounted when it began to struggle, but soon the animal wouldn't go any further.

"Send it home, Finn," said Sofi.

Finn reached out, but, before he'd made a connection, the dagger-tooth cat leapt round as if it had been stung and sped away, a lot more capable over the rocks than it had been on the way up. Finn was left with the sensation that the cat was desperate to get away from something that wasn't very far ahead at all.

The going was difficult, dangerous and slow. Sometimes they scrambled over boulders, sometimes they had to walk up the cold, rushing river. Every now and then they had clear views of the snow-covered mountains that, according to Weeko, they would need to climb.

The gorge narrowed so that both sides were bare, near-vertical rock, and the river passing between was a torrent. At one narrow section, Keef and Wulf tried and failed to carry a rope upstream four times, so they backtracked until they could climb out of the gorge and find a way along the valley side. It turned out to be a serendipitous move, since they found a new, easier path a couple of hundred paces above the river.

The first night in the Shining Mountains they camped in a man-made or possibly squatch-made clearing, where a ring of charred rocks was evidence of previous campfires. Finn slept in his sack alone, as usual. He hadn't been in a sack with anyone else since Bjarni had been alive.

The following day their good path descended to the valley floor and more boulder scrambling and wading. Later, however, the valley opened up into a high prairie.

Wootah and Calnians stopped to marvel. The prairie contained more elk than Finn had thought there could possibly be in the world. They were like the crowd pigeons in deer form. Even more amazing were the snowy mountains, hunkered over the prairie like ogres around a table. The lower slopes were forested but, above a line so neat that it had to be the work of the gods, tree-free bright white snow and dark rock soared skywards.

"Had you expected to see squatches by now?" Sofi Tornado asked Weeko Fang. They were ahead of Finn and Erik, following the riverside path westward. On the far side of the narrow river several dozen fat, furry marmots watched them pass with interest and no apparent fear.

"They've seen us. I'm sure they'll make contact soo—"

Weeko Fang stopped mid-word and fell face first onto the path.

Erik dashed forward and helped Sofi turn him over. He didn't react. A rivulet of blood trickled from his nose.

Yoki Choppa jogged up, crouched, pressed his fingers into Weeko's neck and pried his good eye open.

"What's happened?" asked Wulf, running up with Sassa.

"He's dead," said Yoki Choppa.

"How?" asked Wulf.

The warlock shrugged.

"He said he was exhausted," said Sassa. "Maybe it was just his time and—"

He did not die a natural death, said a wispy, weird voice in Finn's head. *I crushed his mind. I can do it to any of you in an instant.* Everyone looked at each other. They could all hear the voice, too.

"There's a voice in my head!" squeaked Bodil.

"Everyone's hearing it," said Erik. "It's a squatch. Just stay calm and—"

Stay silent. Stay where you are, the voice continued. *Run, and die. Advance, and die. Move at all, in fact, and die.*

"Who are you?" demanded Wulf. "Where are you? What do you—"

Wulf's eyes widened. Blood trickled from one nostril. He fell.

"No!" shouted Sassa. She ran to him, falling down on her knees next to her husband.

I warned you, said the voice. *Stay silent, stay still, or die.*

Finnbogi didn't dare turn his head, but he swivelled his eyes. Several squatches were walking towards them. They were similar to Ayla, the squatch from the Badlands, fur-covered and around twice the height of a man.

Sofi Tornado nodded. She and Paloma Pronghorn ran at them. Paloma got further than Sofi, but both fell before they reached the beasts, and lay still.

Erik blinked at Finn as if to say that they shouldn't try anything. Finn looked at the prone figures of Sofi Tornado, Paloma Pronghorn and Wulf the Fat. He was so shocked, so aghast, that he almost ran at the squatches himself.

Instead he stayed still, wondering what would happen next.

The story continues in . . .

WHERE GODS FEAR TO GO

West of West: Book Three

Acknowledgements

Thanks first and foremost for my wife Nicola's unceasing support. She continues to take my career of writing about monsters and warriors seriously, while she herself moves up the ranks of high finance. She is now director of the American operations of one of Europe's biggest hedge funds, so we have moved to Manhattan. It's an interesting place.

Thanks to my sons Charlie and Otty, who are now four and two and the source of a large percentage of my joy. They've also managed to unearth my previously undiscovered temper, destroyed my social life and are the reason I've been to the cinema only once in the last year, but on balance I'm glad we had them.

Thanks to my beta readers Amy Dean and Tim Watson. Amy particularly has put in an extraordinary amount of work in exchange, so far, for one lunch. She is promised untold riches and golden hats for her chickens when the sales hit the million mark. Tim has received nothing, but he's my brother and responsible for getting me into fantasy in the first place, so it's all his fault that I write these books at all.

Thanks to my editor Jenni Hill at Orbit, excellent as ever, and to Nazia Khatun at Orbit for organising a host of marketing events, and to Joanna Kramer for putting the books together. Thanks to all the others at Orbit who produce such wonderful books and publicise them so effectively, and to their American counterparts at Hachette Publishing, particularly Will Hinton and Ellen Wright.

Thanks to Richard Collins, a diligent copy-editor, who has to wade through and correct my semi-dyslexic spelling.

Thanks to the organisers of Polcon in Lublin and Days of Fantasy in Wrocław, particularly Gosia Uchnast and Maria Chojnacka. These two Polish fantasy conventions shipped me out and put me up in exchange for me talking about myself. I had a wonderful time at both.

Thanks to my agent Angharad Kowal, who works tirelessly selling my books around the world and pitching for those as yet elusive film rights.

Thanks to Joyce Boxall, Eva Gabardo Lorenzo, Dannii Evans and Amber Scardino who have looked after the boys and allowed me to get on with the important business of making up stuff.

Thanks to Sean Barrett who reads the audiobooks. I met him the other day and was not surprised to find that he's an excellent fellow, as charming in real life as he is on tape.

There are probably more people to thank, but I promised Charlie that I would make a Lego car with him when I finished my book. It has ninety-one pieces and every piece needs to be discussed for a good long while, so we'd better get started if we're going to have it done by bathtime.

extras

orbit

meet the author

Nicola Watson

ANGUS WATSON is an author living in New York. Before becoming a novelist, he was a freelance features writer, chiefly for British national newspapers. Features included looking for Bigfoot in the USA for the *Telegraph*, diving on the scuppered World War One German fleet at Scapa Flow for the *Financial Times* and swimming with sea lions in the Galapagos Islands for *The Times*.

Angus's first historical fantasy trilogy is Age of Iron, an epic romantic adventure set at the end of Britain's Iron Age. He came up with the idea for West of West while driving and hiking though North America's magnificent countryside and wondering what it was like before the Europeans got there.

Angus is married to Nicola. They have two young sons, Charlie and Otty, and two cats, Jasmine and Napa.

You can find him on Twitter at @GusWatson or find his website at www.guswatson.com.

Find out more about Angus Watson and other Orbit authors by registering for the free monthly newsletter at www.orbitbooks.net.

if you enjoyed
THE LAND YOU NEVER LEAVE

look out for

SEVEN BLADES IN BLACK

by

Sam Sykes

Acclaimed author Sam Sykes returns with a brilliant new epic fantasy that introduces an unforgettable outcast magician caught between two warring empires.

Among humans, none have power like mages. And among mages, none have will like Sal the Cacophony. Once revered, then vagrant, she walked a wasteland scarred by generations of magical warfare.

The Scar, a land torn between powerful empires, is where rogue mages go to disappear, disgraced soldiers go to die,

*and where Sal went with a blade, a gun, and a list of names
she intended to use both on.*

*But vengeance is a flame swift extinguished. Betrayed by those
she trusted most, her magic torn from her and awaiting
execution, Sal the Cacophony has one last tale to tell before
they take her head.*

*All she has left is her name, her story, and the weapon
she used to carved both.*

Vengeance is its own reward.

ONE

Hightower

Everyone loved a good execution.

From the walls of Imperial Cathama to the farthest reach
of the Revolution, there was no citizen of the Scar who could
think of a finer way to spend an afternoon than watching the
walls get painted with bits of dissidents. And behind the walls
of Revolutionary Hightower that day, there was an electricity
in the air felt by every citizen.

The people gathered in crowds to watch the dirt, still damp
from yesterday's execution, be swept away from the stake. The
firing squad sat nearby, polishing their gunpikes and placing
bets on who would hit the heart of the poor asshole that got

tied up today. Merchants barked nearby, selling everything from refreshment to souvenir so people could remember this day when everyone got off work for a few short hours to see another enemy of the Revolution strung up and gunned down.

Not like there was a hell of a lot else to do in Hightower lately.

For her part, Governor-Militant Tretta Stern did her best to ignore all of it: the crowds gathering beneath her window outside the prison, their voices crowing for blood; the wailing children; and the laughing men. She kept her focus on the image in the mirror as she straightened the blue coat of her uniform. Civilians could be excused such craven bloodlust. Officers of the Revolution answered a higher call.

Her black hair, severely short-cropped and oiled against her head, was befitting of an officer. Jacket cinched tight, trousers pressed and belted, saber at her hip, all without a trace of dust, lint, or rust. And most crucially, the stare that had sent a hundred foes to the grave with a word stared back at her, unflinching.

One might wonder what the point in getting dressed up for an execution was; after all, it wasn't like the criminal scum who would be buried in a shallow grave in six hours would give a shit. But being an officer of the Revolution meant upholding certain standards. And Tretta hadn't earned her post by being slack.

She took a moment to adjust the medals on her lapel before leaving her quarters. Two guards fired off crisp salutes before straightening their gunpikes and marching exactly three rigid paces behind her. Morning sunlight poured in through the windows as they marched down the stairs to Cadre command. Guards and officers alike called to attention at her passing, raising arms as they saluted. She offered a cursory nod in response, bidding them at ease as she made her way to the farthest door of the room.

The guard stationed there glanced up. "Governor-Militant," he acknowledged, saluting.

"Sergeant," Tretta replied. "How have you found the prisoner?"

"Recalcitrant and disrespectful," he said. "The prisoner began the morning by hurling the assigned porridge at the guard detail, spewed several obscenities, and made forceful suggestions as to the professional and personal conduct of the guard's mother." He sniffed, lip curling. "In summation, more or less what we'd expect from a Vagrant."

Tretta spared an impressed look. Considering the situation, she had expected much worse.

She made a gesture. The guard complied, unlocking the massive iron door and pushing it open. She and her escorts descended into the darkness of Hightower's prison, and the silence of empty cells greeted her.

Like all Revolutionary outposts, Hightower had been built to accommodate prisoners: Imperium aggressors, counterrevolutionaries, bandit outlaws, and even the occasional Vagrant. Unlike most Revolutionary outposts, Hightower was far away from any battleground in the Scar and didn't see much use for its cells. Any captive outlaw tended to be executed in fairly short order for crimes against the Revolution, as the civilians tended to become restless without the entertainment.

In all her time stationed at Hightower, Tretta had visited the prison exactly twice, including today. The first time had been to offer an Imperium spy posing as a bandit clemency in exchange for information. Thirty minutes later, she put him in front of the firing squad. Up until then, he'd been the longest-serving captive in Hightower.

Thus far, her current prisoner had broken the record by two days.

The interrogation room lay at the very end of the row of cells, another iron door flanked by two guards. Both fired off a salute as they pulled open the door, its hinges groaning.

Twenty feet by twenty feet, possessed of nothing more than a table with two chairs and a narrow slit of a window by which to cast a beam of light, the interrogation room was little more than a slightly larger cell with a slightly nicer door. The window, set high up near the ceiling, afforded no ventilation and the room was stifling hot.

Not that you'd know it from looking at the prisoner.

A woman—perhaps in her late twenties, Tretta suspected—sat at one end of the table. Dressed in dirty trousers and boots to match, the sleeves and hem of her white shirt cut to bare tattoos racing down her forearms and scars mapping her midsection; about the sort of garish garb you'd expect to find on a Vagrant. Her hair, Imperial white, was shorn roughly on the sides and tied back in an unruly tail. And despite the suffocating heat, she was as calm, serene, and pale as ice.

There was nothing about this woman that Tretta didn't despise.

She didn't look up as the Governor-Militant entered, paid no heed to the pair of armed men trailing behind her. Her hands, manacled together, rested patiently atop the table. Even when Tretta took a seat across from her, she hardly seemed to notice. The prisoner's eyes, pale and blue as shallow water, seemed to be looking somewhere else. Her face, thin and sharp and marred by a pair of jagged scars beneath her left eye, seemed unperturbed by her imminent gruesome death.

That galled Tretta more than she would have liked to admit.

The Governor-Militant leaned forward, steepling her fingers in front of her, giving the woman a chance to realize what a world of shit she was in. But after a minute of silence, she merely held out one hand. A sheaf of papers appeared there a moment later, thrust forward by one of her guards. She laid it out before her and idly flipped through it.

"I won't tell you that you can save yourself," she said, after a time. "An officer of the Revolution speaks only truths." She glanced up at the woman, who did not react. "Within six hours, you'll be executed for crimes against the Glorious Revolution of the Fist and Flame. Nothing you can say can change this fact. You deserve to die for your crimes." She narrowed her eyes. "And you will."

The woman, at last, reacted. Her manacles rattled a little as she reached up and scratched at the scars on her face. Tretta sneered and continued.

"What you can change," she said, "is how quickly it goes. The Revolution is not beyond mercy." She flipped to a page, held it up before her. "In exchange for information regarding the events of the week of Masens eleventh through twentieth, up to and including the massacre of the township of Stark's Mutter, the destruction of the freehold of Lowstaff, and the disappearance of Revolutionary Low Sergeant Cavric Proud, I am willing to guarantee on behalf of the Cadre a swift and humane death."

She set the paper aside, leaned forward. The woman stared just to the left of Tretta's gaze.

"A lot of people are dead because of you," Tretta said. "One of our soldiers is missing because of you. Before these six hours are up and you're dead and buried, two things are going to happen: I'm going to find out precisely what happened and you're going to decide whether you go by a single bullet or a hundred blades." She laid her hands flat on the table. "What you say next will determine how much blood we see today. Think very carefully before you speak."

At this, the woman finally looked into Tretta's eyes. No fear there, she looked calm and placid as ever. And when she spoke, it was weakly.

"May I," she said, "have a drink?"

Tretta blinked. "A drink."

The woman smiled softly at her manacled hands. "It's hot."

Tretta narrowed her eyes, but made a gesture all the same. One of her guards slipped out the door, returning a moment later with a jug and a glass. He filled it, slid it over to the prisoner. She took it up and sipped at it, smacked her lips, then looked down at the glass.

"The fuck is this?" she asked.

Tretta furrowed her brow. "Water. What else would it be?"

"I was figuring gin or something," she said.

"You asked for water."

"I asked for a *drink*," the woman shot back. "With all the fuss you're making about how you're going to kill me, I thought you'd at least send me out with something decent. Don't I get a final request?"

Tretta's face screwed up in offense. "*No.*"

The woman made a pouting face. "I would in Cathama."

"You're not *in* Cathama," Tretta snarled in response. "You're not anywhere near the Imperium and the only imperialist scum within a thousand miles are all buried in graves beside the one I intend to put *you* in."

"Yeah, you've been pretty clear on that," the woman replied, making a flippant gesture. "Crimes against the Revolution and so on. Not that I'd ever call you a liar, madame, but are you sure you've got the right girl? There's plenty of scum in the Scar that must have offended you worse than me."

"I am *certain.*" Tretta seized the papers, flipped to a page toward the front. "Prisoner number fifteen-fifteen-five, alias"— she glared over the paper at the woman—"Sal the Cacophony."

Sal's lip curled into a crooked grin. She made as elegant a bow as one could when manacled and sitting in a chair.

"Madame."

"Real identity unknown, place of birth unknown, hometown unknown," Tretta continued, reading from the paper. "Professed occupation: bounty hunter."

"I prefer 'manhunter.' Sounds more dramatic."

"Convicted—recently—of murder in twelve townships, arson in three freeholds, unlawful possession of Revolutionary Relics, heresy against Haven, petty larceny—"

"There was nothing petty about that larceny." She reached forward. "Let me see that sheet."

"—blasphemy, illegal use of magic, kidnapping, extortion, and so on and so on and so fucking on." Tretta slammed the paper down against the table. "In short, everything I would expect from a common Vagrant. And like a common Vagrant, I expect not a damn soul in the Scar is going to shed a tear over what puts you in the ground. But what makes you different is that you've got the chance to do something vaguely good before you die, which is a sight fucking more than what your fellow scum get before the birds pick their corpses clean." She clenched her jaw, spat her next words. "So, if you've got any decency left to your name, however fake it might be, you'll tell me what happened. In Stark's Mutter, in Lowstaff, and to my soldier, Cavric Proud."

Sal pursed her lips, regarded Tretta through an ice water stare. She stiffened in her chair and Tretta matched her poise. The two women stared each other down for a moment, as though either of them expected the other to tear out a blade and start swinging.

As it was, Tretta nearly did just that when Sal finally broke the silence.

"Have you seen many Vagrants dead, madame?" she asked, unhurried.

"Many," Tretta replied, terse.

"When they died, what did they say?"

Tretta narrowed her eyes. "Curses, mostly. Cursing the Imperium they served, cursing the luck that sent them to me, cursing me for sending them back to the hell that spawned them."

"I guess no one ever knows what their last words will be." Sal traced a finger across the scars on her cheek, her eyes fixed on some distant spot beyond the walls of the interrogation room. "But I know mine won't be curses." She clicked her tongue. "I'll tell you what you want to know, madame, about Lowstaff, about Cavric, everything. I'll give you everything you want and you can put a bullet in my head or cut it off or have me torn apart by birds. I won't protest. All I ask is one thing."

Tretta tensed and reached for her saber as Sal leaned across the table. And a grin as long and sharp as a blade etched itself across her face.

"Remember my last words."

Tretta didn't achieve her rank by indulging prisoners, let alone ones as vile as a Vagrant. She achieved it through the support and respect of the men and women who saluted her every morning. And she didn't get that by letting their fates go unknown.

And so, for the sake of them and the Revolution she served, she nodded. And the Vagrant leaned back in her chair and closed her eyes.

"It started," she said softly, "with the last rain."

TWO
Rin's Sump

You ever want to know what a man is made of, you do three things.

First, you see what he does when the weather turns nasty.

When it rains in Cathama, the pampered Imperials crowd beneath the awnings in their cafés and wait for their mages to change the skies. When it snows in Haven, they file right into church and thank their lord for it. And when it gets hot in Weiless, as you know, they ascribe the sun to an Imperial plot and vow to redouble their revolutionary efforts.

But in the Scar? When it pours down rain and thunder so hard that you swim through the streets and can't hear yourself drown? Well, they just pull their cloaks tighter and keep going.

And that's just what I was doing that night when I got into this whole mess.

Rin's Sump, as you can guess by the name, was the sort of town where rain didn't bother people much. Even when lightning flashed so bright you'd swear it was day, life in the Scar was hard enough that a little apocalyptic weather wouldn't hinder anyone. And as the streets turned to mud underfoot and the roofs shook beneath the weight of the downpour, the people of the township just tucked their chins into their coats, pulled their hats down low, and kept going about their business.

Just like I was doing. One more shapeless, sexless figure in the streets, hidden beneath a cloak and a scarf pulled around her head. No one raised a brow at my white hair, looked at me like they were guessing what I had under my cloak, or even so much as glanced at me. They had their own shit to deal with that night.

Which was fine by me. So did I. And the kind of shit I got into, I could always use fewer eyes on me.

Every other house in Rin's Sump was dark as night, but the tavern—a dingy little two-story shack at the center of town— was lit up. Light shone bright enough to illuminate the dirt on the windows, the stripped paint on the front, and the ugly sign swinging on squeaky hinges: *Ralp's Last Resort.*

Apt name.

And it proved even more apt when I pushed the door open and took a glance inside.

Standing there, sopping wet, water dripping off me to form a small ocean around my boots, I imagined I looked a little like a dead cat hauled out of an outhouse. And I *still* looked a damn sight better than the inside of that bar.

A fine layer of dust tried nobly to obscure a much-less-fine layer of splinters over the ill-tended-to chairs and tables lining the common hall. A stage that probably once had hosted a variety of bad acts now stood dark; a single voccaphone stood in their place, playing a tune that was popular back when the guy who wrote it was still alive. Rooms upstairs had probably once held a few prostitutes, if there ever were prostitutes luckless enough to work a township like this. I'd have called the place a mausoleum if it weren't for the people, but they looked like they might have found a crypt a little cozier.

There were a few kids—two boys, a girl—in the back, sipping on whatever bottle of swill they could afford and staring at the table. Laborers, I wagered; some young punks the locals used for cheap jobs with cheap pay to buy cheap liquor. And behind the bar was a large man in dirty clothes, idly rubbing a glass with a cloth.

He set that glass down as I approached. The cloth he had been using had likely been used to polish something else, if the grime around the glass were any evidence.

No matter. I wouldn't need to be here long.

Ralp—I assumed—didn't bother asking me what I wanted. In the Scar, you're lucky if they give you a choice between two drinks. And if you had any luck at all, you didn't wind up in a place called Rin's Sump.

He reached for a cask behind the bar, but stopped as I cleared my throat and shot him a warning glare. With a nod, he held up a bottle of whiskey—Avonin & Sons, by the look of the black label—and looked at me for approval. I nodded, tossed a silver knuckle on the counter. He didn't start pouring until he picked it up, made sure it was real, and pocketed it.

"Passing through?" he asked with the kind of tone that suggested habit more than interest.

"Does anyone ever stay?" I asked back, taking a sip of bitter brown.

"Only if they make enough mistakes." Ralp shot a glance to the youths drinking in the corner. "Your first was stopping in here instead of moving on. Roads are going to be mud for days after this. No one's getting out without a bird."

"I've got a mount," I said, grinning over my glass. "And here I thought you'd be happy for a little extra money."

"Won't turn down metal," Ralp said. He eyed me over, raised a brow as it seemed to suddenly dawn on him that I was a woman under all that wet, stinking leather. "But if you really want to make me happy—"

"I'll tell you what." I held up a finger. "Finishing that thought might make you happy in the short-term, but keeping it to yourself will make you not get punched in the mouth in the long-term." I smiled sweetly as a woman with my kinds of scars could. "A simple pleasure, sir, but a lasting one."

Ralp glanced me over again, rubbed his mouth thoughtfully, and bobbed his head. "Yeah, I'd say you're right about that."

"But I do have something just as good." I tossed another three knuckles onto the bar. As he reached for them, I slammed something else in front of him. "That is, assuming you can make *me* happy."

I unfolded the paper, slid it over. Scrawled in ink across its yellow was a leering mask of an opera actor upon a headful of wild hair, tastefully framed in a black box with a very large sum written beneath it and the words *DEATH WARRANT* above it.

"Son of a bitch!" Ralp's eyebrows rose, along with his voice. "You're looking for *that* son of a bitch?"

I held a finger to my lips, glanced out the corner of my eye. The youths hadn't seemed to notice that particular outburst, their eyes still on their bottle.

"He has a name," I said. "Daiga the Phantom. What do you know about him?"

When you're in my line of work, you start to read faces pretty well. You can tell who the liars are just by looking at them. And I could tell by the wrinkles around Ralp's eyes and mouth that he was used to smiling big and wide. Which meant he had to have told a few lies in his day, probably most of them to himself.

That didn't make him good at it.

"Nothing," he said. "I've heard the name, but nothing else."

"*Nothing* else?"

"I know whatever they're offering for his death can't be worth him coming for me." Ralp looked at me, pointedly.

I looked back. And I, just as pointedly, pulled my cloak aside to reveal the hilt of the sword at my hip.

"He has something I want," I replied.

"Hope you find someone else who can give it to you." He searched for something to busy his hands, eventually settling on one of the many dirty glasses and began to polish it. "I don't know anything of mages, let alone Vagrants like that...*man*. They're funny stories you tell around the bar. I haven't had enough customers for that in a long time." He sniffed. "Truth is, madame, I don't know that I'd even notice if someone like that showed up around here."

"Birdshit." I leaned in even closer, hissed through my teeth. "I've been here three days and the most exciting thing I saw was an old man accusing his ox of lechery."

"He has a condition—"

"And before I came in here, I glanced around back and saw your shipment." I narrowed my eyes. "Lot of crates of wine for a man with no customers. Where are you sending them?"

Ralp stared at the bar. "I don't know. But if you don't get out, I'll call the peacekeepers and—"

"Ralp," I said, frowning, "I'm going to be sad if you make me hurt you over lies this pathetic."

"I said I *don't know*," he muttered. "Someone else picks them up."

"Who? What's Daiga using them for?"

"I don't know any of that, either. I try to know as little as fucking possible about that freak or any other freak like him." All pretenses gone, there was real fear in his eyes. "I don't make it my business to know anything about no mage, Vagrant or otherwise. It's not healthy."

"But you'll take his metal all the same, I see."

"I took your metal, too. The rest of the Scar might be flush with gold, but Rin's Sump is dry as six-day birdshit. If a Vagrant gives me money for not asking questions, I'm all too fucking happy to do it."

"Yeah?"

I pulled the other side of my cloak back, revealing another hilt of a very different weapon. Carved wood, black and shiny as sin, not so much as a splinter out of place. Polished brass glimmered like it just wanted me to take it out and show it off.

At my hip, I could feel the gun burning, begging to be unleashed.

"As it turns out, asking questions makes me unhappy, too, Ralp. What do you suppose we do about that?"

Sweat appeared on Ralp's brow. He licked his lips, looked wild-eyed at my piece before he looked right back into the ugliest grin I could manage.

Don't get me wrong, I didn't feel *particularly* great about doing something as pedestrian as flashing a gun. It feels so terribly dramatic, and not in the good way. But you must believe me: I was expecting this to go smoothly. I hadn't prepared anything cleverer at the time. And, if I'm honest, this particular gun makes one hell of a statement.

I certainly wasn't going to feel bad about this.

if you enjoyed
THE LAND YOU NEVER LEAVE

look out for

AGE OF ASSASSINS
The Wounded Kingdom: Book One

by

RJ Barker

*The first in a new epic fantasy trilogy set in a world
ravaged by magic, featuring a cast of assassins, knights,
and ambitious noblemen.*

*Girton Club-Foot has no family, a crippled leg, and is
apprenticed to the best assassin in the land.*

*He's learning the art of taking lives, but his latest mission
tasks him with a far more difficult challenge: save a life.
Someone is trying to kill the heir to the throne, and it is up to*

Girton to uncover the traitor and prevent the prince's murder—and his own.

It's a game of assassin versus assassin.

Chapter 1

We were attempting to enter Castle Maniyadoc through the night soil gate and my master was in the sort of foul mood only an assassin forced to wade through a week's worth of shit can be. I was far more sanguine about our situation. As an assassin's apprentice you become inured to foulness. It is your lot.

"Girton," said Merela Karn. That is my master's true name, though if I were to refer to her as anything other than "Master" I would be swiftly and painfully reprimanded. "Girton," she said, "if one more king, queen or any other member of the blessed classes thinks a night soil gate is the best way to make an unseen entrance to their castle, you are to run them through."

"Really, Master?"

"No, not really," she whispered into the night, her breath a cloud in the cold air. "Of course not really. You are to politely suggest that walking in the main gate dressed as masked priests of the dead gods is less conspicuous. Show me a blessed who doesn't know that the night soil gate is an easy way in for an enemy and I will show you a corpse."

"You have shown me many corpses, Master."

"Be quiet, Girton."

My master is not a lover of humour. Not many assassins

502

are; it is a profession that attracts the miserable and the melancholic. I would never put myself into either of those categories, but I was bought into the profession and did not join by choice.

"Dead gods in their watery graves!" hissed my master into the night. "They have not even opened the grate for us." She swung herself aside whispering, "Move, Girton!" I slipped and slid crabwise on the filthy grass of the slope running from the river below us up to the base of the towering castle walls. Foulness farted out of the grating to join the oozing stream that ran down the motte and joined the river.

A silvery smudge marred the riverbank in the distance; it looked like a giant paint-covered thumb had been placed over it. In the moonlight it was quite beautiful, but we had passed near as we sneaked in, and I knew it was the same livid yellow as the other sourings which scarred the Tired Lands. There was no telling how old this souring was, and I wondered how big it had been originally and how much blood had been spilled to shrink it to its present size. I glanced up at the keep. This side had few windows and I thought the small souring could be new, but that was a silly, childish thought. The blades of the Landsmen kept us safe from sorcerers and the magic which sucked the life from the land. There had been no significant magic used in the Tired Lands since the Black Sorcerer had risen, and he had died before I had been born. No, what I saw was simply one of many sores on the land—a place as dead as the ancient sorcerer who made it. I turned from the souring and did my best to imagine it wasn't there, though I was sure I could smell it, even over the high stink of the night soil drain.

"Someone will pay for arranging this, Girton, I swear," said my master. Her head vanished into the darkness as she bobbed down to examine the grate once more. "This is sealed with a simple five-lever lock." She did not even breathe heavily despite

holding her entire weight on one arm and one leg jammed
into stonework the black of old wounds. "You can open this,
Girton. You need as much practice with locks as you can get."

"Thank you, Master," I said. I did not mean it. It was cold,
and a lock is far harder to manipulate when it is cold.

And when it is covered in shit.

Unlike my master, I am no great acrobat. I am hampered by
a clubbed foot, so I used my weight to hold me tight against
the grating even though it meant getting covered in filth. On
the stone columns either side of the grate the forlorn remains of
minor gods had been almost chipped away. On my right only
a pair of intricately carved antlers remained, and on my left a
pair of horns and one solemn eye stared out at me. I turned
from the eye and brought out my picks, sliding them into the
lock with shaking fingers and feeling within using the slim
metal rods.

"What if there are dogs, Master?"

"We kill them, Girton."

There is something rewarding in picking a lock. Something
very satisfying about the click of the barrels and the pressure vanishing as the lock gives way to skill. It is not quite as
rewarding done while a castle's toilets empty themselves over
your body, but a happy life is one where you take your pleasures
where you can.

"It is open, Master."

"Good. You took too long."

"Thank you, Master." It was difficult to tell in the darkness,
but I was sure she smiled before she nodded me forward. I hesitated at the edge of the pitch-dark drain.

"It looks like the sort of place you'd find Dark Ungar,
Master."

"The hedgings are just like the gods, Girton—stories to

scare the weak-minded. There's nothing in there but stink and filth. You've been through worse. Go."

I slithered through the gate, managing to make sure no part of my skin or clothing remained clean, and into the tunnel that led through the keep's curtain wall. Somewhere beyond I could hear the lumpy splashes of night soil being shovelled into the stream that ran over my feet. The living classes in the villages keep their piss and night soil and sell it to the tanneries and dye makers, but the blessed classes are far too grand for that, and their castles shovel their filth out into the rivers—as if to gift it to the populace. I have crawled through plenty of filth in my fifteen years, from the thankful, the living and the blessed; it all smells equally bad.

Once we had squeezed through the opening we were able to stand, and my master lit a glow-worm lamp, a small wick that burns with a dim light that can be amplified or shut off by a cleverly interlocking set of mirrors. Then she lifted a gloved hand and pointed at her ear.

I listened.

Above the happy gurgle of the stream running down the channel—water cares nothing for the medium it travels through—I heard the voices of men as they worked. We would have to wait for them to move before we could proceed into the castle proper, and whenever we have to wait I count out the seconds the way my master taught me—one, my master. Two, my master. Three, my master—ticking away in my mind like the balls of a water clock as I stand idle, filth swirling round my ankles and my heart beating out a nervous tattoo.

You get used to the smell. That is what people say.

It is not true.

Eight minutes and nineteen seconds passed before we finally heard the men laugh and move on. Another signal from my master and I started to count again. Five minutes this time. Human nature being the way it is you cannot guarantee someone will not leave something and come back for it.

When the five minutes had passed we made our way up the night soil passage until we could see dim light dancing on walls caked with centuries of filth. My own height plus a half above us was the shovelling room. Above us the door creaked and then we heard footsteps, followed by voices.

"...so now we're done and Alsa's in the heir's guard. Fancy armour and more pay."

"It's a hedging's deal. I'd sooner poke out my own eyes and find magic in my hand than serve the fat bear, he's a right yellower."

"Service is mother though, aye?"

Laughter followed. My master glanced up through the hole, chewing on her lip. She held up two fingers before speaking in the Whisper-That-Flies-to-the-Ear so only I could hear her.

"Guards. You will have to take care of them," she said. I nodded and started to move. "Don't kill them unless you absolutely have to."

"It will be harder."

"I know," she said and leaned over, putting her hands together to make a stirrup. "But I will be here."

I breathe out.

I breathe in.

I placed my foot on her hands and, with a heave, she propelled me up and into the room. I came out of the hole landing with my back to the two men. *Seventeenth iteration: the Drunk's Reversal.* Rolling forward, twisting and coming up facing guards dressed in kilted skirts, leather helms and poorly kept-up boiled-leather chest pieces splashed with red paint. They stared at me dumbly, as if I were the hedging lord Blue

Watta appearing from the deeps. Both of them held clubs, though they had stabswords at their sides. I wondered if they were here to guard against rats rather than people.

"Assassin?" said the guard on the left. He was smaller than his friend, though both were bigger than me.

"Aye," said the other, a huge man. "Assassin." His grip shifted on his club.

They should have gone for the door and reinforcements. My hand was hovering over the throwing knives at my belt in case they did. Instead the smaller man grinned, showing missing teeth and black stumps.

"I imagine there's a good price on the head of an assassin, Joam, even if it's a crippled child." He started forward. The bigger man grinned and followed his friend's lead. They split up to avoid the hole in the centre of the room and I made my move. *Second iteration: the Quicksteps.* Darting forward, I chose the smaller of the two as my first target—the other had not drawn his blade. He swung at me with his club and I stepped backwards, feeling the draught of the hard wood through the air. He thrust with his dagger but was too far away to reach my flesh. When his swipe missed he jumped back, expecting me to counter-attack, but I remained unmoving. All I had wanted was to get an idea of his skill before I closed with him. He did not impress me, his friend impressed me even less; rather than joining the attack he was watching, slack-jawed, as if we put on a show for him.

"Joam," shouted my opponent, "don't be just standing there!" The bigger man trundled forward, though he was in no hurry. I didn't want to be fighting two at the same time if I could help it so decided to finish the smaller man quickly. *First iteration: the Precise Steps.* Forward into the range of his weapons. He thrust with his stabsword. *Ninth iteration: the Bow.* Middle of my body bowing backwards to avoid the blade. With his other hand he swung his club at my head. I ducked. As his arm came over my head I grabbed his elbow and pushed, making him lose his balance, and as he struggled to right himself I found purchase on the rim of his chest piece. *Tenth iteration: the Broom.* Sweeping my leg round I knocked his feet from under him. With a push I sent him flailing into the hole so he cracked his head on the edge of it on his way down.

I turned to his friend, Joam.

Had the dead gods given Joam any sense he would have seen his friend easily beaten and made for the door. Instead, Joam's face had the same look on it I had seen on a bull as it smashed its head against a wall in a useless attempt to get at a heifer beyond—the look of something too stupid and angry to know it was in a fight it couldn't win.

"I'm a kill you, assassin," he said and lumbered slowly forward, smacking his club against his hand. I had no time to wait for him; the longer we fought the more likely it was that someone would hear us and bring more guards. I jumped over the hole and landed behind Joam. He turned, swinging his club. *Fifteenth Iteration: the Oar.* Bending at the hip and bringing my body down and round so it went under his swing. At the lowest point I punched forward, landing a solid blow between Joam's legs. He screeched, dropping his weapon and doubling over. With a jerk I brought my body up so the back of my skull smashed into his face, sending the big man staggering back, blood streaming from a broken nose. It was a blow that would have felled most, but Joam was a strong man. Though his eyes were bleary and unfocused he still stood. *Eighteenth iteration: the Water Clock.* I ran at him, grabbing his thick belt and using it as a fulcrum to swing myself round and up so I could lock my legs around his throat. Joam's hand grasped blindly for the blade at his hip. I drew it and tossed it away before he reached it. His hands spidered down my body searching for and locking around my throat, but Joam's strength, though great, was fleeing as he choked. I wormed my thumb underneath his fingers and grabbed his little finger and third finger, breaking them. I expected a grunt of pain as he let go of me, but the man was already unconscious and fell back, sliding down the wall to the floor. I squirmed free of his weight and checked he was still breathing. Once I was sure he was alive I rolled his body over to the hole.

"Look out, Master," I whispered. Then pushed the limp body into the hole. I took a moment, a second only, to check and see if I had been heard, then I knelt to pull up my master.

She was not heavy.

For the first time I had a moment to look around, and the room we stood in was a strange one. Small in length and breadth but far higher than it needed to be. I barely had time for that thought to form on the surface of my mind before my master shouted,

"This is wrong, Girton! Back!"

I jumped for the grate, as did she, but before either of us fell back into the midden a hidden gate clanked into place across the hole. Four pikers squeezed into the room, dressed in boiled-leather armour, wide-brimmed helms and skirts sewn with chunks of metal. Below the knee they wore leather greaves with strips of metal cut into the material to protect their shins, and as they brandished their weapons they assaulted us with the smell of unwashed bodies and the rancid fat they used to oil their armour. In such a small room their stink was a more effective weapon than the pikes; they would have been far better bringing long shields and short swords. They would realise quickly enough.

"Hostages," said my master as I reached for the blade on my back.

I let go of the hilt.

And was among the guards. Bare-handed and violent. The unmistakable fleshy crack of a nose being broken followed by a man squealing like a gelded mount came from behind me as my master engaged the pikers. I shoved one pike aside to get in close and drove my elbow into the throat of the man in front of me—not a killing blow but enough to put the man out of action. The second piker, a woman, was off balance, and it was easy enough for me to twist her so she was held in front of me like a shield with my razor-tipped thumbnail at her throat. My master had her piker in a similar embrace. Blood ran down his face and another guard lay unconscious on the floor next to the man I had elbowed in the throat.

"Open the grating," she shouted to the walls. "Let us go or we will kill these guards."

The sound of a man laughing came from above, and the reason for the room's height became clear as murder holes opened in the walls. Each was big enough for a crossbow to be pointed down at the room and eight weapons threatened us with taut bows and stubby little bolts which would pass straight through armour.

"Open the grate. We will leave and your troops will live," shouted my master.

More laughter.

"I think not," came a voice. Male, sure of himself, amused.

One, my master. Two, my master...

The twang of crossbows, echoing through the silence like the sound of rocks falling down a cliff face will echo through a quiet wood. Bolts buried themselves in the unconscious guards on the floor in front of us. Laughter from above.

"Together," hissed my master, and I pulled my guard round so that we hid behind the bodies of our prisoners.

"Let me go, please," said my guard, her voice shivering like her body. "Aydor doesn't care about us guards. He's worse than Dark Ungar and he'll kill us all if he wants yer."

"Quiet!" I said and pushed my razor-edged thumb harder against her neck, making the blood flow. I felt warmth on my thigh as her bladder let go in fear.

"Look at them," came from above. "Cowardly little assassins hiding behind troops brave enough to face death head on like real warriors."

"Coil's piss, no," murmured the guard in my arms.

"Your loyalty will be remembered," came the voice again.

"No!"

Crossbows spat out bolts and the woman in my arms stiffened and arched in my embrace. One moment she was alive and then, almost magically, a bolt was vibrating in front of my nose like a conduit for life to flee her body.

"Master?" I said. Her guard was spasming as he died, a bolt sticking out of his neck and blood spattering onto the floor. "They are playing with us, Master."

Laughter from above and the crossbows fired again, thudding bolts into the body in my arms and making me cringe down further behind the corpse. The laughter stopped and a second voice, female, commanding, said something, though I could not make out what it was. Then the woman shouted down to us.

"We only want you, Merela Karn. Lay on the floor and make no move to harm those who come for you or I will have your fellow shot."

Did something cross my master's face at hearing her name spoken by a stranger? Was she surprised? Did her dark skin grey slightly in shock? I had never, in all our years together, seen my master shocked. Though I was sure she was known throughout the Tired Lands—Merela Karn, the best of the assassins—few would know her face or that she was a woman.

"Drop the body, Girton," she said, letting hers fall face down on the tiled and bloody floor. "This is not what it seems."

As always I did as I was told, though I braced every muscle, waiting for the bite of a bolt which never came.

"Lie on the floor, both of you," said the male voice from above.

We did as instructed and the room was suddenly buzzing with guards. I took a few kicks to the ribs, and luckily for the owners of those feet I could not see their faces to mark them for my attention later. We were quickly bound—well enough for amateurs—and hauled to our feet in front of a man as big as any I have seen, though he was as much fat as muscle.

"Shall I take their masks off?" asked a guard to my left.

"No. Take any weapons from them and put them in the cells. Then you can all go and wash their shit off yourselves and forget this ever happened."

"I think it's your shit, actually," I said. My master stared at the floor, shaking her head, and the man backhanded me across the face. It was a poor blow. Children have hurt me more with harsh words.

"You should remember," he said, "we don't need you; we only need her."

Before I could reply bags were put over our heads for a swift, dark and rough trip to the cells. *Five hundred paces against the clock walking across stone. Turn left and twenty paces across thick carpet. Down two sets of spiral stairs into a place that stinks of human misery.*

Dungeons are usually full of the flotsam of humanity, but

this one sounded empty of prisoners apart from my master and I. We were placed in filthy cells, still tied though the bonds did not hold me long. Once free I removed the sack from my head and coughed out a wire I had half swallowed and had been holding in my gullet. It was a simple job to get my arm through the barred window of my door and pick the lock. Outside was a surprisingly wide area with a table, chairs and braziers, cold now. I tiptoed to my master's cell door.

"Master, I am out."

"Well done, Girton, but go back to your cell," she said softly. "Be calm. Wait."

I stood before the door of her cell for a moment. An assassin cannot expect much mercy once captured. A blood gibbet or maybe a public dissection. Something drawn out and painful always awaited us if we were caught, unless another assassin got to us first—my master says the loose association that makes up the Open Circle guards its secrets jealously. It would have been easy enough for me to slip into the castle proper and find some servant. I could take his clothes and become anonymous and from there I could escape out into the country. I knew the assassins' scratch language and could find the drop boxes to pick up work. Many would have done that in my situation.

But my master had told me to go back to my cell and wait, so I did. I locked the door behind me and slipped my sack and bonds back on. I imagined a circle filled with air, then let the top quarter of the circle open and breathed the air out. I let go of fear and became nothing but an instrument, a weapon.

I waited.

"One, my master. Two, my master. Three, my master…"

5012

orbit

Follow us:

f **/orbitbooksUS**

🐦 **/orbitbooks**

▶ **/orbitbooks**

Join our mailing list
to receive alerts on our
latest releases and deals.

orbitbooks.net

Enter our monthly
giveaway for the chance
to win some epic prizes.

orbitloot.com